PAUL E. HORSMAN

BUILDING A TRADE EMPIRE

BOOK 4

WYRMS OF PASANDIR

I0550032

Book cover and map designed by Deranged Doctor Design
For more info: paulhorsman-author.com

There is a list of names at the back of the book.

## Paul E. Horsman's books:

Zilverspoor Uitgeverij (Dutch Editions):
Rhidauna – Schaduw van de Revenaunt #1
Zihaen – Schaduw van de Revenaunt #2
Ordelanden – Schaduw van de Revenaunt #3

Red Rune Books (Dutch Edition)
De Shardheld Sage

Red Rune Books (English Editions):
The Lioness of Kell
The Road to Kalbakar – Wyrms of Pasandir #1
The Pirates of Brisa – Wyrms of Pasandir #2
The Bokkaners of the North – Wyrms of Pasandir #3
Building a Trade Empire – Wyrms of Pasandir #4
High Merchant (2017) – Wyrms of Pasandir #5
Trade Magnate (2018) – Wyrms of Pasandir #6
The Jinn of Ozzoon (2018) - Wyrms of Pasandir #7

Shardfall – The Shardheld Saga #1
Runemaster – The Shardheld Saga #2
Shardheld – The Shardheld Saga #3
The Shardheld Saga, trilogy

Rhidauna –The Shadow of the Revenaunt #1
Zihaen – The Shadow of the Revenaunt #2
Ordelanden – The Shadow of the Revenaunt #3
Vavaun – The Shadows of the Revenaunt

**The Weal of Four Nations** is the political union of Kell, Vanhaar, Unwaar and the Chorwaynie Archipelago

**Kells:** The tall, bronze-brown people of the Radhaijan Plains in Kell; famed for the fighting prowess of their warriors and the quality of their ordnance.

**Vanhaari:** The warlock people of Vanhaar, masters of magic and learning. They are of small stature and possess curious complexions, ranging from a rare, eerily pale white to dark gray.

**Chorwaynies:** The coppery-brown coastal people of the Chorwaynie Archipelago. A nation of sharp merchants and privateers.

**Jentakan:** The golden-brown inland people of the Chorwaynie Archipelago. Fishers and sailors, their painted fabrics are priceless works of art.

**Unwaari:** The Singers of Aera; priests and mages, living in Unwaar. They are Vanhaar's brother people, though far more religious.

**The People of Malgarth,** the small continent to the east:

**Garthans:** The High Kingdom of Malgarth. A rural people of pinkish-white to beige complexions.

**The Five Tradeports (Brisa, Reveul, Lismer, Dibloon and Veurdel)**: Hotbeds of piracy and crime. Populated by Garthans and renegades of all the peoples in the region.

**Thali:** The dark-brown people of the frozen south of Malgarth; inventors and technicians, who develop wonders like steam engines, airships and other contraptions.

Both Kells and Vanhaari have settlements on Malgarth: Tar Kell, the cave city, and the former warlock town New Winsproke.

Other lands:

**Nanstalgarod (the Hellesands)** is a lost land full of magnificent ruins, totally covered by the desert.

**Hizmyr,** fabled kingdom past the desert lands; olive-skinned people in a land of great riches and a tyrannical Guild

**Qoor**, a mighty empire in the far north of the continent; its people are distantly related to the Vanhaari, but of green complexions.

**Sashuni,** one of the kingdoms that make up Qoor

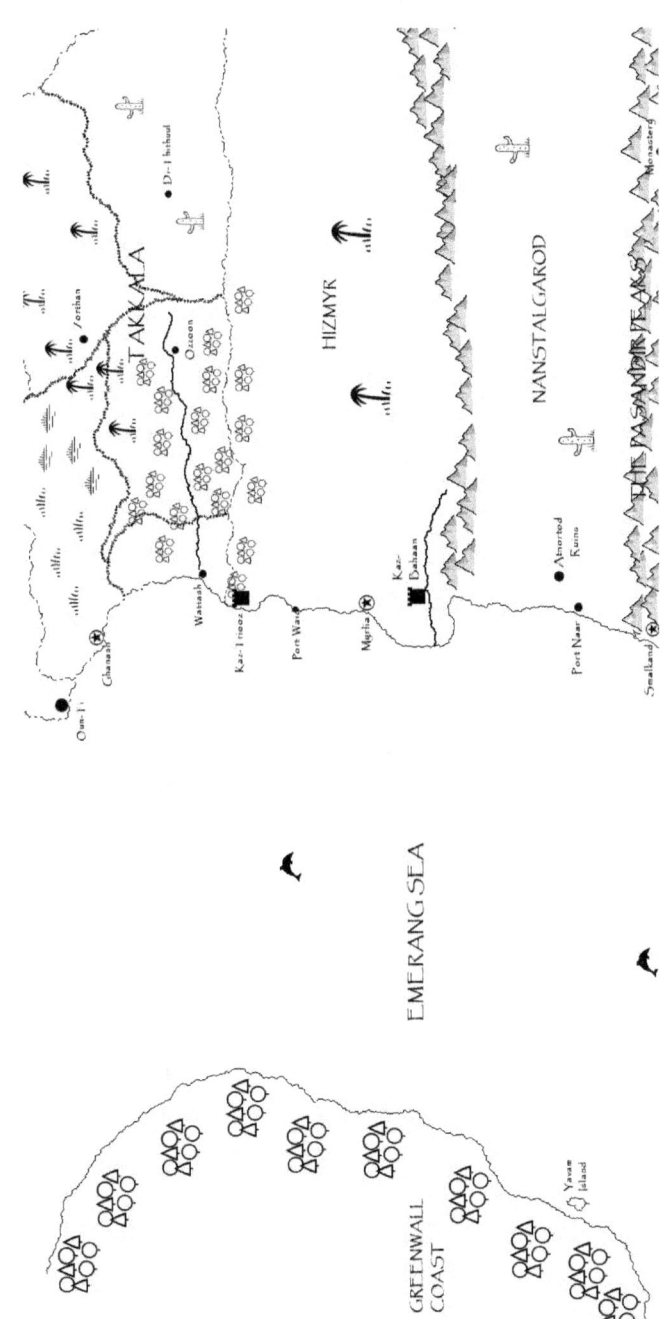

7

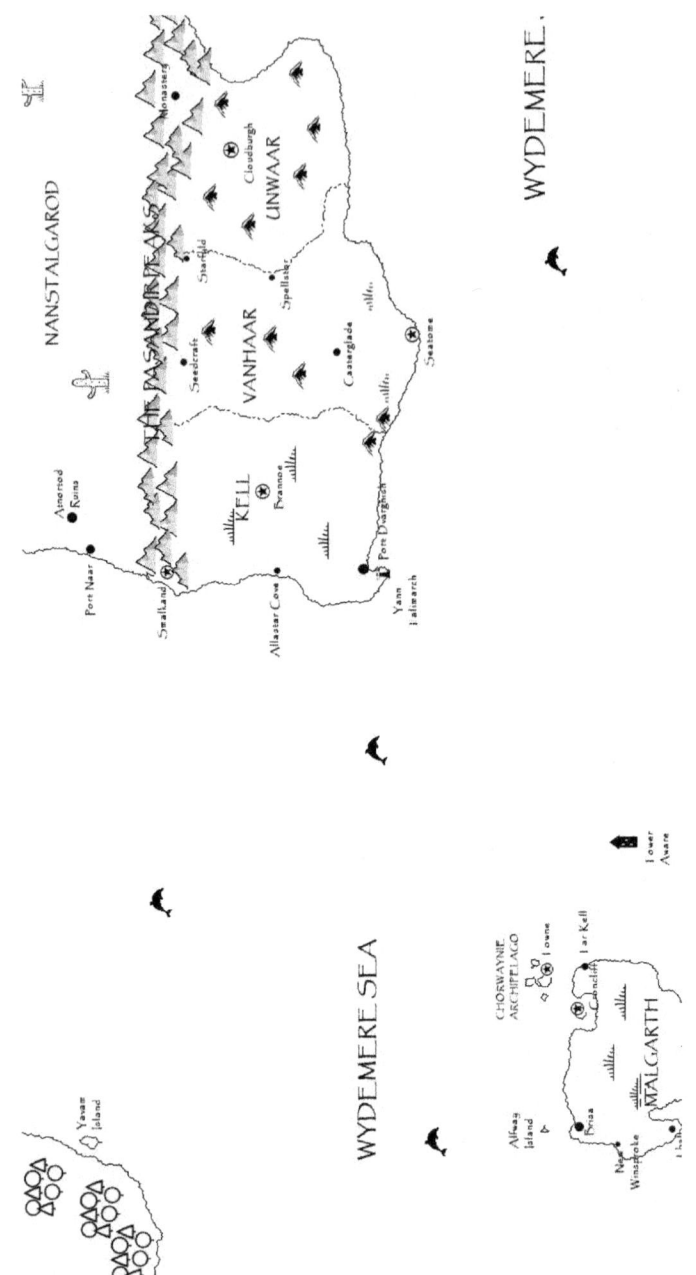

WYDEMERE.

WYDEMERE SEA

NANSTALGAROD

THE PASANDINE AKS

Port Naar

Amerod
Ruins

Smallland

KELL

Evamore

Allastar Cove

Port Dragoun

Yann
Halmarch

VANHAAR

Casanglade

Spellather

Seatone

UNWAAR

Cloudburgh

Starfield

Seedcraft

Monastery

Yawan
Island

CHORWAYNE
ARCHIPELAGO

Towne

Alheas
Island

New
Windspoke

Nessa

Conclave

Tar Kell

MALGARTH

Tower
Aware

8

# INTRODUCTION

The **WYRMS OF PASANDIR** - Series returns the reader to the colorful world of **Lioness of Kell**, twenty-five years later, when the Lioness Maud has become the Queen of the Kell, and the Warlock Basil has settled down as the Spellstor, ruler of Vanhaar.

*#1 – The Road to Kalbakar* introduces Eskandar, a young one-handed ship's boy serving in the old navy sloop *Tipred*, and Teodar, the voice in his head.

Eskandar meets Kellani, the daughter of Lioness Maud, and together they beat off a monster attack on the sloop.

No longer able to hide his magic, Eskandar goes ashore with Kellani, and teams up with Naudin, the son of the Warlock Basil.

Together, they discover a dangerous lich has escaped his crypt and is at large somewhere. They meet Jem, the bodiless granddaughter of the lich, and Lord Amaj, a warrior boy with connections to Eskandar's past.

Eskandar learns the roots of his secret history lie at Kalbakar Keep, a castle occupied by a mad monk cult...

*#2 – The Pirates of Brisa* tells Eskandar that Teodar and the Sleeping God Bodrus are being threatened by pirates, man-eating jinn, and their boss, the mighty lich lord. Eskandar has learned he is the last wyrmcaller, whatever that may be, and Defender of Divine Bodrus.

When the pirates start abducting kids from the orphanage Eskandar once lived in, he knows what to do. Together with Kellani, Naudin and his other friends, he defeats the pirates and rescues the orphan teens, among them a quiet fifteen-year-old girl named Shaw.

Now Teodar tells him he has to collect an army of kid warriors and fight the pirates of Brisa...

**#3 – *The Bokkaners of the North*** sees Eskandar victorious, with the Brisan pirates defeated and their powerful ship in his hands. Just as he thinks to have some peace and quiet, Teodar sends him north, where another bunch of pirates roams.

Teodar knows of a stronghold at the foot of the Pasandir Peaks, Smalkand Keep.

This proves to be a rich former merchants' headquarters, and a veritable treasure room of gold and trade goods.

After Eskandar has secured the keep and the surrounding region, he travels further north, to the mighty kingdom of Hizmyr.

Before he leaves, he agrees to his purser Shaw's plan to build a trade empire that can finance Eskandar's many plans for restoring the Peaks...

**#4 – *Building a Trade Empire*** starts the tale of Shaw, the young purser who dreams of building a mighty trade empire.

She is the one who sells Eskandar's spoils of war, and as she follows the wyrmcaller north to find the old traders keep of Smalkand, she starts building her plans.

When the wyrmcaller Eskandar goes north in pursuit of his enemies, she obtains his blessing to realize her dream. Together with Nate, her business partner, she journeys back to Seatome, the capital of Lord Basil's Vanhaar.

Here, with the gold found in Smalkand's strongroom, and a load of valuable loot from a pirate vessel they had captured, she hires her first warehouse and makes ready to conquer the mercantile world...

# CHAPTER 1 – BIRTH OF A TRADE EMPIRE

The big warship *Drakon of Ilzhar* disappeared from sight in the seaward channel, taking the Wyrmcaller Eskandar on his long-awaited journey to the unknown northern lands.

Purser Shaw turned aside to Amaj and the other chief guys of Kalbakar Keep. 'He's gone.'

She was a slip of a girl, fifteen years of age, with the gray skin of the Vanhaari. Her left eye was the only lazy thing about her, and to correct its squint, she wore a black eye patch over her good right one. It gave her thin face a ferocious look, and helped her shed her natural diffidence.

She slapped her hands and looked at the big youngster standing beside her. Lord Amaj was marshal of Kalbakar Keep now Eskandar had sailed.

'Amaj,' she said briskly. 'I want to discuss the trading business Nate and I are setting up. Department heads only, in my office.'

'Now?' Amaj said, and his face showed her sudden assertiveness startled him.

'Now.' Shaw pressed her lips together. 'There's much to do; I don't want to waste any more time. All right?'

Amaj grinned. 'All right, before you bite off my nose.' He turned to the others. 'Department heads, purser wants a word with us.'

Captain Wylmer smiled. 'She's put enough money in our pockets already; let's hear her plans.'

The purser's office at the back of the second warehouse cave was small, and offered barely enough room to seat all of them.

Shaw sat behind her little desk, pressed against the wall, with the others on chairs filling up the rest of the space.

'My trade plans,' she said and felt her brow contract into a scowl as she tried to read their blurred faces. Automatically, her hand went to the black patch and she cursed as she tried to focus her bad eye.

'Eskandar said I could go ahead,' she added. 'He didn't ask any particulars before he left.'

'He didn't,' Captain Wylmer said pleasantly. He sat across from her, with his hands folded over his ample stomach like a well-fed seventeen-year-old deity. 'Knowing you, I found that rather careless of the boss.'

'He sailed,' Shaw said quickly. 'Too late to call him back now. Instead, I'll tell you.' She tapped the table, as if to underscore her words. 'I'm done with meekness. From now on, I'm Shaw Harwans of the Pasandir Trading Company.'

'What's that?' Lord Amaj said with a puzzled frown on his broad face. A warrior at sixteen, he was a lord's son, with the vague undertone of red in his gray skin that marked the born Peak man. 'Never heard of those fellows. Where do they come in?'

Shaw grinned. 'They are already in,' she said. 'Nate and I are the Pasandir Trading Co. Here in Smalkand we have our main warehouse and stocks.' She frowned. 'But we're far away from our markets in the south. We need a second place in one of the Weal's main ports.'

'And money,' Wylmer said, as he leaned forward. 'You won't get far without a heap of fat golden libers.'

Shaw nodded. 'I have some reserves.' From the loot they had captured, she'd put aside part of the ship's share. 'It's a few thousand libers; not a heap, but enough to get started.'

Wylmer sat back. 'That's a promising begin.'

'The trade goods in *Marigold*'s hold should fetch us more,' Shaw went on. 'With that money I want to set up a base in Seatome.' She looked at Imooga. 'Then could we install one of those spare generators?'

'Sure,' the young engineer said. 'You can have my ice machine prototype as well. I know how it works and I don't need it.'

'That would be great!' Shaw said, as she suppressed an urge to clap her hands in glee. 'If you know how they work, can we build them? I mean lots of them?'

For a fleeting moment, Imooga seemed to retire into herself. She was a Thali, the engineering people of the icy wastes, to whom technology was both their honor and their way of life. Then she gave a formal nod.

'I could build one. We'd need a workshop, technicians and another engineer. Are we going commercial?'

Shaw didn't need to think on that one. 'Yes – if you can produce.'

'I'll give you a letter to post,' Imooga said. 'Ulaataq and I talked it over before he sailed with Eskandar. If we're going to sell those devices in numbers, we need more engineers. I'll call in a few of our friends. You hand this letter to the first Thali airship that's going home, and pay them a liber for their trouble.'

'That would be awesome,' Shaw said softly. She hesitated. 'How's the portal thing going?'

'I almost got it licked,' Imooga said carefully. 'The biggest problem was to overcome my own prejudices. Before he left, Eskandar explained what he did when he ported and showed it in my head. Creepy, but very enlightening! Then I had discussed it with Martha and Tymon; they have remarkably clear minds and after a while I suddenly understood how magic is simply doing technology with your thoughts instead of a machine. That made it easier to translate the magic Eskandar had shown me into a mechanical solution.' She clasped her hands to her chest. 'I might be able to rig a portal to Seatome soon. Keep your fingers crossed, gal.'

'Be sure I will,' Shaw said and she felt a hot glow of excitement spreading through her body. A teleportal! Instant travel between Seatome and Smalkand would make everything *so* much easier!

'When you're going to Seatome, were you planning to travel with the cargo?' Airship Pilot Tangrid asked. 'My crew needs flying time, so we can pop you over if you're in a hurry.'

'Oh, that's great!' Shaw said. 'That would give us time to find a warehouse before *Marigold* comes in.'

She looked at Miyra. 'When could you sail?'

'I'm short-handed,' the big Garthan said bluntly. She was the other captain present, in command of the steam cutter *Marigold*. Then she grinned. 'Don't worry; I can sail when you want me to. Perhaps I'll find more hands in Seatome.'

'Sail, then,' Shaw said, slapping the table. 'How soon will you be there?'

'Day after tomorrow,' Miyra said. 'Weather and pirates permitting.'

'Two days to find a suitable warehouse,' Shaw said, biting her lip. 'I must not tarry.' Everything was coming to a head now, and even quicker than she had hoped.

'Give us an hour,' Tangrid said. 'We have to wheel the girl out of her snuggly bed first.' The airship had her berth in a large cavernous space over the cave entrance that once must have housed the keep's wyrms and it took careful preparations to get her inflated and ready for flight. The pilot came to his feet. 'If you don't need me here anymore, I'll get my crew together.'

'There she goes,' Shaw said. She stood on the beach with Mage Keena and Wylmer, watching *Marigold* disappear over the bay into the seaward passage. Behind them on the field, the big, shark-like bulk of the *Pewbara* airship softly tugged at her mooring lines as if she, too, was eager to leave.

Shaw straightened her new yellow merchant's jacket the women of nearby Pashwend Keep had made for her little crew, with the letters PTC in blue on the lapels.

'A handsome uniform,' Wylmer said. 'You've been planning this a long time, haven't you?'

Shaw nodded, pleased with the compliment. 'From the moment we first met Proprietor Darquine I knew I wanted something like her MCTC. Only the money part made it uncertain, but the pirate loot *Marigold* carries resolved that.'

She turned and watched Nate come trotting across the field and for a moment his fine figure distracted her.

'We can leave,' he said, eagerly. 'Our baggage is aboard.'

'Done, then!' She felt her face glow with excitement. 'Let's go.'

'Good luck,' Captain Wylmer said. They all shook hands solemnly, and Shaw followed Nate and Keena up the rope ladder into *Pewbara*.

The weather was clear and calm. *Pewbara* followed the coastal route south, circumventing the treacherous winds between the Peaks. Below them, the natural sea wall of Kell's Radhaijan Plateau gradually sloped down.

Shaw had pushed her eye patch to her forehead to see anything below. Now she and Nate sat at a window and watched the coastline flow past, unfolding several large villages, each with their own bay or craggy fjord, and a long way removed from anything resembling civilization.

'Sheer loneliness,' Shaw said.

'No worse than Smalkand,' Nate said.

'Sure, but we've got *Pewbara* and the ships. How do these people get anywhere? They don't have an airship tower, and the only vessels are fishing boats.'

'Not that place,' Nate said. 'I see a ship and a shipyard as well.'

Shaw turned back to the window. They were approaching a small town, with a market square at the bayside, and a castle perched on a rock halfway the sheer side of the plateau. There was a ship, an old two-master leaving the bay. Then they were past and the town disappeared from view.

After that the land was empty, but for herds of wild sheep grazing the purplish shrublands.

'There!' Shaw said, punching Nate's arm. 'Hunting cats. They must be big, if we can see them that clearly.'

'Didn't Eskandar tell us about Radhaijan lions once? I seem to remember him saying how enormous they were,' Nate said. 'Big as oxen, or something.'

Shaw nodded and rested her head against Nate's shoulder. She felt his arm against her back and nothing more.

'This is your captain speaking,' Tangrid's voice crackled over the ship's voicepipe, and Shaw sat up abruptly. 'We have arrived at our destination. Thank you for journeying with *Pewbara*.'

'Did I fall asleep?' Shaw said. 'How awful of me.'

Nate laughed and massaged his left arm. 'I didn't mind.'

*Darn*, Shaw thought. *There I was, sitting beside him, and I slept. Idiot!* Angrily she jumped to her feet. 'Let's go to the bridge.'

On the other side of the cabin, Keena opened an eye. 'We're there?' She yawned and came to her feet. 'Good.' Keena wasn't a talkative person. She was a newly discovered mage, and an acrobat by profession; an agile girl of sixteen, with a past even unhappier than most Clam Street orphans.

In the nose of the airship, Tangrid sat relaxed. Beside him, his co-pilot Averson had the con and steered the airship in a wide curve towards the aerodrome. To the right, Byroon the ballast-handler adjusted his floatgas- and water-bags for their landing.

'Seatome Control. What ship?' a lazy voice inquired over the ship's voicepipe.

'This is *Pewbara* from Smalkand, Control,' Tangrid answered.

'Heard of you. First visit, isn't it? Welcome to Seatome, Captain. Mooring Tower Six.'

'Six it is; thank you, Control.'

Tangrid gave a grim smile. 'I know that guy,' he said. 'See those goats below? I know them, too, the hairy monsters. This was the Terrific Tangridis' home base.'

Shaw nodded. She had heard of Tangrid's past. His father and uncle had operated an air show, doing stunts with old airships. There had been a crash, or something terrible, and Tangrid was left alone, without money and with too much pride to beg. He'd been the aerodrome's goatherd then, until Eskandar hired him.

As they spoke, Tangrid took over command and inched the giant airship towards the tower with the large number six nailed to its frame. As they came to a halt, Averson hurried outside to fasten the mooring lines.

'And now you're an airship captain,' Shaw said.

Tangrid didn't look up from his controls. 'Almost,' he said. 'I really should see to that last certificate, to fly passengers.'

Shaw held up a hand. 'We're not passengers; we're crew.'

'Right you are,' he said with a crooked grin. 'Well, we're moored. I'll have the bags refilled before flying back, so we will be here a few hours, in case you change your mind.'

'Don't worry, I won't,' she said with a huge grin.

'Of course not. Good luck, and make us all rich.'

Shaw patted his shoulder, yanked the eye patch over her good eye and hurried to join Nate and Keena at the door.

Outside, it rained, but Shaw didn't even notice as she took the stairs without hesitation. Her stupid eye saw things vaguely, but she'd be darned if she let it slow her down.

At the foot of the tower, a gust of rain blinded her. She crashed into someone taller than she, and smelling of wet wool.

'Ouch!' she said and looked up in the face of a beefy, bushy-haired guy perhaps two years her senior.

'Beg pardon!' the boy said hastily. 'I wasn't looking. You're crew of that airship? I was wondering if she had cargo to unload.'

'I'm not really,' Shaw said, guessing the boy wasn't an aerodrome official. 'And no, she isn't carrying any cargo, only my friends and me.'

'A pity,' the boy said. 'I'm looking for work.' He looked closely at her and Nate. 'PTC? I don't recognize the uniform.'

'We're with the Pasandir Trading Company,' Shaw said carefully.

The boy stared at her. 'Pasandir? Not the wyrmcaller's outfit, are you?'

'We are,' Shaw said with a big smile. 'The merchant side of it.'

'That's great!' he cried. 'You're the talk of the town, running around with wyrms and all that. Say, would you guys have room for an internship?'

Shaw looked at the boy. He seemed earnest enough with his homely, middling-gray face and sturdy built. 'What do you do?'

He blushed darkly. 'Nothing glamorous; I'm a mage, a mover mage.'

'Explain,' Shaw said. 'What I know of magic isn't worth a penny.'

'Ah,' the boy said. 'A mover practices the wonderful art of... well, moving things. Like loading dung into carts without getting my hands dirty. Telekinesis, the instructors call it.'

Shaw felt her heart leap. 'The PTC happens to have a free spot for a caravan mage,' she said nonchalantly. 'Regular pay, free food, and plenty of exercise. You must be able to move cargo around, mindspeak, and summon spelldrakes. Fighting robbers and earning prize money are optional.'

'That means travel?'

'Miles and miles,' Shaw said brightly. 'You've heard of the Pasandir Peaks?'

The boy grinned. 'I'm a Starfyld foothillman; I was born in the shadow of the Peaks. Nobody knows the place; Starfyld is in the far north, near the Unwaari border. I've been at several hunting expeditions across the passes into the mountains.'

'Better and better,' Nate said. 'The PTC has its headquarters on the west coast of the Peaks. Our keep used to be a trading post of the Nanstalgarodians; what's now the Hellesands. We plan to revive their old trading route across the Peaks. The wyrmcaller wants that to bring his people together, and we want us to become as big as Proprietor Darquine's Malgarth and Continental Trading Co.'

'We have several irons in the fire,' Shaw said. 'Nate and I can handle most, but running a trade caravan isn't our thing. We'll be hiring people, we have the wagons and merchandise, and we even have maps, though they're five centuries out of date.'

'It sounds good,' the boy said. 'You said regular pay?'

'Basic wages are six pennies a day, plus one percent of all sales. We provide uniforms, arms and food.'

'That's what I sought,' the boy said eagerly. 'Where can I sign?'

'You don't,' Shaw said. 'Joining the wyrmcaller is a matter of honor, not of contracts.' She offered her hand. 'I'm Shaw, and my sidekick is Nate. The other girl is Keena; she's a newly-discovered mage, unspecialized.'

'Happy to meet you.' The boy shook hands enthusiastically. 'The name is Callogan of Starfyld. Never met an unspecialized mage before. You don't know what you can do yet?'

Keena shrugged. 'Nobody ever taught me anything. Thought I was goin' mad, but then the wyrmcaller told me what was happening. His guys gave me a few tricks to get a grip on it, and that helped. By training I'm an acrobat.' She gave a small smile. 'And other, less lawful things.'

'I can show you how I port,' Callogan said. 'Perhaps you'll pick it up.' He sighed and pulled a printed sheet from his pocket. 'I'm afraid I have something to sign. The Magic Institute wants a written agreement for internships.' He licked his pencil. 'Pasandir Trading Co,' he wrote. 'What's the address?'

'Headquarters at Smalkand Keep, the Pasandir Peaks,' Nate said.

'In case of a nongovernmental position, name the organization's Weal sponsor. I don't know if you...'

Shaw laughed. 'Darquine of Piright,' she said. 'She owes me that one.'

Callogan looked up. 'The proprietor herself?' he said. 'Oh boy, right.' Then he handed the form to Shaw. 'Would you sign this?'

'Sure,' she said, and wrote in her careful handwriting, *Shaw Harwans, managing director*.

'You're the boss?' he said, surprised. 'Aren't you a bit...?'

'We're all young in the Peaks,' Shaw said bluntly. 'Our legal ages are lower.'

'Ah,' Callogan said. 'I heard the wyrmcaller was my age, but I found it difficult to believe.'

Shaw blinked. 'He is,' she said. It was strange to imagine, but Eskandar *was* only seventeen beneath his immense power. 'The three of us are here to open a new warehouse. We expect our first shipment in two days.'

'You want to hire something or buy?' Callogan asked.

'Depends on the price,' Shaw said. 'Why? Would you know of something?'

Callogan wiped away a trickle of water running into his collar. 'I said I did some moving on the side, unloading tramp ships; just to get the feel of it. Most of my friends think it low work for a mage.' He chuckled. 'Being a mover isn't very glamorous, but it paid.' They stepped aside for three grazing goats and walked across the wet field.

'But what I was going to say; I heard things that aren't commonly known. There is a large warehouse on Old Wharf Quay going for sale; forfeited property, to be sold by the Port Authority. It's going cheap, as these things do.'

'Going cheap?' Shaw said. 'I like the word, but their cheap won't be mine. Is that the Port Captain's office?'

'Yes. You know where it is?'

'We were born here,' Shaw said. 'It won't be a secret that most of us in the Wyrmcaller's service came from the Clam Street Orphanage.'

'I'm not,' Callogan said soberly. 'So you'll find your way around the city probably better than me; I admit I didn't frequent *all* areas.'

Nate grinned. 'She never did the seedy places either; not like Keena and me. Thieves and fences, pickpockets and racketeers; we've been there.'

'Then I'll not boast of my tramp ships,' Callogan said.

Shaw thought of the letter in her pocket. 'Before we go anywhere we need an airship bound for Thali.'

'Tower Two,' Callogan said, pointing. 'They didn't need a mover either, they're about to depart. With a bit of luck...'

'Run!' Shaw said.

Out of breath, they arrived at the tower further down the field. It was a WyDir vessel, and a Thali crewman was outside, undoing the mooring line.

'Sorry miss, too late; we're sailing,' he said.

Shaw ran up the wooden ladder. 'We got a letter,' she said, panting. 'From Imooga, our engineer, for her folks in Thali-the-City.'

The crewman put out a hand. 'I'll take it.'

Shaw gave him the letter and the gold liber coin, and the man put both away. 'Consider it done.'

Shaw smiled. 'My thanks; may your flight be smooth as fresh snow.' Her father always told her to pick up local greetings; that showed you cared about people.

Now it got her an answering smile. 'And may the Great Grandmother watch over yours,' the crewman said and disappeared inside. Immediately, the airship lifted.

'That's done,' Shaw said, as she rejoined the others.

# CHAPTER 2 – OLD WHARF

The port captain's office was situated in a pre-war building over a cartographer's shop near the waterfront.

At the top of the stairs was a large room. Inside, a double row of busy clerks greeted them politely, and one of them stepped away from his standing desk to take them into the big man's office.

As they entered his room, a stout, older naval officer turned away from the window. 'Ms. Shaw,' he said, to her surprise. 'You come from the lord wyrmcaller, ma'am? How can I serve you?'

Shaw wasn't about to show his politeness tickled her. 'We are here to trade, Port Captain,' she said, all businesslike. 'One of our ships will arrive shortly with a large shipment of foreign goods. We want to open a base in Seatome, to better serve the Weal.' She smiled slightly. 'I caught a whisper of a forfeited warehouse coming up for sale.'

'That is correct,' the port captain said slowly. 'I was going to post the announcement, so you beat me to it. Old Wharf is a fine building in what used to be a first-class location – until certain criminal elements took it over. Pirates, I'm sorry to say. We have recently cleaned the place out.' Here he paused and gave an old-fashioned half-bow. 'Actually the death of the pawnbroker Llynsing provided the information we needed. So we owe the lord wyrmcaller a favor in this.'

*Llynsing!* Shaw knew the name belonged to the baddest fence in town. Then she remembered Nate telling her how the crook had died at Eskandar's feet that same night a jinni had tried to steal away the Clammers. The wyrmcaller had arrived in time to save the orphans, including Nate. So now something else good came from that night!

'Happy to be of service,' she said firmly. 'How large is the property?'

The port captain laid a finger along his nose. 'Old Wharf is a large warehouse with two adjoining town houses. It is at the outer edge of the harbor district, in the shadow of the city walls. The main building has two storage halls, a workroom and a receiving-hall with loading bays. Upstairs are several offices, a cafeteria and a restroom. Included are the quay, which is part of the Seatome harbor front, and a pier with two cranes, and berths for at least three medium sized vessels. The property goes for the special price of five thousand libers.' He smiled. 'If you wish, we could include the use of Mariner Tower. That's the corner tower of the wall, with room for military stores and a small garrison. It's free of charge, provided you'll bear the cost of maintenance.'

*Darn! Too expensive. Five thousand eats up all my savings,* she thought, chagrined. 'Housing an international company like the PTC would mean a large stimulus to the harbor district. Not only we hire local staff, but we import many goods from places no other traders have access to. I know Proprietor Darquine wants me to settle in Towne. Instead, I choose Seatome, the place of my birth, the place where my parents died.'

'You are from Seatome?' The port captain studied her kindly. 'Harwans. Of Harwans Ship Chandlery?' He shook his head. 'A terrible tragedy, that was. What do you say to a ten-year lease against two hundred fifty libers per year, and automatic ownership afterwards?'

'That is an acceptable suggestion,' Shaw said. Her mind jumped up and down in joy. *More than acceptable!*

'Then perhaps you'd care to inspect Old Wharf. I will have the paperwork ready for your signature by tomorrow morning.' The port captain smiled. 'Normally, you would have needed a few more years to sign any deeds, but the Lord Spellstor waived this rule for the wyrmcaller's officers.' He opened a drawer and produced a key ring.

'There it is.' He hesitated. 'Before you go in the main building, let me warn you it needs cleaning up. We removed the contraband and the bodies, but not the stains or any perishable goods. We offer the buildings as they are.'

'No problem,' Shaw said stoutly. 'In the wyrmcaller's service I've seen it all before. A pleasure doing business with you, Port Captain.'

*This Old Wharf Quay must have been a grand place once,* Shaw thought. She had shoved her eye patch up as she inspected the building. Seatome wasn't known for its architecture, but these buildings looked different, warm and graceful beneath the grime and the bluewing droppings.

'They're beautiful,' she said aloud.

'Yeah,' Nate said, staring narrow-eyed at the two steel derricks on the pier. 'Rusty, though.'

'What? Oh, those cranes.' Shaw sighed. 'When we've cleaned it up, this place will be a proper home for the PTC.'

For a moment she watched the play of the setting sun on the slim pillars lining the front, with the city wall as a grim, solid background. To the left, Mariner Tower watched; a big, square tower with loopholes and a large flagpole on top. Beyond it, sweet-scented honeysuckle turned the city wall in a living bulwark of pink-flowered greenery.

'Yes!' Exhilaration clutched at Shaw's breast as she walked to the main door. To her surprise, the lock opened without a sound and the ever-intriguing smells of a big warehouse greeted her. With pounding heart, she stepped inside.

Nate got out his matches and began lighting the gas lamps. 'We need mage lights, like we have in Smalkand,' he said. 'This isn't efficient.'

'Those stains!' Callogan said, and his voice sounded uneasy.

'Blood,' Keena said with a careless wave. 'That captain guy said there's been a battle here.'

Shaw glanced at the large patches of dried blood, the dropped weapons and a plumed slouch hat. Then she turned her attention back to the tall shelves; many still stocked with old trade goods.

'Ample space,' she said.

'Look, canned fish-bombs,' Nate said, pointing at a cluster of swollen food tins.

'Don't touch them,' Shaw said absently. 'We will clean it all out, keep the good stuff and dump the rest.' She walked into the second room.

'Must have been quite a fight,' Callogan said, goggling at the bloody trails everywhere.

'They were pirates.' Keena had picked up the hat and smoothed out the dents with her hand before donning it. 'Those deserve ten deaths.' She struck a pose. 'Well?'

'Fearsome,' Shaw said, inspecting her friend.

Keena smiled. 'Then I'll keep it.'

Past the empty loading space, where incoming and outgoing goods would be sorted and packed, they walked through the repair workshop. Several workbenches waited for damaged goods, though the tools in their racks looked old and worn.

Then they climbed the wooden stairs to the entresol with the offices.

A clerks' room with two standing desks, a cafeteria that could seat fifty, and a restroom, dirty but strangely modern with its flush toilets. Beyond that a boardroom with a large table and chairs, and at the end the manager's office, wainscoted in redwood, with several paintings of dubious quality and a nice wooden desk.

'Yes,' Shaw said. 'I like the place.'

'I wonder who owned it,' Callogan said. 'It's not at all a Vanhaari building.'

'Whoever it was, they made a special place,' Shaw said. She spread her arms wide. 'Our place.'

'Now we need people,' Nate said as cheerfully as she felt. 'Let's go to the Labor Exchange.'

Callogan pulled a fat timepiece from his pocket. 'It's almost seven o'clock. Are those guys still open?'

Nate laughed. 'They never close. Much of their business is done at night, when employers have time.'

The Labor Exchange was a tall, gloomy building smelling of sweat and cheap lamp oil. Shaw had never been inside before, but she had heard descriptions and she knew how its system worked.

They came into a large room, with a long counter behind which several clerks sat, each with five or six people waiting patiently for their turn.

Shaw walked up to the nearest clerk, a spare, elderly woman in a threadbare robe.

'You kids blind?' the woman snapped even before she could ask anything. 'Stand at the back of the queue if you wanna register, girl.'

Shaw lifted her chin. 'I am hiring.' This must be unusual, for both the clerks and the waiting people stared at her.

'Hiring?' the woman said, and her voice rose in surprise. 'You're but a chit of a girl.'

'I represent the Pasandir Trading Company,' Shaw said. 'I am setting up a warehouse at Old Wharf Quay and I need a crew.'

Her seriousness must have convinced the clerk, for her face changed. 'A moment, ma'am,' she said and slapped a large copper service bell.

A tall man in a dark suit came from behind a desk in the back and hurried over.

'Trouble?' he said, scowling.

'This young lady wants to hire, sir,' the woman said.

The head clerk turned his gaze to Shaw. 'You do, do you? And who might you be?'

Again, Shaw introduced herself, and at the mention of the wyrmcaller, the head clerk smiled, forcing his downward-leading wrinkles into an upward curve they only just managed.

'Now I see,' he said. 'The children's army. Follow me, please.'

*Children's army!* Shaw thought, irritated. *Idiot!*

The head clerk led them past the counter to his desk and offered chairs.

'You are looking for what, exactly?' he asked, his gnawed pencil poised over a blank sheet.

Shaw folded her hands in her lap. 'We are opening a large shipping warehouse at Old Wharf Quay, and I need it manned. Let's start with twenty workers, five guards, five merchants, a repairman and a ledger keeper, and *if* you can find someone, a person who can do the day-to-day running of the establishment. We want only young people. That means senior apprentices and junior journeymen, none older.' *That will mean another hundred libers for the first year*, she thought.

The man peered at her. 'You would need trader apprentices for the warehouse, and merchant journeymen for sales. Can you promise them advancement?'

'Absolutely,' Shaw said. 'We're building a trade network. Capable employees can expect promotions, especially if they are willing to work abroad.'

'We'll put that in the notice,' the man said. 'Guards will be difficult.' He tapped his teeth with his pen as he thought. 'It's not what I'm here for, but I could ask our contact at the Castle. They might have a few soldiers' sons pining for a life of glory; the army isn't recruiting much, these days. I can't help you with a manager as we don't do senior staff; we're here for the poor.' He gave her a tight smile. 'I'm sure that once you're successful, these gentlefolk will beat a pathway to your door.'

Shaw chuckled. 'You could well be right. How much do I owe you?' She paid up without haggling, knowing the Exchange's rates were fixed.

'I need those people tomorrow,' she said in a low voice. 'I'm expecting a ship, and need the place cleaned out first.'

The head clerk sucked in his cheeks. 'A tight call, but I will do my best.'

'Thank you,' Shaw said in all sincerity. 'I will await your applicants tomorrow.'

Back in the street, she sighed. 'What a terrible place. That head clerk means well, though.'

'Yes,' Callogan said with a look of embarrassment on his broad face. 'I barely knew it existed. Those people seemed quite desperate.'

'When you go to the Labor Exchange, you are either very young, or you *are* desperate,' Nate said. 'New journeymen have to register there until they find a permanent job, so for them it's no shame. Older people, though...' He shrugged. 'Once you get a job, you're supposed to hold on to it.'

'I see,' Callogan said. 'Only the young, the incompetent or the unlucky go to the Labor Exchange.'

'That's about it,' Shaw said. 'As long as they weren't Clammers. Even the Exchange wouldn't touch us. Let's go back to the warehouse.'

Keena wheeled around. 'Here, you!' she said. 'Trying to pick *my* pocket? I'll break your nose!'

She pulled a girl of some fourteen years from the shadows. 'Who are you? Not a Clammer, obviously.'

'Clammers are gone,' the girl said. 'Dunno where, but they're all vanished.'

'They struck it rich,' Nate said. 'None of them need to steal anymore.'

'Lucky sods,' the girl said. 'I do.'

'Why?' Shaw said. 'Who forces you to?'

'Hunger,' the girl said. 'What else?' She grunted. 'Not that I'm any good at it.'

'You need food now?' Nate asked.

The girl glanced at him through her long, unkempt hair. 'Yeah. Might you have some?'

'I just remembered we didn't eat either, since breakfast,' Nate said.

Shaw blinked. 'I forget things like that,' she admitted. 'There should be a pastryman around the corner.'

There was, and shortly they were back outside with a large slice of hot, dripping pie.

'Gods,' the girl said as they walked on. 'You're just giving me this?'

'Sure,' Nate said. 'You see, the three of us *were* Clammers. We know how it is.'

The girl stared at him, her mouth full and sauce leaking down her chin. Then she swallowed. 'Clammers? You? Where did you all go?'

'We joined the wyrmcaller,' Nate said. 'Heard of him?'

'Who hasn't,' the girl said. 'The kid with the wyrms. But I didn't know he was hiring.'

'He is,' Shaw said. 'If you're willing to work. What are you good at?'

'Needlework,' the girl said. 'Me mother was a seamstress, and she taught me how to sew clothes and things. She's dead now.' The girl touched Nate's sleeve with a dirty finger. 'I can make robes and jackets just as good.'

'We can use a seamstress,' Shaw said, thinking of uniforms. 'What's your name?'

'Dowa,' the girl said.

'Any relatives?'

The girl uttered a blistering curse. 'Only a cousin,' she said fiercely. 'I lived with my aunt until the gods called her, too. Then her son inherited the house and things. He wanted me to "care" for him.' She spat. 'No way. I'd rather die in the gutter.'

'That's no fun either,' Shaw said. 'But I guess I know what you mean. You can work for us. Three pennies a day plus food, clothes and bed, sewing uniforms and things for the people we'll be hiring.'

'You mean that?' the girl said. 'Three pennies daily for sewing? That's more than my mother ever made.'

'That's what we usually pay,' Shaw said. 'Now let's buy some groceries and stuff, and then we'll go back to Old Wharf.'

Next morning, Shaw and Callogan went to the Port Admiralty building, to sign the lease. When they returned, Shaw found Nate standing in the center of a crowd of people, waving his hands and talking to several people at once.

'Well,' she said, and she felt excitement bubbling up in her chest. 'That's not bad at all.'

'We've been pre-selecting them,' Nate said, wiping his face. 'There were a lot of oldsters, too. I told them no. Only one I kept for you. He's a repairman, ex-navy. Lost a leg and an eye, but he said he'd repair everything that was ever made. I didn't think any journeyman or -woman could say the same.'

'We'll take him,' Shaw said. 'Give him an apprentice to teach his craft to.' She raised her voice to reach over the hubbub. 'Applicants for the warehouse worker jobs first. We want journeymen or senior apprentices.'

She walked over to the porch and sat down. 'The queue starts here. Hold your certificates ready, folks. We're in a hurry.'

Shaw had never ever hired anyone before, but she'd been a keen observer all her life, and could distinguish the serious from the braggart and the active from the slouch. Most of the times, the recommendations on their certificate—or the lack thereof, confirmed her feeling, and the selection went fast. 'Number twenty!' she called and two candidates stepped forward.

'Me!' they both shouted.

Shaw took the first papers thrust under her nose and glanced through them. Good marks and some kind words from a local merchant, enough. She looked up at the applicant. 'You're hired. That was the last one, folks.'

'Drat,' the other boy said so dejectedly that Shaw gave him a sharp glance. Fifteen, sixteen years old; a tired-looking kid with scruffy, often-repaired clothes.

'Show me your certificate,' Shaw said. 'Hey, guy; you're a cook, not a trader.'

The boy sagged. 'I know. But I hoped...'

'We don't need another trader,' Shaw said. Then she grinned. 'But it so happens we *can* use a cook. You make tea? Sandwiches? Prepare fifty meals?'

'Tea and sandwiches,' the boy said. 'I'll not lie; I can do meals, but not fifty, not with only two hands.'

Shaw looked at him. 'Great answer. I want someone to handle the whole eats division. We have a cafeteria, and I want my people fed; there will be extra help for the meals.'

'Then I can do it!' the boy said desperately.

'You're in. Start by looking the place over and clean it up. If you'd manage a pot of tea at the same time, I'd be obliged.'

She turned to the others. 'The warehouse workers can start with scrubbing the floors. You'll find a lot of bloodstains inside.' Shaw grinned, what with the eye patch and all wasn't as soothing as she intended. 'Those stains were *not* made by earlier workers we were dissatisfied with; it was a battle between the city guards and some criminals. Please try to get things customer-friendly.'

Then her free eye narrowed. There were at least another ten candidates for workers left. 'You guys, I'm sorry we don't have a full-time job left right now. If there are any who want to earn a bit extra, I could use temporary house cleaners; two pennies per day. Anyone interested?'

Some six hands went up.

'All right,' she said. 'You start with the house to the left. I want it clean, sparkling and fit for the Lord Spellstor himself. When that's done, there is the house to the right. Which of you can be head cleaner?'

'Me,' a sharp-faced girl said quickly. 'Been cleaning house since I could crawl.'

'You're on,' Shaw said. 'If you need anything, let me know.' She exchanged glances with Nate and turned to the still waiting candidates for the other jobs. 'Warehouse guards next. Anyone here from the Castle?'

'We all are,' a haggard boy said. He stood at the head of a group of boys as scruffy as he, for while his clothes seemed made by a fine tailor, they looked as if he'd been sleeping outdoors in them. His long hair and well-bred gray face could use soap as well. 'Lieutenant said you'd employ us as soldiers. Is that right?'

'We're building a trade network,' Shaw said. 'For the moment we need guys to guard the warehouse. We'll supply uniforms, arms and training. You'll be company troops, not Pasandir army, but the ranks and pay are the same. As we grow, so will your chances on action. Overseas duty, pirate hunting, it can be a part of your job.'

'All right,' the haggard boy said. 'We'll take it if you want us.'

'What's your name? Shaw said.

The boy pressed his lips together. 'Yens Rowe-Yens.'

Shaw sat up. 'You're the...'

His nod was savage. 'The colonel's son. They sacked him for incompetence after the Clam Street fire. I had been training to join the army as an ensign, but his successor informed me that wouldn't be a wise idea. So there I was. I'd gathered these guys, all soldiers' sons, who had wanted to join the army with me, but the garrison ain't hiring. At least not anyone of mine.' He smiled grimly. 'You're our last hope, ma'am. Else we're planning to leave town and seek work as mercenaries somewhere.'

*Who the heck would hire kid mercenaries?* Shaw thought. *Except us, that is.* 'All right,' she said. 'You're in. You'll be squad leader. The Pasandir Army isn't hot on officers; our top field commander is a sergeant, so for now you will be a corporal. Look over the area. Mariner Tower will be your barracks; you must clean it out yourselves. As soon as we're up and running, give me a list of your needs, like bedding, etc. You make up a duty roster. One thing; though we are traders, the Peaks are at war with every pirate and jinni on the Wydemere. That business at Clam Street was a jinn affair; we don't want a repeat here. That's why I expect you to be alert at all times.'

The boy straightened. 'Yes, ma'am,' he snapped and saluted. Then he turned to the seven boys behind him. 'We're in, guys. Get your gear; we'll sling our hammocks inside tonight.'

Shaw watched them march off. *Old Rowe-Yens had been a pompous fool who never should have been made sergeant, let alone colonel. This guy may be his son, but he doesn't look like his father at all.* She shrugged. *He'll get a chance to prove himself.*

'Any ledger keepers here?' she said, hurrying on to the next vacancy.

Two soberly clad individuals stepped forward, one male, the other female, and both in their twenties. Shaw gave a rueful grin. *They won't be youngsters. No kid would have mastered the art of keeping a merchant's books.* She looked at them; both dressed the same, both serious faces, and very much alike as they stood side by side.

'Are you related?' she asked on impulse.

'No,' the young man said, unperturbed. 'Unless slaving for the same usurer means acquiring kinship. I'm Howwil and she's Roza.'

'We've been working side by side to each other for ten endless years,' the young woman said. 'Clerking and keeping books for Pomfrith Bankers of Sturgeon Street.'

Shaw had heard of Pomfrith, bankers of the very wealthy. If you were somebody, you did business with Pomfrith. 'I know the name,' she said.

'You haven't heard the latest? He's dead,' Howwil said.

'Pomfrith?' Shaw sat up straight. *That must have spooked a lot of great people. Pomfrith knew much of many.* 'I hadn't heard that.'

'Last month,' Roza said. 'His heirs didn't want the business, only the money. To their disappointment, once the customers' deposits were returned, what remained was much less than they had expected.'

'Pomfrith had many rich patrons and many rich vices,' Howwil said. 'These balanced, but it didn't leave much. We settled with the clients, burned stacks of documents, tidied up the books, and were out of a job.'

'But I'd think plenty of business houses would want to hire you?' Shaw said.

'I'm sure, but we're not allowed to,' Roza said with a thin smile. 'Our contracts state we cannot accept a job with any Weal trading house for the next ten years.'

'The joke being, there are no non-Weal trading houses,' Howwil added.

'But if the heirs won't take over the business, then what use is that clause?' Nate asked.

'It is not the heirs,' Roza said. 'It's a guild contract, to protect the customers.'

'In short, we know too much,' Howwil said.

'Well,' Shaw said. 'The PTC is most definitely not a Weal trading house.'

'That is what we hoped,' Howwil said. 'Nonetheless, we won't discuss Pomfrith's business, if you don't mind.'

'That's all right with me,' Shaw said. 'I don't think it had anything to do with us. Nate and I are starting up something we want to become as big as the MCTC. We have many trading contacts others haven't and we can bring our customers unheard of luxuries. Would one of you mind moving to our main HQ in the Peaks? With the other here in Seatome, you could between you set up a system for all future business expansions, including a bank.'

'The Peaks?' Roza said. 'You mean camping out? I'm not sure I could.'

Shaw laughed. 'Certainly not! We've a grand place there. Only one thing you should keep in mind. We're a young people's show. Our flag captain is the oldest at 23. Can you handle that?'

Roza looked at Howwil. 'I'm an old maid of 26, but I suppose I'll cope. Why aren't there any older people?'

'I'll explain our history later,' Shaw said. 'Everybody should hear it.'

'All right, count me in,' Howwil said. 'Helping build a big trading company will be a challenge after Pomfrith's eternal skullduggery.'

'We're straight,' Shaw said. 'Our boss is the disciple of Divine Bodrus, the Sleeping God. If there is one thing I know, it's that a lot of gods and men are looking at us. We can't afford anything dishonest.'

'Good!' Roza said. 'I much prefer clean ledgers.'

'They make our work easier,' Howwil said.

'What did Pomfrith pay you two?' Shaw asked carefully.

'One uni a day,' Roza said. 'Would that be too much for you?'

*That's thirty-seven libers per year; a lot of money.* 'We can match that,' Shaw said. 'We can raise it when things go well.' She smiled at the two. 'Welcome. Why don't you have a look at the premises? It's a mess, but we signed the lease only this morning.'

As the two clerks walked inside, Shaw rubbed her hands. *Those guys are class!* She glanced at Nate and gave him a thumb-up.

He winked back. 'Ready for the salesguys?'

'Yes!' she said. There were eight candidates for five posts, three boys and five girls, dressed to kill and eager-eyed.

*Now what?* she thought. Then she chuckled. 'Nate, get me eight different, but useless things from the stock.'

Nate ran, to return quickly with an armful of rubbish.

'Great,' Shaw said. 'Put them away out of sight and set the candidates in a circle. Callogan, you look very much the ideal Gullible Customer. Take a seat in the circle. Oh, and may I have the loan of that impressive timepiece of yours?' She grabbed one of the objects Nate had gathered and walked to the expectant candidates.

'Folks, we only want the top sellers in town. Show me that's you. I will hand you something from our stock. You get three minutes to sell it to our Gullible Customer. My partner Nate and I will judge your performance.' She handed the object to an innocent-faced guy. 'You're first. You can start...' She looked at Callogan's fat timepiece. 'NOW!'

The salesboy lifted the bottle of fish oil people used to burn in lamps and was almost impossible to sell in these days of gas lighting, and started a mighty convincing tale of its benefits in curing hair loss, itchy skin and other conflictions. It sounded wonderful, and Shaw made a mental note not to throw those bottles away just yet.

As the boy sat down, he looked at Shaw. 'You know every word was true? My ma is a witch; she could give you even more arguments.'

*Good,* Shaw thought. *That's a plus.*

The others all did well, and in the end Shaw chose five and wrote down the names of the other three in case they'd be expanding.

'Now we have the people we wanted,' Shaw said, feeling exhilarated.

'Except for a manager,' Nate said. He patted Callogan's shoulder. 'Great show. You did seem eager to buy those rotting fish-bomb tins.'

'I would send them to the proctor at the Institute,' Callogan said. 'With a little extra, to have the whole lot explode right inside his foppish office. Splat-Bam! But I won't, of course. Drat, I'm getting staid.'

'Grown-up,' Nate said. 'That's probably worse.'

As they walked through the second storeroom, they saw a tall, well-dressed fellow standing in the shadow of a lane of storage racks watching the workers scrub the blood away. He wasn't a Vanhaari, or a Kell either; that left Chorwaynie. Shaw frowned. *Darquine wouldn't have sent a spy, would she? Nah, the proprietor knows she only has to ask and I'll show her the whole place. All but the trade secrets.*

'Good day to you,' she said quietly.

The boy, for he was still that, even if he was tall, spun around.

'I beg your pardon,' he said. 'I should have introduced myself, but you were so busy I thought to look over the warehouse first. Varan Lomillor, from Towne Fastness.'

He smiled. 'My family is a competitor of the mighty MCTC, though there is no animosity between us and Darquine of Piright. Lomillor Enterprises is small, and my father plans to keep it that way. No sprawling trade empire for his three sons.'

'How dull of him,' Shaw said, grinning.

The boy signaled resignation. 'We are a cautious family. My eldest brother is the heir and runs the Towne warehouse. My other brother is captain of our single merchant vessel, and I need to find my own way in the world.

'So I came to Seatome, hoping for a golden opportunity. Alas, Seatome is not an adventuresome place, and I had almost given up, when the good port captain told me of you. The wyrmcaller setting up a trade empire? That intrigued me, and I came to see what was going on.'

He smiled. 'I am agreeably surprised. You have a great location; a fine building and enough room to expand. There is a happy atmosphere and even those who weren't hired left feeling you took them serious and appreciated. I wonder, are you up to strength now?'

Shaw looked up at him. He was a handsome chap, had she cared for that. He had easy good manners and seemed seriously interested. Only... could she trust him?

'I'll be blunt,' she said. 'I am looking for one more position to fill; we need a manager for this place. There are other affairs asking for my attention; we are starting up the old trade route through the Peaks, and I should be out breaking open new markets. I want a manager who is discreet, and loyal to us, to the Pasandir Trading Co., to the wyrmcaller and our new country. We have trade contacts no other merchant in the Weal knows about, and I want to keep it that way.'

'Sounds intriguing,' Varan said. 'The Weal is more than ready for new merchandise.'

'We have that,' Shaw said. 'For example a machine that makes ice, and icy cold rooms where you can keep products frozen for months.'

'I could sell a thing like that,' Varan said with raised eyebrows. 'I could sell a lot of them.'

'We cannot *make* a lot of them yet,' Shaw said. 'We're working on it, though.'

'Then we must set up a production line. I should need to see your engineers.'

'You should visit our Smalkand warehouse. Besides the ice machines, our engineers work on a portal prototype, to quicken delivery, but I don't know how far they are.'

Varan stared at Shaw. 'What are you saying? That is the Weal's biggest secret!'

'We found several of the Weal's greatest secrets had been discovered somewhere else as well,' Nate said.

Varan looked flushed now. 'I want to be in on that. And you bet I'll keep it a secret! Gods, we'd blow MCTC out of the water with a few of those things!'

'All right,' Shaw said, happy with his eagerness. 'You're hired. There is one more thing, and that goes for all personnel. Our mindmages must give you a clean bill. We're at war and we need to make sure every one of you is who they say they are and not a jinni.'

'I have no secrets,' Varan said. 'I assume they'll be discreet.'

Shaw thought of Tymon and chuckled. 'Absolutely.' She rubbed her hands. 'We're expecting a ship. *Marigold* brings a load of exclusive printed fabrics, fine hand-painted porcelain, spices and other valuables. And now I remember I still have some hands to find for her.'

'How many?' Varan asked.

'They're sailing her with a skeleton crew,' Nate said. 'We're always short on sailors.'

'How soon do you need them?'

'*Marigold* is a steam vessel, so we expect her tomorrow,' Shaw said. 'Why? Can you find someone?'

'Sure,' Varan said. 'At home, there are several younger sons eating their hearts out for a ship, and Towne Harbor has its own orphanage.' He bit his lip. 'I'd better go if we need them in a hurry.' He produced a handportal.

'Rich kid, eh?' Nate said.

'Not rich like some,' Varan said. 'But well enough off to afford a few of these. I suggest you come along, mister director.'

Away they went, and Shaw turned back to the warehouse. 'We need a sign with our name on it,' she said, looking up at the bare front of the building.

'Do you ever stand still?' Callogan gave a rueful grin. 'Things really move around you.'

# CHAPTER 3 – BURGLARS

Shaw lay stretched out in a chair, still too excited to sleep. Across the room, Keena breathed deep and easily, and in the cafeteria, Cook snored like a one-man sawmill.

There were footsteps on the stairs, hurried footsteps, followed by the faint light of a guard's lantern and a shadow coming toward her.

'Shaw!' a voice whispered. It was Yens, the guard squad leader. 'Shaw, you're awake?'

'What is it?' she said.

'Burglars!' he said. 'Not here; in the house to the right.'

*Darn!* 'Wake everybody! Share out what weapons we have.' She thought for a moment. 'Tell them no lights, no noise.'

'I've alerted my guys,' Yens said. 'What are we going to do?'

'Do? What we always do,' she said, suddenly angry. 'Kick ass.'

He grinned; she could see his teeth glisten in the dark. 'I hoped you'd say that. Good, we'll show them.'

'Burglars?' Keena's voice sounded alert. 'Why now?'

Shaw shrugged. 'We'll ask them.' She sought her shoes with her toes and slipped into them. Then she walked softly to the next room. 'Callogan?'

'Eh? What's wrong?' the mover mage said sleepily.

'Burglars next door. We're going to say hi.'

He made a sound like a waking bear and came to his feet. 'You sure know how to liven things up.'

They hurried outside and found Cook waiting, armed with a wicked kitchen cleaver.

'Whoa, the Old Wharf Butcher!' Callogan said. 'You're a fearsome sight, mate.'

Cook's fifteen-year-old face was hard. 'I got a job,' he said grimly. 'No one is going to steal it from me.'

'That's the spirit,' Callogan said.

'Hush now,' Shaw said. She wasn't a fighter; her bad eye had made her uncertain, and she had left most of the battles in Eskandar's company to the bigger kids. But Cook's words could have been hers a thousandfold. Burgle her trading house? Never!

Downstairs, they found Yens with his seven guards, armed with whatever the warehouse had coughed up, and looking eager for battle.

'There's a small ship at the pier,' Yens reported. 'Must've crept right past us; probably they don't even realize we're here.'

'Came by sea, curse them!' Keena said. 'They're pirates!' She'd donned her plumed hat and looked much like a Bokkaner herself.

'Keep to the shadows,' Shaw said in a whisper. 'We don't want them to spot us.'

The door to the house was ajar and Yens slipped inside, with Shaw on his heels.

'Nothing,' he mouthed.

They crept through the hall and were about to open the door to the sitting room when a crash upstairs halted them.

'Gods!' a voice exclaimed behind them.

'Shut up, idiot!' Callogan whispered.

Yens moved to the stairs, and the others followed him. Near the top, a step creaked with the sound of a tree splintering.

'Wot's that?' a guttural voice said, and a dark shape appeared in the landing.

'Give up!' Yens roared. 'You're under arrest!' He jumped the last two steps and ducked as a sword swung at his head. 'Filthy dog!' he said, as the dark shape crumbled. At the head of his guards he ran across the landing. Shaw wanted to follow, but Callogan pushed her gently back. 'My turn, boss,' he said. 'C'mon, Keena.' Cook barged past next, screaming insults, and Shaw found herself deserted.

'Well!' she said indignantly. Gripping her courage and her knives, she went in.

It was dark in the room; too dark to see properly, but then a clear mage light rose over their heads.

Shaw nearly bumped into a burly ruffian fighting a young guard. Her shin hit a wooden stool and without thought she picked it up. With a savage overhand blow, she broke the seat over the pirate's head and heard him grunt. His knees buckled and he went down.

Shaw dropped the broken stool. 'I've been with the wyrmcaller,' she snapped at the boy, who stared at her in blank amazement. 'What did you think? I was knitting his socks?'

A pirate in a hideous yellow shirt rushed Yens, waving an ax and screaming wildly.

Shaw saw the squad leader stagger. She yelled and crashed her barely 90 pounds into his opponent. The pirate tripped over a table and fell, giving Yens time to recover his stance.

'No killing!' she screamed, and the squad leader nodded. He changed the direction of his blow and knocked the pirate unconscious. 'That's the last one!'

A guard came forward, clutching his arm and cursing, dripping blood from a nasty gash.

'I can do that,' Keena said unexpectedly. She gripped the boy's arm, and slowly the bleeding stopped. The sides of the wound came together, and a clean pink ridge remained.

'Keena!' Shaw said, utterly surprised.

'I ain't a healer,' the girl said finally. 'I been watching our healers at work and it didn't look that difficult, mostly. There, that's the best I can do; your body will do the rest. Bandage it, and light duty for the day.'

'It's a darned good job,' Shaw said.

Keena shrugged, setting her bleached braids dancing. 'I guess I have to train it.'

'Be sure you do,' Shaw said. 'We're always short on healers.'

Yens came back. 'We trussed up the bandits. We found a whole heap of short ropes, so they won't get away in a hurry.'

'Shaw, come and look!' Callogan shouted. He stood bowed over a large coffin. With a body inside.

'It's not human,' he said, tapping the body with his knuckles. It sounded metallic.

'A statue?' Shaw said.

'It looks as if it could move,' Callogan said. 'All those parts are joined much like high-class steel armor.'

'It's not armor,' Keena said.

'It's some sort of machine,' Shaw said. 'We must take it to Smalkand; our engineers will want to see this. Callogan, can you port it to the warehouse?'

'Sure,' he said. 'Those papers part of it?'

A sheaf of documents lay scattered and trampled around the chest. Shaw picked them up.

'Can't read those,' she said. 'Looks like Qoori to me.' She unfolded a crumpled sheet. 'These are orders to some pirate captain. He must send the automaton to the lord Nimmendal in his castle without delay.'

Callogan scratched his head. 'Nimmendal? Who's he?'

'He's very bad news,' Shaw said. 'We first heard the name mentioned as the guy who had united the Tradeports and made himself their boss. After Eskandar bombarded Brisa, he learned Nimmendal was none other than the Angsthafn pirate kingpin, and a jinni prince to boot.'

'Bad news indeed,' Callogan said. 'It means this thingus could be important.'

'I suppose so,' Shaw said. 'Please put the lid back, and move it to the boardroom.'

Callogan closed the chest and ported it away. 'Done.'

'Almost,' Shaw said, whirling around. 'We forget the ship!'

'To the pier!' Yens cried, and they bolted down the stairs like a bunch of eager kids.

In dead silence they ran to the water's edge. The moored ship was a solid, single-masted vessel with round forms and heavy beams, armed with six guns. They ran aboard over her narrow gangplank and spread out.

No one came to meet them, and a quick search of the hold and the cabins told them the ship was deserted.

'Nobody,' Shaw said, panting, as they returned to the deck. 'That would mean we got them all.' She looked at Yens. 'Great job, Squad leader. Send one of your guys to inform the harbor watch. He can take a steamcart; I want those pirates away before daybreak. We're running a business, not a dead house.'

Several hours later, the harbor watch arrived with steamcarts and cages on wheels.

Shaw had finished searching the ship, and was sipping a fresh mug of tea, when one of Yens' boys brought a tall, rawboned lieutenant into the office.

'Are you in charge here?' the man said, his eyebrows crawling into his military haircut.

'I'm the managing director of the PTC,' Shaw said coolly. 'We are the lord wyrmcaller's merchant arm. I must say I don't take it kindly to be attacked by a force of armed pirates right inside the Weal capital.'

'No,' the lieutenant said, taken aback by her reaction. 'I can imagine you don't, ah, ma'am. You are sure they were pirates and not common thieves?'

'They were dressed like pirates, armed like pirates and came by ship,' Shaw snapped. 'By now I have fought enough of their kind to know them, Lieutenant.' She was tired and angry, and the officer irritated her.

'Quite,' the lieutenant said hurriedly. 'Where are they?'

'We left them where they fell, in the house next door,' Shaw said. 'Not all of them survived the battle. I do want them gone before business hours; no need to frighten our customers. I will show you the battlefield.' She put down her mug and rose. 'This way please.'

'I see,' the lieutenant said when they were at the scene. 'And you managed all this with only those, ah, young 'uns?'

'We did,' Shaw said. 'Our people are well-prepared to fight for our organization, Lieutenant. Squad leader Rowe-Yens' lads did excellent work this night.' *There,* she thought. *Do what you wish with that!*

The lieutenant stared at her. 'That will please some and shame a lot of others.' He kicked the nearest pirate, an ill-shaved fellow with a scar on his cheek. 'Get up!' The pirate glared at him, and spat.

'On your feet!' the lieutenant barked, drawing his blade.

The pirate still eyed him defiantly. Then a spasm tore through his body, he opened his mouth in soundless anguish, and went limp.

The lieutenant knelt and sought a pulse. He shook his head and looked up at Shaw in blank amazement. 'Snuffed it.'

Outside, someone screamed, and all at once there was a lot of yelling.

Shaw ran down the stairs and was outside in seconds, with the lieutenant close behind her.

'A jinni!' she cried, as she recognized the enormous blob of flesh. 'Callogan?'

'Knocked out!' Keena cried. 'He walked with that captured pirate when it changed.'

'Help him,' Shaw snapped. 'We need his magic.'

She hadn't fought any jinn herself, but she remembered the instructions. 'Hit the beast low!' she cried. 'Round the mouth and eyes, not higher!'

She saw Yens and his boys rush at the jinni, gripping their swords like pikes.

The jinni laughed and grew an arm. He bowled the young squad leader head over heel aside. 'Give up!' he cried, 'you cannot win, cattle!'

Several harbor guards approached the monster, their faces fearful. Cook ran past them, screaming curses, struck the jinni near the fearsome mouth and darted away again. The harbor guards, probably more used to checking ship's cargoes than fighting monsters, slashed at the jinni face. When the beast jumped at them, they retired in a hurry. Squad leader Yens rejoined the battle, the side of his head gleaming with blood.

'Die, beast!' he cried, striking at an eye. His blow connected, and the jinni screamed. Yens barked an order and his guys ran past the monster, each slashing at the fat body before jumping out of reach.

Shaw moved to the jinni's blinded side, and spurted at him, waving her small wrist-knife. She missed the other eye, but her long slash opened up the jinni's skin. Something slapped her, and she ran out of reach again.

The lieutenant had drawn his saber and confronted the jinni. 'For the Weal!' he said, and slashed the beast twice over the face.

The jinni kicked him, and the lieutenant went down.

Immediately, one of Yens' guys ran up to him, grabbed his booted foot and dragged him away.

The jinni crowed. 'Fools! You edible fools!' he croaked. 'No one can withstand the jinn.'

'What do you know?' a voice said, and Callogan limped forward. 'You're only a lot of lard, with not enough wit to empower a chicken!'

'Callogan!' Shaw whispered, thinking how Eskandar had killed the Brisan jinni. 'Port him into the water! Jinn can't swim!'

'Hah!' Callogan raised his arms. 'You should cool off a little, jinni-boy. There you go.' The monster rose into the sky, limbs flailing, and shot off to splash into the harbor beyond the pier.

For a few minutes, nothing happened. Then the surviving pirates began to scream.

'I think... That did it,' Shaw said thickly. 'Congratulations, Callogan. Your very first jinni.' She staggered, and the mage put an arm around her waist.

'Steady,' he said.

Keena came hurrying, but Shaw waved her away. 'See to the others; I'm tired, no more.'

'You're not,' she said. 'You're wounded.'

Only then Shaw noticed her right sleeve was soaked with blood. 'Darn! How?'

'That beast must've done it, one of his tentacles was razor-sharp,' Callogan said.

Shaw shivered and suddenly her arm hurt like someone was cutting it open with a blunt knife.

'What the heck's going on here?' a familiar voice shouted.

'Nate!' she croaked, and fainted.

# CHAPTER 4 – TO WORK

Shaw moved and then groaned as her stiff muscles protested.

'There you are,' Nate said, from behind her. He lifted her head gently on his lap. 'Drink? It's your own nice lemonade.'

She sipped; darn, it *was* her favorite sweetberry syrup. Shaw sighed and opened her eyes.

'Where did you get that?' she murmured.

Nate chuckled. '*Marigold*,' he said. 'Everything happened at the same time. Varan and I ported back with the crew he'd begged, borrowed and cajoled, *Marigold* arrived and I saw you in Callogan's arms.'

'I wasn't!' Shaw protested, shocked.

'I know,' he said, holding her head as she drank.

She really liked lying like this, propped up against Nate.

'Varan did a great job,' Nate said. 'Without fuss he sent those harbor guards home with the dead pirates, manned the new ship *Fayaafa*, set a crew to cleaning up the house, and had *Marigold* unloaded. Meanwhile Keena healed your arm; then she did Yens' face and several other wounds, and dropped asleep where she stood. Where the heck did she learn all that?'

'She taught herself,' Shaw said as she inspected her arm. Then she frowned. 'That's not my coat.' She looked around at Nate, dressed only in his shirt.

He grinned. 'I didn't want you to catch a cold. Yours is still wet; Dowa washed it for you and repaired the rent in the sleeve.'

Shaw sat up in the grass beside the warehouse. 'The muscles are stiff,' she said as she moved her arm up and down.

'That's what you get from attacking a jinni with a knife,' Nate said drily. 'Silly!'

'At least |I can use a knife. I would've been far sillier had I attacked him with a sword.' Shaw climbed to her feet, leaning on Nate's arm. 'Thanks.'

'Always,' he said. 'For you, always.'

She blinked. *What did he say?* 'Is Chagan around?' she asked hastily.

Nate grinned. 'He is. Do you want him?'

'Only have him look at something,' Shaw said, glancing up at Nate.

'He's in the cafeteria, showing Cook how to brew cawah.'

'Cook fought like a lion. Is he still awake?'

'He? The guy's led an expedition to the grocer's and back; brought fresh bread, meat, cheese and lots more. Cook takes his job very serious.'

Shaw looked at the sun. 'Darn! How long have I been asleep?'

'It's an hour to noon,' Nate said. 'You needed it, girl.'

She grunted. 'Too many hours wasted.'

'Not wasted,' he said calmly. 'You needed to rest.'

'Chagan,' she said, confused by the solicitude in his voice.

Nate chuckled. 'All right.' They walked to the warehouse. 'We found something else. We transferred it to the big safe in your office.' He glanced at her, his eyes sparkling. 'Treasure, ma'am! A good-sized chest full of coins. Many of them bore unfamiliar faces and names, but all were solid gold or minted silver.'

Shaw looked at him. 'Treasure?'

'Heaps of it.' Nate gripped her shoulders. 'Twenty thousand or more. The chest was hidden in one of the rooms. Whoever cleaned out this place the first time did a sloppy job. I don't suppose we'll tell them?'

'No, of course not!' Shaw said weakly. 'Dear gods; I hadn't expected *that*.' She fell silent, thinking of the fight, and twenty thousand coins.

They entered the cafeteria and Shaw sniffed the aroma of freshly made cawah.

'Shaw!' Cook said with a huge smile. 'How are you?'

'Great,' she said. 'What do I smell?'

'It's a beany thing; they seem to like it up north.'

'So they do. The wyrmcaller drinks it all day.' She accepted a mug. 'Smells godly.'

Then she shook hands with Chagan. 'Had a good trip?'

'*Marigold* is fast,' he said. 'We didn't see a pirate until we came here.' He was a young Qoori of seventeen or thereabouts, with the green complexion of his people and a thin, sensitive face. He had been one of *Drakon*'s two surviving officers, a professional naval guy who now served as first in *Marigold*.

'We didn't expect ours,' Shaw said. 'I got something to show you, something those pirates wanted. It is more Xailin's business perhaps, but maybe you can tell me what it is.'

She led him and Nate to the boardroom, where Callogan has moved the chest onto the long table.

'Qoori markings,' Chagan said, studying the chest.

'It came with Qoori papers too. Guys, kindly remove the lid; my arms can't quite reach it.'

'Son of the Gods,' Chagan whispered as Nate and he leaned the lid against the wall. 'An imperial Xo.' His face had turned an even darker green. 'This thing is very, very valuable. Rare, very old, perhaps a thousand years.' He swallowed. 'What the so highborn Xailin builds, are shadows of this.'

'But what is it?' Shaw said.

'An automaton,' Chagan said. 'If it still works, it can walk, talk and think like a man.'

'It is valuable?' Nate said.

Chagan rested his hands on the table. 'All the gold in the Weal, the Peaks and Hizmyr could not buy you a Xo. Such a one must have cost ten annual incomes of Holy Qoor at the height of her power.'

'Then I can't sell the thing,' Shaw said. 'Why would the jinn want it?'

'They mustn't have it,' Chagan said shocked. 'Not ever. They would misuse and dishonor it.'

'No,' Shaw said, impressed by the dismay in his face. 'They won't get it back. Better get Miyra; you'll be taking it to Smalkand.'

Chagan swallowed. 'That will be a nervous journey. I suppose you are right not to keep it here. I'll tell her; my honorable captain will love being made a target.'


Shaw wandered down again. She was still tired and as she moved her arm, her whole body ached. *Those darned pirates!* she thought. *Intruding on her domain. Wrong idea, Mister Jinni!* She stopped and got the eye patch from her pocket. For a moment she waited to refocus her misty eye and then she looked at Nate. 'I'm ready.'

He grinned. 'Good. We need you.'

They stepped outside, and Shaw heard someone call her name. A blurred figure waved and she hurried over.

'Curse it, I can't even see who it is,' she said.

'Varan, with Captain Isambar,' Nate said. 'Your eye will improve, Na'a said. It needs time.'

'I know,' she said. 'But I hate it making me clumsy.'

Varan beamed at her as she joined him. 'You're awake! I'm glad. And sad to have missed such a heroic battle.'

'Nate said you did all the battlefield mop-up,' Shaw said. 'Thank you!'

'It's what I am here for,' he said. 'That harbor lieutenant wasn't too clearheaded when I sent them home with the pirates.'

Shaw swallowed something vitriolic. 'Harbor guards are clerks, not soldiers,' she said. 'Totally clueless.'

Varan smiled. 'Merchant captains like them very much,' he said. 'The more clueless they are the better.'

The strange guy at his side laughed. 'That is the solemn truth.'

'Meet Isambar,' Varan said. 'A particular pal of mine. He's both a trader and a certified mate. He will command *Fayaafa*, if you want him to.'

'Sure,' she said. 'Welcome, Captain Isambar. How do you find the ship?' She studied him as he stood there. She supposed him eighteen years old; almost as tall as Varan, but leaner, with long eyelashes beneath short, reddish-brown curls and a quick smile.

'She's sound,' Isambar said. 'Not much in the way of guns, but sturdy. She is a bomb ketch; we should have her mortars installed, then we could take on Angsthafn if we wanted to.'

Both men laughed at the absurdity.

'Perhaps we will,' Shaw said. 'Angsthafn, that is.'

'Eh?' Varan said, taken aback. 'We can't.'

'That's where Nimmendal is,' Shaw said. 'We want that beast dead. But not today, friends. Varan, if it suits your planning, would you collect all personnel in the warehouse? I must tell them our story first. That is including your crew, Captain.'

'Of course,' Varan said. 'We know something, but not the details. We were wondering about *Marigold*.'

They turned to watch Miyra's crew wrestling with the unfamiliar derrick and the large crate containing the Xo.

'Wait,' Isambar said. He gestured to a guy on *Fayaafa*'s deck. 'Lend a hand there.'

The Chorwaynie sailor ran over and showed them how to handle the crane. Together, they swayed the heavy load on board, where *Marigold*'s people lashed it down.

Then Miyra shouted an order, and *Marigold*'s engine revved up. The cutter's bow swung back to the sea, and she raced away.

Shaw waved, and turned.

'She's in a hurry,' Varan said. 'One darned fast lady, that one.'

'We had some great adventures with her,' Shaw said. 'Get the folks together, and I'll tell you.'

Shaw and Nate entered the warehouse and sat on the hard floor. Cook came and handed them a mug of steaming cawah before joining the others.

'Thanks,' Shaw said gratefully. She leaned against Nate's legs in her back and sipped as they waited for the others to gather round.

Finally Varan joined them. 'We're all here.'

Shaw put her mug down. 'Guys, last night, the first night in our new jobs, we beat off an attack on our business. Pirates and a bold jinni wanted to burgle our property. We didn't let them. Squad leader Yens' guards, Callogan, Cook, and Keena fought and destroyed those blighters. The company and I are proud and grateful for their bravery. Nate told me about the treasure. That will come in very handy, and I want you all to share. A bonus of five libers for every one of you, workers, soldiers and sailors, and another five for those who fought with us last night.'

'That is... uncommonly generous,' Cook said and he looked about to cry at the thought of so much wealth.

'It's only fair,' Shaw said. 'We are in this together, guys.'

For a moment, she was silent, searching for words. 'Yesterday, a dream came true,' she said, and a surge of emotion threatened to choke her off.

'The PTC is in business! Now you all must know what it is you joined. For we aren't just another merchant house. We are part of the wyrmcaller's team. Just as Proprietor Darquine's MCTC finances the Weal countries, shall we do the same for the Pasandir Peaks. I'll tell you our story as the wyrmcaller told us.'

She first gave them a little of Eskandar's background and of his adventures in the navy and in the Hellesands. 'That's how Eskandar became the Lord Wyrmcaller, Wings of the Mountains, and Defender of Bodrus the Sleeping God. His duty, and in a smaller way that of Nate, Keena and me, is to defend the Peaks, our new home.'

'And us?' Squad leader Yens said, staring at her narrow-eyed.

Shaw smiled. 'You're not a Peaks man, so your duty is to the PTC. If you want a chance at building a new life, you can become a citizen and help in the defense of Bodrus.'

She saw him nod. 'But that's for later. There is no hurry.'

Then she went on to tell of their kidnap and Eskandar with his friends coming to their rescue. Most guys knew something had happened to the Clammers, but no details and they listened avidly.

'And then you all became sailors,' Isambar said. 'Just like that.'

'Not exactly,' Shaw said, eyeing his languid skepticism. 'When we came to Towne, Proprietor Darquine lent us Fort Jamril, and her training schooner.'

'Skipper!' Isambar said in a very different tone, and his guys all laughed. 'He's darned good, but not an easy man to satisfy.'

Shaw pulled a face. 'No. But he made us into sailors. At least enough not to sink our ships.'

'All right,' Isambar said good-naturedly. 'With him around, I'll buy it.'

'Well, we haven't lost a ship yet. Quite the opposite.' She then told of the capture of *Pewbara* dirigible, and the Brisa attack that gained them the *Drakon* flagship.

'Burning Brisa made you guys heroes in Towne,' Varan said. 'If you can do that, we want to be in on your enterprise.'

'I've seen *Drakon*,' Isambar said. 'She's fearsome. With her, *Marigold* and our *Fayaafa* you've quite a fleet already.'

'*Drakon* wasn't the last,' Shaw said. She told of their airship crossing the Peaks, and their opening up of Smalkand.

'Across the Peaks?' Callogan said wondering. 'I always heard that couldn't be done.'

Shaw smiled. 'It can be done. There were a lot of crosswinds and whatever, but we have two very good pilots, and we made it.' She went on to the Wastrels they'd fought, the recapture of Pashwend Keep and Eskandar's taking of the *Killarn Ranni*.

'After that, the wyrmcaller took *Drakon* north to fight more pirates, and Nate, Keena and I came back here. The rest you know.' She leaned back, snuggling against Nate's legs.

Suddenly Yens rose. 'I used to make jokes about you Clammers,' he said, his face hard. 'Un-funny jokes, for I didn't think much of you street kids. I wish to apologize; I was wrong.'

Shaw looked at him. He hadn't been the only one, the whole city had made jokes about them, and worse. What surprised her was his admission. 'Thank you,' she said. 'Truth is, we didn't think much of ourselves either. Eskandar, with Kellani and Naudin showed us what we could do.'

'Still, I was wrong,' Yens said doggedly. 'Arrogant colonel's kid, and all that rot. And when I was down, you took me in.'

'We're glad to have you,' Shaw said. 'Forget the past. Fight with us, and we're friends.'

Yens nodded and sat down.

'We have plans,' Shaw went on. 'Big plans. This place will be the southern headquarters, with Varan running it as station manager. We'll also start trade caravans going across the Peaks, connecting all villages and castles in a giant network of grateful customers and loyal friends. Callogan shall be the man for that. Nate and I will go looking for new markets, other places for warehouses. Together, we will grow and prosper. Thanks for being with us, and may Bodrus keep you all.'

That got her a cheer and applause.

'Thank you for telling us,' Varan said. 'We're all with you to make the PTC into a mighty trade empire. Come, my friends; let's get to work.'

Shaw jumped to her feet. 'Mr. Varan, show me what *Marigold* brought us.'

She grabbed Nate's arm and together, they walked to the receiving-room, packed with goods.

'Look at this,' Shaw said, and she pulled away a little of the wrapping to see the fabrics underneath. 'I saw it before in a badly lit ship's hold and found them beautiful. Now by the light of day they're breathtaking.'

'That shipment's for Towne,' Varan said. 'Continentals aren't as much interested in such frivolities.'

'I wouldn't be so sure of that,' one of the new salesgirls said quickly. 'Give me one or two samples; I bet old Clarkill of Fisherman's Lane wants some.'

'All right,' Varan said. 'I'll spare you a bale or two.' He stared at the load, his fingers twitching. 'This is a fortune.'

'I know,' Shaw said. 'What do you hope to get for it?'

'Bottom price? Twenty thousand.' Varan burst out in a chuckle. 'My brother's face when I show him this stuff! He's always telling us how successful he shall be when he is boss, and how much money he will make. Well, he won't make this much.'

They went through the porcelain, the wines and spices, and all the other stuff. As last, Shaw opened the box of sweets.

'I've never seen these before,' she admitted. 'I have no idea of their value.'

Varan stared at the box. Then he sniffed at it and carefully broke off a tiny bit. He put it on his tongue. 'Toffees!' he said, with an awed face. 'How many are there?'

'A hundred,' Shaw said.

'At fifty libers each,' Varan said. 'We had a box like that last year, taken from another pirate. This alone should bring us five thousand libers.'

'Who would pay fifty libers for one sweet?' Nate said.

'Merchants wanting to show off their wealth,' Varan said. 'I better sail to Towne myself, this time. After that, Isambar can handle all the Chorwaynie trading.'

'Then do so,' Shaw said. 'And tell everybody the seas to the north are awash with Bokkaners, lest some adventurous soul would want to go there.'

Varan snorted. 'Most of our merchants aren't the courageous types. If they were, Brisa would never have stood a chance with its piracy. Should I find someone who is mad enough, I'll hire them.'

The *Fayaafa* sailed with Varan and their riches, and life settled down. When the first house was fit to live in, Shaw walked to the second floor and chose a small bedroom with a window to the sea. She dumped her meager possessions on the bed and sat down.

*My place.* She was filled with both sadness and exultation. As a child, she'd had a small cubicle of her own next to her parents' bedroom. After the fire... When she came to Clam Street, she had to sleep in an overcrowded room full of rowdy kids. She had never grown accustomed to the press of bodies, the noise and the smells; the lack of privacy. Later, in Smalkand she bunked with Willow and Hella; that was an improvement. She lay back on the old featherbed, reveling in its softness. At last she had a room for herself again.

*Would I share it with Nate?* She buried the thought as fast as it came up. He wouldn't want her that way, with her boy's body and stupid eye.

She jumped to her feet and hurried down, back to her office and work.

Around noon, a city messenger brought a short note from the Port Authority, thanking them for their assistance, with enclosed a reward of six libers for the pirates they'd caught. Shaw grinned, thinking of the treasure chest in her safe, and put the six gold coins into the cafeteria budget.

In the afternoon, she went with Nate to see a lensmaker, a professional with a handsome office in the city. He read through Na'a's notes, put his fingers to her temples, tuttutted and told her to come back in three days' time.

'Glasses!' she said disgustedly, as they were back on the street.

'They will show you have deep pockets,' Nate said. 'That's good for business.'

She glanced at him, but his face was serious.

'They're ugly,' she said only.


The next day, a steamcart came roaring down the harbor front and screeched to a stop, ejecting two young ladies and a load of heavy boxes.

'Imooga!' Shaw cried, hurrying to greet them. 'Good to see you!'

'So this is your hide-out?' the Thali engineer said. 'It's much bigger than I thought. Here, I bring Oychak, she's another engineer. We got it done, Shaw! We'll be big, rich and famous!'

'Done what?' Shaw was confused for a moment.

'The portal, silly! We got a working portal made!'

Shaw stared at her. 'You don't say.'

'Well, I did, didn't I?' Imooga frowned. Then she smiled. 'Of course; you're surprised. We've been working non-stop to get it done.'

'It was terribly exciting,' Oychak said. 'I never thought to work on a portal; it's such a big warlock secret.'

She was a comfortable girl with ruddy cheeks and a ready smile.

'How it operates will stay a secret,' Imooga said. 'Only this time the secret is ours. We don't think you should go around selling these yet.'

'We won't.' Shaw scratched her neck. 'I don't know what would happen if we did, so I'll leave that for Eskandar to decide. We do want to sell those ice machines, though.'

Imooga giggled and waved at the stack of boxes the driver had piled up on the path. 'Look what we brought. A portal and two ice machines, one working and one in to-be-copied parts.'

Shaw gave a shout, and a worker came running. 'All those boxes are for the workroom. Careful, they're very valuable.' She turned to the engineers. 'Let me show you round. We're doing fine; we already killed a jinni and a bunch of pirates.'

'We heard them talk about it at the aerodrome,' Imooga said. 'And the steamcart driver told it once more. Pirates and jinni! We got that automaton you sent us. It's fascinating, but I'm not going to touch it. I don't know a thing about automata. I put it away beneath a little forcefield, for when my cousin Ulaataq comes back. It's more in his line of tinkering.'

'It's much safer with you than it would be here,' Shaw said.

'I would love to see it working,' Imooga said. 'If it's truly manlike, that would be incredible.'

They walked into the warehouse backdoor.

'Here is the workshop,' Shaw said.

Oychak put her hands to her hips as she inspected the room with its old-fashioned workbenches and tool racks. She didn't say anything disparaging, but her expression told Shaw enough.

'Don't worry, I'll get it up-to-date.' The engineer smiled. 'I will be staying. You got a bed somewhere?'

'Sure,' Shaw said. 'The house next door. It will be small and sober, but it is a single room.'

'That would be perfect,' Oychak said. 'I need workmen, too.'

'We have a repairman and an apprentice. We can hire others if you need more.'

'Let's see what they can do first. You're going to get those machines one at a time, not twenty per week.'

Shaw laughed. 'No indeed! With a model, we'll get a few orders first and make these. I do need an idea of a price.'

'I'll let you know the cost in materials,' Oychak said.

'Now the portal. Where do you want it set up?' Imooga said. 'We'll place it under the stairs, all right? Now go have a cawah or whatever. If you want a portal, we'll be too busy to chat.'

Shaw grinned. 'I have to go into the city, so I won't be in your way.' Then she went in search of Nate.

# CHAPTER 5 – A SPOT OF KEENA'S WORK

Shaw found her partner going through a stack of things she couldn't identify in the semi-dusk between the shelves.

When he saw her, Nate grinned. 'I know; your glasses should be ready.'

They walked outside. 'Our own portal,' he said, as they passed the two engineers. 'We could all sleep back in Smalkand every night.'

Shaw made a face. 'No thanks,' she said. 'I finally have my own room, and I'm not going to share again.' She glanced at his face. 'Not without a lot of persuasion.' She saw a dark blush touch his cheeks. *Gods, what am I saying?*

'Still, that portal is handy,' she went on quickly. 'I wonder if we can get a handcart through. We could send Willow fresh produce whenever she needs anything.'

She caught Nate looking at her and her stomach did a strange flip-flop.

'Sure,' he said, and he smiled slowly. 'A handcart would go through easily. We could tell Willow to arrange it with Cook.'

'Yeah,' Shaw said, and she bit her lip.

Suddenly Nate laughed. 'Silly!' he said, and he gave her a quick hug. 'Let's take a steamcart.'

The lensmaker's office was across the city, on the first floor of a big building. Inside it was a dream of pale blues and greens, with a stern assistant in a spotless cotton robe.

'Ms. Harwans,' she said. 'A moment, please.'

After a few minutes, a well-dressed lady dragging a shrieking six-year-old came out of another door. The boy had a black patch over his right eye.

'Thank you, ma'am,' the assistant said. 'Your next appointment will be over a week.'

The child looked at Shaw. 'You're a pirate, too!' he said accusingly.

'Sure,' Shaw said, touching her own patch. 'We're both big, brave pirates, aren't we?'

'Don't wanna,' the boy said. 'It's stoopid.'

'Not!' Shaw said. 'It makes you look tough, guy.'

The boy made a tough face and growled.

Then the woman dragged the boy from the room and in the hall the shrieking started again.

'Poor kid,' Shaw said to Nate.

'You may go in, Ms. Harwans,' the assistant said.

'Good day, Ms. Harwans.' The lensmaker held up a small cardboard box. 'Your glass, ma'am.' His thin fingers opened the box and produced a round eyeglass, with a gold rim and a chain.

'What's that?' Shaw said. 'I thought it would be a pair, like Naudin has.'

'Oh, but you don't need a pair, ma'am. This monocle will serve to correct the aberrant eye only. Kindly try it on.'

Shaw put the glass into her eye. 'It fits,' she said, surprised.

'It is fully custom made, ma'am,' the lensmaker said. 'After a day you won't even notice you are wearing it. Please return in a month's time. You can leave your check at the desk.'

'Where goes the chain?' Shaw said hesitantly.

Nate clipped it to her tunic. 'Very impressive,' he said. 'A killer's eye.'

The lensmaker coughed, and Nate grinned.

'When we are defending Seatome from pirates, such an eye helps,' Shaw said politely. 'Thank you.'

Back with the assistant she wrote out a check for nine hundred libers. Then she turned and looked in the mirror. It didn't make her attractive, she thought, as she inspected her image. That stupid patch and then the monocle making her idiot eye twice as big. *Darn, no tears!*

Nate gripped her shoulders. 'It's very dashing,' he said. 'It gives you a daredevil look.'

She swallowed and smiled at him. 'Well, I am a big, bad businesswoman,' she said.

'So you are,' Nate said.

'Your next appointment is in four weeks time, ma'am,' the assistant said.

Back at the warehouse, she flaunted her eyeglass, daring anyone to comment, but none did.

'Nice,' was all Keena said.

Feeling vaguely disappointed, Shaw sat down at her desk in the fine manager's office and opened the drawers. They were empty, of course. She picked up a list of old stock Nate had collected from the shelves and read through it, mentally weighing its marketability. Then the door opened and she looked up, screwing the monocle in her eye.

It was Wylmer, smiling and smart in his navy uniform.

'Hi,' she said, surprised. 'How did you come here?'

'Your portal is ready, ma'am general manager,' he said. 'Someone had to try it, so Amaj and I tossed a coin for the honor.'

'And you lost?'

'I won.' Wylmer waved his hand around. 'Grand place this. It looks real classy. Smart eyeglass, too. It fits in with the background.'

Shaw jumped up. 'A *corrective* glass,' she said. 'It is a lovely place; I fell for it as soon as I saw it. Let me give you a tour.'

Excited, she dragged him out of the room. 'Here, boardroom. Next, our ledger keepers.'

Wylmer stepped inside. 'We've met,' he said puzzled, as he looked at the two clerks. 'I know, Pomfrith! My father does business there.'

'No longer,' Howwil said. 'Pomfrith is dead. Thus we came here.'

Wylmer frowned. 'Dead? And the shares?'

Howwil lifted his hands. 'I am not allowed to speak of that.'

Wylmer's light gray face turned splotchy. 'But my father's company?'

Roza looked unhappy. 'I'm sorry.'

'What's the problem?' Shaw asked.

'Pomfrith is... was WyDir's majority investor. If those shares fall into the wrong hands, the gods know what could happen.'

'Could you explain that?' Shaw asked.

Howwil shook his head.

'Treat it as a completely imaginary example, just to show to me how these things work,' Shaw said.

Roza put a finger to her chin. 'As a totally fictional case? A large privately owned business needs money. It finds a wealthy party, like a banker, who is willing to invest capital. In exchange, the banker gets shares that give him a yearly percentage of the business profits and a say in the firm's policy. As long as the banker is a sleeping partner, this will not be a problem; they will leave the running of the business to the management. Should anything unpleasant happen to the sleeping partner...'

'Say he dies, or something,' Howwil added.

'Then the shares go to the heirs,' Roza said. 'If they're honest, that still won't be a problem.'

'But if they're not,' Howwil said. 'If they're crooked ruffians with criminal connections, ruffians who are disappointed with their inheritance and want money, things could get nasty.'

'Strictly hypothetical, of course,' Roza said.

'Of course,' Shaw said. 'Thank you for the explanation.' She hesitated. 'Such shares, do they show the name of the shareholder?'

'They don't,' Howwil said. 'Such shares are to bearer.'

Wylmer nodded. 'It was a strictly unoffiical deal. My father didn't want it known those shares even existed. He saw them as security for a loan, no more; he planned to buy them back later.' He grimaced. 'I know, for I was there. Those days, my father still groomed me for a job in the business, so he had taken me along.'

'You mean nothing was written down?' Shaw said.

'It was a gentlemen's agreement,' Wylmer said.

Roza stifled a snicker. 'Mr. Pomfrith was a lot of things, but never a gentleman.'

'My father discovered that when Mr. Hynks arrived and claimed the position of senior director,' Wylmer said. 'He was livid. And I? If there's one thing I inherited from my mother it's an allergy for business. My father's stupidity, the crooks, the sheer size of WyDir all terrified me. I had to get away, to do a job I could handle. Through friends I met my late naval captain and he agreed to take me on as a midshipman. We sailed the next day, and I haven't seen my parents since. Still...' He slammed Howwil's desk. 'Curse that Pomfrith! I don't want his crooked heirs gutting WyDir. Over a thousand folks are earning a living there!'

'So if the shares are gone, the heirs can't prove they ever had them?' Shaw turned around. 'Let's get Keena.'

They found the mage outside, folding her lean body into tortuous shapes on the narrow strip of grass beside the warehouse.

She smiled as she saw Wylmer. 'Come to inspect the lot?' she said. 'We're doing fabulously.'

'He came to tell us the portal to Smalkand is ready,' Shaw said. 'And now he finds he has a problem.'

Keena straightened out and jumped to her feet. 'Anything we can do?'

Shaw explained the keepers' example, and Keena's thin face grew dark. 'Crooks!' she said. 'Where would we find those share things?'

'Pomfrith's Bankers,' Shaw said.

Keena whistled. 'Sturgeon Street; smack in the middle of the best protected part of the city.'

'Can we get in?' Shaw asked.

'In, yes. Out, that's another question.'

'Because?'

Keena's smile was bleak. 'Alarms, girl.'

'Of course,' Shaw said. She should have thought of that. 'Well?'

'Tonight,' Keena said, and she donned her plumed pirate hat. 'In and out.'

Shaw nodded. 'Just the two of us.'

After dark, two shapes crept from house to lightless house through the stately lane.

Shaw watched Keena, like she dressed in an odd assortment of dark clothes, with gloves and cap to hide her hair. The girl had stopped and seemed to listen. Then she disappeared into the shadows of a narrow porch, drawing Shaw after her.

From nearby came the stamp of booted feet, and two city guards walked past, armed and alert in this wealthy area.

The darkness hid the girls from their suspicious eyes, and the men didn't notice anything amiss. When the sounds of their footsteps had died away, Keena slipped out again.

Shaw followed her to the corner of the street. Quickly they crossed the road and went left until they came to a tall door. Beside it, a placard read *Pomfrith Bankers*.

Something in Keena's hands tinkled, and the door opened silently. The girls went inside, and Shaw closed the door behind her. The beating of her heart was a drum pounding "To Arms" as they tiptoed through the corridor. The first room was a salon, not the place to keep valuable papers. The next was a dining room, and opposite that a large office.

Keena gestured with her head and they went inside. A desk, with behind it a large portrait of a portly gentleman with side-whiskers.

The late Pomfrith, Shaw supposed, though why anyone would have a portrait of himself hanging behind his back was beyond her.

Keena went to the large painting and slid her hand behind it. Then she grinned as the panel behind the dead banker opened, showing a heavy, code-protected safe door.

While Keena tried the various cipher combinations, Shaw listened to the house. For a second she thought she'd heard something, and she stepped back into the shadows beside the door.

Then she heard it again, the sound of soft-soled feet coming their way. A stout, youngish person appeared, wearing a white dressing gown over his nightshirt and brandishing an old officer's saber.

'Caught you!' he said in a sharp voice. 'Burglar, eh? Put your hands up, you scum.'

Keena wheeled around and at the same time Shaw stepped from the shadows. She pressed the mouth of the old pistol she carried to the man's fat neck. 'Drop your blade, hero,' she said contemptuously.

The man made a gobbling sound in his throat and let his saber fall onto the soft carpet.

Keena's hand moved, and the little bludgeon she carried hit the stout man on the side of the head. He slumped and Shaw let him slip to the ground. She took the tasseled cord of the fine dressing gown and proceeded to bind the man's arms to his back.

Then she checked his pulse and felt his heart still beating strongly.

Meanwhile, Keena had gone back to the safe lock. There was a click, another, and a rapid *clickertyclick*, and the safe door swung open.

Keena took the contents from the safe and spread it out over the desktop. A fat roll of banknotes, plenty papers, and a thick folder headed WyDir, containing the twenty shares.

Shaw put the folder inside her tunic. Then, while Keena returned everything else to the safe, she checked the stout man again. He was still out, so she untied him and replaced the cord around his plump waist. Then she waited until Keena had relocked the safe and straightened the portrait.

As stealthily as they had come, the girls slipped out of the house, closing the door behind them. Still without a word, they hastened away.

Two streets on, they stopped and pulled their long skirts from under their jacks, removed their gloves and caps, and walked nattily down the street.

'No servants, no guards; that fellow was begging to be robbed,' Keena said. 'Gal, you should've taken this up sooner; you're a bliddy natural, you know that!'

'The gun did it,' Shaw said. 'I'm glad he didn't call my bluff, threatening with an unloaded fire arm.'

Keena laughed soundlessly. 'No burglar would use a loaded weapon. Better be jailed for burglary than hung for murder.'


Back at the warehouse, they found Wylmer pacing the cafeteria. Callogan lounged in a chair, sipping cawah. Cook was polishing the glasses, while Nate and Squad leader Yens sat playing cards.

They jumped when the girls entered.

'And?' Wylmer cried.

Shaw handed him the folder and Wylmer sighed. 'They're all there.' He slumped into his chair. 'Now what the heck am I to do with them?'

'Give them back to your father,' Shaw said.

'I suppose so,' Wylmer said. 'That won't be easy; he'll not consent to receive me.'

'Did he disown you?' Keena asked.

'Not that I know. Then my awful cousin would inherit, and even my father couldn't stomach *that*.' He grunted.

'Tomorrow morning I'll hop over and give these to his servants.'

He jumped up and embraced both Shaw and Keena. 'Thanks! I'm grateful! I'll not accept a penny from WyDir, but I'd hate seeing it ruined by some greedy crooks.'

Nate took Shaw's shoulders. 'How did it go?'

'There was this guy waving a saber like he'd found it somewhere and didn't know what it was.' She grinned. 'He did know my pistol when I pressed it to his neck. Then Keena knocked him out. We tidied up everything, leaving everything as it was, and left. They'll never be able to prove they held the shares.' She took a shuddering breath. 'It won't be my new job, though. Once was enough.'

'A pity,' Keena said, half-serious. 'We would've made a great duo.'

# CHAPTER 6 – UNEXPECTED EXPANSION

Wylmer Hall was a tall building on Salmon Street, right in the center of the city. It was one of the few surviving pre-war mansions, breathing wealth and arrogance.

Shaw glanced up at the five-story, light-gray facade with its many frills. The sightless curtains behind the balconied windows, and the heavy, forbidding door sent a subconscious shiver of unease slithering down her backside.

Nate glanced at her and winked.

Shaw gritted her teeth. *Wylmer looks ready to vomit.* She saw him swallow a few times and get from the steam cart.

'Wait here,' Shaw said to the driver. 'We'll be back.'

Together, the three of them walked to the big front door, and Captain Wylmer reached for the cast-iron bell. Before he could ring, the door opened silently, and an old servant appeared.

'Master Githeon!' he said in a subdued voice. 'You heard the news?'

'What news?' Wylmer asked, taken aback.

'Your father... He isn't well. He had a stroke, sir.'

'Darn!' Wylmer stood stock still, his face frozen in shock. 'No, I hadn't heard. How is he?'

'One side of his face gave up, he has trouble speaking and moving about. I'm afraid he still won't see you, Master.'

'And my mother?'

'Mrs. Wylmer is at her Art Colony, Master Githeon. She hasn't been at the Hall since you left.'

Wylmer took a deep breath. 'Very good. Please inform my father I have recovered the Pomfrith shares. I will wait.' They stepped into a high, austere hallway decorated in shades of gray, with on both sides closed doors and before them a monumental staircase.

The servant bowed and walked slowly up the stairs.

*What a place,* Shaw thought, staring at the bleak surroundings. *Everything is gray...* She put a hand to the wainscoted wall. *Almost the color of my skin. If I'd run around naked, I would be invisible.*

Wylmer moved and she glanced at him. His lips were a straight line as he faced at the staircase.

'He had a stroke,' he said. 'Now who will lead the company?'

In silence they waited until the servant came back.

'Your father wishes you do your will with the shares, Master,' he said. 'He does not want to see you.'

'Thank you,' Wylmer said. He turned and strode out of the monumental hall, back to the waiting steamcart.

Shaw caught the sigh and the sorrowful face of the old retainer before she turned and followed the captain out.

Once back in the car, Wylmer leaned over to the driver. 'Ride on to the WyDir entrance.'

Next door, WyDir Offices was all stained glass and copper ornaments, blazing lights and top-hatted porters in dove-gray uniforms.

As the driver slowly bridged the few yards from the Hall to the magnificent glass doors of the Office, a porter came hurrying and opened the cart door.

'Mr. Wylmer, sir!' he said, beaming a welcome. 'How good it is to see you!'

'Thank you,' Wylmer said, and Shaw wondered at the desperation in his face. 'Is Mr. Hynks in?'

'Yes sir, Mr. Wylmer. He will be overjoyed you are here.'

'I'm sure,' Wylmer said, and he couldn't hide the disgust in his voice.

A second porter held open the doors with the, well-polished brass WyDir symbol, and they walked inside.

A man in a sober clerk's uniform came running. 'Mr. Wylmer, sir! Mr. Hynks is eagerly awaiting you.'

*Mind reader?* Shaw thought pointedly. *Don't do that to us, mate. It's utterly rude.*

The man stiffened, but didn't speak as he led them up the stairs.

'My father's office,' Wylmer said, as they entered a room marked *President*. Central was a gleaming desk large enough to land one of the airships whose portraits filled the walls.

To the side, nearly hidden behind thick curtains, was another door, with the engraved sign *Senior Director*. Inside was a smaller office, frugally furnished. Behind a desk stacked with documents, a sparse man in an old-fashioned town coat and striped pants looked up as they entered. He jumped to his feet, surprisingly nimble for his age, and stretched out his hands in greeting, looking as sincerely dolorous as a paid mourner.

'Mr. Wylmer, sir! I had hoped you would find time to come by. I am terribly shocked about your father, sir. I can assure you I will do everything I can to run the company as he wishes it while he is indisposed.'

'I have news for you, Hynks,' Wylmer said, his voice stiff with dislike. 'I've got the majority shares right here. I am boss now, not my father or anyone else.'

The sparse man took a step back, and Shaw saw the shock and incredulity on his face were real. 'Pomfrith's shares?' he said hoarsely. 'But how?'

'Does it matter? I hold them.' Wylmer showed him the twenty certificates. 'Eighty percent of WyDir is mine to do with as I wish.' His lips twisted as he said that.

'Yes, I see,' Hynks said; his face a study in chagrin. 'Of course, Mr. Wylmer. You will take charge right away?'

Wylmer's desperation was clearly visible now, as if he were forced to do something terrible.

Without thinking, Shaw put a hand on his arm. Wylmer turned his head towards her and the sun rose on his face. Every trace of fear flowed from him and he smiled.

'No, Hynks,' he said. 'I'm not going to take charge. I am signing over my shares to the Pasandir Trading Company.' He thrust out the file of shares and Shaw took them blankly.

'What?' she said. She heard Nate's sharp intake of breath, but the reason escaped her.

Wylmer grinned. 'You got them, you keep them. For the glory of the Peaks and Divine Bodrus.'

'Dear me, Mr. Wylmer,' Hynks exclaimed. 'Those shares are worth a cool fifty thousand libers each; you can't just give them away to some girl.'

'Not *some girl*, Hynks,' Wylmer said. 'This lady is Shaw Harwans, managing director of the PTC, with a big warehouse on Old Quay Wharf and an even bigger one in Smalkand, the Peaks. That's the lord wyrmcaller's outfit, Hynks; an important Weal ally nation. Now you write a transfer of ownership from me to the PTC. After that, I want to see the whole board of directors. And call me Captain; I'm not my father.'

'Yes sir, Captain Wylmer,' Hynks said, defeated, and picked up the horn of his office voicepipe. He snapped a few orders, and sat down to write.

'Copies to Ms. Harwans, my father, me and the company archives,' Wylmer said. He gripped Shaw's hands. 'My savior.'

Shaw closed her mouth. 'Breath of the Mountains,' she said weakly, as she understood the enormity of what he had done. She took Wylmer's arm. 'Walk with me.'

She glanced at Nate and at Hynks, and her partner nodded.

'This Mr. Hynks; you don't like him,' she said bluntly when they were back in the presidential office. 'Are you prejudiced, or isn't he to be trusted?'

'He's a mean, treacherous crook,' Wylmer said. 'Pension him off or strangle him, then choose one of the department heads in his stead.'

'All right,' Shaw said. 'You really don't want the job?'

'I loathe the very thought,' Wylmer said. 'I'd rather start mudfishing in some distant swamp. Are you angry with me?'

'Of course not,' Shaw said. 'It's a bit much, all at once, but it has its advantages. What about your parents?'

Wylmer shrugged. 'I'm sure my father won't be broke. My mother?' He smiled thinly. 'She fancies herself an Art Patroness. She lives in a village to the north of the city, among a lot of other rich, useless dilettantes, and surrounds herself with rats; ah, artists. She'll find they slink away when my father stops paying her fat checks. Perhaps she will be obliged to come home.' He fell silent as Hynks came in with the documents.

Shaw read the scratchy lines very carefully. It was a clear statement of transfer, and both Wylmer and she signed every one of them.

When it was done, the captain sagged. 'At last! You have no idea, Shaw.'

A young man entered. 'The board of directors is assembled, Mr. Hynks.'

Shaw looked at him. 'Clerk?'

The moment she said it, she knew he wasn't. He looked in his early twenties, with an intelligent face and black hair carefully brushed into a center parting. His darkly elegant tailcoat, burgundy vest and tie, and the fashionable high collar would never be acceptable for a mere clerk.

'I'm Morgan, Mr. Wylmer's secretary, ma'am,' the young man said politely.

'That means you are mine now,' Shaw said cheerfully. She handed him the last two copies they'd just signed. 'One is for the company archives; the other you will have delivered to the elder Mr. Wylmer directly.'

The secretary glanced at the papers and his eyes grew big. 'Y-yes, ma'am,' he said. 'I'll go immediately.'

'Not personally, Mr. Morgan. I suppose you are to make notes at the meeting? I do expect a written report.'

'Yes, ma'am. I'll send someone else.' Morgan hurried out and shouted for a messenger. Then he came back. 'It is attended to.'

'Let us go.' Shaw felt laughter bordering on hysteria bubbling in her throat and she ruthlessly suppressed it.

The meeting room was next-door to the presidential office, and large enough to seat many more than the present twenty people. At the head of the table a high, leather chair waited. *The royal throne,* she thought, killing a giggle.

As a row of puppets, the directors rose when they entered. 'Good day, Mr. Wylmer,' they chorused, bowing like courtiers.

'Allow me, ma'am.' Wylmer disregarded them and escorted Shaw to the high chair. 'Sit down please, Ms. Harwans.' He gave the white-haired gentleman seated at her left hand a stern glance. 'That is Mr. Nate's chair.'

The board of directors stared at him in confusion, but obediently those on the left moved a seat. Nate, trying his darnedest not to laugh, took the corner chair. Wylmer walked to the chair at the low end of the table and sat with his arms crossed.

'Good day,' Shaw said politely. 'I imagine you are confused. I am Shaw Harwans, managing director of the Pasandir Trading Company, the new majority stockholder of WyDir. Mr. Nate is our director of operations, and you know Captain Wylmer.'

The gasp that went round the table nearly set the curtains fluttering.

'But Pomfrith holds those stocks!' a thin man in pince-nez and a flowery frock coat shouted.

'I am sorry to contradict you; we hold them,' Shaw said. 'Twenty shares, giving us the full eighty percent majority.'

'Darn,' a young man halfway along the table muttered.

'Quite,' Shaw said. 'Now I'm sure you know new management brings changes. Mr. Hynks, I must heartily thank you for your many years of devoted duty to Wylmer Dirigibles.'

A collective groan almost broke her sternness and she hurried on. 'Mr. Hynks, you have earned your rest. I will grant you the immediate discharge you must have longed for. Ladies and gentlemen, your applause, please.' She rose and every director with her. The ovation was strangely tentative, only a few clapped with wild abandon as Wylmer came to lead the shocked director out.

Shaw beckoned the secretary over. 'Warn the guards. He is to leave immediately. His rights are revoked; he can't give any orders, and isn't allowed to take, burn or sign any papers. Hand him his hat and have someone arrange for a company car to drive him straight home.'

'Ma'am,' Morgan said, who seemed desperately trying to hide his glee.

Shaw sat down again. 'We will need a new general manager, preferably a younger person with operational experience.'

'That's me,' the young man along the table said, smiling impudently. He was carelessly dressed in a crumpled morning coat and a drooping bow tie.

'Is it?' Shaw said. 'Who are you?'

'I'm Benffald, Supervisor Lines, ma'am.'

Shaw stared at him. 'I'm not used to your terminology yet. What do you do?'

'I'm in charge of the day-to-day running of the Lines Department, ma'am.'

Shaw looked at him. 'And what about the Directors of Lines?'

'Ah,' Benffald said. 'Their responsibility is *oversight*, ma'am.'

Shaw leaned back in her chair and saw round the table. 'So many directors having oversight?' she murmured.

'But of course, ma'am,' the man in the pince-nez said earnestly. 'That is vitally important.'

*He sounds as if he really believes it,* Shaw thought. 'Thank you. Before we go on, a small question. Does WyDir operate its own company steamcarts?'

'But of course,' the white-haired man said. 'We all got one.'

'Why?' Shaw said, surprised. 'Where do you need to go to that you have your own steamcart?'

'Well, to my home, ma'am.'

'You mean we are paying to drive you home? Twenty carts?'

'Yes, ma'am,' he said, as if it was the most commonplace thing in the world.

'What's your salary?'

The man stiffened. 'Ma'am!' he said outraged.

Shaw sighed and turned to the secretary. 'What is the average annual salary of these people?'

'A thousand libers, ma'am,' Morgan said.

'You're kidding,' Shaw said, aghast. 'And you?'

Morgan's face didn't change its polite detachment. 'Thirty-six fifty, ma'am.'

'Thank you. Put it in the notes, will you.' She picked up the pen and paper before her. *'Nate, take a company cart and ask Howwil and Roza to get me a reputable firm of auditors right away. I want accountants to go through WyDir's books today; I am sure we're being fleeced.'* She shoved it under Nate's nose and he nodded. Folding the paper, he left in hurry.

Shaw noted the puzzled looks and smiled. 'Now please introduce yourselves and what your positions with WyDir are. Give me your department, number of personnel and your yearly budget. Try to keep it at fifteen minutes each. Mr. Morgan, make notes, will you?'

After the sixth director had finished, two hours had passed. Shaw sat with her elbows on the table, her hands making a bridge under her chin as she listened and wondered what use those expensive guys were. Why did they need a Director for Executive Training? A Chief Manager Liaison? And what about the woman who sat there explaining she was the Director of Ticket Oversight?

A messenger entered and walked to the head of the table. 'Ms. Harwans?' he murmured.

By now, the Ms. made Shaw feel a hundred years old. She gritted her teeth, and nodded. The man handed her a narrow envelope. 'From Mr. Wylmer, ma'am.'

Shaw opened the envelope and found five printed shares and a short note in a shaky handwriting. *'Don't know how you managed it, but here is the rest; I'm done and past caring. Kick out Hynks and his brood, if you want to prosper. Keep my son well and preferably far away from me. Should you want the house, wait till I'm dead.'*

Shaw took a deep breath. The old man must have given up, abdicating so fully. What a pity he didn't want to see his son. She drew another blank sheet to her and wrote. *'Dear Mr. Wylmer. The house is yours. Your son is a valued captain in the Pasandir Navy and Air Fleet. Thank you, I'm kicking. May Divine Bodrus keep you safe. Shaw Harwans, man. dir. PTC.'* She gave it to the messenger. 'Deliver my answer, will you?'

She looked across the table. 'Your pardon, ladies and gentlemen. Mr. Wylmer presented us with his shares. The PTC is now full owner of WyDir.'

Shaw saw the shock pass over the captain's chubby face and could guess what he was thinking.

Amid the hubbub, Nate returned with two soberly dressed gentlemen.

'Order, please,' Shaw said.

'Ms. Harwans, here are Messrs. Inns from Inns Auditors,' Nate said, wrestling to hide his laughter at the audible dismay his words caused.

'Good morning, ma'am,' one of the two Inns said in a dry voice. 'We have a team of people ready to begin.'

Shaw smiled at him. 'You are most welcome, gentlemen. I am eagerly looking forward to your findings. I expect WyDir's employees to give you all the assistance you require.'

Morgan stared at her with awe in his eyes. When Shaw looked at him, he blushed and returned to his notes.

*They know it now,* Shaw said, watching the directors realize their comfortable sinecures were crumbling around them. Across from her, Wylmer must've got it, too, for he looked as if unsure what was happening.

'You have someone trustworthy to show them where to start?' Shaw whispered to the secretary.

He nodded. 'Mr. Hynks' assistant, if he's done dancing and singing.'

'He's pleased?'

'We both are,' Morgan said. 'I've been here ten years; started as an office boy at twelve. I watched what happened when the Old Man – ah, Mr. Wylmer, sold those stocks for cash, and Hynks brought in his sharks to feed on us. No, we weren't supposed to know that, but Hynks never denied he was Pomfrith's man. Time and time again he and those other hoodlums outvoted the Old Man until he was ready to give up. The auditors will find we're not making much of a profit anymore; most of the money goes into their pockets. Criminals, the lot of them.'

'Thanks,' Shaw said. 'Please bring Messrs. Inns to this other chap; I want those books done. Then come back for more notes.'

The secretary went off with the auditors.

'If you please, ladies and gentlemen,' Shaw said in a sharp voice. It had the right effect, for they fell silent and looked at her.

'What is the meaning of this unexpected investigation?' the white-haired man on her left said angrily.

Shaw hoped her smile reflected the disgust she felt for those brazen thieves. 'I want to know what's going on with my property. Are we making money? How much? Who is functioning less than optimal? Are any things... wrong?'

*Let them wonder what I know,* she thought.

'I see,' the white-haired man said grimly.

'Where were we?' Shaw nodded at a non-descript woman in a severe dark blue dress and a bonnet. 'Your department, please.'

The director spoke at a monotone for nearly twenty minutes, yet when she was done, Shaw still didn't understand her duties, except that the Department of Color Schemes used up a sizable chunk of money.

The next man introduced himself as C&M, Construction and Maintenance, a taciturn fellow who spoke in a drawl. Shaw asked him why they didn't have a Thali in his place, and he laughed.

'No Thali would do it, ma'am. We employ several of them in technical places, but I'm a pen pusher. My job is to keep the engineers happy and give them whatever they need to run our airships, while keeping the costs down. Without me, we would've been broke long ago.'

Shaw caught Morgan's nod, so she supposed the man was right.

When the last of the twenty directors had finished, the afternoon neared its end. Shaw had listed two rows of names, fourteen of which appeared to be deadwood.

'Thank you,' she said, sitting back. 'That was it for now.' She named Benffald and several others. 'Please join me in my office. You too,' she said to Morgan as she rose and strode to the door. She felt strange; ordering kids was one thing, but here she was bossing men around old enough to be her grandfather, and they accepted it. *Stow it. You wanted your own business, now you got it. Only it's a tad bigger than you expected.*

In the presidential office she sat behind the desk. *Gods!* With her hands on the desktop she could only just look over the edge.

'Allow me,' Morgan said. 'The chair is adjustable.'

As she stepped aside, he removed a pin, wrenched the seat up and replaced the pin. 'That should do it, ma'am.'

Shaw lowered herself again. 'Thank you. Mr. Benffald, if we kicked those gold-edged directors out, would that make any difference to the running of the company?'

Benffald coughed. 'No, ma'am. They don't do anything, you see; Mr. Hynks had brought them in to give him the majority vote in a way it looked like a board of directors decided matters. In reality we in this room run the company, and we're supervisors without a vote. We still get our old salary, which isn't much more than what our friend Morgan gets for his mighty efforts. We ain't got a company car either.'

'That's right,' C&M said. 'I'm a supervisor too.'

'I'm Manager Hotels,' the third man said. 'Manager and supervisor share the same pay scale. Me and the lady from Passengers here are of the old crew as well.'

'So we are,' the small, well-dressed woman beside him said. 'We're the old WyDir gang, not those pigs who're here only for the slop.'

'Right you are,' another man said. 'I'm Aerodromes, running seven fields with towers and buildings, most of which I built with my own hands. I'm still earning a master carpenter's wage.'

'We're relics,' the second woman said. 'I'm P&T, Personnel and Training. Darned vital job for an airline, I'd say. Those thousand libers surprised me. I could run a good many safety courses on that much dough.'

Shaw looked at each face, at Nate and Wylmer. 'Write those others their resignation letters, Mr. Morgan. When you're done, call the guards and have them escorted out. No car, no papers, no nothing. Tell them we're going through the books and if we find irregularities, we'll hold them responsible.'

There was shouting outside the office. The door flew open and the white-haired director barged in, brandishing a small pistol. 'Curse you!' he cried, and fired point-blank at Shaw.

Nate and C&M were on their feet first. Nate laid his sixteen-year-old's rage behind the blow that broke the director's nose, while the engineer's years of handling fights added a professional knockout.

'Shaw!' Nate cried and he vaulted on top of the gleaming desk.

'I'm all right,' she said shakily. 'The bullet grazed my ear.'

Two guards burst in with guns drawn.

'We're fine,' Nate snapped. 'Arrest every one of those Hynks directors. Handcuff them and drag them back to the boardroom.'

A healer hurried in, carrying a bag. 'Sit still a moment,' she said. 'It's but a graze wound. You're bleeding, but I'll have it done in a jiffy. Sorry, but it'll hurt, ma'am.' She cupped Shaw's ear with her hand. 'I was a nurse in the war, you know. A witch by profession. I've seen worse.'

'So have I,' Shaw said dizzily. 'I'm with the wyrmcaller; pirate hunting.'

'Ah, so you're a pro too,' Nurse said happily. 'Well, look, it's done already. Keep still for a-while, you'll be wobbly, but it'll pass.' She took her bag and bustled out again without a glance for the felled director.

Nate came back, still fuming, and Shaw felt a warm glow as she saw him. He was angry for her!

'Get him in with the others,' Nate commanded, and C&M laughed.

'With pleasure,' he said. He gripped the director's coat and dragged him from the office.

In the large meeting room, the other directors huddled together fearfully.

'He did it?' one said. 'Shot her? He's mad!'

'You bunch of crooks!' Nate said in a deadly voice. 'We know everything. You were Hynks' pawns, to make it seem WyDir had a real board. Instead, he ruled the company with Pomfrith's shares, while you lot have been sponging on WyDir, creating fat jobs for yourselves, with idiotic wages, company cars and the gods know we paid for your homes as well.'

A director cried out, and Nate shook his fist in the man's face. 'If we did, we'll get it back. We'll have the Lord Spellstor send us some mindmages and interrogate you stooges. It's over!' He marched up and down, snarling at the quaking directors. 'You're fired, the lot of you! And be sure we'll check your past expense statements item for item. We'll demand the unjustified payments back. Guards!' he yelled. 'Take those rats away and throw them on the street. None may return to their desks or anywhere but out! And never let them in again.'

He kicked the unconscious ex-director. 'Call the city guards for that one. Attempted murder on an ally of the Weal Council. I hope they'll hang him!' He lowered his voice. 'Do take him away; he tried to kill my Shaw. I'll not forgive him.'

Shaw saw he was near tears, and she drew her arms around him. 'It's alright. I'm too small for that desk, so he missed.'

'He hurt you,' Nate said fiercely. 'I hate him for that.'

# CHAPTER 7 – POTSHOT MISS

Shaw was watching the sun come up over the harbor. She did that often; her mind was so active she slept no more than four or five hours each night.

She sat in an old chair, thinking a million thoughts as she listened to the cries of the bluewings hunting scraps over the water.

'Morning, Shaw,' the guard said as he passed her on his rounds. By now, he knew better than to stop and chat; his boss wasn't ready to join humanity just yet.

But this time she stirred as the boy walked by. 'Is that a ship?'

The guard stopped and stared at the sea. 'Darn!' he said. 'I believe you're right. Shall I sound the alarm?'

Shaw rose. 'I think not,' she said. 'Follow me.'

They walked to the pier to get a closer look.

'It's *Fayaafa*,' Shaw said.

'Should I have seen her sooner?' the boy asked hesitantly.

'Eh?' Shaw saw his anxious face. 'Not you; we need a lookout on the tower. You better warn Cook. He'll want to make tea and things.'

The boy saluted and hurried inside, while Shaw watched the bomb ketch approach its berth.

Even before the ship had come to rest, Varan jumped ashore and ran to meet her.

'Good news!' he cried exuberantly. 'We made a killing!'

'Who did you kill?' Shaw said, surprised.

'Nobody.' Varan said. 'Only their wallets.' He pulled a sheaf of papers from his pocket. 'Letters of credit,' he said with a meaningful glance. 'Guess how much?'

'Twenty-five thousand?' she guessed. That's what she had supposed those painted fabrics, toffees and things would sell for in Towne.

Varan laughed. 'Wrong!' he said. 'Double.'

Shaw stared at him, her brain suddenly numb. 'Fifty thousand libers?'

'And a bit over. I auctioned the stuff. Bloody noses over the toffees! Two guys would've dueled if the attendant town councilor hadn't stopped them. In the end I sold those sweets in bags of ten for a thousand libers.'

'Crazy!' Shaw said. 'Thirty months' wages for our whole crew, just for ten toffees? That's criminal.'

Varan raised his shoulders. 'That's the way the rich live.' He chuckled. 'My father didn't buy any, though he did bid on a few parcels of fabrics. My silly brother suggested I *gave* them ten toffees, but I had this nasty buzzing in my ears and I didn't hear him.' He snorted. '*Give!* I'm a merchant, dear brother.'

Shaw looked up at him. 'You did fabulously.' Her eyes went to the letters of credit. 'I'll take these to the bank myself.' She gripped Varan's shoulders and did a happy dance. 'I've amazing news, too. We acquired full ownership of WyDir, the airship company.'

Now it was Varan's turn to stare. 'You're kidding! No, of course you're not. But how?'

Quickly she told him all that had passed and several times she had to wait for him to stop laughing.

'Gods!' he said when she was done. 'That's rich. That's really, really rich.'

They walked into the warehouse. In the door Varan stopped. 'I got a letter for you,' he said, suddenly sober. 'From Proprietor Darquine.'

Shaw's heart skipped a beat. *No! Is she angry?*

Outwardly calm, she opened the sealed envelope. Inside were a short note and some official looking documents.

*Dear Shaw,*

*You're doing business in a big way! Good for you, I'm agog with admiration. I got something you might want. I acquired it from the Weal Bank after it happened; your father was never for even a penny beholden to me. I bought it on a whim, in case I would meet you one day. Well, I did, and I think you're great. So I give you back what in better times should have been yours anyway. Do what you wish with it. All the luck and go for it!*

*Darquine.*

The papers were the property deeds to the site of the Harwans Ship Chandlery on Mackerel Square.

'Oh,' Shaw said, and at the sight of them, something broke inside her she'd kept bottled up for years. Standing in the door of her warehouse, she cried like a little girl.

'What's wrong?'

Nate's voice came through the thunder in her ears, and numbly she handed him the papers.

'Oh, girl,' he said.

'I'll see to the ship,' Varan said quickly, and fled.

Shaw let Nate steer her up to the cafeteria.

'Cawah,' he said.

'Bad news?' Cook asked, eyeing her worriedly.

'No, but very personal,' Nate answered. 'It must hurt a lot.'

Her hands clenched the mug and she sipped, feeling the hot drink go down her throat. She shivered.

'I never cried,' she said in a faraway voice. She was vaguely aware of others close by, but she didn't care. She was a Clammer and used to sharing trouble with others. *Only never those troubles,* she thought. She had forced them away, not daring to think of them.

'I never *could* cry.' She gripped Nate's jacket with one hand. 'I must see it.' She looked at his anxious face. 'The seedy side wasn't the only place of Seatome I never came.' She clutched the deed. 'Mackerel Square was the other.'

'If you're sure, we'll go there,' Nate said.

'I want to,' she said. She put the letter and the deed back into the envelope and slipped them into her coat. Suddenly she was anxious to go, to see.

'Come,' Nate said. 'We'll walk; it isn't that far.'

'I'll come with you,' Callogan said. 'You haven't been making friends in the city lately. I... I won't say anything, alright?'

Shaw patted his arm. 'Chatter away.'

They walked along the waterfront, Old Wharf, New Wharf, Tuna Tub, and the other great quays, past the MCTC warehouse, until they saw the great statue of Naudin's father Yarwan the Liberator. Here they turned left, and then right, past an old inn, a bakery and a smithy. Beyond them was a square, with a great scar, a burned out ruin, sixty yards long and at least twenty deep. An old smell of blackened wood and desolation hung over it.

Shaw stood there and stared. 'Things weren't going well,' she said suddenly. 'There was trouble with a bank loan and Father was worried. He'd just lain off our last workman and while we still had stuff to eat, it was often salt meat and beans.' She looked at Nate. 'Off the shelf.'

Nate nodded.

'Then he came home one morning with an order for a tramp ship. A rush order; the ship would sail that same day. So Mother and he went to work. They sent me to the market to buy stuff we didn't have. It took me several hours to get everything. I saw the smoke on my way back, but didn't think of it. When I passed the inn, I saw the flames and I ran until the smith's wife stopped me. The fire watch was there with four carts, fighting to save the smithy and the houses on the other side. Of our store, there wasn't anything left to save.'

'No,' Nate said.

'They were both dead, the smith's wife told me. One of them must've been careless with a lamp in their hurry. We stocked a lot of tar, oil, pitch and even blackpowder. It all burned. I remember running away then.' She waved vaguely ahead. 'Nothing more. It must've been days until Willow and her girls discovered me. They brought me to Clam

Street, washed and fed me, until I was far enough aware to do it myself again.'

She shivered, and felt Nate's arm around her. 'Seven generations Harwans lived here; now it's gone.' She clutched his arm. 'I can't leave it like this; it must be cleared. But what then?'

'Do you want to rebuild?' Nate asked cautiously.

'I...' Shaw stared at the ruins. 'I don't know. Before, becoming a ships' chandler was what I wanted. Now? Old Wharf is much better suited for ships' stores than this place.'

'A workshop?'

Shaw gripped his tunic with both hands. 'Nate! That's brilliant. We could make our ice machines and things right here!' Her eyes grew misty again and she sniffed. 'What a great idea. Harwans' Workery. What would it cost? I've no idea. Where can we get a builder?'

'I don't know,' Nate said. 'Do we have money, apart from those pirate coins?'

'Yes,' Shaw said, with a catch in her voice. 'But I'm not speaking money in the street. Let's go to the bank first. Now.'

'All right,' Nate said and he hugged her.

Shaw smiled waveringly at him and Callogan. 'I'm alright again.'


The Bank of the Weal was a solid building in the city center. Built to impress, it didn't fail. If you could stomach the plush style, Shaw thought.

Its front was made of black stone with yellow accents, and two statues of florid, self-satisfied men in long drapes flanking the doors, apparently symbolizing Sobriety and Wealth. A uniformed porter stood beside a potted tree, waiting for someone he could refuse entry.

Shaw had been here before, so he sprang to life to open the big doors for her.

'Good morning, Ms. Harwans,' he said.

'Good morning, Ms. Harwans,' the liveried servant inside echoed, before leading them to one of the small parlors where customers could conduct their businesses in private.

Shaw sat in an upholstered chair, glancing around the so genteel room with its heavy curtains and the awful ferns in their massive stone urns.

Before she could comment, a woman came in, elegantly dressed in colors matching the drapery.

'Good morning, Ms. Harwans,' she sang. 'How may we assist you today?'

'I have letters of credit to deposit,' Shaw said.

'But of course,' the bank woman said and she accepted the letters with discrete eagerness.

Shaw watched her, and saw her face twitch ever so faintly.

'That is a great deal of money, ma'am,' the woman said reverently.

'One shipload of goods,' Shaw said, with an airy wave of her hand.

'A profitable voyage, my congratulations,' the woman said. 'I will write you a receipt.'

She got out a handsome pen and a slip of paper, and wrote down the various sums, added them up and signed the total with a flourish.

'Thank you,' Shaw said. 'Perhaps you may know. If I wanted something built in Seatome, where should I go?'

'The Guild of Builders & Architects,' the woman said. 'They are straight across from here, the blue building.'

'Thank you.' Shaw rose and immediately the servant appeared to guide them to the door.

'Thank you for your patronage, ma'am,' the bank woman said.

'Thank you for your patronage,' the servant repeated as they walked out.

'Yes, I know,' Shaw snapped to the porter as he opened the door for them.

'Thank you for your patronage, ma'am,' the porter said impassively.

Callogan chuckled at the expression on her face. 'Just try not to notice,' he said. 'The Weal Bank is one of the most pretentious businesses south of Port Naar; from that imbecile porter to the family who owns this mausoleum they're Vanhaar at its worst.'

As they crossed the street towards the blue building, a steamcart revved and came roaring past. Shaw instinctively jumped back, and stumbled. As she fell to her knees, a shot rang out.

Callogan exclaimed and clutched his shoulder as the steamcart tore away around the corner.

'Inside!' Shaw ordered, and together they half dragged Callogan into the blue building.

A porter in a matching uniform came running.

'What's this?' he said. 'You can't...'

'Summon a healer!' Shaw snapped. 'And the commander of the city guard. Quickly now!'

Another man joined them, an older gentleman in a robe.

'It's all right,' he said to the porter. 'Call our healer.'

'And the guard commander,' Shaw repeated.

'I am the guild secretary,' the robed gentleman said. 'I'm afraid I didn't catch your name.'

'This is Ms. Harwans, managing director of the PTC and WyDir,' Nate said. 'Somebody tried to kill her and hit our mage director instead.'

'Lumentis aid us!' the secretary said, shocked. 'Do as she asked.'

The porter ran out and returned with the healer, a slight, nervous fellow in faded robes.

'Shot wound?' he said. 'Long time since I handled one of those.' His face worked. 'Did many of them during the war.'

He sniffed as he unbuttoned Callogan's robe. 'Expensive garment; won't cut it open. Bite on your teeth, soldier.'

Swiftly he pulled the robe down. 'I see. Nice wound. Small caliber bullet. Stand still, please.' He put his thumb and index finger across the wound and moments later something coppery popped out. The healer caught it with a practiced gesture.

'Here,' he said. 'Keep it. Bragging stuff.' As he spoke, the wound closed and the blood disappeared. 'There y' are. Back to the war, old chap.'

Callogan pulled up his robe. 'Thanks.'

'No problem,' the healer said. 'See ya in the mess.'

He brought two fingers to his temple in a vague salute and shuffled out.

'Well,' Shaw said to the guild secretary, and she took a deep breath. 'We were on our way here, but this wasn't in the planning.' She replaced the monocle in her eye and moistened her lips. 'I have a building to build, and the Weal Bank pointed me to you.'

The secretary smiled. 'Rightly so. If you hired anyone else, you would be in conflict with city rules. What is it you want built?'

'I hold the deeds to a plot on Mackerel Square,' Shaw said. 'I want it cleared and a large workshop erected.'

'The Harwans ruins?' the secretary said. 'A family possession, I assume? It will be good to have something new built there.'

'Yes,' Shaw said and she bit her lip. 'It's been far too long.'

'You mentioned WyDir?' the secretary said.

'We recently acquired full ownership. We are the Pasandir Trading Co, the lord wyrmcaller's outfit,' Shaw said.

'Ah, indeed. WyDir of Salmon Street is an old and valued relation, which positively affects our tender.'

'Lord Spellstor named the Peaks an ally of the Weal, and offered us the same prices as a Weal nation,' Shaw said brightly. 'We are fighting the same enemies, such as our blowing up the pirate harbor of Brisa.'

The secretary folded his hands. 'Very noble. I will discuss this with the guildmaster. You have the deeds to the property?'

They were still discussing property boundaries, when the porter came back with two uniformed officers of the city guard. The senior one, a captain with still shiny badges of rank, saluted crisply.

'The Castle sent us. Ms. Harwans?'

Shaw nodded. 'That's me.'

'Perhaps you could explain to us what happened?'

In a few words, Shaw told them, and the captain nodded gravely.

'Have you reasons to suspect it was you they wanted to kill, ma'am?'

'Yes,' Shaw said. She looked around, but both the porter and the guild secretary had left them. 'Please close the door,' she said.

The second officer shut the door and put his back against it.

'I am the managing director of the PTC,' Shaw said. 'Yesterday we acquired the ownership of WyDir.'

The captain lifted an eyebrow, but didn't speak.

'There were a great number of directors on the board who were both overpaid and underproductive. I fired them. One of those gentlemen took a shot at me inside my own office. This matter must have been reported to the city guard.'

'And so it was; I have read the report. The culprit was one of the people you fired?'

'He was,' Shaw said firmly. 'And now I fear he wasn't the only one.'

'So it seems,' the captain said.

There was a knock on the door and the second officer looked outside. He came back and handed his superior a note.

The captain glanced at it, then muttered something dire. 'My men discovered an abandoned steamcart two streets away from here. There was a gun under the driver's seat. It appears a WyDir company cart.' He looked at Shaw. 'We found a body in the back, dressed in a WyDir driver's uniform.'

'Hynks!' Shaw exploded. 'Curse the man! He was the senior director, the one who had brought in those other crooks. I... I ordered him taken home in a company car. The rest of them left on foot.'

'We will have a word with this gentleman,' the captain said. He turned to go. 'I have been told your take-over has the backing of the Lord Spellstor himself, ma'am. Rest assured we will do anything in our power to get our man. We shall return the cart to Salmon Street when we've finished with it. Thank you for your forbearance, ma'am.'

With that they left, leaving Shaw staring at Nate and Callogan.

'Darn that Hynks!' Shaw said wildly. 'To murder his driver! But how did he find us?'

Then the guild secretary came back and she bit her lip. 'Thank you for your discretion.'

'Of course,' the secretary said politely. 'I have made up a contract for the clearance of your property at Mackerel Square. The cost depends on the situation as we will find it, but we guarantee a maximum of three hundred libers.'

Shaw read the contract carefully; then signed.

'Thank you,' the secretary said. 'One of our architects will contact you about your wishes for a new building.'

'That will be fine.' Shaw suddenly felt empty, tired and ready to cry again.

'I will send for the guildmaster's vehicle,' the secretary said. 'He won't be going anywhere and you have had a shock. Just sit quietly for a minute, ma'am.'

Ten minutes later, a sleek blue steamcart dropped them off at the Old Wharf.

When they stepped inside, Yens waved. 'Did that guy from WyDir find you?'

'What guy?' Shaw said.

'An elderly gent driving a big steamcart. He said he needed a signature, so I told him where you'd gone to.'

'He tried to shoot me,' Shaw said tiredly. 'He hit poor Callogan instead. Don't worry; you couldn't have known.' She gripped Callogan's arm. 'I hadn't said how sorry I am and how perfectly wonderful you were.'

'My pleasure,' Callogan said expansively. 'Yens, don't look so shocked man. Come, I'll tell you the whole story. Here, this is the bullet.'

'That healer was right,' Nate said. 'Bullets give bragging rights.' He hooked his arm through hers. 'Let's go up and have a cawah. You were quite wonderful yourself, you know.'

Shaw stared at him. She wanted to ask why, but she was done up. If Nate thought her wonderful, she wasn't going to dispute him.

# CHAPTER 8 – SEWERY

Shaw sat back in her chair and screwed her monocle in her eye. 'Callogan?'

'Hmm?' the mover mage was poring over a copy of the old Pasandir Peaks map and clearly far away in his mind.

'How does one hire a mage? I mean, I can't expect to bump into them all the time, do I?'

'No,' he said, smiling. 'Probably not. Ah, what kind of mage?'

'Well, we have this beautiful portal, but all it does is Smalkand and back. I want more destinations.'

'So you're looking for a portal mage,' Callogan said. 'There is a difficulty. Every one of them works for the Weal; they're in the lower ranks at Casterglade, that's the big center where they build the portals and things.'

'Is that a rule?' Shaw asked. 'I mean, are they forbidden to work anywhere else?'

'No,' Callogan said. 'Only no one else wants them. I mean, the only portals in operation are Casterglade property.'

'Until now,' Shaw said grimly. 'So how do I get to hire one?'

'The usual way, I suppose. Ask around at the Magic Institute. There won't be that many portaller students. It's one of those studies that's a gamble. Most of them are lucky and the Weal needs them, so they're in clover. But now and then fate looks away; if the Weal doesn't have a need for their services that year, they're sunk.'

Shaw frowned. 'What happens to the sunken ones?'

'They're washing dishes in restaurants, or teaching math to school dropouts, or something else that's horrible.'

*A mage?* she thought. *Washing dishes?* 'Why?'

Callogan scratched his unruly mop of hair as he thought. 'Because the Weal only takes portal mages straight out of the Institute,' he said. 'Once you they've passed you over, you are done. I suppose those chaps end up at that awful Labor Exchange.'

Shaw took off her monocle and rubbed it on her sleeve. 'So you're telling me I can go to the Exchange and they have a portal mage for me?'

Callogan blinked. 'I suppose so.'

Shaw leaned forward. 'And what can those guys do?'

'Put coordinates into your portal and operate it for you. Portal mages have memorized all current coordinates. That is another reason the Weal doesn't want those passed-over guys later on. Their coordinates may be out of date and it's too much bother to correct that.'

'Why? If they're so rare, they should be worth a little extra effort.'

'Not to a warlock.' Callogan's homely face had turned to stone. 'They won't accept anything that is flawed; not in tools, not in underlings or... family.' The map in his hands shook a little. 'I know them; my father is Head Theoretician at Casterglade.'

'Your old man's a warlock?'

'To the bone. We avoid each other; that's easier on both our nerves.' He shrugged. 'I know he can't help it; warlocks don't make good parents. I heard the Lord Spellstor is one of the few exceptions, but then, he is still a young man, and happily married. My father is pre-war, nearly a century-and-a-half old. Let's leave it at that, shall we?'

Shaw sprang to her feet. 'All right, come on,' she said as she ran out and down the stairs. 'Nate!'

'Coming!' Nate met her at the foot of the stairs. 'What's the hurry?'

'We're going to find us a portal mage; get the steamcart.' She had arranged for one of the WyDir carts permanently stationed at Old Wharf, and now they rode in style to the Labor Exchange.

Loafers outside the building gaped as the driver held open the car's door. Shaw barely noticed them in her preoccupation and the three of them hurried into the building.

The head clerk came, smiling as he bowed for her. 'Good day, Ms. Harwans. How can I help you today?'

Shaw stared at him through her eyeglass and felt her heart beating faster. 'I have been informed there are unemployed portal mages.'

The head clerk nodded and she sighed inaudibly.

'It is sad but true,' he said. 'At the end of each study year, a great many freshly graduated mages compete for jobs. Most of them end up well, but those you mention are... overspecialized. We have several on our books, yet it is next to impossible to find work for them.'

'I need one,' Shaw said. 'What would such a person cost me?'

'Pennies, ma'am, no more than pennies.' The head clerk looked around. 'There's one of them. He sits here often, simply hoping.' He whistled, and a tall, thin Vanhaari guy of perhaps eighteen or nineteen years came over. His eyes were empty and his voice soft. 'Sir?'

'You are a portal mage?' Shaw said.

The young man's face twitched. 'I-I was trained for it. I had a good head for numbers, eidetic memory, they said. My study mentor advised portaling. A great future, he said. Buckets full of money. Buckets! I studied, got those darned coordinates in my head; and then I graduated. My study advisors promised to get me a job at the Casterglade Center.' The boy snorted. 'It didn't happen. Now I've a head full of numbers and nothing else, and I can't get rid of the lot.'

Shaw nodded to the head clerk. 'Thank you. Leave us alone for a short while, will you.'

'Certainly,' the man said. 'Please call me when you are done.'

'What's your name?' Shaw asked when the man had gone. 'Can you still program a portal?'

The young man shrugged. 'I'm Kier. Program? I think so. But I'm not sure of the data. If a portal moves, the coordinates change and the old one is useless.'

'What happens if you port to a changed coordinate?'

He stared at a point over her shoulder. 'Nothing. No-thing-at-all but a slap in my face.'

'Why can't you get rid of those coordinates?' Nate asked.

'Eidetic memory. Can't forget.'

'But those portal mages Casterglade accepted must have the same problem,' Nate said.

'They got mentalists to help them,' the boy said. 'I don't, and I ain't got the money to hire one. Study broke me. I'm not a rich guy, I worked for my future.'

'You're not the only one,' Shaw said. She mustered the shabbily dressed portal mage thoughtfully. 'I'm willing to take a risk on you.'

'You're not the Weal government,' Kier said with a tired shrug 'You ain't *got* a portal.'

Shaw grinned. 'We're the Pasandir Peaks, mate. We do.'

'You think you can do it?' Nate said. 'Mind we're not going to pay you buckets of money. We *can* arrange for a mentalist to help you forget.'

'I can try,' Kier said doubtfully. Then, with a raised voice, 'I darn well can try!'

'All right, you're hired.' Shaw walked to the counter and the head clerk came over.

'We'll take a chance on him,' Shaw said. She counted out the regulation fee. 'How many others could you supply?'

'Three more,' the head clerk said.

Shaw nodded. 'If this works out, I'll come back for them.'

'Thank you,' the head clerk said. 'We see many sorry cases here, but these young people bother me. It is such a waste of talent.'

Shaw looked at him. *He cares,* she thought, surprised. 'I agree; the Weal is a harsh place for some.'

'For too many,' the head clerk said. 'There are always too many looking for work, and too few employers.'

When they were outside and the young man saw the company steamcart, he sighed. 'They'd promised me one like that. It was part of the job, they said.'

'It's not.' Callogan said as they got in. 'Portal mages earn good money, but no buckets full of gold and free steamcarts. Not even my father gets that. Who promised you such nonsense? Surely not the Magic Institute.'

'No! The Institute never promised anything. My study advisors said so.'

'Fine advisors,' Shaw said. 'How did you come by them? Is it usual to engage such people?'

'I've heard it happen,' Callogan said. 'Not the kids with parents and money, but the poor ones. These study advisors help and coach them, against a percentage of future earnings. Some even pay for the study.'

'Mine didn't,' Kier said. 'I paid both my study and them from the money my father left me, and they'd get a quarter of my future salary. In exchange they would get me accepted by the portal organization.' He grunted. 'Tarradiddle.'

'And then?' Shaw asked.

'They denied me. They didn't know me, didn't admit me into their office. It was a bust.'

Then the steamcart arrived back at Old Wharf.

'This is our Seatome base,' Shaw said. 'We got a bigger one up north in the Peaks, and of course there is the WyDir building in Salmon Street. Let's go in by the back door, and I'll introduce you to our engineer, Oychak. She's one of the Thali who worked on our portal'

They found her studying an old tool.

'Quaint,' she said, looking at Shaw. Then she put the tool down and grinned. 'Not you.'

'That stuff is old,' Shaw said. 'I bring you a new one; I got us a portal mage.'

Oychak stared at her. 'You did what? Where did you find him? Drifting on an ice floe in the wilds?'

Shaw told her about Kier's bad luck, and the engineer cursed violently. 'Criminals!' she said, with no indication whether she meant his study advisors or the warlocks at Casterglade, or perhaps both. 'They should hang them!' She turned to Kier. 'You're blown in by the blizzard, friend. Well come, I'll show you the portal.'

One of the workers called Nate away, and Shaw walked upstairs to her office. She dropped in her chair and stared at the papers on her desk. She felt too restless to pick them up, and wandered back to the ground floor, where Oychak and Keena watched the new portal mage apparently doing nothing.

'Look at that,' Keena said, scratching with her fingers under the rim of her hat. 'Dunno the guy, but he's talking to our portal. It's like his mouth is spewing numbers and that portal swallows them.'

'I wonder,' Shaw said. 'Would Casterglade consider these codes secret?'

'We'll find out when he is done,' Oychak said. 'Most coordinates can't be a secret. If he has any that are confidential, I'd suggest wiping them.' She grinned. 'If one of your kids pops into the holiest of the Great Grandmother, her priests kill them first and ask later. And you won't like their questions.'

Shaw sighed and returned to her office and the waiting paperwork until Keena called her.

'He's done,' the mage said. 'It took him over two hours to unload. He's a bit upset now.'

Shaw hurried downstairs and found Kier prone on the floor, crying his heart out.

She knelt beside the portal mage. 'What's the matter?'

'Darn,' he said, slapping the ground. 'Darn. Relief.' He took a sobbing breath and turned onto his back. 'I did it.'

'Good work,' Shaw said calmly. 'Now you need food?'

'I'm exhausted,' he said. 'Hungry, too.'

'Come to the cafeteria,' Shaw said. 'Cook will feed you.'

'One thing,' Keena said. 'The Smalkand portal, will it still port here automatically?'

Kier nodded. 'If it's the same as this one was, it can't go anywhere else yet. From now on, your portal needs a porter. So if you want to go anywhere, call me.' He rubbed his eyeballs.

'Perfect,' Shaw said. 'We also wondered about secret coordinates.'

Kier snorted. 'We don't get *those*. Nah, you'll not end up in Queen Maud's bedroom.' He scowled at Shaw. 'If you have coordinates you want to keep a secret, don't use them in this portal. It remembers them and then I'll automatically pick them up the next time I operate this thing. Use handportals. They're easy to make and I can show you how to enter the coordinates yourself.'

'Will Casterglade object to your giving us those coordinates?' Shaw asked.

Kier shrugged. 'Don't know. No one ever told me not to.'

They sat down and Cook brought Shaw a mug.

'What can I get you?' he asked of Kier. 'Tea, cawah, milk or lemonade. No booze.'

'What's that you're drinking?' Kier asked.

'Cawah,' Shaw said. 'It's brewed from roasted beans. It keeps your mind active.'

'I'll try it. Now, about that other portal.'

'Can you do it?' Shaw asked.

'Better not. The Exchange has a girl I know, who could do the other place.'

'I heard there were three more portal mages on the Exchange,' Shaw said. 'I want to hire them. We'll be expanding, so I will need them before long.' She stared at Kier. 'What else can you do?'

He stared at the cawah in his mug. 'I don't know. I'd prefer not to sweep floors.'

Shaw grinned. 'I get that. Don't you have any other magic?'

'It's stupid,' he said. 'From the first I focused on portal magic. I never studied anything else, convinced I'd be making it big as a portal mage. I was sure I didn't *need* any other magic.'

'You can mindspeak?'

'Yes. That and lighting a candle is so basic we all can do it. But that's it.' Kier looked away. 'It's not much for six years of the Magic Institute.'

'You take it easy for a few days. Walk around; meet the others and see what is going on here. We'll discuss it later.' Shaw downed the last of her cawah and went in search of Nate and Callogan. She found the mover mage staring at the portal.

'This thing drives me crazy,' Callogan said. 'I see those coordinates milling around and I can't grasp even one of them. It's awful.'

'You should go out more,' Shaw said. 'Don't stare at that thing. Will you go to the Exchange and tell them to send over the other three portal mages today or else the day after tomorrow?'

'Sure. No mage should end up sweeping floors. I was constantly thinking, *that could have been me.*'

Shaw patted his shoulder and went to find Nate.

She found him in discussion with Varan. As she joined them, he turned to her. 'We were talking about uniforms.'

Shaw lifted an eyebrow and nearly dropped her monocle. 'Dowa is working on them.'

'That's the point,' Nate said. 'She's drowning in work; she needs help.'

Shaw sighed in exasperation. 'That girl is too quiet. Where is she holed up?'

'One of those little rooms at the back,' Varan said.

'Darn,' Shaw muttered. 'I should've kept an eye on her. Nate, let's see how she is.'

They found the young seamstress in an airless, badly lighted hole, squatting on a table while she hand-sewed a pair of trousers. Around her were stacks of cloth, boxes of buttons, needles and whatever.

'Mountain's Breath!' Shaw said. 'This won't do, girl! You'll go out of your mind in this place. Do you take breaks? Eat and silly things like that?'

'No time,' the girl said, looking hot and sweaty. 'I got another thirty-five uniforms to make.'

'Not like this,' Shaw said. 'Put down that needle, go for a meal and relax. You'll not do another stitch today, you hear?'

'But then I'll never finish!' the girl wailed.

'I should have thought this through,' Shaw said. 'You can't do all that on your own, you'll need help. Do people really sew by hand anymore? I remember seeing those clever machines tailor shops use.'

'But we don't have them,' Dowa said.

'So we'll buy them. Let me think on this. You'll go outside and chat, sleep or whatever you fancy; no more work today.'

'You're angry,' Nate said.

'Yes!' Shaw took the monocle from her eye and rubbed her skin. 'I'm angry at myself.' She lifted a hand. 'Wait! Who makes WyDir's uniforms? Let's ask them. We'll walk.'

'What's with the steamcart?'

'Callogan took it to the Exchange. No matter; I need to lose energy.'

Nate grinned. 'You don't say!'

'Our uniforms?' Morgan repeated. 'I have to check; one moment, please.'

He walked to a large filing cabinet and leafed through a series of yellow folders. Then he wrote something on a sheet of paper.

'Here it is,' he said. 'Pilots and stewards uniforms come from Clarkill in Fisherman's Lane. Masters of Elegance, they call themselves. Ellars in Kell produces the uniforms for our ground crews. They give our people the slightly military look that is typical WyDir. Ah, that's Personnel's slogan, ma'am, not mine.'

'Sure,' Shaw said absently. 'I know Clarkill; they're overpriced snobs. Ellars may be fine, but I prefer a local business. I remember there was another one in the city, near Whales Gate.'

'Ghol's,' Morgan said. 'They went out of business. I believe their place is for sale.'

Shaw looked up. 'Is that so? We'll pay them a visit. Thanks, you've been a great help.'

Morgan grinned. 'It's what you pay me for, ma'am.'

'True.' Shaw gave him a sweet smile. 'That's why I'm glad to see the money isn't wasted.' She gripped Nate's arm. 'Let's hurry a bit.'

'Did you have another speed then?' Nate asked innocently.

'Oh yes, a dead run. But not in here; I must think of my position.'

'Right,' Nate said. 'You are a person of consequence.'

Moments later the big steamcart roared off, to the other side of town.


Whales Gate was a narrow bit of road connecting the fish market with Weigh House Square, where traders have their goods weighed free of charge.

Ghol's Sewery was a low building with glass windows looking into the large rooms where the seamstresses had worked.

All sewing machines were there, but the place looked dusty and somehow sad.

'Funny,' Nate said. 'I've been to the fish market often enough, and to the Weigh House, but I don't remember this building.'

Shaw grinned. 'It must have been those women staring at your masculinity put you off.' She walked to the two identical doors. The one should lead to the sewery, so she firmly pulled the bell at the other entrance.

After some time a lady answered. She was ancient, with a dark gray, leathery face, and dressed with old-fashioned dignity. Her hands holding her cane were stiff, with knobby fingers.

'I am sorry; we are no longer open,' she said. 'So we don't need either girls or customers.'

'But you might need a buyer,' Shaw said politely. She had taken off her eye patch and pocketed the monocle, and managed to look very young all at once.

The woman looked her over. 'But it would cost money, dear,' the woman said. 'I don't think you could afford that.'

'How much?' Shaw said.

The old woman smiled slightly. 'Ah, five hundred libers should do it. Too little for an established name like Ghol's, but way too much for a young girl.'

'But not for the Pasandir Trading Company,' Shaw said. 'We are looking for a place to make our uniforms.'

'Uniforms.' The old woman laughed softly. 'Your uniform was not made by a professional.'

'No,' Shaw said. 'By a sewing-maid in a castle far, far to the north of here. The Pasandir Peaks lack the proper skills. That is why we come here.'

'The skills we have; the hands no longer.' The woman lifted hers. 'Old rheum got me.' She peered at Shaw. 'You have a lazy eye, dear.'

Shaw grinned. She got the eye patch and fastened it over her good eye. Then she replaced her monocle. 'I know, but I wouldn't alarm strangers looking like a storybook villain.'

'You're clever,' the old woman said approvingly. 'You really have five hundred libers?'

'I do,' Shaw said. 'In letters of credit, not in a bag over my shoulder.'

'Yes, of course,' the old woman said. 'Let me show you the premises.' With troubled hands she took a long key from a ring and opened the other door.

A dry smell of dust, cloth and faded lavender embraced Shaw. There was a small hallway with wooden stairs, and a second door.

'Two rooms, each for ten girls,' the old woman said. 'All machines worked to the last, now three months ago. There are plenty scissors and other necessities available. The mannequins look their age as much as I do, but they will do. Beyond are a small restroom and a place to make tea and such.'

She shuffled back to the hall. 'Upstairs are the stores. You can go look if you want to; I find it too much of an effort.' She turned to Shaw. 'That's it. Will it serve?'

'Perfectly well,' Shaw said.

'I have the contract ready.' The old lady pulled a stiffly rolled document from her sleeve. 'Here it is,' she said, smiling. 'A woman's sleeve can hide much.'

Shaw nodded. Her cuff hid a knife strapped to her arm, but she couldn't very well acknowledge that.

'Then all that remains is the payment,' the old woman said.

Shaw got her letters of credit and a pen, and wrote one out for five hundred libers. Carefully she blew the ink dry.

'Pasandir Trading Co,' the old woman said, staring at the slip of paper. 'What a strange name.'

'The Peaks are what Vanhaar calls the Borderlands,' Shaw said.

'I have never been away from Seatome,' the old woman said. 'Not even during the war. This town is all I know.'

Shaw pocketed the sales contract. 'Seatome is a great place,' she said.

'It used to be.' The woman stirred. 'One request. Please remove the name from the shop front. Ghol's Sewery is no more and you will want to use your own name.'

'Of course,' Shaw said. 'I have a request, too. I will hire seamstresses. Should any lack experience with the machines, would you instruct them? We will pay for your time.'

'I can do that,' the old woman said. 'I will not ask money for it; the pride in my profession demands I teach others.'

'She must have run a classy business once,' Nate said as they got into the steamcart.

'That's one smart woman,' Shaw said, not hiding her chagrin. 'She had me pay what she asked, darn it. I didn't even think to get the price down.'

Nate looked at her and laughed. 'You can't win them all!'

'But I want to,' she said, and then realized how childish that sounded. She ground her teeth and looked outside.

'The driver wants to know where to go next,' Nate said with laughter in his voice.

She turned to face him. 'I'm an idiot.' She touched his arm. 'Sorry.' She picked up the tube to the driver's cabin. 'To the Labor Exchange, please, and thanks for your patience.'

'Seamstresses,' Nate said. 'That supervisor guy will wonder if we're trying to hire the whole city.'

When they arrived back at Old Wharf, they found Dowa in the sun with two workers, peeling potatoes.

'I can't sit and do nothing,' she said apologetically. 'My hands need to be busy.'

'As long as you do it willingly,' Shaw said. 'Nate and I just bought us Ghol's Sewery and hired a team of women to run it. They can do those uniforms and I plan to have them make WyDir's clothing as well. If you want to, you can join them, or if you want to stay here, you can have a go at making flags and things like that. We'll need a lot of flags; here, at the WyDir aerodromes, at Smalkand and on our ships. And badges, too, if you think you can do that.'

'Sounds fun,' Dowa said. 'I'd rather stay here; that feels safer, you know. I like embroidery, so I'll do the flags and things.' She embraced Shaw. 'Thank you.'

'What's that for?' Shaw asked, surprised.

'For caring,' Dowa said. 'No one ever did for me.'

'That's the Clammer way,' Shaw said. 'We quarrel and fight, but we always care for each other.'

At the portal they ran into Callogan and Kier with three other young people.

'There's the boss,' Callogan said to the strangers. 'We got us a strong portal team, Shaw.' He introduced the others; Beth for the Smalkand portal, Mott and Tomar.

'A portal,' Beth said hungrily. 'I despaired so long, thinking all was lost, but there it is.' She was a starved-looking twenty-odd, with her dark hair randomly cut off with a knife, and intense eyes.

'For the moment we've got only the two of them,' Shaw said. 'Don't you worry; we'll build more. With Beth in Smalkand, I shall need you other guys someplace else. Would that be a problem?'

'My home is where my portal is,' Mott said. He was a chubby fellow in a stained robe that looked as if he'd been sleeping out in it.

'We understand,' Beth said with barely checked urgency. 'Shall we go?'

Shaw looked at Callogan. 'Come with us; I'll show you around Smalkand Keep. We're not ready to start the caravans yet, but at least you'll have an idea of the place.'

'I'd love to,' the mover mage said.

'You got an escort already,' Nate said. 'Then I'll stay and do some dull work here.'

Shaw looked at him quickly, but the laughter in his eyes put her mind at rest. She sniffed. 'Port us over, Mr. Kier.'

# CHAPTER 9 – SMALKAND

They came out in Smalkand's entry hall, facing the cave opening to the bay.

'Shaw!'

She waved at the other girl, dressed in the red-and-blue of the wyrmcaller's service. 'Willow! How's life going?'

'Nice and quiet,' Willow said. 'With the boss away, nothing happens here. You bring us visitors?'

'Only him,' Shaw said. 'At least for now. Meet Callogan, our porter mage. He'll be doing the Trans-Peak caravan route when we get to it. These other three are new hires; portal mages. Beth is to handle your portal, and will fill it with coordinates so you can hop all over the Weal. The other two are to assist Imooga's crew for the moment. They will take over the next two portals when we're ready for them.' She turned to Callogan. 'Willow is our keepmistress. She runs the place with a sweet smile and an iron fist. If I am mean, she taught me.'

'I'm not mean,' Willow protested. 'Welcome! Beth, you will be popular. Now our kids can go to Seatome whenever they want.' Then she frowned. 'I don't think we'll do it like that, or nobody will get any work done.' She stared at the portal mage. 'You and I shall work out a routine. Come and meet the engineers.'

'I'll show Callogan around and after dinner we'll go back. We have a busy day tomorrow.'

'Shaw,' Callogan said. 'Your days are *always* busy. Darn it, you could power a portal yourself.'

'Hah,' Willow said. 'She used to be a quiet girl. But once she got going, not even Eskandar could stop her.'

Shaw sniffed. 'I got things to do.' She grabbed Callogan's arm. 'Let's start with the view.'

She half dragged him through the entry hall to the natural cave entrance that hid the keep from view.

'Oh,' Callogan said a moment later. He stood inside the cave entrance and gazed out over the bay. 'Yes.'

Shaw looked at him and darn if he didn't have tears in his eyes. 'Homesick?' she asked.

He moved his shoulders. 'I never settled down in Seatome. It's a nice enough place, but it always makes me restless. Never thought I was missing this, though.' He grunted. 'Stupid thing to discover at my age.'

'Seventeen?' Shaw guessed.

He grinned. 'For another few months.' He gestured at the mountains. 'Starfyld looked like this. Not the bay, obviously, instead she has a large plain, the Field. But from the village, there is a path leading up to just such an escarpment, and the peaks rising up behind it.' He turned away. 'Then my mother died, and I left for the Magic Institute, seven years ago. I haven't been back since. Curious vessel, that,' he said, as if eager to change the subject.

Shaw blinked and looked at the ship at anchor half a mile away. It wasn't very large, but looked fast. One mast, lateen rigged – she smiled at remembering that—with four guns to a side. It would make a nice explorer ship.

'Are those fishing boats?' Callogan said, pointing across the water.

'I can't see them,' Shaw said grimly. 'Not anything far away.'

'Sorry,' Callogan said. 'I forgot.'

'No matter, I'm used to it.' Shaw took the patch from her pocket and covered her eye. Then she dug out her monocle. 'Let's set a fashion,' she said.

'It does add an air of elegance,' Callogan said.

Shaw laughed. 'Elegant? Me? Scrawny is the word, mister.'

'Slender,' Callogan said.

'Let's go inside.' Shaw turned around. Flattery always made her feel awkward; she never knew whether she was made game of. Not that she believed that of Callogan, but still.

In silence, they crossed the hall into the cafeteria.

As he took in the spacious room, the white walls and tiled floor, the mage lights, the coppery counter with its stools and the many little tables and chairs, Callogan stared around open-mouthed.

'Oh my,' he said. 'That's living in style.'

They walked to the counter, where Averson was doubling as bartender.

'Hi,' she said, glowering at Callogan. 'Drinks?'

'The girl is Averson, our airship third pilot,' Shaw said. 'Drinks are like those at Old Wharf, only lemonades and such. They do serve terrific ices and milkshakes which we don't have yet.'

'Tangrid wants you,' Averson said. 'Urgently. He's at the ship.'

'We'll go up. Averson is a great gal,' Shaw said as they walked away with their glasses. 'Not very sociable; she's worked as a miner for years. Tough and strong, but no graces. She's a good friend and deadly in a fight.'

'You folks are impressive,' Callogan said.

'Some,' Shaw said. 'A lot of us are just, well, kids. But a few are special.'

On *Pewbara*'s ledge, they found Tangrid sitting in the open door, pouring over a slim manual. 'Shaw!' he cried as she walked along the small catwalk past the airship's bulk. 'I need you.'

'So we heard,' she said. 'This is Mage Callogan. Tangrid is our principal pilot. Officially, Wylmer is first, but he prefers the sea.'

Tangrid turned to her. 'I heard the news; I still can't believe it. When Old Wylm told me, I nearly slammed his silly nose, sure he was having me on. You bought WyDir?'

'Bought isn't the word,' Shaw said. 'But yes, we are full owner. Why? You want a job?'

'No!' he shouted. 'I want my certificates.'

'No problem,' Shaw said. 'Come over when you're ready and we'll have a word with Personnel and Training.'

'Free?' he said.

'Of course not,' Shaw said coolly. 'We'll bill the Pasandir Armed Forces. They should be a separate thing by now, not Eskandar's toy.' She giggled. 'We'll organize things for him, while he's out there catching nasties. But you won't have to pay, don't worry.'

He sighed. 'We'll come over. Averson, Byroon, some other guys we're training, and me.'

'Give me a shout first; I'm running around a bit these days.'

Shaw dragged Callogan down again, and went to look for Roza, the ledge keeper who was organizing Smalkand's administration. She used Shaw's little office, and broke into a smile when they came in.

'How is it going?' Shaw asked.

'It's gigantic,' Roza said. 'I've been counting the money in the safe, but halfway I had to stop. It's simply too much. Several hundred thousand libers, at least. We need a banker. We must know how much money there is, we must reserve some for wages, food and things, and ideally we should get at least enough income to cover the expenses. I can't do both that and get the warehouse side in the books. Besides, I'm a clerk, not a banker.'

'Where do I get a banker?' Shaw asked. 'I don't suppose they go through Exchange.'

Roza laughed. 'Not precisely. It's by word-of-mouth. You could advertise in the *Weal Gazette*; it's read by many upper class citizens.'

'Newspaper!' Shaw cried. She remembered several Clammers had earned a meager penny selling those printed sheets they couldn't read themselves. 'I never thought of that. What would I have to pay a banker?'

'Out here?' Roza wrinkled her nose as she considered the question. 'Fifteen libers per week at least. Do stress the, ah, somewhat primitive circumstances.'

'Are they primitive?' Shaw said surprised.

Roza smiled. 'For a city banker? Very much so. No servants, no mansions, no business clubs, nothing but the company of a bunch of kids. Abysmal, actually.'

'Does it bother you?' Shaw said. 'I hadn't realized...'

'No,' she said. 'I find I like it. After Pomfrith and his clients, this is a relief. But then, I said I'm not a banker.'

Shaw managed to show Callogan everything and everybody in time before the meal bell called them to the cafeteria.

'It's a grand place, this,' he said, when they joined Amaj and Wylmer's table.

'It is,' Amaj said. 'Jem's people knew how to do things in style.'

'They even died in style,' Jem said sourly, popping out of thin air onto the last empty chair. 'Pathetic show-offs. A lot of this stuff was made by the Qoori. My grandfather's people only paid for it.'

'Qoori,' Shaw said, her mind jumping subject again. 'That reminds me. I need copies of your maps, guys.'

'All of them?' Wylmer said. 'You got a month or so?'

'For the moment, everything north of here. I can't expect you guys to keep supplying us with booty, so we'll have to go up there ourselves and trade.'

'We can copy those,' Wylmer said.

'Thank you.' Shaw swallowed a bite of fish. 'This is nice,' she said. 'Where did you get it?'

'They told me it's halibut,' Wylmer said. 'It is a fastidious beastie; doesn't come next to or near Seatome. We got half the Port Naar fishing fleet. They've settled across the bay, and provide us with ample fish.'

'So that's what you saw out there,' she said to Callogan. 'If you guys have got a surplus, I'm buying. And that brings me to something else. That ship in the bay, is she navy?'

'*Raffix*? No, she's not.' Wylmer grimaced. 'The boss captured it near Port Naar, and had those fishers sail it here. I haven't got a crew for her, and she's undersized for a warship. Do you want her?'

'As a gift?' Shaw grinned. 'I was thinking it would make a nice explorer ship. Big enough for a trader and a load of samples. We could send her out to discover new markets; there is so much of the world we don't know.'

'You can have her,' Wylmer said. 'You must come and take her yourself; I have no hands to spare.'

'How large a crew does she need?'

'Six and two officers,' Wylmer said. 'Any bos'n or master's mate would do.'

Shaw nodded. 'I'll pass it on to our Captain Isambar.'

## CHAPTER 10 – NEWSPAPER

'Advertising?' Nate said the next morning as Shaw dragged him outside to the steamcart. 'What for?'

'A banker,' Shaw said with a small smile.

Nate fell down in the leather seat and stared at her. 'Would that work?'

'We'll find out,' Shaw's smile turned determined. 'It's worth a try, I think.'

The *Weal Gazette (Voice of the Free Weal)* had its headquarters in a dingy building not far from Clam Street. A large sign over the door declared *Barlett & Son, Printers.*

Past the scratched double doors, they stepped into a different world.

'Darn,' Nate muttered. 'It's like *Marigold*'s engine room.'

A man was standing over a long machine, with several boys waiting, arms crossed. Apart from his steady cursing, the silence was deafening.

At their entrance, the man looked up. 'No newsies right now,' he barked. 'Be back at midnight.'

Shaw smiled. 'I wanted to buy – is that the word? – an advertisement.'

'Eh?' the man said. 'Oh, apologies. Advertisement, sure. I won't make it tomorrow, I'm afraid. That blasted press broke down again.'

'What's wrong with it?' Nate asked.

'Money,' the man said, and he stepped from the machine's platform. 'Name's Barlett,' he said. 'Owner, publisher and printer of the *Weal Gazette.*'

'If we can get that thing working again,' the eldest of the boys said. 'Else it's done with the *Gazette.*'

'Money is tight?' Shaw said, and she felt excitement rise in her chest.

'Yes,' the man said bitterly. 'Ever since the Clam Street disaster.'

'Why?' Nate asked, looking up in surprise.

'Why?' the man said. 'Because that bleepin' wyrmcaller took away my newsies. My sales dropped, and I got bills to pay but no money. Now the press died again; John the Smith got replacements made, but he wants four unis I ain't got. Unless you'd want for four unis worth of advertisements?'

'What would that get me?' Shaw asked nonchalantly.

'A full page for ten days,' Barlett said.

'But you haven't enough buyers,' Nate said. 'So who will read our advertisement?'

Barlett sighed. 'I need more newsies, but with the orphans gone, I must hire other kids. Those cost me more, an' I'll be running at a loss.'

'Subscriptions,' the boy said. Shaw thought him sixteen, with a sharp, darkly gray face, matching eyes and the wavy hair that was rare in Vanhaari.

'Sure,' the man said, as if they'd been going over this a hundred times already. 'But who's going to pay the investment?'

'Explain,' Shaw said.

The boy looked at her. 'Subscriptions. Buy one; get the *Gazette* delivered to your home every day.'

'Sounds great,' Shaw said. 'What would it cost?'

The boy snorted. 'We worked it out,' he said. 'Twelve libers fifty for a year. But we'd need at least a hundred libers to have the system up and running first. Delivery boy wages, free copies, salesmen, things like that.'

Shaw looked at Nate.

'Why not?' he said. 'It sounds promising.'

Shaw nodded. 'I'm willing to invest the money you need,' she said. 'For starters here is one liber to get those parts for the press. Then I suggest you come to our office and we'll set up something official. Pasandir Trading Co, at Old Wharf.'

'You mean that?' Barlett said. 'Why? What do you get out of it?'

'Advertisements,' Shaw said. 'We could use a way to get our name out.' She grinned. 'Besides, we're the Clammers the wyrmcaller stole away. If our good fortune meant your bad luck, we can at least help you out. You employ journalists?'

'That's me,' the boy said. 'Emmett Barlett; the son. I'm doing cats in trees, ox cart accidents, lost wallets, and other exciting happenings.'

'Do people want to read that?' Shaw asked.

The boy shrugged. 'Nothing ever happens in Seatome. Yeah, the Clam Street fire, but my mother forgot to wake me up that night. I did do an out-of-my-butt story on the scene the next day that got us a few letters.'

'Angry letters, because you blamed the colonel,' his father said.

'They sacked him afterwards, didn't they?' the boy said. 'So the *Gazette* was right.'

Shaw grinned. 'If you're interested, you could write something about our headquarters in the Peaks. Maybe people would find it interesting for a change.'

The boy sat up. 'You mean, go out there? I'd like that!' He looked at his father. 'But the local news...'

'Hire someone else for the cats and wallets,' Shaw said. 'Now, our advertisement.'

With their business done, Shaw turned to leave, when her eye fell on a notice board full of small cards, each with a person's head and a few lines of text.

'What are these?' she asked curiously.

'Business cards, ma'am,' Emmett said. 'Very chic, with your face on it and your company's details.'

'You make these?' Shaw looked at Nate. 'That's just the thing we need when we go inspecting WyDir's enterprises.'

'I can do that, ma'am,' Emmett said proudly. 'I have a photo camera. I could do them now, if you have time to spare, and have the cards ready tomorrow.' He took them to the back of the workshop. 'Sit down please.'

Shaw sat on the narrow stool, while Emmett walked to a small box on three legs, covered with a black cloth such as a barbers used.

'It will take ten minutes, and you must hold perfectly still.'

Nate laughed. 'Now you're asking! She couldn't sit still if you'd paid her.'

Shaw sniffed and with a mighty effort of will managed to prove him wrong.

'Done!' Emmett said, and Shaw jumped up.

'Nah nah!' she cried to Nate. 'Your turn, mister!'

Another ten minutes later they were both immortalized.

'He bought that camera of his own money,' the elder Barlett said. 'He'd like to do them photographs for the papers, but the apparatus is clunky, what with those legs and things.'

'It takes too darn long,' Emmett said. 'You can't expect accidents to wait happening for ten minutes.'

'Talk it over with our engineer,' Shaw said. 'She's a Thali. Take your camera; you can take a few pictures of the premises as well, for our next advertisements.'

The next morning, Shaw and Nate were discussing plans, when Emmett appeared, carrying his camera. He handed her two copies of the *Weal Gazette*, with a handsome half-page advertisement calling for candidates to start up a new major banking institution in the Peaks. Only for the intrepid banker!

'Beautiful,' Shaw said. 'That should do it.'

'And here are your cards,' Emmett said. 'I made a larger print of both pictures as well. You could have them framed, or something.'

Shaw stared at her likeness. 'Is that me?' she said finally. 'I'm so angry.'

'Fierce,' Nate said. 'That face had those useless directors quaking in their too expensive socks. It's a lot better than my silly smile.'

Shaw picked up Nate's photo. 'It's... beautiful,' she said slowly. 'That's no silly smile! That look is how you keep me from doing stupid things.' She sighed. 'Great job, Emmett. If you want a tour of our place, find Mage Callogan. He'll be pleased to show you around. Don't forget to ask him how he killed a jinni. That should make a rousing story.'

'A real story?' Emmett said. 'Not a thumbs-tale?'

'Very real,' Shaw said. 'A jinni and a bunch of pirates thought to burgle us. We of the wyrmcaller's folks don't take kindly to things like that, so we took them down and handed the survivors to the harbor guard.'

'Our readers will love that!' He grinned at Shaw. 'Don't worry, ma'am. The *Gazette* will bring you fame!' Then he ran out, swerving past Varan, who entered the office with a stack of papers.

'What the heck?' Varan said, staring after the boy.

'He's a journalist and a photographer,' Shaw said straight-faced, shoving the newssheet under the warehouse manager's nose. 'Yesterday, we bought a half-partnership in Barrett & Son Printers, who publish this paper. Young Emmett Barrett is sure their readers are breathlessly waiting for his reports of our great deeds.'

Varan pulled a face. 'I stubbed my toe this morning. Would that...?'

'Only if you allow me to saw that toe off,' Shaw said. 'Seriously, I think it will help the business to advertise. What are you clutching so triumphantly?'

'The first orders our salesguys brought in,' Varan said, and he handed her the sheets.

'Hey!' Shaw said, leafing through them. 'These are for Kell products.'

'You told our salesguys to take all orders,' he said. 'That's what they did.'

Shaw felt a giggle coming up and suppressed it ruthlessly. 'I thought we'd catch one or two foreign ones; not a whole shipload of them.'

Varan smirked. 'Every one of those guys complained MCTC is very slow these days; every Kell order they placed with them went way beyond its delivery date. They came to us to see if we would do better.'

'Does MCTC have its own people in Port Dvarghish?' Nate asked.

'They don't,' Varan said. 'They work through Jelvaren, a local trading house.'

Shaw tapped the desk. *Kell – that's the next step.* She didn't need to think, it was that clear to her. 'Then we will. Tell Captain Isambar to get his *Fayaafa* to Port Dvarghish immediately. Nate, Keena and I will port thataway and see about a warehouse and things. You guys keep rolling here.'

Varan laughed. 'Off to conquer Kell you are. Good luck, ma'am general manager.'

'Drums!' Nate said. 'Trumpets! Blow the advance.'

'Just get moving!' Shaw grinned and hurried out. 'Keena?'

The mage stepped from the cafeteria and raised an eyebrow.

'There y'are,' Shaw cried. 'Come, we're off to Port Dvarghish.'

Keena didn't ask anything. She simply drained her cawah and turned to Cook, behind the counter.

'Catch,' she said and threw the mug at his head. The boy plucked it out of the air and waved.

'You're getting better,' Keena said approvingly and donned her pirate hat.

Downstairs, Kier the portal mage looked up. 'You want a port? Mind to take a handportal for the way back.'

'Thanks,' Shaw grimaced and pocketed the slender rod; in her hurry she would've left them stranded in Kell. 'The three of us are for Port Dvarghish. When you've sent us over, please warn the engineers I'll need a new portal soon.'

'I'll tell them,' Kier said. 'Ready? Off you go.'

They found themselves in an alcove to the side of a soaring corridor of massive redstone walls and a high, vaulted roof. From somewhere far away Shaw heard the sound of soldiers exercising and closer by the noise of a big city.

A tall Kell woman in burnished armor hurried past, and then stopped in her tracks. 'Well now. Strangers? Who might you be, youngsters?'

Shaw eyed her carefully. 'This is the port captain's office? A public building?'

The woman unbent a little. 'It is, but we seldom get portal visitors from outside the country.'

'We're here on business,' Shaw said. 'None of us have ever been in Kell, though we flew over it once. We're with the wyrmcaller.'

At that, the woman's face cleared. 'His people are always welcome here,' she said. 'He spared us a great deal of grief with those two wyrms recently.'

'I know,' Shaw said, smiling. 'I was with him then. Shaw Harwans, of the Pasandir Trading Co. We are looking for markets.'

'That's always useful,' the woman said. 'Did you have anything special in mind?'

'We trade in everything. First we'll need a warehouse, then we will start hiring. In the meantime I have a few orders I need filled.'

'You want a guide,' the woman said. 'You won't find your way around the city without one. If you look across the street, you will see a tall building with two towers. That is the Workers' Market. They can supply the people you need.'

'Thank you,' Shaw said gratefully. 'That will be the first place to visit.'

The woman saluted and strode away.

Outside, everything was too big. The houses, the doors, the shop windows, and everything around were made for people far larger than a five feet tall Vanhaari girl. Shaw grunted. She screwed her monocle in her eye and gripped Nate's arm.

'We'll show them,' she muttered, chin in the air.

Nate briefly touched her hand and she knew he understood.

The Workers' Market had been built of the same red stone as most other buildings, and looked as sternly humorless.

Inside, everything was ordered like a military camp. Even the queues in front of the counter clerks were straight and their clients lacked the desperate poverty of their Seatome counterparts.

*Of course,* Shaw thought. She remembered what Kellani had once said of her country. *With us, the clan takes care all its members are fed and clothed.* The jobseekers looked just as unhappy, though.

The atmosphere was subdued and besides the soft voices of the clerks, no one spoke.

As they looked around, a young woman stepped from the shadows. She was dressed in a short, dark robe that seemed the official clerking uniform.

'Your business?' she asked.

'I'm hiring,' Shaw said.

The woman's lips unbent in a smile. 'We can help you with that. What do you seek?'

'To begin, the port captain's office told me I need a guide.'

'If you are here for the first time that certainly would ease matters. Do you wish for someone military, admin or menial?'

'We're a trading company. I need a person who is both young and knows the way around businesses.'

The woman turned around. 'Wyon, report!' she said in a raised voice.

A Kell boy of some fourteen years came running.

'He will assist you,' the woman said. 'He is a Dvarghish of trade descent and knows all the merchants and artisans in the city. Don't you, lad?'

'Almost, Supervisor,' the boy said solemnly.

'This lady needs a guide. She will hire you. Perform well, and you can do great things.'

The boy let his already considerable biceps roll. 'I will, ma'am.'

'Good. He requires three pennies a day, one of which is our fee. When you are finished with him, you can send him back. Or you can hire him permanently, in which case he will leave us.'

Shaw looked at the boy. He was taller than she, with a golden sheen to his brown skin and broad in the shoulders as most Kells. His straight hair was cut short and his nose sharp as a bluewing's beak. He wore a sleeveless tunic open at the front, and a boy's kilt with laced boots. His answering look was frank, as if he weighed her as well.

'You'll do,' Shaw said. 'Let's go outside and sit somewhere we can talk.'

The boy saluted. 'As you wish, ma'am,' he said. 'I would suggest the harbor, to impress you with our fine ships.'

'I don't impress easily,' Shaw said. 'But try by all means.'

Wyon brought them to a stone bench and they sat down.

'Well now,' Shaw said. 'I'm Shaw; mistress is only for official moments. Nate is my partner, and Keena our company mage. We run the Pasandir Trading Company. We have a warehouse in the Peaks, and one in Seatome. Now we seek to open one here as well.'

'A warehouse,' the boy said. 'Are you superstitious?'

Shaw looked at him. 'No; why?'

'I know of one, going cheap. But they say there's a ghost inside.'

'A ghost? In Kell?' Nate said.

Wyon grinned. 'Yeah, funny, isn't it. We've rules for everything, but not for ghosts.'

'Let's have a look at this spooky place,' Shaw said. 'Do we need a key?'

The boy looked at her. 'A key? Why? We don't lock our buildings.'

'Now you do surprise me,' she said. 'Alright, show us the ghost.'

# CHAPTER 11 – BRANCHING OUT

The warehouse was almost a mile down the road, where the piers looked older and less well cared for. It was a solid-looking building of gray stone, not the usual red. When Shaw commented on that, the boy looked grave.

'This once was M'Arrangh property,' he said. 'They liked dark things.'

'So they did.' Shaw knew the history of the Arrangh Warlock and Traitor Vystyn. 'That was a time of betrayal and treason.'

'And great deeds,' the boy said.

Shaw laughed. 'I can't say we lack these. Now, lead the way.'

Inside the warehouse, all was dark. The air was still and smelled vaguely of dust mixed with exotic merchandise. Then, a bright glow rose and chased the gloom away.

Wyon stifled a curse. 'I'm not used to magic,' he said sheepishly, watching the little light drifting over Keena's head.

'It's a terrific magelight!' Shaw said.

Keena muttered something, but her plumed hat couldn't hide a pleased smile. With a twist of her shoulders she strode deeper inside.

The warehouse was large, with long rows of empty shelves. In the center was a narrow steel staircase leading to a platform with what looked like an overseer's office. Nothing moved, and they walked slowly on.

As they passed underneath the platform, a creepy hand touched Shaw's leg, something heavy came crashing, and bits of sticky red goo splattered all over them.

'Darn!' Nate shouted, and he ran to the stairs. The others followed him up, but the platform was deserted. Then a shrill, high laughter somewhere ahead sent shivers along Shaw's back.

'What's that?' their young guide said, turning his head left and right. 'I don't believe in ghosts, but...'

'Ghosts exist,' Keena said. 'But they don't bother people.' She stared at the broad wooden railing. 'See that lighter spot there? It's free of dust. That's where the pot must've stood.' She grinned. 'Strawberry jam and no old stock either.'

Shaw rubbed her finger in a red stain and tasted. 'You're right. What a waste!'

They went down again, and Keena wandered into a lane between the shelves. The others followed her. Suddenly she knelt and touched an end of rope on the ground. Then she nodded grimly. 'Let's see if there's more.'

Shaw's senses were vibrating as they walked to the back of the long hall.

Again, a shrill cry made Shaw's blood run cold, but Keena only chuckled.

At the back of the warehouse was a hatch in the floor.

Keena pulled her lip as she stood staring at it. 'Ghosts don't leave footprints,' she said.

Shaw looked at her and then at the hatch. There were faint marks there. Tracks in the dust?

Keena stooped and gripped the hatch. It lifted without a sound. 'Stairs.'

Something below chuckled, and Keena smiled. Then, without a word, she climbed into the hole.

Shaw hesitated.

'I'll go first,' Wyon offered, but she clenched her fists and followed Keena.

The cellar was dry, and clean, with several stout beds, a desk and a large birdcage with a big, gaudily colored bird inside.

Shaw burst out laughing. 'Was that the scream?'

As if in reply, the bird screeched again, and buried its beak beneath its wing.

Keena walked over to some clothes hanging from nails on the wall. One piece was a long, pale gray cloak, with a hood and a creepy mask.

'Ghost ain't at home,' she said.

Wyon cursed. 'That's it?' he said, and he sounded offended. 'A robe and a booboo mask? But that crash...'

'A tripwire,' Keena said. 'It's all a big trick.'

'Why?' the boy asked.

Without answering, Keena walked to the other side of the cellar. Above her was a large hatchway, for loading goods directly from a cart into the cellar. Underneath were many crates and barrels stashed. Keena opened a one of the wooden boxes.

Shaw looked past her shoulder and saw a mass of pink seeds the size of her little finger. They gave off a pungent smell she couldn't identify.

'What's that?'

Wyon came closer and gasped. 'I heard of these!' he said. 'They're Jabisk seeds, and forbidden! Bad guys use them to make slaves of other people. Dunno how, but the queen forbade them. Shucks! There's so *many* of them.'

'We've seen enough,' Shaw said. 'Let's get the authorities in on this.'

'Wait!' Keena said, and they all froze as a harsh voice came from upstairs.

'Fool! You let the hatch open again. You don't want that cat among the jabbies, idiot.'

'I didna,' another voice declared angrily. 'I always close the hatch.

'Darnation!' a third voice said. 'Someone's in the cellar?'

'What's that light?' the second voice said.

'Down! Whoever it is, kill them!' the harsh voice commanded.

Shaw moved her hands, and two daggers appeared in them. She wasn't a fighter, but Willow had trained her in the use of throwing knives and she never went anywhere without.

Nate gripped his trusty cudgel, and Keena looked around, as if searching for something.

Three men jumped into the cellar.

'Intruders!' the harsh voice said. 'Who the hell... Vanhaari!' He was a heavy built pale man with the slight stoop and dangling arms of the harbor brawler.

'They're only kids,' the second voice said. He was an overdressed man, with golden rings on his fingers.

The third Garthan laughed. 'They're *dead* kids.' He was thin and walked with a jaunty air that ill fitted his skull-like head.

'Who are you children?' the brawler said. 'How the heck did you get in here?'

'We're the wyrmcaller's agents,' Shaw said coolly. 'You're caught in the act, bud.'

'So?' the brawler said. 'But you're not going to tell, sis.' He walked slowly forward, his enormous hands twitching.

Keena sniffed with so much derision that the brawler's coarse face reddened. He snarled and moved faster. At the same moment, Keena took a flying leap at the man. Her fine hat went sailing, then her stretched boot crashed into the bandit's face and her body arched forward. Her hands gripped a gas pipe running along the ceiling, and she swung herself over the falling body into the natty fellow.

Shaw's knife flashed, and the third man clutched his shoulder. Then Nate was at him, and the man dropped like a stone.

The brawler sat up, blood running down his face. Keena lashed out with her foot and the Garthan folded without a sound.

Shaw turned to Keena. 'Two out in one move,' she said, embracing the other girl. 'You're a secret army on your own.'

Keena shrugged. 'Done that forty feet up,' she said. 'Those dastards who stole me did a big show, and I was their throw and catch girl. If I didn't catch, I'd be dead. You will learn tricks that way.' She picked up her plumed hat and donned it resolutely.

'You were great,' Shaw said. 'Now we need the authorities. Let's try that hatch up there.'

'Wyon, old chap, climb on my shoulders and push,' Nate said, and he put his back to the wall. The guide clambered onto his shoulders, and Nate groaned.

'Like lifting a young ox! Hurry, guy.'

The hatch opened easily, and Wyon climbed out.

'I'll warn the guard,' he whispered and let the hatch slam shut.

Soon, loud military voices and heavy boots in the warehouse told of the approach of someone soldierly. The large hatch was wrenched open and three big, armed women dropped in.

One of them was a grizzled leading tigress with a deeply lined face. 'You this trader woman?' she barked.

Shaw lifted her chin and glared through her monocle.

'I am Shaw Harwans, managing director of the PTC,' she said.

The tigress relaxed slightly. 'What was your business here?'

'We are in Port Dvarghish to seek a location for a new trading post,' Shaw snapped. 'The Workers' Market hired us a boy as a guide and he advised us of an empty warehouse for sale. He warned us about a ghost inside. Instead, we found a lot of foolery and what looks to be clandestine wares. Then these three ruffians appeared. We duly warned them we were part of the wyrmcaller of Kalbakar's people. They nonetheless attacked us, and we knocked them out. Then we sent our guide to get the authorities.'

The tigress smiled and it changed her face. 'He found us; we told him to wait outside, just in case anyone would try to be funny.'

One of the other tigresses opened the crate with the seeds. 'Divine Gorm! Jabbies! If they'd gotten this load out of the country...'

'Who the heck would need so many slaves?' the leading tigress said.

'Bokkaners and their jinn masters,' Shaw said harshly.

The tigress looked at her. 'You youngsters are pirate hunters, aren't you? We never expected them here in one of our major cities.'

'That's what the authorities in Seatome thought. Yet those dogs walk in and out like they own the place,' Shaw said bitterly.

'At least these won't.' The leading tigress regarded the three unconscious pirates thoughtfully. 'Attacking our allies would have earned them a life in the mines. Those Jabisk seeds hang them. You did us a great service, Ms. Harwans. We will remove the contraband; the rest is for the warehouse operator. If you want this place, you better hop over to the castle. The building has stood like this ever since the end of the war. It is a prime location, but no Kell is anxious to use a former M'Arrangh possession. As a foreigner, you won't mind, but if you want any customers to come here, you better have a wisewoman purify it before you open.'

'That's a helpful suggestion,' Shaw said. 'We'll go over to the castle first.'

'We can take a steamcart, if you wish,' Wyon said, looking in through the hatch.

Two hours later, they arrived back at the warehouse with the lease in their pockets and a crew of young workers hired, and found the tigresses gone.

Shaw went down into the cellar. 'There's quite a lot of stuff left,' she said. 'That should be ours then.' She lifted the lid off a chest. 'Seasoning herbs. Well, we had an order for those. What's this?' She stared at a crate filled with small, beautifully cut glass bottles, filled with a golden fluid. She opened one and a lovely smell greeted her. 'Perfume!'

'Snake oil,' Wyon said. 'It's made from real snakes. Very expensive, but the ladies like it. Seen those bottles sold for twenty libers or more.'

'Good!' Shaw said. 'We should get even more for them at home.'

There was a large box of brightly colored candied fruits much prized by the wealthy, and then she looked up as she heard Nate curse.

'Wastrel loot!' he said as he stared at two crates of golden tableware.

'At least it's not a load of stones,' Keena said, as she waved at a barrel full of bits of purplish gleaming rock.

'Not stones,' Wyon protested. 'Them's garnets; I seen these in jeweler's shops. They're made into neck chains, rings and stuff. At ten for a penny you could sell the lot for a thousand libers.'

Keena glanced at him and closed her mouth.

'That's nice,' Shaw said. 'My mother had a garnet ring.' She grabbed a handful of stones and let them dribble through her fingers. 'I wouldn't have recognized these.' She bit her lip. 'What's in the last crates?'

'Tinned preserve,' Nate said. 'Crocodile steaks.'

Shaw suppressed a shudder. 'No thanks.' She rose and dusted her hands. 'A handsome reward for a fight. This stuff will get us going here.'

'What'll we do with the bird?'

'We could place the cage near the entrance, with the spooky robe, to tell tall stories to our customers,' Nate said.

Wyon gripped the cage and lifted it. It was heavier than he'd expected, and the bird showed its resentment at being shaken by jabbing at the boy's head.

Keena sighed. 'I'll help you,' she said. Together, they manhandled the cage to the main entrance.

As they came to the front door, they found a small group of girls peering inside.

'Oehh!' A massively muscled girl with her hair tied up in a mass of little tails looked scared. 'This is the ghost place! Spooks ain't hiring, are they?'

'It's creepy,' another girl said. 'I heard awful screams in here, of people murdered.'

'You didn't,' Wyon said, laughing. 'It was a scam. A bandit scam. I seen them. Big, stupid bandits they were, in a ghost suit and a booboo mask.'

'Don't kid me,' the girl said, scowling and bunching up her shoulders.

'I'm not,' Wyon protested, stepping back carefully. He wasn't small, but these girls were two, three years older and they loomed over him.

The bird uttered a long, shuddering cry.

'There,' he said. 'That's your people murdered. Come on in, I'll show you the mask.' They ran off, to reappear ten minutes later, giggling and relieved.

'No ghosts,' the big girl said. 'We'll go to work then. There should be water here, and brooms.'

'At the back,' the girl who had heard people murdered said. 'Kitchen, bedrooms, everything.' She grinned. 'Been inside, all the way. Then we heard the scream, and ran. That bird sure fooled us!'

Shaw handed the big girl a handful of silver coins. 'You'll be head girl. If you need any gear, buy it.'

The head girl puffed out her cheeks and fixed the others with her eyes. 'Let's get this place cleaned up.'

'Not me,' Wyon said hastily. 'I'm a guide.'

The girl sniffed. 'You're too small for real work.'

'There's more at the back, that girl said.' Shaw walked around the building, over a path of flagged stones, now overgrown by grass. A long row of small stone poles connected by chains marked the borders of their territory.

Near the end of the building was a pair of double doors. 'Stuck,' Shaw said as she tried to open them.

'Let me,' Wyon said. He gripped the door and pulled mightily. With a loud shriek, one door opened. He saluted. 'Ma'am.'

'Thank you,' Shaw said with a queenly smile and stepped inside.

'My,' Nate said over her shoulder. 'Transport!'

It was a wagon shed with an assortment of vehicles, from a small handcart to a big dray.

'They'll need checking up, I suppose,' Shaw said. Her parents hadn't owned any wagons, so this part of the business was unfamiliar. 'We'd better paint them over, too; Arrangh black lacquer won't make us popular.'

'Someone at the door, ma'am,' one of the girls bellowed.

'Coming.' They hurried back to the front door and found two young women waiting. Both were dressed in short robes of some tan fabric, their hair cut the same way, making them look very much alike.

'You were looking for salespeople?' one said soberly. 'We were with Jelvaren of Brannoe Lane, general merchandise. A competitor recently took over our company. The whole sales department and many others got laid off. I daresay more of us will come to see you.'

Shaw looked at Nate. 'Jelvaren. Wasn't that MCTC's agent?'

Nate nodded. 'It was.' He grinned. 'This can be interesting.'

'Tell me of your sales experience,' Shaw said to the girls.

'We've both been with the company for several years,' the second girl said. 'We were five, a team, working well together. After a time, things seemed to slow down. The boss wasn't a young woman; then her daughter died, and it was as if the company died with her. We did what we could, but when the Purchasing Department no longer filled our orders, we were sunk. Two weeks ago, the boss sold everything to a competitor who didn't need us.' The girl spread her hands. 'So here we are.'

'We're the Pasandir Trading Co out of Seatome and the Peaks,' Shaw said. 'That's the wyrmcaller's outfit. We are branching out into Kell and I need good, loyal salespeople.'

She handed the first girl a paper she had prepared. 'This is a list of goods I have, with amounts, quality, and prices. They are in our Seatome warehouse, so remember to take account of the distance. We can handle rush orders, but they'll cost more.'

The girls both studied the list. 'We need help,' the second girl said. 'If we have others working on this with us, ma'am, would you hire them too?'

'The five of you,' Shaw said.

The first girl gave a curt nod. 'We're off then.'

'Good luck,' Shaw said solemnly, as the two girls hurried away.

Wyon looked at her. 'You trust them a lot,' he said. 'Those girls couldn't deliver before, that shredded their reputation. Many merchants will hesitate to accept them.'

'They deserve a chance,' Shaw said. 'We got a chance; why not they? With luck, the wyrmcaller's name will help them. And us as well.' She sat staring at the harbor. 'Do you know anything about this Jelvaren Company?'

Wyon scratched his head. 'They weren't large, but their reputation was fine. They were MCTC agents for Kell; that's bi-ig business.'

'I know MCTC,' Shaw said. 'Big indeed. Go on.'

'Brynnyr Gunny Co are the guys that bought Jelvaren. Dunno anything about them. Suppose they only wanted that MCTC agency, if they fired everybody in the office.'

'Guess so,' Shaw said. 'Nate...'

'Workers' Market?' he said.

She stretched out her hand to him, then froze, her brain working furiously. After a moment she stirred. 'See if you can find out what happened to their office building. If it's still for rent, take it. Then get us the former Jelvaren personnel. I sniff a chance.' She tapped their guide's chest. 'Go and keep him out of trouble.'

'Sure,' Wyon said. 'Come on, boss!'

'Spending money, aren't we?' Keena said. 'Won't we run out?'

Shaw looked at her. 'PTC's capital is seventy thousand libers. Our ledger keeper in Smalkand tried to count what was in Eskandar's safe. She stopped at half a million libers. We'll not run out of money any time soon.'

Keena sighed and a slow smile pulled at her lips. 'Nice!' she said.

More workers arrived, and Shaw sent them to join the others. Then a battered steamcart came roaring, and dislodged two women in blue tunics.

'Gas Board,' one said. 'We come to inspect your building. You need a new safety certificate, ma'am.'

They disappeared inside, and one after another the lights went on.

After that someone came to check the water, a woman from the Port Authority brought a file with harbor regulations and placed a sign at the pier saying *Private; No Fishing, No Swimming.*

'We changed the pier's name, ma'am,' the official said. 'It was Arrangh Pier, but now the official address is Peaks Pier. Please note the change in your records.'

Lastly, an old wisewoman arrived who went round the building, chanting and waving her hands. When she was

138

done, Shaw wondered how to ask if there was a fee involved, but the wisewoman helped her.

'No donation needed; the Arrangh spirit was very faint,' she said with a small smile. 'There is another power in here, a divine force. My Lady Gathea welcomes the other presence, though she refuses to name him. Seeing you are a follower of the wyrmcaller, I suppose mysterious Bodrus is watching over you.'

'Bodrus?' Shaw said, confused. 'Why would he do that?'

'Don't ask for a reason, girl,' the wisewoman said gently. 'Accept his blessing and do his work as best as you can. Even if that work is as mundane as trade.' She moved her shoulders and the green robe she wore shimmered like a cascade of spicy autumn leaves. 'I must go. May Gathea walk with you.'

When the old priestess had left, Shaw sank down on one of the small poles lining the path. Bodrus? She had mentioned him and his works, but always in connection with Eskandar. Never thought there could be something between her and the Sleeping God.

*'Teodar?'* she thought in impulse.

*'Don't ask.'* The familiar voice sounded peevish. *'Do what the holy woman said and accept it.'*

*'Are* you *watching* me?' she said, confounded.

*'Yes.'*

*'Why?'*

*'I said you shouldn't ask,'* he said.

*'But I do,'* she said. *'I'm not Eskandar; you're not my lifelong almost-older-brother and I want to know. Why are you watching me?'*

He grunted. *'You're direct, aren't you? Fine. Because what you do is important for Eskandar and for the Peaks. I want to be sure you're not doing anything idiotic to spoil it.'*

*'I won't,'* she said.

*'That's what they all say,'* he retorted.

Shaw had to laugh at that. *'All right. Are you coping?'*

*'Yes,'* he said. *'I have to.'* For a moment he was silent, and Shaw wondered if he'd already gone. *'Following you and Eskandar helps. But I'd love a walk in the open air, and normal food instead of what Bodrus creates for me.'* Then he made a sound halfway between a laugh and a choke. *'You go on getting rich, girl. As long as I'm not yelling at you, you're not doing too badly.'*

*'Thanks!'* she said, not hiding a chuckle. *'If you do yell, I'll come and scratch your face open. Keep well.'*

*'Same.'* He was gone.

'Shaw!'

She wheeled around and saw Nate come in, wreathed in smiles, and her heart leaped at the sight of him.

'Yeah?' she said coolly. 'You're back.'

He grinned, not at all taken in. 'We got the Jelvaren building for six hundred per year, furnished. The Workers' Market had most of the former Jelvaren personnel in their books, and I hired them. We even got their financial manager, an old gal who had taken her ledgers home when she left. It seems those Brynnyr Gunny fellows who bought the company only wanted the name and the MCTC agency. I got a carpenter to make a new sign with our handle on it. I told him to come along and do another one here as well.'

She relaxed. 'Brilliant,' she said gratefully. 'Simply brilliant.' She looked around. 'Where's Wyon?'

'I sent him to get something edible for all of us. To celebrate, like.'

'That's a great idea!' she said, staring at him in awe. Somehow, she never thought of such things.

Nate looked around. 'Lights!' he said. 'I wondered if they still worked.'

'We got them inspected,' Shaw said. 'I've seen more officials in one afternoon than I've encountered in Seatome in ten years.'

Wyon came back, carefully balancing a large box of sweet pies and six bottles of lemonade. 'You made one baker very happy, boss,' he told Nate. 'Especially the lemonade, it's import, and expensive! He normally sells a bottle per month.'

'Really?' Shaw said. They drank the same Chorwaynie syrup at home, and she hadn't thought of it as something extraordinary. She filed it away like she did so many things.

Nate coughed. 'Ah, I didn't think of that, but are there any glasses?'

'I wasn't sure either,' Wyon said. 'So I borrowed a set of the baker's. He wants them back; I paid five pennies deposit for them.'

'Smart thinking,' Shaw said. 'Let's call the others; they have worked hard all day.'

'Pies?' the head girl said. 'Oh, that's nice! We were getting hungry.'

'I forgot,' Shaw said. 'Arrange for someone to bring groceries; bread, meats, tea and things. You can't work on empty stomachs. And if you need anything, don't hesitate to ask. We're busy, but never that busy. I asked for a cook to run the cafeteria, but I haven't seen anyone yet.'

'Guess they'll come this evening,' the girl said. 'Many of those looking for work have got extra clan responsibilities instead, so they'll be busy.'

'Nate and I won't be here tonight,' Shaw said. 'So if any come when we're gone, tell them to be here at eight tomorrow morning. If they want a job, that is. With all due respect to their clans, but if I am to pay their wages, I want them here when I need them.'

'I'll tell them,' the girl said. 'Some will put their clan duties first, I'm afraid.'

Shaw shrugged. 'Their choice; then I won't hire them.' She wiped the sticky pie crumbs from her mouth.

'I'll stay over tonight with the others,' the girl said. 'We'll do the kitchen and one of the bedrooms.' She grinned. 'If I go home now, I'll have clan duties waiting, too. I'd rather work here.'

'Keep a note of your hours,' Shaw said. 'Then we'll pay you overtime, like we do in Seatome.' She gripped Nate's arm. 'Time to go back; what with the difference in hours it's been a long day. Besides, I got to tell you something.' She turned to Wyon. 'You go home now. Be back tomorrow at eight.'

'You gonna hire me then?' the boy asked casually.

'We already did,' Shaw said. 'Three pennies per day, all yours. You will be the warehouse guy; greet customers, run messages, feed the bird and things. With that sort of job you can end up as warehouse manager.'

'Oehh!' Wyon said. 'I can do that. Great! I'll be there.'

'Tell me,' Nate said when they were alone. 'I'm all ears.'

Shaw repeated the wisewoman's words, and her conversation with Teodar.

When she was done, Nate stood watching her, his eyes thoughtful. Finally he relaxed. 'You don't surprise me. At least not with Teodar. You are bringing big changes and I understand him wanting to make sure you won't disrupt his plans. Bodrus now, that's another story.... Or perhaps not; I get the feeling he is playing games of his own. Dunno what; didn't Eskandar say something about the gods quarreling?'

He shrugged. 'Let them play their games. We've got other things to do. Though it *is* nice to know us getting filthily rich is the will of our god.'

Shaw hooked her arm through his. 'You're right. Let's find Keena and go back to Old Wharf before you have to carry me.'

Without a word, Nate picked her up.

# CHAPTER 12 – THE AXED

The next morning, Shaw and Nate returned to Port Dvarghish. As they didn't have their own portal yet, Mage Kier sent them to the port captain's hallway and they walked the last bit.

At the warehouse door, two burly tigresses stopped them.

'You can't come in,' one said. 'The business is closed.'

'I'm the manager,' Shaw said quickly, with her heart in her throat. 'What's the matter?'

The tigress gave a shout, and the same grizzled senior they had met the day before came to meet them.

'Ms. Harwans,' she said. 'You were not here last night?'

Shaw shook her head. 'We had gone back to Seatome. What happened?'

'Some more bandits thought to force entry,' the leading tigress said. 'They hadn't counted on your people, though.'

'Curse it!' Shaw said. 'I should have expected something. Is everyone all right?'

The tigress' smile was grimly appreciative. 'You got stout girls there, ma'am. They fought like true Kells and the bandits lacked a fitting answer. The girls got four of them; a fifth tried to get away, but ended up in the harbor.' The tigress smiled unexpectedly. 'He must've run into that new "No Fishing" sign in the dark, for there is a bloody smudge all over it. We got him out; we don't need drowned bodies cluttering up our harbor. Your girls are fine. Some minor wounds, but we'll request a wisewoman's assistance. That will fix it.'

'Thank you,' Shaw said. The leading tigress saluted and departed with her women.

The workers had gathered in the kitchen, looking bloodied, shocked and triumphant at the same time.

'Ma'am...' the head girl said, and she swallowed.

'I heard,' Shaw cried. 'You've been heroic! Defending our territory against bandits. That leading tigress was right, you did very well. You girls have earned a fat bonus.'

'And free healings?' the head girl asked. 'Those wisewomen cost money.'

Shaw blinked at her. 'Of course, our people get free healing; that's standard.' She kicked the door in her anger. 'Curse those bandits! How can I defend this place? What are the local rules?'

'You can hire guards,' Wyon said, who must have come in unnoticed. 'Some merchants with expensive stuff employ their own guards. You can get them at the castle. Or...'

'Or what?' Shaw asked.

'You can hire some other boys like me.' He grinned. 'All right, a bit older. We've got bedrooms, so they could sleep during the day and guard at night.'

Shaw stared at him. 'You know such guys? Honest guys?'

He nodded, very serious now. 'Six of them. They'll tell you about themselves, but they're terrific. Big, strong and idiotically honest. They're the best, and they don't ask much.' He hesitated. 'They would serve for food and lodging, but that wouldn't be fair, would it?'

'No,' Shaw said. 'I pay normal wages. They don't have a home now?'

'They do,' the boy said. 'Every Kell has a home. But not all homes are happy places.'

Shaw thought of the Clammers with drunken or abusive parents. 'No, some homes aren't happy at all. Go get them. I'll decide when I've spoken with them.'

After an hour, the warehouse crew was laughing and joking again, healed and proud of their strength, and happy with the bonus Shaw paid them.

Then Wyon reappeared, with six lads who looked and moved like soldiers.

Shaw saw them come in and watched the workers turn away from them. The boys didn't seem to notice, but walked on, not exactly like they were on parade, but definitely as a unit.

As she went to meet them, they halted, and the foremost boy brought a hand to his heart in what was almost a military salute.

'Here they are,' Wyon said and he sounded strangely subdued.

Shaw lifted her chin and stared at the lead boy, her blurry eye magnified through her monocle. 'Morning,' she said. 'And who are you?'

'We're the Axed, ma'am; I am Kennan.' He eyed her with a quiet defiance she didn't understand.

'And what are the Axed?' she asked.

The nearby workers froze. 'Traitor kids,' one of them said without turning.

The six stiffened. 'Kids of traitors, please. There is a difference,' Kennan said softly.

'Sure there is,' Shaw said cordially. 'One of our friends in the wyrmcaller's service is Justym. He is Vystyn's great-grandson. The ultimate kid of a traitor, and he is as loyal as any of us to his goddess and to the wyrmcaller.'

Kennan stared at her, his eyes weighing her words. 'Yes,' he said. 'My mother was in the army; an officer. I was brought up as an aspirant, destined to follow in her footsteps. Something happened. Let us say cowardice, killing a lot of her troops, but not her. She was court-martialed and shot. The same sort of thing goes for the others. After that we were disrated and kicked out of the army. It was a very public ceremony – the whole city knows we're tainted; named untrustworthy. Yet it wasn't through our own fault. Maybe my mother was a traitor,' he said coolly. 'But me?'

'True,' Shaw said, sensing the massive hurt in him, but she kept the emotion out of her voice and face. 'You are trained?'

'Melee only, ma'am; no archery or firearms. Swords, spears and axes. There are still those willing to train us, for a fee that is.'

'Would you do ship duty? Overseas duty? Dangerous things?' Shaw asked.

'Of course,' Kennan said without moving a muscle.

'And you would be loyal to the PTC and the wyrmcaller's service?'

'To the death,' he said.

'Then you're hired,' Shaw said. 'Forget that Axed, you're now proud members of the Pasandir Trading Cos Troops.'

She turned around. 'Folks, listen well. I hired these guys to help defend us and our property. Their past is dead, their future are we. I want us to work together. Am I understood?'

'Sure,' the head girl said, turning to face them. She didn't smile, but there wasn't any hostility in her words either. The boy had professed his innocence, and like a true Kell she was prepared to judge them for herself.

'Welcome, guys. The next round of bandits is yours, all right?'

'We'll get them,' Kennan said harshly. 'I promise.'

'Excellent,' Shaw said. 'You'll be squad leader. We're still building up this place, so for the moment your barracks are a six-bed room at the back. I don't suppose you possess arms?'

'Cudgels, ma'am,' Kennan said. 'We're not allowed any weapons.'

'We'll bring swords and things over and put them in a closet somewhere.' Shaw sighed. 'You will get uniforms, but not today. Or tomorrow. Now settle in, get to know the others, and I'll leave the rest to you.'

By the time it was noon, she had hired enough people to fill the warehouse, including a cook and a clerk. Then Nate dragged her to the cafeteria.

'Enough; take a break before it takes you,' he said.

'Tea, cawah or lemonade, ma'am?' the new Cook called.

'Cawah,' Shaw said.

Cook brought two beakers and Shaw sniffed gratefully. 'I needed that.' For a moment she sat in silence. 'Now we have a warehouse and nothing in it.'

'We do,' Nate said. 'I asked the head girl to move that stuff from the cellars and prepare it for transport. When *Fayaafa* comes in, she can take it back. I had the amounts checked, and some samples packed. We'll take that back ourselves, for our salesguys.'

'Good. Next stop that office you hired. Those salesgirls will work from there, of course. And there is WyDir as well.'

Wyon came in, goggle-eyed. 'Ma'am!' he said breathlessly. 'They come to install a portal!'

'Already? Darn!' Shaw looked at Nate. 'Where do we want it?'

'To the side of the cafeteria,' he said. 'Plenty space, and there is that little office next to it, for the portal mage. If we'd want to move a wagon, we'd better use a handportal.'

'You're right,' she said. 'I'd been worrying about that, but a handportal *is* much easier.'

'You stay here,' Nate said. 'I'll go tell them. Show me where they are, Wyon.'

Alone, Shaw stretched out her legs and closed her eyes for a moment.

When she opened them again, Oychak came in with Callogan and a stout young man Shaw recognized as Mott, one of the portal mages.

'Asleep?' the Thali engineer said. 'It's such a beautiful day.'

'She's been running like mad for hours already,' Nate said. 'Sorry to wake you up. Your portal is ready.'

Shaw groaned as she straightened. 'Great,' she said. 'We need it.' She shook hands with the portal mage. 'Hi, Mott; accommodation is not yet what we want it, but we'll get there.'

The portal mage shrugged. 'I'm not particular. A bed, a heap of sacking, that's all the same to me. I was *almost* sleeping under a bridge, lately, so anything you offer is better.'

'There are beds.' Shaw said. 'You're far too valuable to us to let you sleep on the floor.' She looked at Callogan. 'How do we get a healer? This place got attacked last night; pirates again. Our crew managed to catch them, and there were several wounded. The guard sent a wisewoman to patch them up, but we should do that ourselves. Any suggestions?'

'The Magic Institute has a Healing Faculty,' Callogan said. 'To do regrowth and near-death restoration, you need a mage. These are rare and expensive. For simple wounds and broken bones, a witch would do. I could get you one, if you want me to.'

'We have a healer mage at Smalkand,' Shaw said. 'Tymon would come for anything serious if we asked him. I think for resident healer a witch would be enough. I'd like you to hire one for here and another one for Old Wharf.'

'Good,' Callogan said. 'That one could help Keena develop her healing as well. I'll get onto it.'

'Thanks,' Shaw said. 'Tell them free healing for our people and their direct family. Before they start, ask them to see Tymon at Smalkand and arrange for emergencies.'

Callogan nodded. 'Will do. Free healing for family is quite generous, I'd say.'

'We don't need our people worried about their relatives,' Shaw said. 'They'll work better when they are happy.'

'True,' Oychak said. 'The same goes for machines.'

Her face was serious when she said that, and Shaw was sure she meant it. But... happy machines?

'Any idea where you want the next portal?' the engineer added.

'North, probably,' Shaw said. 'But that's all I can say.'

'No problem, we got a second one ready, and more to come. I'll be off then. Callogan, ready?' She waved her handportal at them and the two of them disappeared.

'That's our sign to get a move on,' Shaw said. 'Wyon, call us a steamcart. Nate and I have places to go.'


'Your steamcart, ma'am,' Wyon said, when they stepped outside.

For a few heartbeats Shaw stood blinking against the bright sunlight. She'd gotten used to the luxurious company vehicles and this hired hack was shabby. Then she laughed. *Getting spoiled, already?* She got into the back and nodded to the female driver. 'To the new office.'

'Brannoe Lane number 12,' Nate said quickly and they both laughed as the steamcart roared off.

Compared to Seatome, traffic here was much more disciplined, keeping carefully to the right. There were separate walkways for pedestrians and at several busy intersections Shaw noticed two city guards keeping an eye on things.

The steamcart halted in front of an identical series of office buildings. Number 12 had a dark blue door, opening onto a narrow hall with a wooden counter, where an older Kell woman stood talking to a younger man. When they heard the door open, both turned.

'Mr. Nate!' the woman cried. 'And... Ms. Harwans? How happy I am to see you, ma'am. I am head of Finance.' She introduced the younger man as the receptionist mage and general factotum and then gave them a tour of the building, ending in a shadowy office.

'This is your office, ma'am,' Finance said.

'Not mine,' Shaw said firmly. 'We will need a general manager.' She looked at the older woman. 'How does one go about hiring senior staff in Kell?'

'An advertisement in the *Dvarghish Legends* and the *Trumpet* would do it,' Finance said. 'They're newspapers.'

'I'll see to that,' Shaw said. 'Now, who handles Purchasing at the moment?'

'That was young Ms. Jelvaren's job,' Finance said. 'There is a girl who assisted her, but she cannot act, as she lacks the necessary authority.'

'Call her in, will you?' Shaw said. She sat down behind the desk and opened one of the drawers. It was empty.

'We cleaned all out before we left,' Finance said. 'We need to restock before we are operational.'

'How much money do you need?' Shaw asked.

'A hundred libers would do it.'

Shaw wrote her a letter of credit. 'I made it for a thousand. That gives you the wages for the whole year as well.'

There was a knock on the door, and a young woman entered. She was tall and soldierly like many Kells, but walked with a slight limp.

'You asked for me, ma'am?'

'Not I, this is Ms. Harwans of PTC, the new owner. She wanted to see you.'

Shaw rose and shook hands. 'Mr. Nate is our operations manager. You are running the Purchasing Department?'

'Running isn't the word,' the woman said. 'After Young Ms. died, I watered her plants and things, but without authority I'm as useful as the office cat.'

Shaw smiled. 'Let's rephrase the question. You think you can run the Purchasing Department?'

'Yes,' she said. 'I've been doing the work for the last five years. Young Ms. was a very sick woman, and she couldn't handle much. Signing papers, mostly.'

'You will begin as Acting Purchaser,' Shaw said. 'You are hereby authorized, in coordination with Finance.' She produced a list of the orders she had to fill. 'I need this urgently. I expect my ship to arrive tomorrow, and I want these things on board without delay.'

She looked up at the Purchaser. 'I will be open with you. Many MCTC customers in Seatome complained about bad deliveries of their Dvarghish orders. They came to PTC to see if we could do better. As Jelvaren was MCTC's agent in Dvarghish, the cause of the delays must have lain here. Now I expect things to go smoothly again. If you disappoint me, you will never hold any position of authority again anywhere in the Weal.'

'That is blunt enough,' the Purchaser said. 'It is good to be open about those matters. I will not disappoint you.'

'You are but one. If you need another buyer, hire one,' Shaw said.

'Certainly, ma'am,' Purchaser said. She nearly saluted as she left.

Finance smiled. 'You show remarkable insight, ma'am. Now she knows what is expected of her, she will do well.'

'It's a Kell thing,' Shaw said. 'Even my friend Kellani sometimes needs things spelled out to her. We Vanhaari have plenty other failings.' She smiled. 'I spoke with the girls from Sales already. Actually it is thanks to them I knew what had passed here. They are out selling some of our Seatome stock. Wasn't there a sales manager?'

'There was,' Finance said. 'But he retired when the company closed.'

'I see. We'll let the results of their work decide who will replace him. I expect you to keep an eye on things for the moment. You could start informing your old customers you're back in business. Don't forget to mention you are now the Kell Headquarters of the Pasandir Trading Co, owner of WyDir Airship Lines and other companies. The PTC just opened a warehouse in the harbor district, with a portal connection to all major locations within the Weal, and we got a bigger one in the Peaks.' Shaw grinned. 'And that's only the start.'

'It will cause a stir in the city,' Finance said. 'The wyrmcaller's actions capture a lot of attention and that will reflect on us.'

'It also means we can't afford big mistakes,' Shaw said. 'I'm traveling around a lot; if there are any questions, our Peaks Pier warehouse will know how to find me. Now we'll see about advertising.'

'The *Trumpet* is almost dead,' Wyon said softly as they walked from the office building. 'Last I heard they couldn't compete against the *Dvarghish Legends*.'

'Is that so?' Shaw looked at the others. 'Let's start with them.'

They found the *Trumpet*'s building full of people. A gray-haired Kell woman, an older man, three girls and a whole bunch of others, every one of them looking glum.

'It's finished, clan sisters and brothers,' the first woman was saying. 'We're done; the *Trumpet* issue on the press will be the last one. *Legends* has won.'

Then she saw Shaw and frowned. 'Who're you?'

'Shaw Harwans, PTC,' Shaw said. 'I came for an advertisement.'

'I'm sorry,' the woman said. 'You better go to the *Legends* office. We're out of business.'

'Why?' Shaw asked. 'Isn't there a place for two newspapers?'

The woman shrugged. 'We thought there would be. But it was a pipedream; we had too little money. The *Dvarghish Legends* have rich backers; we don't.'

'Well,' Shaw said. 'We can do something about that. My company is half-owner of the *Weal Gazette* of Seatome. We might be willing to do the same here.'

Those present stared at her in blank incomprehension.

'You would invest in us?' the woman said slowly. 'Why? We're broke.'

'Broke, but not broken, I hope,' Shaw said. 'PTC is a trading company; advertisements will be good for our business. I expect you would be more willing to experiment than *Legends*.'

'I know! You're the wyrmcaller's people!' a tall girl exclaimed. 'I had planned to check up on your new warehouse.' She grinned. 'We're Clan M'Dannish; that's Naval Ordnance. Only my aunt and we are not interested in guns, and this newspaper seemed a great alternative. Our clan didn't think so. If we can silence their ridicule, we're game! I'm Yerene. We'd be pleased to talk business with you.'

Two hours later, PTC was the proud half-owner of the renamed *Weal Trumpet*.

'That's a great idea, to swap stories with the *Gazette*,' Yerene said when they were done. 'People want to know things. Normally we get the news from the other nations too late, but with your portals we could exchange our tidbits every day! My aunt does the printing part, and I'm the news side. I'll look in on this Mr. Barlett, to discuss things with him. Ooh, to bring the wyrmcaller's adventures! The people will want to hear all about you!'

'I wonder what Eskandar will say,' Nate muttered.

'We're doing Bodrus' work, aren't we?' Shaw said innocently.

# CHAPTER 13 – AERODROME

At the aerodrome, the gate guard stepped from her booth and saluted. 'Welcome, Ms. Harwans!'

Shaw's surprise must have shown, for the woman's hard face relaxed in a smile.

'WyDir sent a letter round all divisions and facilities, announcing the change of management, with a photograph of you and Mr. Nate. Can I help you with anything?'

'How efficient of Mr. Morgan,' Shaw said. 'Perhaps you can tell us where everything is around here?'

The guard's stance changed subtly from grim soldier to a jovial guide. 'Dvarghish Hall is the aerodrome's main building,' she said with a wave of her hand.

'Passengers enter the field through its ground floor. There are the ticket office, a comfortable lounge and a first-class restaurant. The Hall also houses the AerMan offices on the first floor and above them is the control tower.

'The building next to it is the Drome Inn. It is mostly used by crews and those who prefer affordable comfort. For those passengers who want more luxury, we offer special arrangements with several of the city's best inns.

'Across the field are the hangars of WyDir Mines. They do the freight runs to and from the mines to the north.

'Further east are the hangars and filling stations of AerMan Maintenance, whose mechanics take care of the airships. Beyond them are a few hangars and offices used by the Weal Government. On the far side of the field is the sheep farm that's keeping the grass short.'

'And everything is WyDir?' Nate's face was uncommonly serious as he looked around and Shaw agreed silently. Until now, it had been... not exactly a joke, but abstract. True, they had marveled at the big office, but that business with Hynks and his cronies had killed the feeling it was the headquarters of a sprawling company.

'Every aerodrome is the property of AerMan, Aerodrome Management, a WyDir company,' the guard said proudly.

'How many aerodromes are there?' Nate asked.

The guard held up her fingers. 'Dvarghish and Brannoe in Kell, Traitor's Field in Seatome and smaller ones at Spellstor Center and Casterglade. Then there are the original ones in Towne, Tar Kell and New Winsproke. That's eight. We don't operate an aerodrome in Unwaar. The Singer religion doesn't hold with air flight, so we only have a mooring tower just outside the high temple at Cloudburgh. I'm told we still own a field at Brisa, but well...'

'I know, the pirates,' Shaw said. 'You are a fount of information.'

The guard smiled. 'I get a lot of visitor duty, so I wanted to have something to tell them.'

'Very good,' Shaw said. 'You said "the original ones" when you named the Malgarth aerodromes.'

'Yes; the island of Malgarth is where WyDir started, fifty-six years ago. Old Mr. Wylmer's father was the first to build and operate a dirigible. That was in the time of exile, of course. After a while, he had airships flying to all main locations on Malgarth. After the war, the importance of the island dwindled. The high king didn't want our presence in his land, so we discontinued our lines, leaving only the connection between our colonies New Winsproke in the west and Tar Kell in the east.

'Old Mr. Wylmer moved the business to Seatome. With the queen and the Lord Spellstor rebuilding our lands, transport became of the first importance, and WyDir grew rapidly. Several others tried to get a foot in as well, but Mr. Wylmer absorbed them.'

'Thank you,' Shaw said. 'So where do we need to go? We're checking up on contracts, both passengers and cargo.'

'You will find the line agents for Dvarghish in the Hall,' the guard said. 'Any of the porters will take you to the admin floor.'

They followed one of the white gravel paths criss-crossing the field to the towering main building.

'It's impressive,' Nate said, gazing up at the square tower with its big windows and large frontal balcony. Below it, an unknown sculptor had decorated the façade with stone airships flying off and on, and some doing things only Pilot Tangrid's late father would have dared with his air show, but no sane airship captain should imitate.

The passenger hall was immense, airy and luxurious; built of gray and black basalt, with potted plants giving the impression of strange gardens. Every servant Shaw saw wore a smart two-part uniform, and she remembered Morgan's words, "...with a vaguely military look", except for the porters, who were in top-hatted dove gray like their colleagues in in Salmon Street.

Shaw sighed. 'Not precisely for the common folks,' she said.

'Those can't afford a ticket, I suppose.' Nate got out a little notebook and made a quick note.

'Now what?' Shaw said. 'Where do we get to the first floor?'

Then she spied a tall porter with a gold cockade on his hat scanning the hall from a position between two large potted palm trees. Then his searching glance met hers, and she saw recognition stiffen his face. He crossed the hall to receive them and saluted stiffly.

'Ms. Harwans and Mr. Nate! Welcome! I am the chief porter; can I be of service?'

'How do we get to the first floor?' Nate asked. 'I don't see any way up.'

The chief porter bowed gravely. 'The door is behind the ticket booths; we do not want any visitor accidentally wandering into the control tower.'

The booths were three round pavilions amid a sheer forest of foliage.

The chief porter nodded to the nearest booth, and the ticket operator inside lifted a hand.

'She will inform the secretary there are visitors coming up,' the chief porter explained. He opened a door half hidden behind the shrubbery, showing a narrow staircase. At the top, a tall, almost slender Kell woman waited for them.

'Thank you,' Shaw said to the porter. 'It is very efficient.' The man beamed and saluted before returning to his post in the hall.

'I am the aerodrome secretary, ma'am,' the woman said. 'I'm afraid the manager isn't in; she worked the night shift. I shall have her called.'

'Don't,' Shaw said quickly. 'We'll meet with her another time. I want to know about lines and cargo.'

'The line agents can tell you,' the secretary said. 'This way, please, ma'am.'

The agents were two young men; one big and impressively muscled, the other smaller but intense. Both jumped to their feet, looking shocked and anxious at the unexpected visit.

Shaw smiled at them. 'Don't worry, this ain't a surprise inspection. I'm hunting information, not heads.'

'Phew,' the small one said. 'We heard of the take-over, ma'am, but we never expected you to come in person.'

'Dry reports don't tell me everything,' Shaw said. 'I want to meet the faces behind them.' She thanked the secretary and sat on the corner of the nearest desk. It wasn't a bad place, she thought as she looked around. Modern desks, with a chair and a fine view over the aerodrome. On the big one's wall were two posters of some singer whose name Shaw vaguely recognized and behind the small man a colored announcement of a match between two imposing female wrestlers.

'We're pleased to tell you everything we know, ma'am,' the small one said. 'I'm Cargo and he does Passengers.'

'You're the guys I need,' Shaw said. 'How is business? How are the contacts with the head office?'

'To begin with the latter, there aren't any,' the small one said. 'I truly couldn't tell you who handles the Kell lines these days.'

'Same goes for me,' the big one said. 'We see to our own business here, selling tickets, signing contracts and everything, with no help from Salmon Street.'

'How many lines do you run?' Shaw asked.

'Four passenger lines; Brannoe, Seatome, Cloudburgh, and the Trans-Wydemere to Towne and Malgarth,' the small one said. 'That one is once every two days; across the sea to New Winsproke, Tar Kell and then to Towne with a stop for refills and maintenance, return flight the next day. It's not a very busy flight; a few Weal officials, one or two navy people, and the occasional fisherman. Rich fellows who want a stuffed shark in their salon.'

'We're operating at a loss?' Shaw said.

'Passenger-wise, we do,' Passengers said. 'My buddy Cargo makes it profitable, with the yield of the Winsproke Crystal Mine. A small cargo; a crate at a time, but it pays enough to offset the passenger losses.'

'That's better,' Shaw said. 'Sorry; go on.'

Passengers smiled. 'The Brannoe Line is only a short trip; mostly crown officials, warrioresses and businesswomen. Seatome has both business and luxury flights and does very well, but Cloudburgh is a bust. No one ever goes there. We still do one run per day, only because the Weal wants it. It's a terribly long route, as well; with a stopover at Spellstor it is nearly twelve hours, and we need to carry an extra crew for the return flight.'

Shaw frowned. This didn't sound very good. 'Do we have another flight to Cloudburgh?'

'Oh, certainly. Spellstor has a direct flight that sees a reasonable number of passengers.'

'So if I wanted a flight from Dvarghish to Cloudburgh, I would get there?' she asked.

'Definitely,' the big agent said. 'Dvarghish to Casterglade, change for Spellstor, change for Cloudburgh. It would cost you a day, but you'd get there.'

'How many passengers have used this connection last year?' Nate asked.

'One,' the agent said. 'An Unwaari merchant in Brannoe, who does the trip every quarter to pray at the high temple.'

'Inform whoever needs to know these things we're discontinuing the direct connection. Tell them we have a very good connection with stopovers at Casterglade and Spellstor. Give the Unwaari merchant a one-time free ticket for the longer route. If any Weal officials complain, refer them to me. Do send me a report on costs and benefits over the last years.'

'Yes!' The big agent beamed. 'Finally someone to take a decision.'

'Perhaps you could help me with a problem too, ma'am?' the cargo agent said. 'You see, my traffic is threefold. The general merchandise could be more, but it is not giving me trouble, nor do the freight contracts running personnel and small stuff to the mines inland. It is the third kind. We used to do the bulk transports, carrying the weekly output of the mines in the north. The freighter is stationed at Brannoe Aerodrome, but the contracts are my responsibility. It is a highly profitable business, so you can guess my surprise when Salmon Street sent me a letter last month I was no longer to bid on the bulk contracts. Mr. Hynks found it too risky.'

He snorted. 'I wondered if someone paid him to say that. It's idiotic; we're the only commercial airship line with the

159

capacity to carry ores in bulk. Now some outfit called Brynnyr Gunny Co. got the job. They clearly haven't got bulk ships and had the whole thing subcontracted to the Weal Transport Board, of all people.'

'Brynnyr Gunny again,' Shaw said. 'They're the same guys who bought Jelvaren Co. to get the MCTC contract. And who is this Weal Transport Board? Another shady outfit?'

The agent laughed. 'Not really. WTB is government. They're the Weal airships service, running officials and equipment across the four nations, they're doing army transport, and that work. They're not supposed to take commercial business, but one of their bulk carriers was seen loading ore a few weeks ago.'

'Funny,' Shaw said. 'Have you ever heard of this Brynnyr Gunny before?'

The agent shrugged. 'I only know they got that contract for far too much money.'

'Mr. Hynks and his cronies are no longer with us,' Shaw said. 'Go after those contracts. Undercut any other bidders, see what they do. And inform me of the results.'

The cargo agent brightened visibly. 'Good! A second contract is due to expire in a few days. The new one has just been published, with Gunny as the first bidder. We'll shake things up and add our own offer.'

Shaw rose. 'You will shortly hear from Salmon Street,' she said. 'Discuss any further problems with them and what they can do to help you.'

'Thanks, ma'am,' the small agent said. 'You made our day, you did.'


As they arrived back at the warehouse, they found a large oxcart barring the path to the side entrance.

From inside the building came the sounds of angry dispute, and Shaw jumped out of the steamcart even before Nate had time to open the door.

Inside, they found Wyon, hot and flustered, confronting an agitated person in a dark suit.

'No money, no goods!' the man cried. 'This ain't no way to do business, boy; ordering goods without coin is swindle!'

'What is the problem?' Shaw said as she strode in, eye patch and monocle in place.

The manufacturer proved a strangely stout Kell. He wasn't tall either, and his excited voice was higher than even Wyon's boyish voice.

'My man came to deliver an order of copper appliances,' he almost shouted. 'Top quality, the best you can get. Order came from your Brannoe Lane office only an hour ago. Now we're here and there's no money!'

'Of course there is,' Shaw said smoothly. 'Only I hadn't expected such fast delivery. I handed the orders to our office less than two hours ago. This is quick work, sir. Step inside, and I'll write you a letter of credit.'

'That's better,' the man said, mollified by the promise of payment. 'You are new here?'

'Very new in town,' Shaw said. 'We're officially not even open, but I have some rush orders to fill for our Seatome location. We're the PTC, of Smalkand in the Peaks; the wyrmcaller's outfit.'

'The pirate hunter. Heard of him. You're one of his people, ah, ma'am?'

'I am,' Shaw said. 'I was with him when we burned Brisa.'

'Ahh, Brisa!' the man said. 'You made a lot of poor businessmen happy with that deed.' He produced a crumpled bill. 'Here it is; prices as agreed upon.'

Shaw glanced at it and saw Brannoe Lane had managed to get the amount due nicely down. 'Excellent,' she said, getting out a check and her pen. Carefully she copied the details, and signed. 'Your payment, sir,' she said, 'and my thanks for your fast work.'

'Pleasure,' the man said. 'I'll tell my man he can unload.'

Shaw waited until he was out of sight, before she soundlessly collapsed into laughter.

'Sorry,' she said finally, gripping Nate's arm. 'He was right; I should have thought they want payment on delivery.'

'I'll go to the local Weal Bank and get some cash,' Nate said. 'The warehouse clerk ought to be able to pay for things.'

'You're right,' Shaw said. 'I had simply forgotten.'

Shaw watched him go and then went to the back for some cawah. In the cafeteria she found Kennan staring at a mug.

'Awake?' she asked.

He nodded. 'I was thinking.'

Shaw grinned. 'Ouch.'

'Yeah,' he said. 'My thoughts have done that for a long time.'

'You're angry?'

'You could say that.'

'At your mother or the army?'

'My mother is dead,' he said. 'They never told me what she did. Cowardice? Before, I couldn't imagine her other than being brave.' He shrugged. 'Now, I don't know. Still, I'm not angry at her. It's the army, mostly. For being rejected. Humiliated.' He looked at her. 'Can you see it? Probably not.'

Shaw snorted. 'You don't know us. Most kids in the wyrmcaller's outfit are rejects. Not me, I'm an orphan; my parents died in a fire when I was ten. But I'm from the same orphanage.' Cook brought her a cawah, and she said thanks absently.

Then she explained Clam Street, the keepers and their neglect. She told of her parents and Eskandar's wandering, and of Aya, Willow, and Jornyll. While she spoke, Kennan sat watching her, listening.

When she was done, he nodded. 'I'm glad you told me. Apparently the world is rotten everywhere.'

'But we're making our world better,' Shaw said. 'We have taken our lives in our hands and we're better off than before. We're earning money, we are working for ourselves and our friends; we have food, clothes, respect. What was, is behind us; only the future counts. And the future is ours.'

Kennan sighed. 'I don't know. Maybe it's me; I'll think on it.' He rose. 'If you don't mind I'll have another few hours shut-eye before my watch begins. Thanks for talking to me.'

Shaw patted his sleeve. 'Sleep well.'

She leaned back in her chair. *I should call Amaj,* she thought. *Maybe we could hold some exercises together; that'll shake him out of his gloom.*

Then Nate returned. By the time they had arranged the money matters with the warehouse clerk and complimented Wyon on his handling the irate supplier, it was time to port back to Old Wharf and dinner.

'That guard captain was here,' Callogan said, as he met them in the hall. 'He left a message; it's on your desk.'

'Grub first,' Nate said firmly. 'Messages can wait.'

'You tell her,' the mage said. 'She's looking peaked.'

'It's been a tough day,' Nate said. 'What's on the menu?'

'Rabbit stew with potatoes and fresh peas,' Callogan said. 'Not bad at all.' He grinned. 'I got you two witches. Our healer set up office in the little room next to Dowa's sewing room. The other one will be in Dvarghish by now.'

'I must've missed her then,' Shaw said. 'Thanks, Callogan. You're fantastic.'

After dinner, Shaw went to her office. There was a white envelope marked "private" and the seal of the city guard, but nothing from Salmon Street. She grunted and slid open the envelope. She read the note and froze.

'Nate!' she shouted, urgently enough to set him running, with Keena and Callogan on his heels, looking alarmed.

She handed him the guard captain's note and watched him stiffen as he read.

'So they interrogated that white-haired would-be assassin, discovered someone had tampered with his mind, and saw him die in his chair,' Nate said. 'No trace of Hynks yet.' He handed the letter to Callogan. 'Sounds just like the pirates.'

'Jinn work! We'll keep it silent,' Shaw said in a hard voice. 'Darn, we should have Naudin here. We need a mindmage.'

'Not my department,' Callogan said.

Keena shrugged. 'I can mindspeak, but that's about it. I'll ask Martha and Tymon.' She walked outside and leaned against the wall.

'This Hynks,' Nate said. 'He looked very convincing.' He cursed. 'So did that captain at Clam Street.'

'But why would a jinni take him?' Shaw muttered.

Nate grimaced. 'What would happen if WyDir went belly-up?'

'Chaos,' Shaw said. 'The Weal would have to take over, or all air transport would stop.'

'And chaos in the Weal means they won't come to help Eskandar against the jinn,' Nate said.

'You mean the jinn are working to create confusion,' Shaw said absently. She was watching Keena, who was gesturing and pulling faces. Martha and Tymon were twins; a brilliant pair of elementalist and healer, but very touchy.

'Phew.' Keena came back, wiping her forehead in exaggeration. 'Those two stuck-up snotties ask a lot of my patience.' Then she grinned. 'But they'll help. Martha will contact Ruth.'

Shaw stared up at her. 'And who's that?'

Keena's eyes opened wide. 'Who? Ruth of Spellstor, Naudin's sister and Lord Basil's youngest daughter. Martha always goes on about how Ruth as a senior student was her mentor at Magic institute. I bet she wasn't the only one; a highborn gal like this Ruth must be chummy with scores of people.'

# CHAPTER 14 – RUTH

Past midnight that evening, Shaw lay down her pen.

'Enough,' she declared.

'Really?' Nate looked up from where he sat reading. 'Not a last report to evaluate? Not a final letter to write? Darn, girl; you've done more work in one day than most managers do in a week.'

She rose and stretched. 'No matter; I love it.' She loved the dusky office, the quiet, and him being with her as well, but she couldn't tell him that. 'Let's stroll around a bit before bed.'

They walked outside and stared at the moon coming up over the harbor. Here, away from the city center, the night was silent. Most of their crew had gone to bed, and only the guards did their rounds. With Nate beside her, she felt a contentment she hadn't known since her parents died.

Suddenly, she sensed something move behind them. A shadowy figure appeared, wearing a wide-brimmed hat and a long cloak.

'Evening,' a girl's voice said, carrying an echo of laughter.

'Who're you?' Shaw snapped.

'I'm Ruth of Spellstor,' the girl said. 'Martha called me.'

'You're Naudin's sister.' Shaw returned her knife to its arm sheath. 'Why the creeping-up act?'

The girl laughed. 'Because I wanted to see you without the house knowing.'

'About what?' Nate asked.

'Me,' Ruth said. 'You wanted a mindmage, I'm not precisely that, not like my brilliant little brother, but I can read minds. I can recognize a jinni and a compulsion, and there's one other thing we urgently need – I'm an agent of the Weal.'

'A spy?' Nate said bluntly. 'And we need *that*?'

'An agent,' she corrected him. 'I do more than spying; I represent my father Basil. Unofficially, of course. Nor am I spying on you people; we want the same things, after all. I'm a contact.' She glanced at Shaw. 'Let's go sit on the pier, out of earshot.'

Shaw tried to pierce the shadows surrounding the girl, but only a pair of eyes and a hint of a Vanhaari face were visible between her hat and cloak. Without a word she walked onto the pier.

'You're not the one I saw in Clam Street,' Nate said.

The hat shook in denial. 'That was another agent, with another purpose,' Ruth said.

*She doesn't sound enthusiastic about that other guy,* Shaw thought as she squatted down and waited for Ruth to fold her legs and cloak beneath her.

'I'll be blunt,' Ruth said. 'My father and Aunt Maud both feel there are things not going as they supposed. Remember it's only twenty-five years after the war. When they defeated Vystyn and signed peace with old Eghol, they became boss over two ruined countries. There was nothing; no infrastructure, no commerce, no magic, no food. They had to rebuild both Vanhaar and Kell from scratch, and drag Unwaar up with them. By now, things are going more or less smoothly. But not always.'

'Clam Street,' Nate said. 'Our lives there, not the jinni.'

'The orphanage's shameful failure shocked my father,' Ruth said. 'He doesn't show it, but the knowledge the Weal had neglected those kids for so long was a blow. It set him thinking, for if this could happen without him knowing it, what else might have gone wrong?'

A sudden splash in the water had Ruth pause. Then she chuckled. 'A bluewing snatching a late meal.' She shifted slightly. 'For Aunt Maud it's the same. When she became ruler, Kell men were dying out and the women did everything. The clans were only a shadow of their former self, and the heavy hand of the M'Arrangh was everywhere. These days, young people want to marry again, and build a family. But many of the older generation of women resent the changes. They can't accept men taking part in what they see as their affairs. As a result, things happen Maud doesn't get told about.

'Both you and Eskandar are running into problems the Weal Council – the Family, as we call them – feel they should know. Now they want me to find out why they don't.'

'Darquine?' Shaw said sharply. 'Where does she come into this?'

Ruth grinned. 'Aunt Darquine is both MCTC and de facto ruler of the Chorwaynie Archipelago. As her father's deputy, she sides with Basil and Maud. As boss of MCTC, she needs competition to keep her people on their toes. The company has become too big, too slow, and there, too, things happen she doesn't hear until it is too late. Darquine wants you to become an active competitor. That should turn her people looking outward again. She's cheering you on with every deal you make.' For a moment she sat in silence.

'The fourth ruler,' she said in a flat voice. 'Singer Eghol is an enigma; the Unwaari high priest is over two centuries old, and my father isn't sure we can still trust him – if we ever could.'

'We heard of that Wador guy trying to kidnap Justym,' Nate said. 'Was Eghol involved in that?'

'He strongly denies it,' Ruth said. 'But we can't be certain. Wador was highly placed, but even at his level, singers aren't usually acting without orders.' She shrugged. 'Eghol is not my direct business. The jinn are. Originally, the Family was content to leave them to Eskandar, certain our lands were secure. But the Clam Street fire and your recent affairs showed them different. Obviously we can't have jinn and pirates running all over the Weal. In this, my father places his hopes in Eskandar and the prophecy. He realizes there is something big going on that's out of his hands and in Eskandar's lap. It doesn't make him happy, but he accepts it and does what he can to ease the wyrmcaller's way – and yours.'

She took off her hat and showed herself a young lady only a few years older than Shaw, with a soft gray skin and the flaming red hair of her Spellstor father and uncles.

'One thing must be clear. I will not speak of your company business or the wyrmcaller's affairs with the Family or anyone not authorized to know. That was my condition to come here, and the Family agreed.'

Shaw watched Ruth as she spoke. A direct line to the Weal rulers could simplify a lot of things.

'All right,' she said briskly. 'I assume the world isn't aware of your, ah, profession?'

'To outsiders I am the Lady Ruth of Spellstor, Warden of Winsproke and an earnest young mage just out of school.'

'What did you study?' Nate asked.

'Economagics,' Ruth said dramatically.

'Great,' Shaw said. 'I'm home schooled; what the heck is economagics?'

Ruth smiled. 'Making magic pay. That's something many mages don't think of until it's too late.' She sighed. 'Of course warlocks never think of money. Yet every one of them needs income; they can't call up a fat bag of libers to cover their expenses. That's a crime and they'll end up behind bars pretty darn quick.'

'So why did you become a spy?' Nate asked.

Ruth shook her red hair. 'I was bored. Economagics isn't an exhilarating study, and when I graduated, I wanted something else for a while. Basil needed a high-level spy; family preferred. Well, m'sister Argyra is too conscious of her position as the Spellwarden and heir, and too much the dedicated theoretician warlock to do anything unorthodox. Kellani... Let's say she won't do it. Naudin is too lazy, besides, our fathers think him too young. That left me.'

'You'll be management secretary,' Shaw said. 'I won't mind you help making money for us as well.'

Ruth smiled. 'I'll be pleased to. One small thing you should know; because of certain spells I carry I will not leave the Weal.'

'What spells?' Nate asked.

'Protective ones,' Ruth said. 'Like no one can listen in when I'm around. I would break them if I went abroad.'

'In that case you can read the reports when I'm away,' Shaw said. 'Give me your opinion on them. Now, let's show you around the place. We'll even have a little room for you. I'm sure it won't be Spellstor House, but it has a bed. Tomorrow... Nate, would you go to Kell alone? I want to show Ruth the Salmon Street office first. I'll follow later.'

'Sure,' Nate said. 'It will be dull, but I'll probably survive if it's only a few hours without you.'

'Don't you kid me,' she said, poking his shoulder.

'I'm not kidding,' Nate said, and something in his voice made her stare at him.


The next morning, Shaw introduced Ruth to the whole crew.

'Wow,' Callogan said, with a comical look of awe on his homely face. 'The Winsproke Warden? She'll be working with us?' He sighed. 'I mean, Shaw told us about Kellani and Naudin, but they're out there and you... you are in here with us. Perhaps now my father will believe I'm on to something good.'

Ruth grinned. 'Your old man's a warlock, right? Developing teleportals at Casterglade? Hah! This portal Shaw's people produced is just as fast, far cheaper and far smaller than anything your father and his folks built.'

Callogan answered her grin. 'I'll leave it to your dad to tell him, if you don't mind.'

'He did,' Ruth said. 'Believe me, he did. He descended on the Casterglade chaps like a raging glacier – both hot and icy cold. Basil doesn't anger easily, but if he does, the seas hide under their beds. He asked the big guys why a bunch of Thali graduates keep outwitting the mightiest brains of the Weal. I never saw senior warlocks cry before.'

'The answer's simple,' Kier said sourly. Shaved, with a decent haircut and dressed in a simple blue suit with a mage's badge, he looked very different from the ragged figure Shaw had hired. 'Because those fellows aren't the mightiest brains. They're bureaucrats, creeping around in each other's footsteps. There isn't an original thinker among them.'

Ruth stared at him. 'You... you're a portal mage! How in the world... Wait! So it is true Casterglade didn't always take all of you guys?' She turned to Shaw. 'You got more of them?'

'Another three,' Shaw said with a faint smile.

Ruth cursed. 'Heck and Darnation! Four portal mages! Now you'll be training others, I suppose?'

Shaw hadn't thought of that. 'Can you train people?' she asked of Kier.

'Other eidetics?' he said. 'With a live portal and an engineer at hand? You bet I could. It took us three years at the Magic Institute because we worked with simulators instead of the real thing. Now I can do it in half the time.'

'Do you need an eidetic memory?' Nate asked. 'Can't you simply write those coordinates out?'

'Sure, but there are thousands of them,' Kier said. 'And we checked every one of them in person.'

'But we don't need so many destinations,' Nate said. 'Not in all portals. Most would go no further than other PTC portals. Only the central ones, like Smalkand and Seatome, would need the lot.'

Kier shrugged. 'Me, Beth, Mott or Tomas, each of us can teach any half decent hedgemage how to do that in a week.'

Shaw looked at them in awe. 'You guys are *good*! You're flippin' *brilliant*. Callogan, can you get us a bunch of fledgling hedgemages? I want half of them in Seatome, and the rest here.'

'As you command, ma'am,' Callogan said gravely. 'You'll be their goddess, you know. There's hardly any decent future for a hedgemage, so they'll murder each other for the chance.'

'I only want living ones!' Shaw shouted at his disappearing back.

'For sale, one majestic property at Casterglade,' Ruth said. 'Will go cheap, because outdated.'

'Cheap?' Shaw said. 'Three thousand and it's sold.'

'We'll keep it in mind,' Ruth said. 'This is a nice place you have here. Nice, clean minds, too.'

'Glad you say so,' Shaw said. 'I'll show you WyDir. Let's hope you'll say the same.'

'Morning, Shaw,' Squad leader Yens said as he came in. He looked at Ruth, his face stern. 'Kindly don't creep around in the nightly dark, m'lady,' he said. 'After that jinni pirate, my guys are quick on the draw. My archer nearly shot you when you went up to the boss in that funny way.'

'Archer,' Ruth said slowly. 'I had observed your guards for some time, but I saw no archer.'

'You're not supposed to,' Yens said. 'Luckily I recognized you in time.'

Ruth stared at him. 'You knew me already? I'm afraid it is not mutual.'

'I'm Yens Rowe-Yens,' he said and clenched his teeth.

'Ah,' Ruth said without a change of tone. 'Now I remember. Weren't you in the army?'

'I was going to,' he said. 'But the new garrison commander canceled my appointment.'

'Oh dear,' Ruth said. 'Yes, I can imagine his reasons, but it was mighty cruel.'

Yens shrugged. 'The whole situation was less than happy. I haven't seen my family since. There's talk of them moving to New Winsproke. Good riddance, I'd say.' He looked around the hall. 'I found a new crowd, so why bother?'

'We're pleased you are here,' Shaw said. 'Warn your guys that Ruth has joined the staff.'

Yens saluted. 'I will tell them, ma'am.' Then he relaxed. 'After you went to bed last night, some gent from WyDir brought a stack of notes. I put them on your desk.' He grinned. 'A Mr. Morgan it was; he didn't seem to want to shoot you.'

'He won't,' Shaw said. 'Ruth and I will have a go at his notes right away.'

'Take some cawah and sandwiches. No good gadding about on an empty stomach,' Cook said.

With her hands full of breakfast, Shaw went to her office, sat down and got out her eye patch and monocle.

'I need them,' she said, noticing Ruth's quizzical look. 'Na'a told me I had to wear them, to repair my lazy eye.'

Ruth smiled. 'If Na'a says so, you blippy well wear them! They make you look ferocious at the same time.'

Shaw growled and opened the file. 'It's a report from Mr. Morgan, our management secretary at Salmon Street. It should tell me what our airline managers are about.'

She scanned each sheet carefully, before passing it on to Ruth.

'What are those fellows supposed to do?' Ruth asked a while.

'Manage a bunch of airship lines, get freight and passengers, long-term contracts, and such. I spoke with our agents in Dvarghish. They said they hadn't heard from the Salmon Street office for years. These notes confirm the line managers don't do much. Why not?' Shaw leaned across her desk. 'Let me tell you how we acquired WyDir.'

Ruth listened intently, her face growing darker by the minute. 'This is terrible,' she said when Shaw was done. 'That Hynks and his guys are criminals. And the guard captain reported that guy who shot at you was under a compulsion?'

'Yes. Hynks is still out there somewhere.'

'I should inspect the whole office,' Ruth said. 'Better make sure all are clean.'

'We'll port,' Shaw said, as she stuffed the report into her inner pocket. 'I've asked Kier to add the coordinates of Salmon Street and the Seatome aerodrome station to our portal.'

# CHAPTER 15 – WRONGNESS AT WYDIR

As they came out of their port in the stained-glass hall of WyDir Offices, Ruth stepped back and looked around.

Shaw followed her glance. Nothing seemed amiss. The porters, the hall clerk, the secretaries chatting beneath the potted butterfly trees, everything looked normal. Still, a shapechanged jinni *did* look normal.

'Well?' she said.

'I'm cautious,' Ruth said slowly. 'There is a feeling...'

Her voice trailed away as they climbed the central stairs to the management offices.

They found Mr. Morgan at work in what had been Hynks' room. Shaw hid a grin; why not, he was doing the job of senior director, after all.

He jumped up to greet them, spruce as ever in spite of working late the evening before.

'Ms. Harwans,' he said. 'I am happy to see you.'

'I got your report,' Shaw said. 'So I thought to come over. This is Lady Ruth of Spellstor, PTC's new management secretary.'

Morgan's eyes grew large. 'Lady Ruth! An honor to meet you!'

'So pleased to meet you,' Ruth said effusively. 'It's very exciting! My first real job! I'm an economage, so this position is *perfect* to get to learn the ropes. Besides, PTC is such a promising company.'

'Indeed it is,' Morgan said enthusiastically.

*'He's clean,'* Ruth said. *'And so is that other secretary chap.'*

*'Good,'* Shaw thought, as she would with Eskandar. Apparently it worked, for Ruth winked ever so slightly.

'I was in Port Dvarghish the other day, Morgan,' Shaw said. 'I spoke with our agents at the aerodrome, and I came away wondering what our line clerks did, if the local people had to go after all contracts by themselves. Now I got your report, and I still don't know.'

'Ma'am,' Morgan said. 'Nor do I. That's why it took so long. I interviewed everybody in the line department, and I didn't understand the answers. I can't imagine what is going on in there.'

'The line managers are writing reports and memo's and the gods know what and file them,' Shaw said. 'Nothing they do goes anywhere.'

*'There is a fog around this place,'* Ruth said. *'Let's have a look at those clerks.'*

'We'll visit the Lines Department,' Shaw said. 'Lead the way, Mr. Morgan.'

Lines occupied a large area of open floor, divided into separate workspaces by beautiful hand-painted screens. Men and women were sitting at wooden desks, scribbling busily, and there hung a massive silence in the room.

*'Wrongness!'* Ruth snapped. *'There's a jinni in here.'*

'Ah, yes,' Shaw said. 'Back to the office, Mr. Morgan.'

He gave her a puzzled look. 'Ma'am?'

'I have some other matters to attend to first,' Shaw said quickly, and walked away. *'Ruth, call Kier. Tell him to contact Mott in Dvarghish. I want Kennan with his boys. Tell Kier to port both the Kells and Yens with his guys into the president's office up here, fully armed. Tell them jinni fight; he has fifteen minutes.'*

Back in the office, she whirled around. 'You will go on with your work, Morgan! Whatever happens, you will not think of it. Attend to your job, if you want to keep it.'

Morgan's expression blanked out and he went without a word to his own office, closing the door behind him.

Ruth shook her head. 'Blind obedience; that's not good either,' she whispered. 'While we wait, I will check the other departments.'

It weren't fifteen minutes, when a mass of armed guys appeared inside the office. Yens and Kennan, Nate and young Wyon, with *Fayaafa*'s Captain Isambar and two of his lads, Keena and Seatome Cook.

'A jinni?' Nate snapped. 'Who?'

'Someone in Lines,' Shaw said tersely. 'The other departments are clean. We'll find out who it is; let's go.'

They ran back to the Lines office.

'Wait here,' Shaw commanded and she stepped into the office.

Inside, all was as before.

'Let's do some magic,' Ruth said at her shoulder.

Not a soul stirred when she swung up a hand and called something Shaw didn't understand.

A clerk screamed and clutched his head. 'What's happening?'

'Outside!' Shaw snapped, and the man staggered to the door, where several hands dragged him away. One after another, the others followed. Finally,, the door to the line manager's office flew open, and young Mr. Benffald came out, without his coat, and with his bow tie slightly awry.

'What's going on?' he said. The frown on his face relaxed into friendly acceptance. 'Ms. Harwans?'

'Jinni!' Ruth said.

Benffald grinned. 'So you finally caught on. What fun it was, corrupting those fools. What jolly laughs I had! Now comes the final accounting. Behold!'

His form blurred, and turned into something only vaguely humanoid; half man, half something else, with a sharp-toothed mouth and mad eyes grinning in his nether regions.

'At him!' Shaw screamed and found herself roughly shoved aside as her little army rushed inside.

'Go for the belly face!' Nate bellowed.

The jinni snatched up a Kell fighter and threw him at Shaw. She jumped aside to escape being flattened. The boy crashed into the wall and as she knelt at his side, he shook his head, blew his nose between his fingers, and without a word ran back, in a beeline for the jinni's smirking mouth.

'First blood!' he croaked as he stumbled away, and green fluid leak from the jinni's bulk. Side by side, Yens and Kennan went for the creature, to be slapped aside by a nonchalant wave of the jinni's crooked left arm. Captain Isambar laughed. 'Yoho!' he shouted, and hurled a chair at the creature's belly. The beast evaded the projectile, but in the confusion, several blades slashed and drew more green blood.

Wyon; the warehouse lad's young face twisted with terrible concentration as he jumped past the creature's arms and laid open a cheek.

The jinni squealed and waved its limbs. Cook ran up from behind, and slashed with his meat cleaver. A girl fell, her arm a bloody mess, but Keena drew her away and Shaw saw the wound close again.

The jinni screamed a mad challenge. Two yards away, Kennan gave an answering roar. 'Axed Ones! To the Deathblow!'

As one, the six Kells ran forward, their blades clasped in both outstretched fists, and skewered the jinni.

With a loud explosion, the beast imploded into nothingness, and the six Kell tumbled over each other into a heap.

Shaw ran forward. 'Well done!' she cried, and she found she was crying. 'Oh, well done!'

Kennan picked himself up and saluted. 'Ma'am!'

Yens came and slapped his shoulder. 'Good fight, mate! We must do this more often.'

Kennan's brown face glowed with sudden pride. 'I'm game.'

'It was fun.' Isambar joined them. 'I've been in some bar fights, but this was a bit different.'

'A bit,' Wyon said. 'Just a bit different.' Then he laughed till he cried.

Mr. Morgan made his way through the crowd. 'That was something!' he said, his face strained and sweaty. 'That was darned something! A jinni? Here inside WyDir? How...?'

From the corridor came loud voices. The gaping employees jumped aside as the tall guard captain burst into the room at the head of a unit of armed city soldiers.

He lifted his hand and his men stopped as he stared at the ravage and the battered fighters. 'Your people called us. There was a brawl, Ms. Harwans?'

'A jinni had infiltrated our staff,' Shaw said. 'When we confronted him with it, he attacked us. It's settled; we came prepared.'

'Everything is under control, Captain,' Ruth said.

The officer looked at her and suddenly smiled. 'If you say so, my lady. I will leave it in your hands.'

'Ms. Harwans says so,' Ruth said resolutely. 'Her word is as good as mine.'

The captain bowed. 'My lady.' He paused. 'Ms. Harwans, I must inform you we found Mr. Hynks. He was dead.' His eyes rested on Ruth. 'I will send you a full report, ma'am.'

'Thank you, Captain,' Shaw said. 'You had better look in on the other directors I dismissed. I fear there may be more deaths.'

The captain looked around the room. He was clearly burning with curiosity to know what had happened here, but somehow Ruth had claimed seniority, so he saluted politely and left.

*Hynks is dead,* Shaw thought. *Would the jinni have killed him? He was a tool, then. Hynks, Pomfrith, those other fine gents the jinni used to try and destroy WyDir were no better than the lowest drugged pirate.*

'Ma'am.' Kennan's stiffly formal voice burst through her thoughts. 'Have you any further orders? Else I'd like to return to the Pier; we need to prepare for the night watch.'

Shaw looked at his expressionless face; tired or not, they would stand that watch if it was the last thing they did.

'Certainly, Squad leader,' she said as officially. 'You have the company's gratitude.'

'We'll walk with you to the Old Wharf portal,' Yens said. 'I don't suppose you will know your way around Seatome.'

'My guys will take a steamcart,' Isambar said. 'We were busy loading when your call to battle came. Of course we couldn't leave it to the soldiery.'

Yens snorted. 'As if we needed a couple of harbor thugs.' They exchanged grins and left.

Morgan looked at the field of battle. 'This must be cleaned up,' he said. 'How are we feeling, people?'

'Lightheaded,' an elderly clerk said.

'Like leaning from an open window in a smoky room,' another said. 'I haven't felt as clean in years.'

'What was that beast?' a third said. 'And where is Mr. Benffald?'

'I'm afraid he is dead,' Shaw said carefully. 'The jinni who had taken his place killed him. He bewitched you all to sabotage the company, as he had done with Mr. Hynks and the other directors. Not old Mr. Wylmer, nor Mr. Morgan, though even their wits were befuddled.'

'I need a drink,' a man said, holding his head in his hands. He went over to a bronze tripod in a corner of the room, holding a large upside-down glass bottle with a tap in its neck.

'Wait,' Shaw said. 'What's that?'

'That's our water dispenser, ma'am,' the man said. 'Mr. Benffald had it installed two years ago, to provide us with a nice drink when we wanted one. It has a faint taste of the herbal medicine it contains. The first time is strange, but you get used to it soon enough.'

'Give me that glass,' Shaw said. She sniffed at the water. 'I've smelled that before.'

Nate took the glass from her hand and immediately his face tautened. 'Jabbies!' he said. 'It's the same stink.'

'So that's how he did it,' Shaw said. 'That water is poisoned.'

The line clerk turned splotchy. 'P-poisoned? But nobody died of it.'

Shaw didn't hear him; she was thinking of the pirates and their endless thirst. Would that rotgut they drank be tainted too?

'Not all poisons kill,' Nate said. 'This stuff made it easy for the jinni to influence your mind. Have someone take the bottle and tap down to the cafeteria. It must be cleansed with plenty of soap and hot water to make it safe again. Check the building for any other dispensers.'

'I got one,' Morgan said softly. 'I don't use it often, but its water smells the same. The demon!'

'That's your jinni for you,' Shaw said. She looked at the acting director, and at the other supervisors huddling in the corridor.

*The building is clean,*' Ruth said. *'There was some befuddlement in other departments; enough to confuse and slow down. I removed that too.'*

*'Thank you,'* Shaw said gratefully. 'Can you manage here, Morgan? I want the line managers to meet with every agent in their territory and discuss what Salmon Street can do for them. I think we'll find it is thanks to the line agents' efforts we're still in business. Mage Kier at Old Wharf can arrange ports to every destination. She slapped her thighs. 'Warn the people their jobs will become much more active. Any line manager who cannot cope will be replaced. Not fired, if I can help it, but it will mean a demotion.'

Morgan took a deep breath. 'I can manage,' he said hastily, probably supposing Shaw's last comment was meant for him as well.

'Thank you,' Shaw said. Then she thought of something else. 'Ever heard of Brynnyr Gunny Co.?'

'No, ma'am,' Morgan said slowly. 'The name is new to me.'

'I want to know everything you can discover of them. Ask the line clerks to check with our agents as well. Discreetly!'

'Of course,' he said. 'Anything wrong with those guys?'

'That's what I want to know,' Shaw said. 'We found them shouldering their way into our territory in Kell. But nobody had heard of them before.'

'I'll see what I can find out,' Morgan promised.

'Good,' Shaw said. 'Ah, to be on the safe side. Throw out everything edible and drinkable in the building, and buy new stuff. After that, order a huge stack of pies for all, to celebrate we're a clean business again.'

He swallowed. 'Clean! We're WyDir, darn it. How deep did we fall?'

'It wasn't your fault. Not truly anyone's fault, except the jinn's,' Shaw said. 'We're still WyDir, and we'll prove it.'

'Yes,' he said, biting his lip. 'Thank you, ma'am!'

Shaw grinned. 'We'll be off, then.'


Back at Old Wharf she warned Kier of the horde of WyDir clerks about to descend on him.

He nodded. 'No problem. I'll probably be able to send them somewhere close, with a handportal. Those thingies are designed to remember where one is. Simply twist the blue ring in the handle and a new coordinate is made. When I get the handportal back, I'll add their information to the portal, and we've got every one of our stations within reach.'

He waved a languid hand at four kids busily writing. 'Old Callogan delivered, by the way. Four freshly hatched hedgemages, still wet behind their ears.'

'Aren't they a little young for graduates?' Shaw said.

'Fourteen,' Kier said. 'Most kids start the Magic Institute at ten. Regular mages finished their primary study at sixteen, do another year of internship, and are ready to conquer the world. They're the lucky ones. The less fortunate get summoned to their mentor's office to hear their powers ain't up to snuff. They'll be hedgemages for life. Lots of crying and tearing of hair, that. All their beautiful future crashed at their feet. Imagine the horror of it, ma'am.'

'Don't!' one of the boys said. 'Or I'll start bawling again.'

'Why?' Shaw said. 'Because you won't be called a mage? I've met plenty mages I wouldn't ask the time of day for fear of getting five different answers. You guys make the big mistake to think mages are the only ones to get rich and powerful. They're not. Actually, most of them won't, even if they have magic. You should forget your childhood dreams. Refocus. Become a general, a statesman, an artist. Or be clever and become a merchant. Use the magic you have as an extra, a bonus. But don't feel sorry for yourselves; it's childish.'

The four looked at her. 'That's harsh!' a thin white-haired boy said.

'It's true, though,' Shaw said. 'You guys are healthy, smart, and probably not born in the gutter. You have an education, with hard work and determination you can become anything you wish.'

'Like you?' the boy said skeptically.

Kier grinned. 'She's the boss around here, kid. Building a multi-mega business from scrap, and paying your splendid largesse as well.'

'Oh gods,' the boy said in dismay. 'Did I put my foot in it?'

'Because you're questioning something?' Shaw said. 'Of course not. I'm giving you my take on things; you can do with it what you like. Just remember that while I want you guys to run a portal somewhere in this big bad Weal of ours, it would be nice if you could do more than that. So keep your eyes open, your brain active and don't hesitate to ask. We need plenty managers; stationmasters, merchant ship's officers and top salesguys, every one of them a well-paying job. Being a hedgemage is an extra, not a failure.'

'Well,' the boy said. 'That's not how the Magic Institute told us. They acted as if we were worthless, we'd never amount to anything.'

'Forget the Magic Institute,' Shaw said, remembering Naudin's stories. 'Most of those instructors don't know the world outside of their precious school. To us, you are very valuable and I'm glad you are here.' She grinned. 'That was Mother Shaw's sermon; I'm for some cawah, before we go to Dvarghish.'

'I didn't realize it was that bad,' Ruth said as they walked up the stairs. 'I was a peer mentor, but all my students were super clever.'

'Nothing but the best for a Spellstor,' Shaw muttered. She saw Ruth bristle. 'That is not a dig at you; it's a fact of life; just as your father doesn't get told the negative things. And thinking back to things Naudin said about the navy, the same goes for your dad Yarwan. The Magic Institute sees those boys as failures, so they want to keep them away from you and Basil, and if they can manage it, out of their statistics.'

Ruth cursed. 'They're fools! Though to be honest I wouldn't have thought to tell those kids what you told them. We magic-users do tend to see our power as the measure of all things.' She grunted. 'I must talk with Mother; I bet she'll say you are right.' She sat down, looking unhappily at Shaw. 'I will put this in my report to Basil.'

Shaw nodded. 'Tell him.'

## CHAPTER 16 – BUYING A BOAT

Filled with restlessness, Shaw wandered down again. Everybody was hard at work, as she should be. Her head was too full of plans and ideas. Suddenly she stopped halfway the stairs, with one foot in the air. *Kennan and his Axed.* She nodded grimly and walked quickly to the portal below the steps.

'Smalkand, please,' she said absently.

Mage Kier must've noticed her preoccupation, for he didn't say anything, and whisked her away before she knew it.

She stepped from the portal, said hi to Smalkand's portal mage and walked into the cafeteria, greeting familiar faces. She avoided everyone who wanted to stop and talk to her, and strode to the wyrmcaller's office.

Inside the marble-and-gleaming-copper room she found Amaj and Wylmer playing cards.

'Bored, gentlemen?' she said, hands to her hips. 'Let me help you.'

'Hey, Shaw. Grab a chair, then we'll deal again,' Amaj said. He sat relaxed, with his sleeves rolled up and his helm within reach beside his hand.

'This girl ain't playing, Marshal,' Shaw said. 'I'm busy. I wondered if I could interest you in organizing some joint military exercises.'

'With whom?' Amaj said, putting down his cards in surprise.

Shaw gave him a monocle stare. 'My troops, of course. For the good of the Peaks and all that.'

'What troops do you have?' Amaj asked with a hint of condescension in his voice. 'Are they any use?'

Shaw bared her teeth. 'My six Seatome boys are sons of Castle soldiers and they know their job. Our Kell guys are at least as good as Benwar's lads and very tough. All of them have fought and killed jinn. We haven't had time to teach them broomriding, though.' She pulled a chair back and sat down. 'Kit them out with guns as well. And brooms, of course. You can bill the PTC.'

Amaj looked at Wylmer and grinned. 'They're tough, you say? All right. Bring them here two days from now. We'll start with the brooms and take it from there. Will you be attending?'

'Nate, Keena, Callogan and I. We'll use that time to go through the warehouse and things,' Shaw said. 'Maybe visiting the nearby keeps.' She put both hands on the table and leaned forward, giving Amaj a flat stare. 'One thing, bud. You will not goad Kennan's lads into proving how tough they are. This will be a friendly contest, my lord marshal; not the all-out war you don't want. Apart from the fact I will personally disembowel you if you try.'

Amaj flushed. 'I wouldn't,' he said stiffly.

'As long as you remember I told you,' Shaw said. 'Those guys have been badly used in the past; they are suspicious, touchy and *very* dangerous.'

'Have you plans for getting a caravan together?' Wylmer said hastily.

'As soon as possible,' Shaw said, relaxing. 'A small one, for starters. They need to scout the route and lay contacts. By that time I will want *Pewbara* on standby, in case we find any more robber keeps.'

Amaj nodded. 'Pilot Tangrid will like that.'

'Now I only need a new warehouse manager here,' Shaw said. 'I'd like to ask Sylas, if that doesn't upset your scheme of things.'

'If he wants to do it,' Amaj said. 'He has his classes, but he should be able to fit them in.'

'All right,' Shaw said. 'I'll go ask him. Don't let me stop your card game, guys. I'll see you in two days' time.'

She grinned as she hurried out. Poor Amaj, she thought. But she had to warn him; it wouldn't do if the exercise ended in a bloody battle.

Sylas had just finished class when she found him in the schoolroom, a utilitarian place with tables, chairs and a large blackboard.

'Hi,' he said, slipping down from his desk onto his broom. 'How is business?'

'Booming,' Shaw said. 'I got a job for you, if you're interested.'

'A teaching job?' He grinned and lifted his body up on his arms to straighten his lame legs. 'I've got a few more hours to fill.'

'Something else. You've been assisting in the warehouse often enough, would you be interested to making it official?'

'Warehouse worker?' he said, raising an eyebrow.

'Warehouse manager,' Shaw said. 'Overseeing the workers, coordinating with the caravan masters and ship's masters, buying and selling stuff, and things like that.' She grinned. 'It's a boss job, paying in silver; three unis per day.'

He whistled softly. 'I'm interested. As long as it's clear I signed up with Eskandar, so I'm not abandoning him.'

'That goes for all of us,' Shaw said without hesitation. 'Our task is to give the Peaks an economy. Every bite you guys eat is money going out what doesn't come back in. We don't want Eskandar reduced to washing dishes to pay for his meals.'

'He'd probably do it with magic,' Sylas said. 'But you're right; we must make money. I'll have a go at it. When do you plan to start those caravan runs?'

'No fixed date, but soon,' Shaw said, jumping to her feet. 'Callogan is studying the matter. Well, I'm off.' She grinned. 'Welcome to the PTC. Write me a business plan, will you?' With a wave of her hand she hurried back to the entrance hall.

'Whereto?' the Smalkand portal mage asked.

'Dvarghish Warehouse,' Shaw said.

'You say it.' Beth had a strange habit of clapping her hands as she sent someone away, like she did now.

Then Shaw was in Kell.

'Boss!' Mage Mott cried. 'There was a girl asking for you a second ago.' He turned and bellowed. 'Wyon! See if that gal is still around; the boss came in.'

Shaw smiled. 'What did she want?'

'She had an offer,' the portal mage said. 'Something you might be able to use.'

'She didn't say what?' Shaw shrugged. 'All right. First I need Kennan, if he's awake.'

'That guy barely sleeps,' Mott said. 'Half the day he sits staring at a mug of cold cawah.'

'I'll order him not to,' Shaw said. 'Thanks for telling me.'

She went to the cafeteria and found Kennan hunched over a stone mug, his eyes dead.

'There you are.' Shaw dragged up a chair and sat across from him. 'Orders. The day after tomorrow you'll report to Lord Amaj, the wyrmcaller's marshal at Smalkand, for three days of combined exercises with Squad leader Yens' chaps from Seatome and Leader Benwar's guys of the Pasandir Peaks Army.'

His empty face had gone rigid. 'You're asking a lot,' he said. 'We don't mix readily.'

'I know,' Shaw said. 'I warned Amaj I'll remove his guts if he tries to be funny. He won't, he isn't that kind of guy, but I wanted to make sure. Yens' troops are Vanhaari; Benwar's boys are Sons of the Army.'

Shaw saw his whole upper body stiffen. 'The lucky ones,' Kennan said.

'If you can call it that,' Shaw said. 'I'm not sure they had a pleasant time in the army.'

'Probably not,' he said. 'But they weren't totally rejected.' He touched his mug with a strong finger. 'Three days of it.'

'I'll be there to cheer you on,' Shaw said. 'They will teach you how to ride a broom.'

'They will *what*?' he said, looking up..

'Ride a broom. It's standard in the wyrmcaller's outfit. We all do it.'

'Oh,' he said, and a little of the life returned to him. 'That would be something.'

'It would. You must be fit, Squad leader. Now you're not. Go to bed and sleep.'

'Yes, ma'am,' he said, and gave her half of a smile before going back to his squad's room.

'Darn,' Shaw said softly.

'It's real cruel,' Cook said from behind her counter. 'At first I doubted them Axed, but no longer. Something is not right there, ma'am. Those boys weren't traitors or anything.'

'I don't believe they were,' Shaw said heavily. Those guys hadn't been treated well; if only she knew what she could do about it.


'There she is,' Mott said as she stepped from the cafeteria, and nodded to a tall Kell girl in a blue sea officer's uniform.

Shaw walked over. 'Hi, you were looking for me?'

'You're the boss?' the girl said. 'I was told you were young, but...' Even for a Kell she was tall; not massively so, but lean and agile.

'I'm the general manager,' Shaw said. 'My age is irrelevant.'

'Sorry,' the girl said. 'You're right. I'm Leolynn, second officer and supercargo of the *Allastar Maiden*, flagship of the M'Allastar clan.' She sighed. 'That sounds very grand, but the Allastars are only a small clan, clinging to past glory. The *Maiden* is a twenty-year-old steamer, running general cargo between Allastar Cove and Towne. She is a stout ship and good for many more miles.'

She stared at Shaw as if uncertain how to go on.

'Drat,' she said. 'It seemed such a good idea, but now I'm here it's absolutely idiotic.'

'Let's hear it first,' Shaw said, wondering what it was about.

'The clan lady died last month,' Leolynn said. 'The Allastar, as we call her, was over a century old, and her health had been failing. Still, she kept us together, and now she's dead, the clan is falling apart. The Allastar's heir doesn't care for our long history; he has other interests and wants to sell the *Maiden*. Only who would buy a big steamer like her? The knacker yard offered five hundred libers for her, and I fear the heir will take the offer, only to get rid of the ship.'

'And?' Shaw could imagine the pain. Probably the ship had been their home for years, perhaps the only life she knew.

'We, that is her crew, we heard of you starting up warehouses and we wondered if you'd be interested in buying the *Maiden*.' Leolynn sighed. 'Ah, just say no and I'll go away. It *is* a stupid question.'

'How large a crew would she need?' Shaw asked.

'Her standard number of hands is twenty-five,' the girl said. 'We have those; we only lack a captain and first mate. Those decided to quit; they were of the old generation. We, the crew, the officers and me, we're younger. The bos'n is the eldest at thirty-two.'

'You mean the ship would come almost fully manned?' Shaw said. She took off her monocle and polished the glass to give her time to think.

Leolynn nodded. 'Yes. If you'd want to see her...'

'I'd have to go to Allastar Cove?'

'No, ma'am; she's outside the harbor, in case you were interested. The heir gave me until tomorrow to sell the ship. After that, I'm to sail her to the knackers.'

'I do want to see her,' Shaw said, replacing her eyeglass. 'Can you signal her?'

'I've got my boat here,' the girl said hastily. 'I'll go and bring the old gal in myself.' She almost ran to the door.

Shaw turned to Mott. 'Would you call Smalkand and ask both Captain Wylmer and Engineer Imooga to come over? After that, call Nate; tell him I got a little surprise.'

'Buying him a boat?' Mott said. 'That's nice.'

Shaw grinned. 'Tell them I'll be at the pier.'

She walked outside and saw a six-oar jolly already past the light at the pier's head, speeding towards the shadowy mass that was the Yann Talimarch promontory.


Nate arrived first, and came running down the long pier to join her, his eyes glowing as he gripped her shoulders.

'There you are!' he said, his voice gruff. 'I missed you. Kier said you had gone to Smalkand.'

'Sorry,' she said with a pang of remorse at the relief in his face. 'Everybody was hard at work and I felt a bit jittery. I went to see Amaj, and arranged for exercises between our three squads. I hadn't planned to stay away long, or I'd told you. Then I came here to tell Kennan, and other things happened.'

He gave her one of his brief hugs. 'It's all right. Now, what is this about a surprise?'

Relieved, she grinned. 'You'll have to wait a bit.'

'Is it coming over sea?' Then he chuckled as he saw Wylmer and Imooga coming to join them. 'It is.'

'You wanted us?' the captain asked.

'Yep,' Shaw said. 'But it ain't here yet.'

'Wait, there's a ship,' Imooga said, staring at the sea. 'A steam vessel.'

The others turned and they watched a large iron threemaster steamship approaching fast.

'She's breathing nicely,' Imooga said, her eyes narrowed as she watched the ship.

Shaw agreed, noting the clean white clouds coming from the ship's smokestack.

'She looks trim,' Wylmer said appreciatively. 'Built a few years after the war, I'd guess.'

'She's big,' Nate said. 'She won't outshine *Drakon*, but she's big enough. Twelve heavy guns, no less!'

The ship lost speed rapidly, and came alongside the pier no less gently than *Marigold* would have done.

'Good show,' Wylmer muttered.

Four girls in trim blue ran out the gangway, and Leolynn strode down to the watchers.

'She looks very well,' Shaw said. 'I asked some people to join me.' They shook hands.

'The *Allastar Maiden*; she is for sale.' Shaw looked at Nate. 'Including the crew.'

'How much?' he said without taking his eyes off the ship.

Shaw pursed her lips. 'If our experts agree, I'd pay double for what the knackers offered. And full pay for the crew.'

Now Nate looked at her. 'Double is not an answer.'

'One thousand libers is,' Shaw said, planting a soft elbow into his ribs. 'That's only the ship, smart boy; not the crew's pay. Let us look her over, shall we?'

Nate shut his mouth. 'All right.' He guffawed and touched her chin softly with his fist. 'I knew I wouldn't catch you out on a bargain.'

At the entry port, the three remaining officers waited to receive them. The third mate was a jolly, sharp-eyed girl who seemed barely past the required minimum age for merchant officers. The cadet beside her was younger; a lanky girl with worried eyes and a slightly overlarge uniform. Number three, the engineer looked in her late twenties, and seemed a taciturn, unflappable woman.

Together, they went all over the ship. The sweeping quarterdeck was even larger than that of *Drakon*. Past it, her gun deck looked clean and freshly painted, with the cannons ready for action.

'This is my department,' the third mate said. 'I am acting gunnery officer as well.'

'It looks very neat,' Wylmer said. 'Have those guns seen any action?'

'Twice,' the mate said. 'Both times we chased the pirates off.'

'Sink them or take them is our motto,' Shaw said.

'I would need more hands for the latter, ma'am,' Leolynn said.

Shaw nodded. 'Gunners and marines,' she said. 'Do you have room for extra hands?'

'The ship was designed to carry passengers as well as cargo; we have ample accommodation,' Leolynn said.

A wooden hatchway the size of a wardrobe led them down into a narrow, dimly lit corridor. Leolynn opened a door to a large cabin with a bed, a desk and several chairs. It wasn't opulent, but to Kell notions comfortable and clearly meant for a person of authority.

'Captain's cabin?' she guessed.

Leolynn smiled. 'No, the captain beds across from here. This one was reserved for the Allastar, though she never sailed with us. It will be the owner's cabin.'

'Oh,' Shaw said. 'I see.'

'On this side are the passenger cabins,' Leolynn said. 'The port side ones are for the officers. The last door is the sick-bay, though we at present don't carry a healer.'

They walked on to the next bulkhead.

'Here is the dining-room,' Leolynn said. 'Officers and passengers; the crew have their own accommodations in the bow.'

The room looked like any well-furnished cafeteria; not precisely a military mess, but not a restaurant either.

Past the counter they came into a well-equipped kitchen. 'This is the galley,' Leolynn said. She smiled. 'With Cook and Cook's Mate.'

A woman and a younger girl in the same blue uniforms saluted smartly.

'Welcome, ma'am,' Cook said. 'If you are in need of a bite, just holler.'

'Not yet,' Shaw said. 'But thanks.'

'Beyond the galley is the engine room,' Leolynn continued. 'There is an emergency door here we don't generally use. Let us go a deck lower.'

Another door opened on a staircase leading down.

'Cook's stores,' Leolynn said. 'Beyond are a series of smaller compartments we use for ship's stores. For any longer voyage we need to carry more stock; our elders didn't want to spend any money, considering.'

'I understand,' Shaw said.

Nate looked around. 'We seem to have lost our engineers,' he said.

Leolynn smiled. 'Ours is rather single-minded. To her the purpose of the ship is to give her an engine room.'

'That's an engineers' habit,' Shaw said. 'Imooga and her gals are the same.'

'Our engineers aren't the only ones suffering from single-mindedness,' Nate said drily.

Shaw gripped his arm. 'I know.' Then she punched him. 'Meanie.'

'Ouch!' he said and grinned. '

Shaw sniffed. 'Let's go on. I'll believe the storage compartments. Show us the crew quarters.'

They walked back to the gun deck and down another hatchway into a second corridor, with small cabins on each side.

Leolynn opened one, showing five hammocks slung bow to stern, and over them another five, port to starboard. There were a table with two benches, and ten chests lined the back wall.

'There are five such cabins to a side, for a hundred hands. Each girl has a chest for her belongings. Here, they eat as well. There is a second galley at the end. Each day, two girls have cook's duty, one from each cabin.'

'Your crew is fully female?' Shaw said.

'Yes,' Leolynn said. 'It's a tradition in our clan. The women went to sea and the men stayed at home. I know the queen wants to change that, but our clan elders objected.'

'And you?'

'I wouldn't mind male sailors,' the third mate said with a sly grin.

'No, I didn't think you would,' Leolynn said. 'But you will remember you are an officer, won't you?'

The mate flushed. 'Of course.'

'I don't hold with boys,' the cadet said softly. 'They're weak.'

Leolynn ignored her. 'What is your policy, ma'am?' she asked.

Shaw screwed her monocle more firmly in her eye. 'Remember whom you are selling your ship to,' she said. 'We're not Kell, not even the Weal. We are the Pasandir Trading Co, of the Peaks, the wyrmcaller's people and followers of Bodrus the Sleeping God. And...' She couldn't help but smile. 'They call us a children's army. If we decide to buy the *Maiden*, be prepared for that. Our guys are fifteen, sixteen years old and so are most of our officers. We make no different between girls and boys. Our rules state no alcohol under eighteen and no sex. Can you handle that?'

Leolynn grinned. 'We discussed that. Most of our girls are three or four years older, and frankly said, unused to mixing with other peoples. We will have to adapt and we're willing to do so.'

'We ain't got no alternative,' the third mate added. 'Adapt or seek a job ashore. None of us wants that.'

The cadet made a small sound in her throat.

'The idea of boys scares you,' the mate said.

'I'm not scared!' the girl said. 'It's only...'

'Strange,' Shaw said. 'Don't I know it. Relax and accept things will change. How far are you with your studies?'

'Another few months,' the cadet said defensively. 'I haven't had much time lately.'

'We're two officers short,' Leolynn said. 'That leaves us little spare time.'

The third mate raised an eyebrow, but she didn't say anything and Shaw didn't ask either.

Imooga rejoined them, clearly satisfied. 'The engine room looks fine. Everything is well maintained; the crystal alignment is at eighty percent maximum and that's as close as a non-Thali can get it. Your engineer is a professional.'

'What do the others think?' Shaw asked.

'I'd say buy her,' Wylmer said.

'Nate?'

'She'd be perfect for the northern run.'

Shaw slapped her hands together. 'So we are agreed. One thousand libers.'

Leolynn sighed. 'She's worth ten times as much, but the heir won't know that. He never took any interest in ships and the sea. If you come to the officers' mess, we can sign the papers.'

'Do you want coins or a check?' Shaw asked.

Leolynn pulled a face. 'Coins. The heir sent someone to fetch the gold. They're not savvy enough to accept a check.'

'I'll ask the warehouse clerk,' Nate said. 'He can advance the money.'

He hurried away, while Shaw sat down. Like all of the ship, the officers' mess wasn't uncomfortable, but utilitarian in the Kell way. Which meant everything was just that bit too large for her.

When Shaw had signed the last of the papers and Nat had returned carrying a heavy bag, Leolynn gave a shout. A girl rose from her chair in a corner. Shaw had seen her watching the proceedings, and wondered who she was, sitting slumped in her chair with her feet on the table.

'Is it done?' the girl said. 'Finally; I'm dying of boredom in this stupid bucket. Gimme the gold; that'll please daddy.'

Leolynn handed her the heavy bag. 'Now hurry home,' she said. 'And don't tell anyone you're loaded.'

The girl made a rude noise and without a word ran from the cabin.

Leolynn sighed. 'Useless chit. Well, it's done. Now what is next?'

'Are you qualified to command her?' Wylmer asked.

'I have my master's ticket,' she said. 'I lack another three years for the required age, though.'

'That's the Weal law,' Shaw said. 'The Peaks ages are lower, so you can take command right away. And you?'

The mate sighed. 'I'm a licensed third, but I'm still working on my command certificate. I will need that for any higher rank.'

'You will have to hurry then,' Shaw said. 'You're Acting First Mate. Captain, I want you to make an appointment with the dockyard guys in Seatome to have the ship inspected. You are her supercargo?'

Leolynn nodded. 'I handled the buying and selling in every port.'

'You'll continue to do so, but now for the PTC. You will first acquaint yourself with our organization. Visit our Brannoe Lane office in Port Dvarghish, speak with the salespeople. After that take their portal to our Seatome warehouse and meet the people over there. Engage any officers and hands you need. When the ship is ready to sail, you will take her to Smalkand. That will be your official port of registry. After that, we will probably want you to sail north, to the lands beyond the Hellesands desert.'

'Very good,' Leolynn said.

'Great. With the *Maiden* in dock, your girls won't get bored. Send them to Smalkand. We have a small ship, *Raffix,* to be sailed to Seatome. Do you have a subofficer capable of taking command?'

Shaw saw the cadet open her mouth, but Leolynn ignored her.

'My bos'n could do that.'

The cadet flushed, but didn't speak. As a cadet and with an experienced crew, the girl should be able to manage a ship like *Raffix*. Didn't the captain trust her? Shaw shrugged. It wasn't her business.

'Excellent,' she said. 'I'll leave it to you. For accommodation ashore, Keepmistress Willow at Smalkand will put you up. If you need me, Ruth at Old Wharf will find me.'

'I'd suggest using a large net to catch her,' Nate said. 'Shaw's like a butterfly, always flitting around.'

'A wasp,' Shaw said. 'Butterflies haven't got a sting.'

# CHAPTER 17 – KEENA TAKES CALLOGAN OUT

Smalkand Keep hummed with activity as Shaw ported in with Nate, Callogan, Keena and Kennan's squad.

Yens had arrived before them, and Shaw saw him halfway across the cafeteria with his men. He had brought Emmett Barlett of the *Weal Gazette*, who was eager to do a series of stories for his newspaper.

'This place is more grand than I expected,' Yens said when they met. 'If this is a warehouse, I wonder how their cities looked.'

'I've seen images from the ruins of Atnortod,' Shaw said. 'That was impressive; raw wealth screaming in your face.'

Then Amaj came forward, wearing full armor.

'Lord Amaj of Kalbakar, Marshal of the Pasandir Peaks Armed Forces,' Shaw said formally.

Both Yens and Kennan saluted.

'Welcome,' Amaj said briskly. 'Follow me and I'll introduce you to some people.'

'Amaj,' Shaw said. 'You haven't met Emmett Barlett yet? He's a journalist from the *Weal Gazette*, doing a series of stories. He'll probably want to interview you, as one of the wyrmcaller's closest friends.'

'Sure,' Amaj said expansively. 'Walk with me and ask what you wish.'

'That tickled him,' Keena said calmly. 'Journalists! I wonder if they'll ever become regular visitors at happenings like this.'

From a distance, Shaw watched Kennan meet Benwar. Both were Kell; tall, muscular guys, though Benwar was perhaps a year older. With their brown complexions, short, straight hair and their aquiline noses, they could have been kin. They eyed each other like two wrestlers looking for strengths and weaknesses.

'Poor Yens,' Callogan said. 'He'll be outclassed by both of them.'

'He knew that before he came,' Nate said. 'He sets his own standards and his men must match those.'

'For Kennan it's different,' Shaw said. 'To him this is a matter of survival.' She turned away. 'We'll leave them to it. I want to introduce you to our neighbors at Pashwend Keep and High Morv. You can discuss their needs and perhaps they have a few restless souls who would want to join your caravan.'

'Great idea!' Callogan said. 'Ah, I never rode a broom before.'

'Come with me,' Keena said quickly. 'Let's get one and I'll teach you.' She waved at Shaw. 'I'll call you when we're done.' With that, she steered Callogan away, the plumes on her pirate hat flying in the wind.

'Oh?' Shaw said, staring after them.

Nate laughed. 'She has her own plans. Don't be surprised if she joins his caravan. Running after you isn't what she wants of life.'

'No, of course not,' Shaw said. 'I know that. It's just that I hadn't seen this coming.' She hadn't even thought of it; she had taken Keena's assistance for granted, without asking what her friend wanted.

'It probably surprised Callogan as well,' Nate said. 'I don't believe he'll mind, though.' He took her arm. 'Let's grab a bite of food. I didn't see you at breakfast again.'

She nodded, her mood ruined. She'd been blindly thoughtless, and that bothered her.

An hour later, Keena called. *'Shaw? We're at Pashwend. I can introduce Callogan as well and he needs to work this business out for himself. You got your hands full, so let him and me do this caravan thing, all right?'*

Shaw took a deep breath. *'Hey, that's fine with me,'* she said. *'You two make a go of it! If you need anything, ask Roza. Do give me a report now and then, gal.'*

*'Will do,'* Keena said, and Shaw thought she sounded relieved.

Shaw looked at Nate. 'They're off on their own.'

Nate shrugged. 'You hired Callogan to run that caravan thing. I'd say let him.'

'Yeah,' Shaw said uncertainly. 'But Keena?'

'She made a choice,' Nate said. 'She's always been a loner, guarding Willow. With you she was in a larger team and that didn't suit her. This way, she'll be back guarding someone else.'

Shaw was at a loss for words. *What should I do now?*

'We'll visit Imooga,' Nate said cheerfully, hooking his arm into hers. 'About that workshop you want to build. Unless you made a plan already?'

Shaw bit her lip; somehow her mind always avoided it. 'No,' she said. 'I don't even know where to begin.'

As she walked away with Nate, the idea of Keena and Callogan running the caravan fleetingly returned. She gave a mental shrug. If they can do it, good luck to them.


'Busy?' Imooga said when they cornered her in the large workroom at the back of the keep. 'Ha! I should think we are.' She had to speak loudly, for the whole place was filled with clanging, hammering, and cheerful shouting. 'Come.'

They hurried to a side room and Imooga kicked the door closed behind her. The noise abated far enough to speak without raising their voices.

'You had something to discuss?' Imooga said, as she wiped her oil-stained hands on her trousers.

Shaw sat on the edge of a long table and told her of the plot of land at Mackerel Square.

'A new-built workshop?' the engineer said. 'That sounds fabulous. Who's doing the building?'

'The local guild,' Shaw said. 'Point is, I know nothing about these things.' She pulled a face. 'Neither from the builder's side nor from what must be in it.'

'Leave it to me,' Imooga said. 'You give Oychak the dimensions of the plot and we'll make a design.' She was silent for a moment. 'It will surprise your architect, for we'll include some strange features like a concealed room. For the mana pump, see?'

Shaw remembered the old store, the rose bushes her father had planted, the... *Put it away! It's all gone now*, her mind cried. She forced a smile on her face. 'All right. I'll show Oychak the deed and leave it to you girls.' She sighed. 'Now I'll slink back to the mess and doze a little. It's nice to be back here for a few days.'

# CHAPTER 18 – JOINT VICTORIES

'Good morning,' Shaw said as Nate joined her on the early-morning beach, yawning like a tired whale. 'Slept well?'

She knew he had been up and going strong when she went to bed. Life at Old Wharf wasn't dull, but she suspected he missed the other Clammers who had been part of his life for so long.

He grunted.

'My!' Shaw said brightly, peering at his face. 'Do you need a *shave?*'

Nate colored and brought a hand to his chin. At sixteen, shaving was far from his mind, unlike Amaj, who was fostering a hopeful mustache.

'I'm teasing you,' Shaw said and she patted his cheek. 'You look a bit crumpled, that's all.'

'Hmpf,' he said. 'I'm awake, ain't I?'

'Are you?' She laughed. 'I know, silly. You just had some fun last night.'

This last morning of the exercises the two of them stood on the path into the hinterland. Below them on the beach three little flags waved in the wet sand, a red, a blue and a green one, about a hundred yards apart.

Above them on the mountain's ledge, the others waited; the three squads of Smalkand, Seatome and Dvarghish, and most of the keep's populace.

To the left on the beach hovered Sylas, the referee.

*'A silence replete with expectancy hung over the mirrored lake,'* Emmett muttered as he came to stand with them, writing furiously. *'The crowds wait, their breathing hushed in the early morning dusk...'*

They well ought to be quiet, Shaw thought. This would be the final race, the end of three active days. Now it was between the three squad leaders, between Benwar, Yens and Kennan.

They had been flying for hours a day, solo, in squads and in formations. They had been running, swimming and diving; entering the schooner, fighting mock duels, and in all these the two Kell squads ended up equal.

Yens and his Vanhaari didn't even come close, but they were content. Their archer had won them the shooting contest. He was a sharp-eyed lad from one of Seatome's outlying farms, and had been hunting rabbits ever since he could walk. The bobbing targets in the bay had been easy, and none escaped his arrows, so they'd go home with their honor intact.

Then a sharp whistle pierced the silence.

*'There they come. From the high ledge of the keep, three valiant young broomriders swoop down the beach...* Fine! Oh, fine, what a story!'* Emmett said.

Each boy was lying low over his broom, hand stretched out to grab the first of the little flags planted in the hard sand.

Shaw screamed in glee as Kennan snatched up the first flag. Benwar, the Smalkand leader, took his loss and without a second's hesitation raced on to the second flag. Yens looked like he hoped to pass both Kells, to position himself for the third.

Kennan disregarded the safety rules as he shot at the second target. His broom nearly collided with Benwar's handle and his shoulder gave the other a massive shove.

Sylas hovered over them with his whistle between his teeth, but he didn't interfere.

Both boys staggered in midair. For a long second, it seemed Yens wanted to pass between them, but he swerved to prevent himself from being mangled. Kennan went for the second flag a fraction faster than Benwar. His broom's brush almost touched the ground, what would have meant disqualification, and Shaw gasped. But he'd judged it rightly and snatched up the second flag.

Shaw jumped up and down in excitement. 'Go! Go!' she shouted.

Kennan and Benwar both dove for the third flag. Yens wasn't about to be nut-cracked between the two massive Kell boys and drifted to a halt.

Both riders closed in on the final target. Now Benwar's knee hit Kennan's broom and knocked him spinning.

The rules were flexible, and again Sylas kept his silence.

Kennan turned around and around, seemingly helpless as he gyrated towards the green flag. Benwar's mouth opened in a triumphant shout as he stretched out his hand. At the last moment, Kennan broke from his spin, grabbed the target and shot up across his opponent's nose, straight into the air, leaving Benwar clutching nothingness. Then he straightened out, turned his broom and raced for the finish, with Benwar after him, hoping to tackle him before he could reach Amaj. Kennan looked over his shoulder and grinned mirthlessly. Shaw saw Benwar's face twist in a curse as with a mighty sprint he forced his broom beside Kennan. His big hand gripped the other broom and pulled. Kennan went into a spin, forcing Benwar to rotate with him, dragging him out over the bay. Then he miraculously stalled in midair. The shock as they unexpectedly went motionless made Benwar lose his grip while his broom, without orders and confused, for a brief moment lost flight. As rider and broom plunged into the bay, Kennan shot back to the beach and landed at Amaj's feet.

'There you are, sir,' he said thickly, handing him the three flags, and saluted.

Amaj took a deep breath. 'Thank you.' He eyed Kennan. 'Took some risks, didn't you?'

'He's mad,' Benwar came down beside them, soaking wet and grinning broadly. He slapped Kennan's shoulder. 'You're stark, raving bananas, mate.'

Kennan shrugged. 'I wanted to win.'

'You got a death wish,' Benwar said. 'That flag ain't worth it.'

'Our lives ain't worth anything either,' Kennan said. 'Win or die, that's all.'

'But...'

'Leave him alone,' Shaw said, as she reached up to grip the tall boy's shoulders. 'It was a great victory, Squad leader Kennan.'

'So it was,' Benwar said. He laughed out loud. 'Idiocy, but brave idiocy. I salute you, warrior.'

Yens joined them, broom over the shoulder. 'I won't play with you two,' he said. 'You're too rough, you bullies!' Then he laughed. 'Gods, what a show! Madcap Kells, you are.'

'A fitting end to a great training,' Shaw said. 'They all did well, I'd say.'

'Eskandar can be proud of them,' Amaj said. 'Now go inside and relax; you earned it.'

The other warriors joined their squad leaders amid laughter and cheerful backslapping.

'Beautiful,' Emmett whispered, still writing. 'Flippin' beautiful! Readers will love these boys! Darn it! Sports in the newspaper! We'll be settin' a fashion.'

'Benwar is right; they do have a death wish,' Shaw said as they watched them go. 'How do we talk them out of that?'

Nate shrugged. 'I don't know.'

'We must convince them they aren't worthless,' Shaw said. Then she fell silent as she saw Wylmer come running to where Amaj waited. The stout young captain wasn't built for athletics and never moved at anything faster than a walk, so the sight alerted her and she hurried over.

'Where did you go so suddenly?' Amaj asked. 'You missed all the excitement.'

'Flag signal from Bighead Rock,' Wylmer said, breathing hard. 'You guys won't have noticed, but I did. We're getting visitors; the look-out up there reported a ship heading for the passage.'

Amaj frowned. 'Enemies?'

'Probably.' Wylmer gave a wolfish grin. 'They're not the Weal Navy, and not even our badass Shaw would use chained rowers in her ships. I've alerted the gunnery kids on the *Killarn Ranni*.' He waved a hand at the schooner at anchor half a mile away.

'Whoever it is, they'll find us at maximum strength,' Shaw said.

The young lord slapped his hands. 'True. *Jem, have Willow sound the alarm.*'

Princess Jem didn't answer, but moments later, Shaw heard the bells peal throughout the base, calling all assigned defenders to the cafeteria, while the young and their caretakers went to their dormitory in the back.

The three squad leaders turned as one man to Amaj, and broke into a run back.

'Enemy ship,' Amaj said. 'This is not an exercise. You guys and I will fly to the schooner. Captain Wylmer, take command here.'

'Aren't we swapping places?' Wylmer said mildly. 'The *Killarn Ranni* is my ship, after all.'

Amaj grinned. 'I'm not going to sail the bucket; she's just a convenient place for an ambush. We need information. I'll ask Jem; bet you she's already on to them.'

'*Course I am,*' the ghostly princess said in their heads. '*It's an old ship, a row-and-sail trading vessel; dunno how else to call her. Twenty crew, looking like pirates; they're armed to the teeth and smelly. Forty rowers, all kids – tough-looking types, no older than us. There's a bearded buffoon with a whip standing over them. I hope you'll do something nasty to that one. Those kids, they are...*' Her thoughts faltered for a moment. *'They look familiar, but that's impossible.'*

*'Ship's guns?'* Amaj said, his thoughts clearly by the ship.

*'Yeah, but the only manned one is a little fat bigmouth in the bow; it has four pirates standing by it.'*

'Twenty pirates,' Benwar said. 'Piece of Cook's homemade cake that is.' He grinned at Kennan. 'My guys could do it alone.'

'But you won't,' Kennan said coolly.

'Mount up.' With a wave of his hand, Amaj jumped into the air.

Shaw didn't say anything. She glanced at Nate and grinned as he was readying his broom. They were the wyrmcaller's warriors as much as the others, she thought as she mounted.

As they landed on the schooner's deck, Rawe, the former Rocks boss in charge of the ship's guns, received them with a sigh of relief.

'Am I glad you guys are here,' he said. 'We know how to fire those beasties, but never done it for real.'

'With luck you don't need to,' Amaj said. 'We'd rather not sink a ship in our bay. You loaded them?'

Rawe grinned. 'I know that much. We're ready to fire them one after another and our bow chaser prepared with a blank, for a warning shot.'

'Good.' Amaj rubbed his hands in anticipation. 'Jem says they've got only the one gun manned. From her description it sounds like a carronade. That could mean grapeshot, so you'll keep your heads well down.' Then he stared in surprise at young Emmett, still writing. 'What are you doing here?'

'Begged a lift,' the young journalist said. 'I must be in on the action! This will sell, Marshal! A true report, live from the scene of your magnificent action. My readers will *eat* this! He wrote hastily. "Heads well down," said the marshal, twirling his brave mustache.'

'Don't overdo it!' Amaj said.

'I'm not overdoing it, Marshal,' Emmett said without looking. 'Those are superlatives.'

'Oh, superlatives,' Amaj said, out of his depth. Then a cry saved him.

'Enemy ship!'

Shaw's broad grin faltered at the sight of a long, mean-looking vessel entering the bay. She had three masts, but carried no sail. Instead, her twenty oars propelled her swiftly towards the beach.

*I'm standing on the quarterdeck,'* Jem said in their heads. *'The pirates appear surprised. They know the bay and both ships, but never expected them together.'*

*'The rowers?'* Amaj asked, staring at the ship and trying to twirl his budding mustache.

*'Apathetic,'* Jem said. *'They're just rowing, as if they don't care about anything.'*

*'We're coming,'* Amaj said. *'Will you sing for us?'*

*'Sure,'* Jem said. *'I'll sing them to death.'*

Amaj banged his fist against the railing. 'Let's go,' he said, baring his teeth in a grin. 'Benwar, your guys take care of the men at the carronade. The others stay with me. Rawe, when we're in the air, fire your warning shot.'

Shaw gave her guys a thumb-up and followed Amaj. Moments later, a deep boo-oom rolled over the placid lake, sending flocks of bluewings into the air, squawking in anger.

Shaw saw the pirates running around, gesturing and shouting. The four men at the carronade were frantically trying to light the slowmatch.

'Fools!' Shaw shouted into the wind. The pirates hadn't prepared! Then Amaj waved; they swooped down like a flock of mountain eagles, and she stopped thinking.

From around them came Jem's voice, singing a song of death and defeat that shook the pirates.

Shaw sheathed her broom and ducked a pirate's blow. 'Idiot!' she said, and slashed the shirtless ruffian across the chest with her dagger. The blow sent him staggering backwards into the rowers. Chains rattled, and the pirate's scream ended in a strangled gurgle.

Shaw stared at the nearest rower; a tall, rawboned girl with a scarred, olive-skinned face and a haphazardly set nose. For a moment, their eyes met, and then Shaw nodded.

'We'll get you free,' she said, and turned around to another enemy. The pirate stumbled a moment and Nate reached past Shaw's ear, slamming the hilt of his sword in the side of the pirate's unshaven head.

'Nice,' Shaw said, and her partner grinned tersely.

Standing together, they paused for a few seconds to watch the Kells fight. Those guys, not even full warriors yet by their people's standards, slammed their opponents about with the ease of a worker stacking bags of grain in the warehouse. It was beautiful!

Then a rower yanked her leg from under her. As she fell, something swished downward through the spot her head had been, and caught the rower's shoulder instead. The boy screamed once, and sagged against his neighbor, with blood spreading down his chest. From somewhere, Kennan yelled. He shoved Nate aside, drew his arms around the pirate and wrestled him down in the narrow gangway between the rowers' benches. Livid with anger, the young squad leader gripped the man's throat with one hand and rammed him hard against the planking. As the pirate groped for his knife. Kennan brought his knuckles down on the man's hand and Shaw heard the pirate's bones break. Then Nate's cudgel flashed and the man flopped like a dead fish.

'That was the last one,' Amaj called. 'Nice little fight.'

'Any wounded?' Shaw asked.

'Cuts and bruises,' Kennan said indifferently. He came to his feet. 'Nothing serious.'

Shaw turned to the boy who had saved her from a busted head or worse. 'How's the shoulder?'

'Shattered,' the rower next to him said. 'We'll have to kill him to spare him suffering.'

Amaj looked over his shoulder. 'Nothing so drastic, we have a healer who will help him.' He looked around. 'Row us to the beach, friends. Then we can see to those chains.' He looked around. 'Jem? Tell Healer Tymon to get his ass over here.' Only then he saw Emmett standing behind the ship's wheel, writing.

'Spare him suffering. The noble mercy-death in battle, how beautiful,' he said.

'You find this beautiful?' Amaj said.

Emmett looked at him, his face drawn. 'No, it's ugly and terrifying, but it's too good a chance to let pass because I am scared. My readers want this, Marshal. That means we'll sell more newspapers, more people see PTC's advertisements and Ms. Shaw knows we're not failing her.'

Amaj nodded. 'All right. Remember we can't protect you the whole time.'

'I know,' Emmett said.

Then the scarred girl rattled her chains. She shouted something and as one, the rowers went to work. Without breaking her rhythm, she turned her head to Shaw. 'Who are you people?'

'We're the Pasandir Peaks Armed Forces,' Shaw said. 'Or rather, they are.' She nodded to Amaj. 'My guys are the Pasandir Trading Co.'

'We'll explain later,' Amaj said. 'Welcome at Smalkand Keep.'

'Keep?' the girl said. 'Where?'

'Over there,' Amaj said vaguely.

'I never...' The girl gave a command, and the ship came to rest close to the beach. 'Anchor's over there,' she said, nodding with her chin to the bow.

Without a word, Amaj walked over and wrestled with the heavy capstan.

After a second, Benwar sent his guys to help him and moments later, the ship was secure.

'Those chains,' Amaj said. 'Do they have keys, or must I send for a smith?'

'There's one key,' the girl said. 'That beast with the whip carried it.'

'The fat one? He went overboard,' Kennan said. He turned to his squad. 'Let's get those bodies out of the water.'

Before Shaw realized what he meant, all six had jumped over the side and swam back to the dead pirates.

Beside her, Benwar shook his head. 'What are they trying to prove?'

'They're Axed,' Shaw said. 'They always have to show they aren't cowards.'

Benwar's face tautened. 'I didn't know, I thought they were the same as us. So they got it worse; kicked out, ridiculed, spat upon. Gods! No wonder they're a prickly bunch.' He shivered as he turned to his squad. 'Guys, let's lend a hand, shall we?' His boys laid down their swords and things, and slipped into the sea.

'Are we supposed to do the same?' Yens muttered.

'No,' Shaw said. 'Leave it to them.'

Amaj stood watching how they wrestled the dead pirates onto the beach. 'I'm missing something. What is that between Benwar and Kennan?'

Shaw told him.

'Axed? The army kicked them out for what their parents did?' Amaj said. 'What kind of stupid cruelty is that?'

Right then Kennan's head appeared beside the ship. With one hand he gripped the gunwale and heaved himself up. In his other hand he held a neck chain. 'The key, ma'am,' he said calmly.

'Thank you, Squad leader,' Shaw said. 'You may return to the keep and get dry.'

'Ma'am,' he said, and swam to his mates.

'Here's the key,' Shaw said.

Amaj took the chain and wrapped it around his wrist. 'Before we unchain the lot of you,' he said to the big girl, 'we must talk. We're awfully nice and trusting, and all that, but first tell me who you are, where you come from and things like that.'

The girl's lips twisted in what could have been a grin. 'Sure; we don't look much like honest folk, do we?'

Amaj looked her over. 'Mwah, I've seen worse.'

The scarred girl snorted. 'You must keep terrible company. I'm Grimthailla of Yavam Island. Before the pirates came, I was Thailla, a cheery child in pigtails. She died with my family; now you may call me Grim, all right?'

Amaj nodded. 'I know that story.'

'Yeah?' Grim said skeptically.

'Yeah. I'm Amaj, of Kalbakar Keep. In my case it were jinn, though. And I didn't wear pigtails.' He lifted a balled fist. 'We're fighting back. Leave your guys here for a bit; we'll step inside and have a talk.'

The girl lifted her chains and Amaj unlocked them. Then he handed the key to Yens. 'Keep an eye on that lot. We'll be back when we've reached an agreement.'

Yens saluted. 'Yes, m'lord.'

'You a lord?' Grim said.

Amaj stepped over the railing into three feet of bay and turned. 'Second son,' he said. 'M' brother has Kalbakar now. I'm in command of the Pasandir Army. We're small, but tough.'

Shaw followed him into the water and looked back for Nate and the young journalist.

'Can't do that!' Emmett said urgently. 'I must keep my notebook dry!'

Nate smiled and got his broom out. 'I'll fly you to the beach.' He winked at Shaw as she waded through the surf.

'I never was here before,' Grim said. 'Don't know where we are.'

'Where is that Yavam place?' Amaj asked without answering. 'I never heard of it.'

'North, I think. It's near the coast.'

They walked to the keep.

'Caves?' Grim said. 'Not living rough, are you?'

'That's Smalkand Keep,' Amaj said. 'And no, we're not.'

'Gormighty!' Grim said when they entered the posh cleanliness of the cafeteria. 'That's some darned place y' have here.'

Then Captain Wylmer and Willow came to meet them.

'We got the ship,' Amaj said with an offhand air. 'This is Grim. Her name, that is.' He turned to the girl. 'Wylmer commands our schooner and Willow is boss of the keep.'

'Welcome,' Willow said, mustering the girl. 'Are you alone?'

Amaj grinned. 'She's not; there's a full crew of rowers with her, forty at least. Both of you join us in the office; we must discuss things.'

The wyrmcaller's office was a palace of smooth marble and seemingly fragile, copper furniture. Grim looked about her, mouth half open.

'Are you the lord of all this?' she asked with some difficulty.

Amaj laughed. 'Not me. The wyrmcaller is lord here; I'm only his marshal.'

Then Wylmer and Willow entered and they sat down at the large meeting table.

'It was a beautiful operation,' Amaj said. 'Everything went as planned. The ship came in under oars, as Jem had said. While we flew to the attack, Rawe almost overloaded his bow chaser – it sounded way too loud to me, but it shocked the heck out of those Bokkaners. Them fellows were unprepared, and we got them easily.' He grinned at Grim. 'With some great help from the rowers.' Then he folded his arms and frowned. 'Forty guys; that's a lot. What shall we do with them?'

'Give us the ship and let us go,' Grim said.

'What would you do then?' Willow asked.

The girl put her fists on the table. 'Go back to Yavam and liberate the rest of us.'

'There are more of you?'

'Oh yes, many more. Those pirates have been collecting kids for a year or more; some were sent to Angsthafn, and the rest was housed at Yavam.'

'Why?' Amaj asked. 'What do they do with those kids?'

Grim shrugged. 'Let us work the land, fish, cook and die of misery. There is no...foolery, though; the captains are very strict about that. They do beat us regularly, but that's all.'

'How long have they been at this Yavam?' Amaj asked.

'They came when I was ten,' Grim said in a bleak voice. 'Killed the grown-ups, but none of the children. Everybody under eighteen is safe.'

Amaj rose and walked over to the big map on the wall. It was one of their own, showing the Continent from Vanhaar in the south to Port Naar in the north. 'Where is your place?'

Grim joined him. 'Where are we now?'

'Here.' The marshal pointed at Smalkand, at the foot of the western mountains. Then he moved his hand all the way east. 'This stretch of mountains is our land, the Pasandir Peaks. To the north are the Nanstalgarod deserts, and past that a place called Hizmyr.'

'We've seen the desert,' Grim said. 'That's a bad stretch for a rower; too flippin' hot. It was to our left, so we must've been going south.' She stared at the map. 'We're not on this thing.' She tapped the left edge, about halfway the Wydemere Sea. 'There are lands on this side, too.'

'The Greenwall Coast,' Wylmer said. 'That's all jungle.'

'Sure,' Grim said. 'But not our island. It's hills and grass, but most of it rock.'

'I have a map on board the schooner,' Wylmer said. 'That shows the Greenwall as well.'

'Later,' Amaj said. 'The big question is those other kids.' He looked at Wylmer, Miyra and Shaw. 'Can we do it?'

'How many pirates are there?' Wylmer asked. 'What are the island's defenses?'

'They aren't all that many,' Grim said. 'About two hundred. Half of them are on board the old frigate, the others holed up on the island.'

'A frigate?' Wylmer said sharply. 'How many guns?'

'Thirty-two,' Grim said. 'She's old, and worn, but she can shoot.'

'We can't cut her out,' Wylmer said decisively. 'We could never sail her. So must destroy her.'

'How?' Amaj said.

Wylmer scratched his chin. 'Fire. Darn, it's been done before. Would Martha know how?'

'We'll have a meeting,' Amaj said. 'Shaw, are you playing?'

Shaw had been sitting back in her chair, hiding behind her eye patch as she waited for the question. Now it was asked, and she had to decide. She screwed her monocle in her eye. 'What do I get out of it?'

Amaj blinked. 'What do you mean?'

'I'm running a trade business, Amaj. Squad leaders Kennan and Yens are employees of the PTC, not the Pasandir Army. If they're to help, I want something in return.'

'I told you she had strangled and buried meek little Shaw,' Wylmer said. 'She's changed into a boss.'

'I noticed,' Amaj said. 'What do you want?'

Shaw grinned. 'I'll be moderate; I want everything. Seriously, I want *Kokkacir*; I want these guys to crew her, and a first chance to offer the other kids a job. You can keep your soul, Lord Amaj.' She smiled sweetly. 'For now.'

'What are you that they are not?' Grim said, looking from Shaw to Amaj and back.

'I'm Shaw, I run the Pasandir Trading Co, the Peak's merchant arm, and I might be able to offer you jobs.'

'I must speak with the guys,' Grim said.

Shaw jumped to her feet. 'Let's go ask them.'

Back on board the pirate ship, they found most rowers asleep over their oars, while Yens' guys watched them with pity and wonder in their eyes.

'That's the first sleep they had in two days,' Grim said. 'No more than quick naps at sea.' She put two fingers to her lips and gave a piercing whistle. Automatically, the rowers straightened and put their hands to the oars.

'At ease,' Grim said. 'Listen well, you lazy no-good softies. Merchant Shaw has a proposal you should hear.'

A host of bleary, red-rimmed eyes turned to look at her. Shaw stared back through her monocle and smiled, balancing like an old hand in the narrow space between the two groups of rowers.

'Whichever deity steers your way did a good job today,' she said. 'You sailed to the last place a pirate should want to go, straight into the headquarters of the Pasandir Peaks Armed Forces. To be clear, that's them; Lord Amaj commands here, Captain Wylmer is senior naval officer and Boss Willow is your friendly hostess. Me, I'm Shaw; I run the Pasandir Trading Company. But all of us here are pirate hunters.'

'Good,' someone muttered.

'It's part of our job,' Shaw said. 'Grim wants us to go to Yavam Island and liberate your friends.'

Every one of them was wide awake now.

'Of course we will do that,' Shaw said calmly. 'We expect you to help, but we'll get your friends free. After that, I will use *Kokkacir* for trade, and I want you to man her. Without the chains.' She grinned. 'I'll shackle you with money; three pennies per day, free meals, clothing and medical help.'

'You'll join us in freeing our friends?' a curly-haired boy said.

Shaw lifted her hands and let her knives appear into them. 'We kill pirates. Now we're going to sail against the dogs who keep the rest of you capture. We'll sink their bleepin' frigate and bury the others six feet deep.'

'Won't work,' the curly-head said seriously. 'Burying them must be at sea; the whole rotten island is too rocky for digging.'

'That's fine with me,' Shaw said. She thought of something. 'That broken shoulder?'

'Here,' a voice called. 'Your healer came on board. Funny fellow, but he did a great job. My arm is good as new.'

'Excellent,' Shaw said. 'Well, what about it?'

'It sounds fine,' the curly-haired boy said. 'Grim, whaddoyasay?'

'I think it's a grand deal,' she said. 'But you decide for yourselves.'

'Then I say let's do it,' the curly-headed boy said. 'If you're after that scum at Yavam, I'm with you.'

That opened the sluices and a wave of ayes followed.

'Squad leader Yens,' Shaw said. 'Unlock those chains. No friend of ours should be shackled.'

In minutes, the chains were off, and several kids sat rubbing their bare wrists in unbelief.

'If there's anyone among you who think they can command this ship, come and tell me later,' Shaw said.

'Enough talk,' Willow said sternly. 'You follow me to the beach. I will show you your bunkroom for the night, and the washroom. Then I'll have you supplied with other clothes. They're pirate castoffs, but clean.'

Grim hesitated. 'Do you have any... girl stuff?' she said, and her cheeks turned red.

Willow glanced at her. 'It's your period? Sure, come with me.' Without another word, she slipped into the sea and made for the beach.

As Shaw watched them go, she noticed Kennan and his lads still on the beach, dragging the bodies together and undressing them without a moment's hesitation. *Guard duty won't suit them for long,* she thought. *That's all right for regulars like Yens, but those guys need more.*

# CHAPTER 19 – COUNCIL OF WAR

Nate met Shaw as she returned to the mess. 'And?' He eyed her sharply. 'You look satisfied; what did you get for us?'

'*Kokkacir* and all those guys,' Shaw said. 'But first we'll sail to that island of theirs and go kill pirates.' She put her arm around Nate. 'Let's have some tall, cold drinks,' she said. 'Those pirates always leave a bad taste in my mouth.'

'Bad smell in my nose as well,' Amaj said, as they made for the cafeteria counter. 'They're filthy.'

They barely sat before the curly-headed boy marched up to Shaw.

'You need officers,' he said. 'What's the deal?'

Shaw and Nate exchanged glances.

'We're building a trade empire,' Shaw said carefully. 'We own several warehouses and a large airship company. But they're all in the Weal.'

'Weal?'

'That's a few countries to the south. They've joined forces as the Weal of Four Nations. We of the Peaks are another country, though we are allies. We want to start trading north, past the Hellesands desert. For that, we need ships and people to sail them. We prefer guys our own age. What's your name? Are you qualified as a ship's officer?'

'I can learn,' the boy said harshly. 'Name's Jakopanari; call me Jakop. I've been rowing that blippin' bucket all over the Emerang Sea. I... have been studying those pirates. A few of us waited for a chance to take over, so we needed to know how to get her home.'

'Yeah,' Shaw said. She studied the boy and liked what she saw. He had a big, strong face, with the strange, olive skin all Yavam islanders had. 'Are you guys literate?'

'Most of us locals are,' Jakop said. 'We went to school until the pirates came.' He pressed his lips to a thin line. 'Our parents... Our elders were monks, so we got lots of schooling. We were on Yavam for... for a Life of Study, my ma used to say. Twelve generations of monks, and then the Bokkaners wiped them out. We had schools and an academy, but no defenses. We trusted in our god. In our need, we called him, but he didn't come. Now we have nothing.'

'Why did the pirates keep you guys alive?'

Jakop shrugged. 'They weren't sure. The orders came from up high, from their boss Nimmendal on Vulcan Island.'

'What?' Amaj said. 'Nimmendal... That was the top guy in Brisa, the one who is the pirate boss in Angsthafn.'

'Nimmendal is a jinni,' Shaw said. 'We've encountered his stooges before.'

'Angsthafn is an island with a volcano,' Nate said. 'Do you know where that Vulcan Island is?'

Jakop scratched his curls. 'Only that it's farther north somewhere.'

'That narrows the search,' Nate said.

'Shouldn't we tell Eskandar?' Amaj said.

Shaw was silent for a moment. 'Not yet. We need more information.'

'We're not tackling Angsthafn on our own,' Wylmer said.

Amaj stared at him. Then he chuckled. 'I won't; I've seen Ozoezd, mate. Nimmendal is Eskandar's job, not ours. But if we were to find Angsthafn's location, I wouldn't mind surprising the boss with it.'

'True. Let us start with Yavam. Very, very cautiously. They've got a blipping *frigate*, Marshal. That's dangerous enough for me.' Wylmer turned to Jakop. 'Can you draw a map of the island?'

'I'm not much good at drawing,' Jakop said.

'Ask Chagan to help you,' Wylmer said. 'He's the *Marigold*'s lieutenant.'

'The Imperial?' Jakop said. 'I mean the green guy?'

'Yes. Why Imperial?'

'That's what our elders used to call them, on account of them being an empire. We got a kid like him, back on Yavam; his folks were mechanics, I think. He doesn't handle being a... a slave well, seeing he's only a scrawny fellow.'

Amaj touched Jakop's shoulder with his fist. 'You go get Chagan and make that map for us. After dinner we'll hold a bosses' meeting to discuss plans. You and Grim are invited, but we need that map done then.'

'Got it,' Jakop said. 'Chagan?'

'Try the library,' Wylmer said. 'He's working on a manual of arithmetic.'


'Monks!' Amaj growled. 'I hate monks! The lich king's first servants were the monks of our local monastery. He made them into madmen and sent them to conquer Kalbakar Keep. Eskandar and I kicked them out, but the thought of monks makes my blood boils.'

'These won't be the same ones,' Wylmer said soothingly. 'Besides, the guys we found aren't very pious, I'd say.'

'Not really,' Shaw said. 'I wouldn't hold it against them, Amaj.'

The marshal grunted. 'I won't, of course. It's just the idea of mad monks makes my hand itching for my sword.'

'Say,' a gruff voice said behind them. 'I heard that sheep-haired punk Jakop beat me to it. Where do I sign?'

'You don't,' Shaw said, turning around. 'You simply agree to join; we trust your word. We will train you, pay you, and expect you to stay, but we won't force you.'

'Nice,' Grim stood with her legs apart, arms crossed, and scowling, looking very un-monk-like. 'In joining you guys, would we become – what do you call yourselves?'

'We're the people of the Pasandir Peaks,' Amaj said. 'We never had a name for that. The boss and I are Ma'aweshi, Wylmer and Shaw are Vanhaari, and your people?'

Grim scowled and the scars in her face tightened. 'I dunno. The parents told us we came from somewhere else, but we'd learn more about our people's history at an initiation when we turned eighteen.' She hesitated. 'There is a book. We keep it in the mill, but we can't open it. Somehow, the pages stick together.'

'Sounds magical,' Amaj said. 'That's out of my province. You people look like my girl Jem, and she's from Nanstalgarod, across the sea from Yavam. It doesn't matter, of course. If you want to join the navy, you must become a Peaks citizen first.'

'Not for the merchant marine,' Shaw added. 'Though it would be great if you did, it's not an obligation.'

Grim gave a curt nod. 'Understood. I don't mind joining, but I'd rather choose Shaw's outfit. We don't mind a fight, but we're scholars at heart, not warriors.'

'Do I smell money?' A small, brown boy with a sharp face and big ears wrung his way past Grim. 'I want to apply.'

'If only you could reach the wheel,' Grim said with a small smile. 'This is Tamyas; one of those guys the pirates stole somewhere and dumped with us. He's the guy who taught Jakop and me what little we know of commanding *Kokkacir*.'

'I was apprentice on a trade vessel out of Port Waid in Hizmyr,' the boy said. 'Them bliddy pirates captured me ship and locked me up. The others...' He shrugged. 'Divine Chottapan has them, I suppose.' He looked at Shaw. 'I'm a trader, but I wanna kill pirates, too. Shoot them, sink them, and see them b-burn.'

Shaw recognized the anger in the boy's eyes. 'Our ships won't avoid a battle,' she said. 'So you might do both. Have you been at sea long?'

'Eight years,' the boy said. 'Since I was eight. Captain had promised me I'd be third mate next year.'

'You can hand, reef and steer? Stand a deck watch?'

'Sure, even if some think I'm too small.' He cast a dark glance at Grim.

'I was kidding you,' she said soberly. 'No offense meant.'

Tamyas touched her arm. 'None taken.' He looked at Shaw. 'I do a bit of navigating, pointing a gun and stowing cargo, too. We merchant officers are supposed to be good at everything, unlike those stuffed jackets of the navy.'

'Not *our* navy,' Wylmer said quickly.

Shaw smiled. 'Now the big question. Can you sail the *Kokkacir?*'

'I can,' Tamyas said confidently. 'I've had plenty of time to study her.'

'You're in,' Shaw said. 'Captain Wylmer, would you test his readiness for a mate's license?'

Wylmer nodded. 'See me after the evening meal.'

'You got sunk by pirates?' Nate asked.

Tamyas cursed. 'A big fourmaster; a Qoori boat. We couldn't fight *her* in a million years.'

'*Drakon of Ilzhar?*' Wylmer said.

Tamyas' eyes spat fire. 'Yes! Captain Bliddy Luzon's ship.'

'No longer,' Wylmer said. He shook the last nuts in his hand and put down the empty bowl. 'She's ours now. We captured her at Brisa, and the lord wyrmcaller has taken her north, to bring that kid Hizmyran prince home they picked up along the way.'

'You guys captured *Drakon?*' Tamyas said, staring at them. 'Gods! So I *had* seen that Qoori lieutenant Chagan before. I wondered, but those guys look much the same to me.' He took a deep breath. 'And a prince? You don't say that's young Jazzaunt, is it? I heard the king gave him a ship as a toy.'

Wylmer grinned. 'And the Weal navy out of Port Naar sank it from under his feet, thinking the lad a pirate.'

Tamyas burst out laughing. 'Sunk it! Kid won't be half mad. It's common knowledge Jazzaunt fancies himself a great sailor.' Then he sobered. 'Still, to lose your ship is awful, even if you're a prince.' He made a sound halfway between a sob and a snort.

'I know,' Wylmer said in a low voice. 'The same *Drakon* sank my sloop as well. Luzon left a trail of destruction three thousand miles long.'

Tamyas slapped his hands. 'I suppose you'd like a sketch of *Barcute*'s decks?' he said hurriedly. 'Ah, that's the pirate frigate.'

'Yes!' Wylmer said, relaxing. 'Have you been on board her?'

'Three months day crew,' the boy said. 'Months I'd rather forget. I'll draw you a deck plan if you promise to sink her. Don't cut her out; she's rotten; both her planks and her soul.'

'I'm planning to burn her,' Wylmer said. 'We'll have a meeting tonight; you come and bring that drawing.'

The meeting that evening was Amaj's first as commander, and he sat in Eskandar's chair at the head of the table, looking embarrassed.

Shaw grinned at his discomfiture; the guy was a fighter, and chairing a meeting didn't come natural to him.

At his side, Wylmer sat at ease, legs stretched out under the table and arms clasped over his ample stomach. Round the table were Smalkand's department heads, the three guys from *Kokkacir* and the squad leaders.

Shaw sat facing the marshal, with Nate. Uninvited but unchallenged, Emmett sat away from the table, scribbling.

Amaj cleared his throat, and colored as they looked at him. 'Great to see you here,' he said lamely. 'We, well, we got plans to make. There's a lot of kids waiting to be rescued, and we're the only ones who can do it.'

'Any idea how many?' Shaw said.

'About ninety,' Grim said.

Tamyas shook his head. 'More. You forget those thirty-odd countrymen of mine that came just before we sailed.'

'You're right,' Grim said. 'I heard a whisper but I ain't seen them.'

'They're artisan types; smiths, carpenters, stonemasons, coming from a guild penal school.' Tamyas pulled a face. 'You don't want to fall foul of the guild in our land; they got lots kinds of nasty laws they wrote themselves.'

'We're running out of bed space,' Willow said. 'There's no way we can house another two hundred guys.'

Nate looked at Shaw. 'Nor can we.'

'We'll hire another place,' Shaw said. 'There are several unused buildings on New Wharf we could convert into barracks and such.'

'Shaw, we can't take them to Seatome,' Nate said. 'Not as artisans; you'd create a riot. There are too few workplaces as it is already.'

*He's right, darn it.* Shaw grunted. 'Lemme think on it.'

'We must get them out first,' Amaj said. 'We know where we must go to?'

Wylmer grinned. 'Yes, we have Yavam Island on our maps. And we have a nice sketch of the island itself, made by Jakop and Chagan. It shows the locations of the important buildings, and where the big frigate *Barcute* is moored.'

'A frigate,' Captain Miyra said. 'We're not going to cut her out, are we?'

'No!' Tamyas said fiercely. 'She's a hell ship.'

'We haven't got the hands to sail a frigate,' Wylmer said. 'We must burn the bitch.'

'How?' Captain Miyra said.

Amaj turned Martha. She was Tymon's twin sister; a rotund, unattractive Vanhaari girl with a bad haircut and a self-righteous manner. 'You're the elementalist mage,' he said. 'Can you light fires inside a ship's hull?'

'Me?' Martha said, and her gray face turned splotchy. 'But I'm a teacher, not a... an adventurer.'

'You're a daughter of the Revolution,' Sylas said. 'You're always telling us how brave and resourceful your folks were in the war. Surely you are no less heroic?'

'No, of course not! But...'

'Well then,' Wylmer said not unkindly. 'Can you do it from outside?'

'I... must touch the ship; make contact,' Martha said in a strangled voice. 'Then, yes, I could.'

'Excellent,' Wylmer said. 'You will be the star of the whole operation!'

'Will there be kids on board?' Captain Miyra asked. 'You wouldn't want to roast them, too.'

Tamyas shook his head. 'The pirate boss doesn't want any youngsters around. There's no room, either, with all his crew sleeping on board at night. He's got only his fetch-and-carry-girl, who brings his wine and slippers and sings bawdy songs for him.'

'Do they keep her locked-up or anything?' Shaw said.

'Nope, she can walk around freely; wouldn't dare to run away.'

'I can slip on board and tell her to get out,' Jem said.

'Yeah?' Tamyas said doubtfully. 'How will you do that?'

'Like this,' Jem said, and faded from sight, to reappear behind the smaller boy's back.

'Booo!' she said, and Tamyas cursed as he wheeled around to face her.

'You! How did you do that?'

'She's under a spell,' Amaj said heavily. 'Jem can go anywhere; no one can see her.'

'Unless he is a jinni,' the princess added.

Tamyas shivered. 'You people are creepy,' he muttered. Then he brightened. 'Still, all that magic makes me feel it could work.'

'Of course it will work,' Wylmer said. 'You got that sketch of the frigate?'

Tamyas waved a slip of paper.

'Good. Show it to Jem and Martha, and point out the best spots to light a fire. Powder magazine, sail room, captain's cabin, all the flammable places.'

The Hizmyran boy grinned. 'Gladly.'

'When the ship's a-blaze, where would the rest of the pirates be?' Shaw asked.

Jakop touched the map he had made of the island. 'By night most of them will be sleeping. A bunch of them is using the academy as a bunkhouse; it's just outside the village. The pirate camp is on a hill overlooking the path to the armory, about a mile to the north. The camp is only tents, but they can house a hundred men. And no, there aren't a hundred men; not when you do away with the frigate crew at night.'

'Where are the kids?' Shaw said.

'They hole up in the houses,' Grim said. 'There's a bell in the village center to summon them each morning.'

'A bell...' Wylmer said.

'Near the armory?' Amaj finished. 'How nice of them.' He slapped the table. 'All right, so here's how we'll do it...'

# CHAPTER 20 – TO KILL A FRIGATE

The next morning, *Killarn Ranni* and *Marigold* left the bay.

'We're not taking *Kokkacir*,' Wylmer had said. 'Grim's guys have never sailed her and this isn't the moment to start. Let them cut their teeth on the schooner, where I can see them.'

The others couldn't fault his logic, and so there were only two ships sailing for Yavam Island.

Shaw stood on the schooner's quarterdeck with Wylmer and Amaj, and watched the ship make her way through the narrow passage. Several times, she held her breath as the relentless cliffs came close. Captain Wylmer however stayed cool and seemed to take the clumsiness of his new crew all in his stride. As a self-respecting merchant boss, Shaw couldn't do less and she kept her face impassive.

When they came from the passage still in one piece, Wylmer nodded. 'Well done, guys,' he called out. If he was relieved, Shaw couldn't read it in his face.

'We'll take it easy.' Wylmer turned his bulk to the curly-haired Jakop clutching the wheel with sweaty hands.

'Watch the compass. Hold the needle on that bit between North and Northwest. Relax; the wheel isn't a pirate, don't fight it. Go with the motion of the ship.'

He shouted an order to young Tamyas on the main deck, who was acting first officer. Then he watched as Tamyas explained things to six other boys, before they all went aloft.

Jerkily, the main sail rose, and the schooner gathered speed.

'Steady the wheel,' Wylmer said. 'Keep one eye on the compass, helmsman.'

Jakop clenched his teeth. 'It feels like she's running away from me.'

'You're not *that* ugly,' Wylmer said. 'Keep her on course; I'll take care of the rest.' He winked at Amaj. 'They learn fast.' He peered at the masts. 'You remember Skipper's sail-handling instructions, Marshal?'

'Oh gods, yes,' Amaj said. 'Why?'

'Take a few guys and set me the fore sail, will you?'

Amaj sighed. 'I hated that part, y' know.' He hurried off, calling names.

Wylmer and Shaw exchanged glances.

'Don't ask me, Captain Wylmer,' she said. 'I'm not going up there.'

'He does,' Wylmer said, pointing at a small figure following Amaj and his guys into the foremast shrouds.

Shaw lifted her eye patch and looked at the mast. 'Emmett?' she said, aghast. 'Even there he's writing his stories?'

'He's taking his job very serious,' Wylmer said. 'The guy's been asking my ears off for the right names of everything.'

The sun rose palely on the third morning, when Shaw thought she heard the sound of guns in the distance.

'Sea fight?' she said, cupping her ear. On the other side of the quarterdeck, Amaj stood peering at the horizon.

'Signal to *Marigold*,' Wylmer said. 'Let's investigate together.'

Tamyas flipped through the signal book, an adapted version of the one Eskandar had rescued from Wylmer's late navy sloop, and moments later a string of flags ran up.

'*Marigold* acknowledges,' the boy reported.

Wylmer grinned and gave an order to the helmsman.

'Prepare the guns?' Amaj said, unable to hide his eagerness.

'That's Rawe's job,' Wylmer said. 'If you behave, I'll let you go with the boarding party.'

'You're an overbearing fellow,' Amaj complained.

'I am senior naval officer,' Wylmer said. 'When we're on land, you are just as overbearing, Marshal.'

Amaj couldn't help but laugh. 'I can't deny it.'

Half an hour later, they came to the scene of a desperate battle between a tall, antiquated merchant vessel and a red-painted cutter with black sails.

'That merchant is Hizmyran,' Tamyas shouted, and he sounded shocked. 'She's a guild ship!'

'Losing the battle,' Wylmer said grimly. 'She's far too slow; that pirate is toying with her.' He turned to the main deck. 'Mister Rawe, we're engaging the red vessel. Have your guns fire as they bear.'

Rawe waved and soon a ragged volley went off. Most balls went over, as the inexperienced crews had forgotten to compensate for their schooner's roll, but one shot plowed through the red ship's railing, cutting a swathe through the pirates. The gunners cheered, while Rawe gestured to reload.

From nearby, another volley echoed theirs, and *Marigold* steamed past the red cutter, sails furled and guns blazing. She, with her Skipper-trained crew, didn't miss, and sudden smoke billowed from the cutter's afterdeck.

*Marigold* made a sharp turn and Wylmer whistled. 'Taut move, Captain Miyra,' he said. 'Well done!'

Then *Marigold* barked her opposite broadside. Hot flames sprang up over the cutter's deck, and turned her rigging into lines of fire.

'Heated shot?' Wylmer said. 'Does Martha warm them up? Helmsman, steer for the merchant. Amaj, hop over and ask how she is doing.'

'I'll go,' Shaw said in a steely voice. 'I've never seen a Hizmyran merchant before.'

Amaj opened his mouth, but one look at her face made him reconsider. 'Sure,' he said. 'Be my guest. If they try to eat you, holler.'

'I'll buy them,' she said darkly.

Shaw took her broomstick and flew towards the merchant. Her experience with ships was limited, but her torn decks, the splintered railings, and several ragged holes in her mainsail told her the vessel had taken a beating. She was the *Gilded Hind*, with an old-fashioned figurehead of a gold-colored deer under her bowsprit. Shaw steered for the quarterdeck, where an elderly officer in a gold-crusted uniform was shouting orders. At his side an apprentice stood, sword in hand.

As Shaw's feet touched the deck with a thud, the boy turned on his heels, waving his blade. 'Who the heck are you?'

'Shaw Harwans, Pasandir Trading Co,' she said. 'My ships are engaging the pirate. How is your situation?'

The captain turned and regarded her in surprise. 'A girl? You arrived in the nick of time, young lady. I fear that rascally pirate was too fast for my ship. My thanks to your captain for his timely assistance.'

'I am the PTC managing director,' Shaw said. 'We don't like pirates cluttering up our shipping lanes.'

'You are in command?' the captain said. Then a flash of understanding came over his face. 'Of course; you must be of the wyrmcaller's people. Everyone in Myrlia, our capital, talks about him and how his troops aided Prince Jazzaunt in recapturing the royal keep of Kas-Bahaan.' He bowed. 'I will tell our people his other forces are as brave.'

Shaw hid a smile. 'Thank you,' she said. 'Will you be all right?'

The old captain watched the pirate. 'She is done for,' he muttered. He took a deep breath and glanced at Shaw. 'I will return to Myrlia for repairs. There will be a reward; I am sure the owners will want to show their appreciation of your help.'

'That is very good of them,' Shaw said. 'I hope to have an agent in Hizmyr shortly.'

'There she goes!' the apprentice shouted. Still burning, the red cutter slipped into the sea.

'A fitting end for any pirate,' Shaw said. 'If you are all right here, I will return to my ship.'

'Certainly,' the captain said. 'I will make it back safely; thank you.'

As they walked to the companion ladder, a sailor came up to them and saluted. 'The guildlady requests a moment of your time, ma'am.'

Shaw looked at the captain, whose face had stiffened into a mask. 'A guildlady?'

'Guildlady Jathira is a passenger,' the captain said stiffly. 'She is an agent of the guild in Myrlia. It would be better if you...' His words trailed away in embarrassment.

'If I saw her?' Shaw said. 'Very well, I can spare a few more minutes. Where is this guildlady?'

'In my cabin,' the captain said, clearly relieved. 'This way.'

The captain's cabin was in near darkness as Shaw entered. All lamps had been doused at the start of the action, to prevent fire.

'I'm glad you came,' a female voice said. 'Wait!' There was a sound of a match struck, and a single small folding lantern illuminated the cabin.

By its light, Shaw found a tall, slender figure watching her; she seemed in her early thirties, dressed in a dark uniform. She had a sharp, brown face, with dark hair tied into a knot in her neck. There wasn't any clear sign, but Shaw got the impression she was nervous.

'I'm Jathira, special agent to the Grand Guildmistress Satthyba,' the woman said. 'That triple darned pirate you so obligingly sank forces our hen-hearted captain to return to Myrlia. My mistress will never forgive him, but he thinks his life more important than his continuing in command.' She pulled a face. 'Stupid fool.'

She smiled. 'But now there is you, brave lady. I need your help. I am ordered to a certain island that houses a band of Bokkaner pirates. They had the temerity to abduct my mistress' grandson and they hold him captive. I am supposed to get him out without any fuss and with no ransom paid. A tough task made even more difficult now our incompetent captain lets a tiny pirate ship cow him. He will disobey his orders and sail home like a whipped cur, thereby ruining my task. Back home he will be broken, dismissed his ship and for all I know fed to the hunting lions as a snack, but that won't help me.'

She paused for a moment. 'Your arrival saved my task. In the craven captain's stead, you will take me to this island, wait until I have got the boy out, and sail us back to Myrlia.' She looked at Shaw triumphantly. 'How's that for a deal? No risks and good money.'

'What island might this be?' Shaw said, trying hard not to laugh. She was sure she already knew the answer.

'Yavam,' Jathira said. 'It used to be some kind of religious place, until the pirates captured it. Now it is a prison.'

'A prison for kids,' Shaw said. 'And your mistress couldn't spare a warship to liberate all of them? No matter, that's our part. You can come along, but we are under way to free all prisoners, not only that rich guild kid.'

Jathira's face turned red. 'The rest of them are street urchins. They are of no account.'

'I wouldn't say such aboard our vessels,' Shaw said. 'Most of our crew members are street kids. They make the best sailors and merchants in the world, guildlady; tough, clever and independent.'

Jathira walked up and down the cabin. 'I'm sorry,' she said after a moment. 'In Hizmyr we think of them as worthless.'

'We don't.' Shaw looked around the fine cabin, breathing an old-fashioned grandeur that rhymed badly with the life of the kids they were going to save. 'If you want to come, grab your luggage; I must return to my ship.'

'That's quickly done,' the guildlady said. 'My bag is always packed. When my mistress says "Go", she means now, not in an hour's time.' She pulled a backpack from underneath her bed. 'Ready. You have a boat waiting?'

'I have not,' Shaw said, unclasping her broom from her back. 'I'm a broomrider.'

Jathira frowned. 'I don't understand?'

'We'll fly.' They walked to the door and found the captain still waiting outside.

'I will move to the merchant lady's ship,' the young woman said. 'You can continue running.'

The captain gave a jerky nod. 'As you wish, guildlady.'

Shaw mounted her broom. 'You can sit before me,' she said. 'The spell will hold both of us.'

Gingerly, Jathira sat down. 'Hey,' she said. 'That's better than I thought. Does this thing really fly?'

'It really does,' Shaw said, and they rose in the air.

'All right?' she asked.

'Sure,' Jathira said. 'You won't scare me.'

Without another word, Shaw steered back to the schooner.

There was a lot of wreckage in the water, and several bodies. Something caught her eye, and Shaw noticed a small figure waving frantically.

'Somebody still alive down below,' she said and dove down for a closer look.

She saw long, black hair plastered to a thin brown boy's face, and eyes full of terror as the kid wrestled to keep his head above the water.

'It's a boy,' she said. 'Sorry, guildlady; you'll get your feet wet.' She lowered her broom into the water. 'Grab him round the waist; I'll help.'

Without a word, Jathira drew an arm around the boy and heaved. The castaway had passed out and lay as a dead weight in the water. Shaw's arms were too short to reach him, and Jathira alone couldn't manage.

'Won't work,' she said through clenched teeth. 'Abandon the beast.'

Then a second broom appeared.

'Nate!' Shaw cried, and a wave of relief filled her.

Without a word, Nate sank into the water up to his chest and simply shoved his broom under the boy.

'Up!' he grated, and with a sucking sound the two of them broke free from the sea's grasp.

Shaw followed and they returned to the *Marigold*.

'Thank you,' Shaw said, with a glance at Nate's stormy face.

'Share!' he exploded. 'Don't cut me out! You can't do every cursed thing alone! Take me with you, darn it!'

'I'm sorry,' Shaw said unhappily. 'I didn't think.'

Nate grunted. 'Try it now and then, thinking ain't that hard.' He relaxed. 'Idiot!'

Shaw hugged him. 'I know.'

Nate patted her cheek. 'It's all right.'

Meanwhile Amaj had turned the pirate boy onto his back on the deck and checked his life force.

'He's still breathing.' The marshal came to his feet. 'Healer Tymon will help to him.'

Movement behind her reminded Shaw of her passenger. 'This is Guildlady Jathira, an agent of the Hizmyran guilds,' she said. 'We have the same destination, so I thought to give her a lift.' She smiled at Jathira, who regarded her without expression, dripping water.

'You weren't afraid,' Shaw said. 'Welcome to the *Killarn Ranni*; I'm sorry I got you wet.'

'I've been wet before,' the guildlady said. 'But never to save a pirate who had tried to kill me.'

'I don't think he is that,' Shaw said. 'We'll find out.'

'Step aside please,' Tymon's dry voice said, and obediently they made way for the healer. 'Get some dry towels and a blanket.'

Shaw looked up, but Tamyas was already moving.

Tymon put his pudgy fingers on the boy's chest. 'Empty the water from your lungs,' he said, and a trail of slimy seawater streamed from the slack mouth, while the chest heaved laboriously.

While he worked, a white light grew around the healer's hands, spreading to his arms and upper body, and flowing over to engulf the boy on the deck. A vague tingling made Shaw sneeze.

As she watched, the bluish pallor drained from the boy's face, and his cheeks tinged a healthy red. The body relaxed and the labored heaving of the chest became an easy breathing.

It took only a few minutes before the light dimmed and disappeared.

Tymon wiped his hands on a small cloth from his sleeve. 'Rub him dry, wrap him in the blanket and put him to bed, with somebody sitting at his side. I don't expect trouble, but you never know what shock can do. His mind is free of compulsion and lacks the warped madness that characterizes the usual pirates. He is – in common words – just a kid.'

'Well done,' Shaw said with awe in her voice.

Tymon glanced at her and nodded. 'He'll be out for a long while. After that, we'll see.' He turned around and walked away.

'Thanks,' Shaw called after him.

'If we're done here,' Amaj said to no one in particular.

Shaw felt an irresistible giggle coming up. 'I am.'

Amaj scowled at her. 'Let's get a move on. How far is it?'

'Another halfday,' Captain Wylmer said. 'We lost a few hours; it should be way past midnight when we arrive.'

'Good,' Amaj said. 'That's how we want it. Do we have a cabin for the guildlady?'

'She can have mine,' Tamyas said. 'I'm on deck most of the time anyway.'

'You are Hizmyran?' Jathira said.

'I am,' Tamyas said. 'I was an independent trader.'

Jathira looked at him. 'Independent – a smuggler, you mean.'

'An independent trader,' Tamyas repeated. 'That we wouldn't trade through the guild didn't make us criminals, guildlady.'

'That is a point of view,' she said. 'No matter; such is no business of mine.'

'What is?' Tamyas asked point-blank.

'I'm Guildmistress Satthyba's troubleshooter,' she said. 'Independents are not my concern.'

'What is your present concern?' Wylmer said.

Jathira sighed. 'This *is* supposed to be a secret.' She shrugged. 'Darn, what a mess! *Hind*'s captain should have sunk that pirate; then all this wouldn't have happened.'

'Your precious guild should've sent a better ship,' Tamyas said. 'Even the greatest captain afloat wouldn't have won in that old tub. What is the big secret?'

Jathira pulled a face. 'The guildmistress' grandson got abducted by robbers. I am charged with recovering him. I found his trail leading to a royal keep in the Iron Reaches, and from there into the hands of a bunch of pirates from Yavam Island.'

'How did they manage to lay hands on the guildmistress' kin?' Tamyas said. 'Her relatives live locked away in golden cages, don't they?'

'This particular relative isn't very fond of cages,' Jathira said. 'He is rebellious. To show him what the guild does with unruly youngsters, his grandmother sent him to the Zamidra Syndicate Institute.'

'That's a penal camp,' Tamyas said. 'I have heard of it. It's a... harsh place.'

'Very harsh,' Jathira agreed.

'Then what happened?' Amaj said.

'Those robbers I mentioned,' Jathira said. 'They captured the camp, killed the guards and dragged off the youngsters.'

Tamyas opened his mouth, and laughed till he cried. 'They kidnapped her grandson! Gods, what a jest!'

'Unless you are the boy,' Jathira said.

He took a deep breath. 'Sure, it's no fun; I had months of it.'

Jathira gave him an arrested look. 'You've been with them?'

'All the way,' Tamyas said. 'They captured my ship, killed my mates and took me to Yavam. The last months me and forty others were rowing their bleeding galliot all over the Wydemere. Here, look.'

Tamyas showed her his wrists, still raw from the iron shackles, and his red and calloused hand palms. 'Now we joined Shaw and the wyrmcaller, earning good money for our efforts.'

He gave her a straight look. 'I'm glad Shaw picked up that guy from the pirate ship. Ten-to-one he's another victim like me and old Satthyba's whelp. It seems those pirates collect kids like a beggar fleas.'

This made Jathira start. 'Do they? Why?'

'They want them,' Amaj said. 'Why, is a question for another day.'

'Pirates *are* my concern,' Jathira said. 'My mistress' business contains a lot of sea trade and the Bokkaners are bad news for merchant ships.'

'The wyrmcaller shall wipe them out,' Amaj said. 'We are sailing for Yavam Island, put an end to their base there and liberate the prisoners. If your boy is among them, you can have him.' He grinned at Shaw. 'For a price.'

'Money?' Jathira said. 'I didn't think you were mercenaries.'

'I'm a lord of Kalbakar,' Amaj said harshly. 'I fight for honor, duty and glory. Nor am I fool enough to ask money of a merchant.'

'Prices are my department,' Shaw said. 'We speak of trade, guildlady; deals.'

Jathira laughed. 'Ah, my mistress is always interested in talking trade. And deals are a proper way of showing gratitude.'

'Exactly,' Shaw said. 'I represent the Pasandir Trading Co. out of Seatome. We need to talk.'

Amaj grunted. 'You've got time before we're there.'

It was nigh on two hours past midnight when they arrived; with the moon playing peek-a-boo behind the clouds and the frigate a bloated silhouette against the lighter sky. Yavam harbor was a sheltered bay with a long pier and a large building that could be anything.

Once inside the bay, *Killarn Ranni* and *Marigold* anchored with all lights doused, invisible against the background of the headland.

'My sister is coming over from *Marigold*,' Tymon said. He had changed his customary healer's robe for a pirate suit, which made him look... out of place, Shaw thought. Not funny; there wasn't a thing funny about Tymon.

A bump and a soft-voiced stream of curses announced her arrival.

'Over here,' Amaj said, and a dark figure almost fell into his arms.

'I... I can't...' Martha said, her voice and face shaking.

'You can do it,' Amaj said. 'I know you can. Think of your spells. *Jem, ready?*'

*'I'm flying over the frigate now,'* the princess broadcasted. *'No jinni. I'm searching for any children on board. Found one... I'm going to talk to her now. You can listen.'*

'Hey,' Jem broadcasted, 'Wake up, girl.' To Shaw it was as if she was there with her, in some oppressively dark place inside the frigate's bowels. Through Jem's perception, the pirate captain's girl servant looked a heap of sacking in the dark.

'Wake up,' Jem said, louder.

'No!' the girl sat up. 'Please don't! I'm coming, Master.'

'Hush,' Jem said. 'I'm a friend.'

'What?' the girl said confused. 'How did you come here? You're mad! When the guards find you, they'll beat the heck out of you.'

'They can't,' Jem said with a chuckle. 'I come to warn you. Can you get off the ship?'

'I'm not allowed to,' the girl said.

'But you can, can't you?'

'Y-yes, of course. I could tell them I carried a message for someone on land and the guards will let me pass. But when they find out...'

'They won't,' Jem said. 'I'm part of a troop coming to attack the pirates. We're going to blow up this flippin' bucket, but Tamyas warned us you were aboard, and I came to get you out first.'

'Tamyas? He's with Kokkacir.'

'I know; we captured the ship. Tamyas is with us now, waiting to attack, as are Grim, Jakop, and a heap of others. Now you get up and jump ship, girl. I'll come with you; nobody can see me, but I will speak in your mind. Like I'm doing. You think back at me and I'll hear you.'

'How? You... you're a mage? Then you're not from here.'

'I'm not from here,' Jem agreed. 'Now, time presses. Get up and walk.'

Through Jem's mind, Shaw saw the girl stumble to her feet and walk out of the little space. She crossed the deck to the gangway. A burly pirate stirred.

'Where you goin'?' he said.

'*Captain sent me ashore with a message,*' she said, trembling.

'*He did, huh? Stupid; captain should've warned me. Nah, get goin' and be back quick, ya hear!*'

'*I will,*' the girl said, and hurried down the plank, while the guard returned to his somnambulant state.

'*Well done! I must go back. You run on, girl,*' Jem said. '*Tell all kids you meet not to hang around here. When she blows, they could get hurt. Tell them to assemble at the armory.*' She stopped broadcasting and Shaw blinked as the images disappeared.

'Our turn,' Amaj said to Martha.

Shaw looked at the shaking mage. 'You sit down before me,' she said. 'I'll do the flying.'

Without a word, Martha sat down.

'Off we go,' Amaj said, and they flew away across the bay to the dark bulk of the frigate. '*Jem?*'

'*The girl left. I'm standing at the sail room. Martha, come in.*'

Shaw nearly bumped into the frigate's hull as Jem's view of the ship's hold interfered with her own sight and she muttered a curse.

Martha stretched out her hands, her eyes tightly shut. '*Gods, what a place. What is this stuff?*'

'*No idea,*' Jem said. '*Try if it burns.*'

The mage muttered an incantation, and flames appeared out of nowhere. A heavy coil of tarred rope started to smolder, then another, and another. Soon, the fire grew and the planking blackened.

'*Ni-ice,*' Jem said. '*Now follow me and strew your fire around like a bridesmaid her blossoms. They do that in the Weal, I hope?*'

Shaw chuckled at the question.

'*Eh? Yes, sure,*' Martha said. '*Big, white blossoms. Not... not red ones.*'

'*No, but you don't really want to marry the pirates, do you?*'

'*Of course not!*'

Shaw stifled a snicker at the thought of prim Martha walking out with a dirty old Bokkaner.

'*Here's the powder magazine. It's locked, but you and I don't care for locks, do we?*'

They had discussed this. Firing the powder room, where they kept the blackpowder and ammunition for the ship's cannons, would be the high point of the show. But it would be difficult, as the room was well protected against fire.

'*No,*' Martha said, seeing the room through Jem's eyes as the princess turned around slowly. '*Everything is stowed fireproof; I need more heat,*' she said. *There's a way. A dangerous way. Tymon, get your butt over here, twin. I need backup.*'

The healer grumbled. '*Why? Can't you light your little fires alone? WHAT? You're not going to... You know the ritual? Sure? All right.*'

'*What are you thinking of?*' Jem said.

'*A fire elemental,*' Martha said. '*I know how, but I never done it. Elementals are dangerous; if it got loose, it could destroy the whole island.*'

'*I'll sing for you,*' Jem said.

Shaw had no real idea what they were talking about. They waited until Tymon flew in to join his sister.

As Shaw watched, she saw what Martha saw, as Jem was still broadcasting everything. The powder room was a cramped place, sheeted with copper, the floor packed with some hard material, and lined with barrels of powder, boxes of lint, small ammunition and things whose purpose even she with her ships' chandler's knowledge didn't recognize.

Suddenly a glowing circle appeared on the floor, and words appeared inside; incomprehensible words, line after line until the whole circle was full.

*'I'm ready,'* Martha said. *'Ty, gimme your strength. Jem...'*

Shaw heard a clear note, and a strange song followed, rousing and hearty, full of strength and promise. Through it came Martha's voice speaking, or perhaps reading the words she had written. A dancing flame appeared inside the circle, jumping like an acrobat. It grew, broadened, and turned into a giant, flaming man.

*'Burn!'* Martha shouted. *'Burn the ship and return whence you came, great elemental!'* She clapped her hands over her head. *'Now get away from here! Fast, Shaw; run!'*

Without a moment's hesitation, Shaw ran. Her broom flashed away from the frigate on maximum speed back to the schooner, but as quick as she'd been, Tymon already dropped onto the deck.

When she dove to land, there was a giant explosion. Hellish light turned the night world into orange brightness as the frigate exploded. A fist of hot air bowled Shaw and Martha head over heels, dumping them ungently onto the *Killarn Ranni*'s deck.

'Duck!' Wylmer shouted as small bits and pieces of the frigate came down in an endless hailstorm. Then it was quiet again.

'Phew,' Wylmer said. 'I hadn't counted on an explosion. Luckily we were on the outer edge. Anyone hurt?'

Marta sprang to her feet and ran to the railing. 'The elemental!' she said. 'Is he...?'

'Gone,' Jem said, as she materialized beside her. 'He obeyed your command.'

'I did it!' Martha cried. 'I showed the nasty gossiping losers I am a mage!' Then she burst into tears.

'Hey, you did great,' Amaj said, shaking her gently. 'You twins are the greatest and I'm proud you are with us.'

Martha blew her nose. 'The others at school always said I wouldn't be worth much, because our dad is only a hedgemage. Well, I'm no hedgemage! I'm a true elementalist.'

'And so we'll tell the world,' Amaj said. He turned to Wylmer. 'How is everyone?'

'Shaken, but raring to go,' the captain said.

'They won't have to wait. Martha, tell the guys here and on *Marigold* we're riding to battle. Shaw, you and Kennan take the armory; I'll capture the pier. Mount up, all!'

'I'm coming with you, Shaw,' Martha said. 'I can fight, too.'

Suddenly they heard someone cursing.

'What's that?' Amaj barked.

'I'm running out of notebooks!' Emmett said. 'Just as it's getting serious.'

Wylmer grinned. 'A tragedy! Go to my cabin; you'll find one or two in my desk.'

'Don't leave without me!' Emmett raced to the main deck, to reappear within minutes waving two fresh notebooks. 'Got them,' he panted.

Moments later, a mass of kids lifted from both ships and rode to the coast.

Shaw's guys landed in front of the armory. It was a large barn, built of the dark stone dominating the barren landscape. Some twenty local kids waited outside, scared, but gripped by elation.

A ragged girl in a dirty dress jumped up and down. 'They're here! They're here as I told you!' She clutched Shaw's arm. 'Did you get the grumpy snake out?'

'What snake?' Shaw said while she tried the door handle. 'Darn, it's locked.'

'It was in a cage,' the ragged girl said. 'I had to feed it, but it barely spoke. Real bad-tempered, that poor snake was.'

Shaw only listened with a half ear, her mind on the action, and didn't answer as she rattled the door.

'I'll fix that,' Martha said fiercely, and she waved a fist at the door. A small bolt of lightning burst the lock, and the door crashed open.

Inside, the pirates had stored rows of arms; swords, spears, long muskets and armor too, a motley collection they must've stolen from places all over the Wydemere.

'Arm yourselves, guys,' Shaw shouted to the waiting kids. 'Everyone who can fight, grab something that suits you and join Lord Amaj at the pier.'

'Pirates coming!' someone screamed.

Kennan's squad rushed outside. Six pirates came hurrying across the field, waving cutlasses.

'For the Axed!' Kennan shouted, as he ran to meet them. With his Kells and a handful of crazed local kids, they dispatched the pirates quickly.

Screeching like maniacs, the locals ran along the stony path to the pier and the burning remains of the frigate. Here, the Marigolds were battling a large group of Bokkaners.

'Come,' Shaw said, and they hurried to assist them. More youngsters joined them, straight from the armory, screaming and excited.

A kid came running, shouting. 'They're loading the guns!'

Shaw halted. 'What guns? Where?'

The kid pointed. 'On the hill; two guns guarding the village. New captain brought them.'

Shaw looked around. Kennan's Kells, Martha, Nate, and two boys were all; the rest were fighting in the street.

'Come,' she said, and mounted.

The hill was clearly visible as it was the highest place in the landscape, but they saw the men only when they were close enough to draw their fire.

Martha shouted something terrible and threw a mass of flames at the assembled pirates.

'At them!' Shaw shouted amid the cries, and was first on the ground. Eight men and two swivel guns, she thought, and slashed at a darkly brown pirate with a beard.

'Ha!' the Bokkaner bellowed. 'Your puny attack ends here, child!' His body swelled and turned into a mighty blob of flesh with a mouth full of sharp teeth and two mean eyes all where you'd expect the navel.

'Jinni!' Shaw cried. 'Not puny, we're the wyrmcaller's outfit, fool.'

'But he's not here, child,' the jinni answered with an awful leer. 'I am, and I will dine well on you; very well.'

'No way,' Martha cried, and a hot beam of fire splattered against the massive body. The flesh rippled and the terrible mouth contorted, but that was all. Nate used the moment o dash at the jinni and a gaping wound opened, leaking green stuff.

The jinni cried out and the six Kells attacked, while the two other boys circled around, to attack from the rear. Martha threw another bolt, and one of the eyes shriveled. The jinni cried out, and a Kell boy rammed his sword in the other eye.

Again the jinni screamed, twitching and flailing with a mass of thin tendrils.

Blindly, the jinni attacked, mouth wide open, and caught two long Kell swords in its gullet. The blob of flesh heaved and imploded with a force that had them all fall forward.

Then he was gone, leaving only a large white stain on the rocks.

'We got the beast!' Shaw shouted. 'Bless you all, guys! Martha...' She turned around and found the mage sprawled on the ground. Shaw hurried over and knelt at her side. 'Martha?' She felt the girl's heart beat faintly, but her hand was cold and limp.

'She used too much magic,' Jem said from nowhere. 'Take her to her brother; he'll know what to do.'

Shaw nodded to Kennan. 'Have her carried to Healer Tymon.'

'Mana exhaustion,' Nate said. 'It should be familiar; Eskandar did that all the time.'

Shaw nodded. 'So he did. If we're done here, we'll go back to the others.' They flew toward the little harbor, where the bulk of the fighting had been.

Now there was silence. Everyone was looking at one house, a small stone dwelling with a broken roof.

'What's going on?' Shaw asked.

'The last pirate holed up with one of the new boys as hostage,' Tamyas said. 'The poxy dog wants us to take the two of them to Hizmyr, and put them ashore there. If not, he'll kill the guy.' He waved at a hand at a downed body. 'The guildlady tried to jump him as he dragged the boy inside, but caught a bullet for her troubles. We can't get at her, because that guy inside shoots at anyone coming too close.'

'I'll sing this one,' Jem said, still invisible. 'Like Martha, I haven't much energy left, so be prepared to act fast.'

It took a long time, but finally she whispered. *'Amaj, come. Now!'*

Shaw ran inside with Amaj and Kennan on her heels. The door opened on a small room with all the furniture pushed to the back and several heaps of bedding on the flagstone floor.

Here she found a pirate sitting cross-legged, dazed by Jem's song. He had a large dagger in his fist, and a bound and gagged boy lying over his knees. In the background, Shaw heard Jem sing faintly.

'Get him,' Shaw said to Kennan. With a tigrish leap, the squad leader cleared the helpless victim and crashed into the pirate's face, slamming him back. Without a sound, the man's head broke as he hit the floor and his body sagged into death.

'We got him, Jem,' Amaj said. 'Jem?' The singing had died away and all was silent.

*'Bottle,'* her voice seemed to come from a great distance.

With a sudden, dreadful panic in his face, Amaj looked around. There, half buried beneath the pirate's bulk, was the glass bottle that was Jem's body she always carried somewhere. He snatched it up and stood staring at it, tears streaming over his face.

'Jem?' he cried. 'Gods, no! Jem!'

# CHAPTER 21 – YAVAM ISLAND

Shaw watched Amaj as he sat on the porch of a ruined house, turning Jem's bottle round in his hands. He didn't speak, his whole being frozen in misery.

'She'll be all right,' Shaw said. 'Give her time to recover. She used a lot of power today, and she's exhausted herself, just as Martha did.'

'She's gone,' Amaj said dully. 'I can't hear her; I never before had a moment I couldn't hear her.'

'Has she ever used so much power?'

Amaj shrugged. 'She never said.'

'Perhaps she didn't realize before. She didn't have proper mages' training, remember.' Shaw peered at Amaj. 'You do care for her? I mean, more than the old she's-my-girl thing?'

'Yes.' Amaj wiped his nose on his sleeve. 'It's such a mess, her being in that bottle and all, but I care for her and... and she for me.'

Soft footsteps on the gravelly path made Shaw look up. Healer Tymon's round face looked tired as he stood there, rubbing his pudgy hands.

'Jem will be asleep right now, Marshal,' he said stiffly. 'Give her a day or so to wake up.'

'Will she wake up?' Amaj said, wrestling with his desperation.

'I don't suppose she *can*, ah, die, just like that,' Tymon said. 'The bottle spell keeps her alive no matter what.'

Amaj looked up. 'You think so?'

'Of course, Marshal. The one who did that to her wouldn't allow her to escape his grip by killing herself.'

'That rotten dog Wrachazd!' Amaj shouted. 'Her own blippin' grandfather!' He cradled the bottle in his hands and burst into tears.

'You should blow your nose,' Tymon said calmly. 'The children need you, Lord Amaj. Jem will wake when she is ready and she wouldn't want you neglecting your duty.'

'No.' Amaj kissed the bottle and put it carefully away inside the leather breastplate that was his mark as a Kalbakar lord.

'How's your sister?' Shaw asked of the healer.

Tymon grinned unexpectedly. 'Sound asleep. She never worked as hard as today. I'd expected her to fold when she'd blown up that frigate, but something must've got at her and she went on to fight those pirates.'

'She said she was truly an elementalist, not a hedgemage.'

Tymon nodded. 'You may find hedgemages useful, Shaw, but for us it's different. Our father is one of them and he has never held a paying job in his life. If our mother wasn't a moderately successful minor merchant, we'd have starved. Somehow, Martha and I were born with real magic. To compensate for this blunder, Fate made certain we don't look like serious mages. As an elementalist, Martha always had to prove herself. She hated to be called hedgemage.' He frowned, and his face turned cold. 'She has a sharp tongue, but she isn't as mean as me. *She* wants to be liked.'

'Well, neither of you are a hedgemage,' Amaj said. 'You're both great guys, and I hope we can be friends.'

Tymon sniffed. 'You are not ill; return to your duties, Marshal.'

Amaj nodded. 'You're right; thanks. You too, Shaw,' he added. 'We got the island; now what? You're the empire-building gal, I'm only a soldier. The next stage is yours.'

'I'll have to inspect the place first,' Shaw said. 'Be sure I will let you know.'

Shaw walked to the pier, where Nate joined her.

'I've been looking at things,' he said. 'There's a lot of useful stuff left lying around.'

'Do we want the island?' Shaw asked.

Nate stared at her. 'As a base? Would this be better than Port Naar?'

'It's less hot and it has a great harbor. Point is; can we live here?' She turned to watch a large crowd of kids gaping at the sight of *Killarn Ranni* and *Marigold* sailing across the bay with their wyrm flags proudly visible in the light of the dawning sun.

'They're the ships I told you about,' Jakop said to a tall, massively built boy who was old enough to be unshaven. 'The ones that took *Kokkacir* and got us free.'

'The mysterious strangers,' the tall boy said. 'Who the heck are they?'

'Friends,' Shaw said, walking over to them. 'The ships are the Pasandir Peaks Armed Forces. Me, I'm Shaw, of the Pasandir Trading Co. We promised Jakop, Grim and the others we'd come to help you.'

The boy's eyes narrowed in his heavy, olive face. He rubbed his stubbled chin with a big hand. 'So you did. Why? Thinking to sell us again?'

Shaw snorted. 'If we wanted that, we wouldn't have armed you, would we?'

'There's that,' the other said. 'But you don't help us because you're such nice guys.'

'Why not?' Shaw said. 'We're committed to wiping out the Bokkaners wherever we find them. So when *Kokkacir* sailed into our headquarters bay, we captured her and liberated your friends. Then I hired them, paying them good money, and came here.'

'You *hired* them to free us?' the boy said, stiffening.

Shaw eyed him coolly. 'No, I had to promise I'd free you before they allowed me to hire them.'

The boy relaxed. 'Yeah. Now what will you be doing?'

'I'm not sure yet. If you're interested, I will hire all of you as well. I'm not decided what to do with the island.'

The massive boy grunted. 'This used to be a nice place. Now it is ruined. We were peaceful folks. I wanted to be a technician. We had a workplace across the hill, until some idiot pirates smashed it. Now, I dunno what to do.'

'We can rebuild things,' Shaw said, thinking hard. 'What's your name? Perhaps you and Jakop would show us around?'

'Sure,' the boy said. 'I'm Uthur.'

'I'm Shaw,' she said. 'And this is my partner Nate.' She turned and saw Emmett. He looked haggard and dirty, with bloody stains on his face, but he was still scribbling. 'That's Emmett, he's writing it down for his newspaper.'

Then *Marigold* came alongside the pier and they watched her crew securing her lines.

Uthur shook his head. 'I can't believe those beasts are gone,' he said. Then he wheeled around. 'All right. Let's start as visitors do, at the inn.'

The inn was stout, built of stone and wood with a porch at the long sides. Inside, they came into a large common room that would have been pleasant if it hadn't been so dirty.

Three gangling boys were eyeing the bottles in the wooden bar.

'Brandy?' one of them said. 'Must be good stuff if those pirates managed to live on it.'

'None of that!' Shaw snapped. 'I'll kick the butt of the first one who touches a bottle. Pirate booze is poisoned to keep them docile. Drinking it would turn you into sheep.'

'Poisoned?' one of the boy said, startled. 'But...'

'Not a kill-you-dead poison, but a mind-stealing one,' Shaw said. 'Jinn use it to keep their followers enslaved.'

Uthur nodded curtly. 'You heard the lady,' he said. 'Forget the booze. Now get to work; I want this place clean by darkfall.' He looked at Jakop. 'Go get a few guys to collect the wine and spirits, and pour them out. Bring back the bottles and stoppers; we can use those.'

From the inn he led them along a graveled path with small, homely houses on both sides. In the light of the moon they looked ruinous, with broken shingles on the roofs and overgrown gardens.

'The kids use them mostly,' Uthur said, his face hard. 'The pirates were holed up in the academy, those that weren't on board the frigate.'

Shaw thought of the burned-out ruins of her parents' ship's chandlery, and she marveled at his composure. To live here, among the houses they'd been born in, been happy... She felt like bawling.

'Who works that?' Nate asked. He pointed at the contours of a large farm, with cultivated fields and a mill, its sails stilled.

'We do,' Uthur said. 'We need the food. Most of us have a little vegetable garden as well.' He colored a little. 'We're quite self-sufficient, you know. Our parents taught us that; living the simple life of study, close to the earth. We got a smith, a cobbler, a baker and others. The pirates for the most part let us be; they didn't need us for anything. I have no idea they even knew why they were here; they sure didn't need the island either.'

The academy was a large building, with a second floor added later, in a different style. Inside, there were several classrooms, a library, workrooms and even a gym, extremely filthy and smelling like pig sties.

Behind it were several other buildings; a smithy, and a totally smashed workshop.

'I had hoped to work here,' Uthur said, and there was a bitter echo of rage in his voice. 'Now there's nothing left.'

'It has possibilities,' Nate said. 'We can replace the instruments and tools. The building itself isn't too damaged. What about water?'

'We got a water tower,' Uthur said. 'Even those rotten dogs weren't stupid enough to ruin that.'

'Who owns this island is this?' Shaw asked hoarsely.

Nate glanced at her, but he didn't say anything.

Beside him, Uthur shrugged. 'We do, I suppose. I never heard anyone saying otherwise.'

Shaw coughed and swallowed against the constriction in her throat. 'How many of you would stay here, if we agreed to repair everything?'

'Would it be safe?' Uthur said. 'What if more pirates come?'

'You're armed. We can build a teleportal connecting you to Smalkand and Seatome, and give you a mage to operate it, and to yell for help if you're attacked,' Shaw said. 'Port Naar is straight across from here. We could arrange with the navy there they'd extend their patrol to include this island.'

'We must ask the others,' Uthur said. 'Let's get them together.'

It was still dark when they all met in front of the armory; tired, dirty, ragged and free.

Uthur addressed them, with the moonlight illuminating his broad, stubbled face.

'Guys,' he said. 'It seems there's something like good fortune after all. She's called Shaw, and she came with her mates to help us. She's a powerful lady who runs a big company across the sea, and she's got plans you should listen to.'

'Now the fortune lady wants to rebuild this place and turn it into a kids' wonderland, right?' some quipster called.

Shaw stared round the circle, using her eye patch and monocle to its fullest effect. 'Right,' she said, in deadly earnest.

'Ha, ha,' the voice sounded less assured.

'I want to rebuild this place and turn it into a way station for my company,' Shaw continued. 'You have a great harbor, with fresh water and an inn, and you're much better situated than Port Naar. We'll give you a teleportal, build a warehouse and get that workshop running again. *If* enough of you guys are interested we could hire the lot of you as technicians, working with our engineers to build magic machines. Or else you could work the farms, and run the inn and the warehouse.'

'You serious?' a girl said.

'I'm perfectly serious,' Shaw said.

The girl looked around at the buildings and there was a look of longing in her face. 'Many bad things happened here,' she said. 'We buried our parents, our elders, we were as nothing. But this is our home; I... wanna stay.'

'Me too,' another said, and a third one.

Grim's crew kept themselves apart; they had made their choice already and no one wanted to go back.

Seventy-two Yavam kids elected to stay and rebuild. The third group, forty-four kids from other places, hesitated.

'I'll tell you why I'm going with Shaw,' Tamyas told them. 'This wasn't my home. I could go back to Hizmyr, but I see opportunities in this PTC business.'

'As I do,' a tall boy said.

Tamyas looked at him. 'You?' he said, surprised. 'But...'

'Me,' the boy said. 'A monkey in a golden cage is still a monkey in a cage, ain't it?'

'You're the one Jathira sought,' Shaw said, eyeing him closely. He was older than she had supposed; sixteen or seventeen at least, with a proud head and stern eyes.

The boy looked at her. 'Yes. I know Hizmyr; if you want to do business there, I could help you. But I'm not going back with Jathira.'

'Why not?' Nate asked.

'Because I want to be my own man,' he said. 'I don't care to jump to the strings of a guild puppeteer. Not my grandmother or anyone else.'

Shaw shrugged. 'It's your life. All right; I'll not send anyone back into a cage. Nate, did you have a spare handportal to make a coordinate of this place? Then return to Old Wharf and ask Oychak to bring me a portal and a hedgemage. I'll wait for their arrival. You'll take – drat, guy, what *is* your name?'

'Amsalon,' the boy said, with a slight bow.

'You'll take Amsalon with you, feed him, and tuck him into bed, or whatever he needs. Amsalon, you can join us, but remember I'm not your grandmother; I'm not a puppeteer, I am your boss. I pay your wages and what I say goes. Any insubordination and you're out. Got that?'

He grinned. 'Perfectly clear.'

'Fine. You can offer comments and suggestions; I promise to listen and think about them, but in the end I decide. Unless the wyrmcaller has other ideas, but that's my problem.'

'Don't forget to kiss her feet before you leave,' Nate said drily.

'Throw that man to the wolves!' Shaw said grandly. Then she embraced him. 'I know; I'm awful.'

'You're not,' he said. 'You're my own brave Shaw.' Then he kissed her and left her staring speechless.

'Coming, Amsalon?' he said, and both disappeared.

Shaw sat down hard, her mind awhirl. Nate, he...

'Shaw!' Tymon's voice cut through her wild thoughts. 'Jathira asks for you.'

'She'll have to wait, I'm not done here yet,' Shaw said. She turned to Emmett. 'You're not writing that kiss in, you hear.'

'I don't do romance,' he said. 'Don't write of business deals and things either. Action, foreign lands, treasures; that's the stuff.'

Shaw jumped up and strode to the last group.


Tamyas' people huddled together on the inn's porch, haggard boys and girls, all more or less similarly dressed, and hollow-eyed from exhaustion.

One of them, a boy with a pattern of diagonal scars over his face, rose and bowed to her. Then he staggered.

'Sit down,' Shaw said. 'You guys look done in.'

'We haven't had much food or rest the last week,' the boy said. 'I want to sleep, but we must decide first. I will explain to you why you must not tell Guildlady Jathira about us. You see, those you see here were "freed" from the Zamidra Syndicate Institute.'

'I heard the name mentioned,' Shaw said. 'But what is it?'

'It is a school. That's what they say. A correctional school for Hizmyran street children. And it is true, they do teach a profession. I am a metalworker, journeyman level. For the Syndicate taught me, but they also kept me, beat me, misused me and would never ever have let me go. It is a penal camp, ma'am, and they work you till you're dead. It's part of an iron mine, and we did most of the work. Mining, melting, refining, shaping, everything. We made things, from sword handles to lamp stands, everything iron we made, for twelve hours a day.

'Then the robbers came. Our bully guards were unprepared for armed men, and they died. We children were dragged through the woods until we came to a ship. They dumped the lot of us in their hold, in the dark, with sporadic food, and when the hatches opened, we were here.'

'That was just before we sailed,' Tamyas said. 'I had managed a few words with them, enough to know who they were.'

'The Zamidra Syndicate is owned and operated by the guilds. Grand Guildmistress Satthyba knows all about it; she even sent her grandson there, to warn him to behave.' The scarred boy gave a hoarse laugh. 'Amsalon didn't budge, I give him that.' He moistened his lips. 'I beg of you, when you speak with the guildlady, do not tell her about us. She will demand us back, and we will not go.'

'If you join us, no one can demand your return, for you will be citizens of the Peaks.' Shaw paused. 'Whatever you choose, I will not betray you to Jathira. But I will trade with her people.'

The boy nodded. 'We will trust you in this. We shall talk it over and let you know what we decide.' He looked at her. 'There is another group of us, a smaller group. They were to be sent to another ship. Should you hear anything of them, we would like to be told.'

'If I do, I will let you know,' Shaw said. Then she saw a thin Qoori boy staring at her.

'Hi,' she said. 'May the Son of the Gods be with you.'

The boy didn't answer the ritual greeting, but continued to stare at her unblinkingly.

'What's your name?'

Now he stirred. 'Wanei,' he said.

'Tymon examined him,' Tamyas said. 'He was in a bad way. Not a fighter guy, are you, mate?'

'No.' The boy's skin was pale green and looked soft, like a young child's cheek. *A rich kid face*, Shaw thought.

'You're from Qoor,' she said.

'Sashuni,' he said.

'Is that a city?'

'A *tingon*,' the boy said.

'What's that?' Shaw asked.

'King, minor king, is *ting*. Father's brother is ting of Sashuni.'

'Does that make you a prince?'

The boy shrugged. 'Very minor one. I'm navy lieutenant in *Royal Sashu*, sailing for Oun-ti, the southern naval base. Then pirate schooner came; captured ship at night. Took me away and stole our cargo. Now cargo gone, Qanan my brother gone, I am dead. Dead. All dead. No more honor.'

He sat down again and retired back into himself.

'Leave him be,' Tamyas said. 'We'll keep an eye on him.'

Jathira sat up, looking wan and pale under her brown skin. 'There you are!' she said. 'Have you found him?'

'Amsalon?' Shaw said. 'Yes, I did.'

'Then where is he?'

Shaw looked at her. 'You won't like my answer. He refused to go back to his gilded cage. So I hired him and sent him away.'

'You did WHAT?' Jathira's eyes opened wide with dismay. 'I can't tell that to his grandmother!'

'Sure you can,' Shaw said. 'Explain to her the opportunities. Her grandson entered the wyrmcaller's service. He'll hobnob with the mightiest rulers; he'll be part of a great trade empire and acquire a business experience she would never have been able to buy for him on her own.'

'Yes, but now he is gone, he'll never want to have anything to do with her, so how does she profit?'

'First, you don't tell her he won't. Second, I am perfectly happy to deal with her for profit, on an exclusive basis. Of course, if she isn't interested, I will deal with her markets directly.'

'You can't!' Jathira said, aghast. 'She would forbid it.'

'Even if I had the king's permission?' It was a wild shot, but Jathira recoiled.

'Rashaunt wouldn't give it! He's financially dependent on the guilds. We pay for his fine armies and navies!'

Shaw grinned. 'Or I could pay for them, in exchange for some benefits. After all, we share the same enemy.'

'The guilds aren't his enemy!'

'I didn't mean the guilds,' Shaw said. 'I was speaking of the jinn.'

Suddenly Jathira shivered. 'Ah, the jinn,' she muttered. She sat back. 'I'll tell her. She won't like it; Satthyba isn't used to being thwarted.'

'I daresay. Maybe if she'd treated the boy better, he wouldn't have run away.' Shaw rose. 'How do you plan to return home?'

'Lord Amaj agreed to put me ashore in Port Naar. I can hire a fishing boat to sail me north.'

'Does Hizmyr have an airship service?' Shaw asked.

'A public service? That would be too expensive,' Jathira said. 'The king's father bought a few airships in Qoor, second hand, but there are none for commercial use.'

'Yeah, they're expensive,' Shaw said, but as she went in search of Tymon, her mind was dancing on the table in joy.

As she joined the healer, Shaw paused to calm her racing heart. *I'd give a thousand libers for a portal to Hizmyr right now!* she thought. 'Tymon, would you check if *Drakon* is still in that Hizmyr place?'

'It's called Myrlia, the capital,' the healer said. 'They're still there.'

'If you have a moment, I got an urgent message for Ricco.'

Ricco was the purser she'd hired to take her place aboard the flagship. He was a small, happy youngster with a keen intelligence and a nose for trade.

After a screamingly long few minutes, Tymon nodded. 'Ricco is standing by.'

'Tell him to start earning the salary I pay him. He's to go triple quick to Abia and request her to take him to the king, or as high as they can manage. Tell them I want a WyDir concession for the whole of Hizmyr, exclusively, independent of the guilds. Ask them what it would cost me.'

As she spoke, Tymon's face lost a little of his studied pose. 'Ricco is looking for his heart, he says; it jumped out of his mouth when he understood your demand. All right, he caught it under a chair. The crown prince is pretty chummy these days, he said. Would that be high enough?'

'I'll leave it to him,' Shaw said. 'As long as he produces that concession.'

'He's already running,' Tymon said. 'Probably calculating the size of his bonus.' He stared at her, for the moment free of his studied pomposity. 'A concession for the whole of Hizmyr? A monopoly? That would be big.'

'It is. Very big. If the maps don't lie, Hizmyr is larger than Kell, Vanhaar and Unwaar together.'

Shaw sat down with a bump. 'Darn,' she said. 'Another ball in the air.'

Unasked-for, Tymon started massaging her shoulders. 'You show amazing depths, so I would say you can do it.'

Shaw groaned as the fatigue drained from her. 'What a madhouse,' she said. 'So many things happening at the same time.'

*'Fight times,'* a voice in her head said. *'Times of ends and beginnings. You do right; grabbing every ball fate throws at you.'*

'Who are you?' Shaw said, looking around.

*'Look high, high; scorched wyrmling I am. Haai-Bo, boomed from his cage, flying free again.'*

A small shape came spiraling, to land in Shaw's lap. It was a red-and-golden wyrmling, about the size of an ax. Here and there, his skin showed blackened patches.

'A wyrmling,' Tymon said. 'You are hurt; do you require healing?'

'No need, hurt is drawing away,' the wyrmling said. 'Caught me by surprise, you did. Snoozing in my cage of silver, your beautiful explosion threw me up, up, away into the dark night. Wyrmling skins are strong, so I did not shatter like the cage. I flew a big way and rested on top of the water tower. I watched, did not understand, first. Now I do, a little.'

'You're the grumpy snake that little girl mentioned?' Shaw said. 'She was worried about you.'

'No snake! Grumpy I was, for the food she offered was pirate-poisoned and I would not eat. Tell her no worry, Haai-Bo is safe.'

'You are Haai-Bo? But where do you come from?' Shaw looked closely at the creature. 'You're different from Lothi-Mo; she is all flashing colors.'

'Sparkling, many-colored she is?' Haai-Bo exclaimed. 'Then it was no dream; a princess came verily? I did sense something, but too far away for my small powers. Oh happy day! Would you... Would you please let me into your mind, so I might learn what happened? I will be so, so discrete.'

'Sure,' Shaw said, without knowing why. 'Go right ahead, but don't tattle.'

'I promise! Haai-Bo serious advisor, he no tattler. Yes... I see... How beautiful she is! And him at her side... Jinnbane! Memories of old.' He lifted his long head and looked at Shaw. 'Thank you. Now you will ask me... Who is Haai-Bo? So I will tell you. I was first-born to a sept across the sea, in jinn-land! Bad men caught me and sent me here as a present to a jinni prince. Then you came and blew up the bad ship, with little me inside. Hah! Haai-Bo is free and he will advise you now. For you are a world shaker, as is Jinnbane. Not, perhaps, quite as violently, but just as enduring. The soft power of words and libers are no less dangerous than the might of swords and steel.'

'True,' Shaw said. 'But a world shaker?'

The wyrmling chuckled. 'You will find you did when you're done, Shaw-girl. Enough, others will claim your attention. I will return to that tower. You can reach my mind even without magic.' The little creature flapped his wings and shot away.

'Now you have a wyrmling.' Tymon shook his head. 'These are strange times.' He hesitated. 'I had a glance at the book that big guy Uthur keeps hidden. No, I cannot open it. The book is locked by priestly spells, sealed by a name: Zenyunthalata.'

'Who's he?' Shaw asked.

'The vanished God of the Lands, one-time patron of Nanstalgarod.'

From the inn Amaj's voice yelled, 'Jem!'

The translucent form of Nanstalgarod's princess ran out, followed by Amaj.

'Jem!' he cried. 'Wait! Jem!'

She stopped abruptly and turned to him. 'Amaj?' She sounded shocked. 'Why are you crying?'

'Darn!' he said wildly. 'I thought you were gone! That you were dead.'

'What?' she said, staring at him. 'I can't die... I'm sorry; that last song used up my last energy. I had to sleep, I couldn't even speak anymore. I thought you'd understand.'

'When I saw your bottle, I wanted to kill myself,' Amaj said simply. 'I can't go on without you, girl.'

'You're not going to, silly. I won't abandon you; not ever!' Jem said fiercely. 'Never think that, you hear!'

He nodded. 'Then all is fine again.' He smiled at Tymon. 'You were right; I shouldn't have panicked.'

Jem's hands seemed to touch his shoulders. 'You shouldn't,' she agreed. 'Never panic again, my love.' Then she turned to Tymon. 'What did you say just now?'

The healer told her of the book.

'Sealed by Zenyunthalata,' she said. 'That would mean... I must see this book.'

'Uthur,' Tymon said. 'He has the key to its chest.'

They found Uthur at the farm. 'The book again?' he said. 'Come to the mill.'

The chest was hidden underneath the lower millstone, covered in dust and chaff.

'It doesn't get out much,' Uthur said apologetically. 'We can't do a thing with it.'

He opened the chest and took out a folio the size of his underarm, and a full hand-and-a-half thick. It had a brown leather cover, with unreadable green letters, and emitted a vague light.

'*The Tale of the Followers*,' Jem read aloud. 'Its spell is bound to Zenyunthalata's blessed. None of you were blessed?'

Uthur shook his head. 'We were too young. At eighteen we would have been initiated.'

Jem stared at the book. Then she swallowed. 'I've been brought up to keep this a secret; it would have made my position at court impossible. It won't make any difference now, of course.' Her hands moved over the large book as if they were independent, and under their touch the light went from the book. 'You can open it.'

Uthur closed his mouth. 'You are a blessed Follower of Zenyunthalata? But how? Who are you?'

'I am Jemyanyailatha, granddaughter and heir of Wrachazd King of Nanstalgarod,' Jem said. 'My mother had me blessed in secret, to protect me from my grandfather's wickedness. I suppose our god did protect me, but I'm not impressed by a deity who let his whole people be murdered.'

'We're not that religious, either,' Uthur said. 'I mean, he wasn't here when those pirates killed our parents.'

'That's what I mean,' Jem said.

Uthur opened the book. *This is the Tale of the Zenyunis, the Blessed Followers of Zenyunthalata, God of the Lands, who led them out of the Mad King's clutches into the isle of Yavam,'* he read. *'Protected by their god against Vile Wrachazd's curse, they survived and prospered in the holy name of Zenyunthalata.'*

'The Zenyunis,' Jem said. 'They were mendicant monks, always railing against the sins of Nanstalgarod's rulers. When the sands came, they disappeared. We assumed them dead and in my heart I grieved for them.' She made a curious gesture, half greeting, and half benediction. 'We are of one people, you and I, Master Uthur.' She sighed deeply. 'The Mad King. That's Wrachazd, my grandfather.'

'He's dead, isn't he?' Uthur said.

'Yes and now; he turned himself into a lich, an undead horror,' Jem said. 'The pirates and jinn are his minions.

Shaw and her crowd, the wyrmcaller and all of us fight them.'

'He is an undead?' Uthur said. 'What a terrible thought.'

'Yet to me, this is a moment of joy,' Jem said. 'I believed I was the only one left of my people. Now I found you and yours, and that gives me hope. Perhaps, one day, we can restore Nanstalgarod to what it was before my grandfather's madness.' She turned and looked at Shaw. 'I must reclaim my country. I didn't care before, but now there are more of us, I cannot let my lands be plundered by strangers.'

'Do you want to be queen?' Shaw said.

'I don't know!' Jem said. 'Amaj and I have talked of this before. I'd be perfectly happy being his keep lady; I don't need to rule Nanstalgarod. But I hate what it became; I hate it being a useless desert, picked empty by Wastrels and Reclaimers.' She slammed her fists into an invisible surface. 'I want to see the corn grow outside Atnortod; I want to walk in the grass along the Port Naar river and watch the red storks hunting fish. Darn, I want my home back, and I'm stuck in this cursed bottle.'

'The Weal doesn't want Nanstalgarod,' Shaw said. 'I'm sure if you offered to buy Port Naar and exploit it yourself, they would hand over the reins and be pleased. Naudin said once his navy dad found the place a drain on his budget.' She grinned. 'You could give the reclaimers a royal concession to do what they already do; on the condition they share the magic with Eskandar and the gold with us.'

'The gold?' Jem said. 'What do you want with that?'

'You will want it,' Shaw said. 'If you're thinking of rebuilding, you will need money. With that money you can hire us. We'd start building up Port Naar. Perhaps some of Uthur's guys would be interested in helping, if we'd pay them?'

'I must think,' Jem said, anguished.

'There is no hurry,' Shaw said. 'We need to discuss this with Eskandar first.'

# CHAPTER 22 – ROYAL JUSTICE

At daybreak, Shaw walked from the inn and stared around the island. There wasn't anything left for her to do here. She had claimed the island for the Peaks and PTC, and two flagstaffs flew both the wyrmling flag and the company banner. Oychak had installed a portal in the armory, and brought a hedgemage to operate it and act as island communicator.

Jathira had left for Port Naar and home. *Marigold* and the *Killarn Ranni* had sailed, taking with them the dead pirates, every one prepared for burial in sailcloth found in the armory. Kennan and Yens had ported back to their posts and Emmett had gone back to his newspaper, battered but jubilant. Wanei was apathetic, wrestling with the loss of his brother, his ship and his honor. He had stopped eating, and Shaw had sent him to Smalkand and Tymon's good services. The Hizmyran kids had gone with him, and so had the pirate boy she'd rescued. He was still out; a coma, Tymon called it, caused by all the water he'd swallowed.

Tamyas and his new crew had followed them, to sail the *Kokkacir* to Seatome.

Shaw had done what she could, and now she, too, wanted to go home and Nate.

*'Haai-Bo, I'm leaving.'*

*'Wait for me-e!'* the wyrmling cried.

Shaw turned to Uthur, now the Yavam stationmaster. 'Good luck,' she said as they shook hands. 'I'll get to work on everything you need.'

'Thanks,' the big guy said. 'We'll do our darnedest to repay what you did for us.'

The wyrmling braked with a flutter of wings. 'Going?'

'Yes; ready to see the world?' Shaw said to Haai-Bo.

Haai-Bo made a crowing sound. 'Bring it on, girl.'

Shaw nodded to the interested hedgemage. 'To Seatome.'

'This is Old Wharf,' Shaw said. 'It... Nate!' She forgot the wyrmling as her partner came running down the stairs.

'You're back!' he said breathlessly. Then he stopped in his tracks and stared at her, arms outstretched. 'A wyrmling? Where in the Name of All the Divines did you find that one?'

'Explode me, you did,' Haai-Bo said. Then he lifted his head. 'I smell... I smell... food? Whooo! Let's go say hi to the nice food-boy.' He jumped in the air and disappeared to the cafeteria.

'That one knows his priorities,' Nate said, finally finishing his embrace. 'He wasn't on the island, was he?'

'In a cage on the frigate,' Shaw said. 'Luckily he's a tough little fellow.'

'We did blow him up then? Poor chap! And he still wants to come with you?' Nate grinned. 'He's brave.'

They met Ruth on the stairs, hurrying to greet her. 'I am glad to see you,' she said. 'I find running a growing business quite...'

'Exciting? Confusing?' Nate guessed.

'Terrifying,' Ruth said.

'I know,' Shaw said. 'Did anything happen?'

'Nothing tremendous,' she said. 'It's just that so much is coming at you. I've prepared notes.'

With a sigh, Shaw dropped in the chair behind her desk. 'I've missed this,' she said, looking around at the paintings on the wall, the tall standing timepiece in the corner and the beckoning stacks of reports filling the in-basket.

'Nice place you have,' Haai-Bo said as he flew in, chewing mightily. 'No mice, that's a pity.'

Ruth goggled at the sight of the wyrmling. 'My!' she said breathlessly. 'You're gorgeous.'

'Naturally,' Haai-Bo said complacently. 'I'm a wyrmling of high degree; advisor to dukes and merchant princes.'

'You're not shy either, are you?' Nate said.

'No, my high state is part of my strength,' Haai-Bo said. 'I must overawe with the excellence of my bearing, blind with my beauty and silence with my wit.'

'Ah,' Nate said. 'I will never match that.'

'You will not, for you are no four-fingered wyrm. But don't despair; you too have your place in the scheme of things.'

'Like gnats and lice and such,' Nate murmured.

'Precisely,' Haai-Bo said stately. 'And now I will take a nap.'

He winged out and disappeared into the cafeteria.

'Wants to stay near the food stores, I suppose,' Nate said. Shaw grunted. 'We'll find out what he can do.' She studied the reports in silence.

'We're making a profit,' she said finally. 'That's good.' Then she looked up and found Nate staring at her.

He grinned at her surprised glance. 'Have you done anything interesting while I was gone?' he asked nonchalantly.

Shaw felt her cheeks grow hot. 'Nothing much,' she said, as careless as she could. 'Jathira wasn't happy with my enlisting her guildmistress's son, I claimed Yavam for the PTC, and Jem discovered the local kids' ancestors were refugees from Nanstalgarod.'

'That's all?' Nate said. 'Nothing much, you call that. Tell us more.'

So Shaw settled in her chair and told them.

'Jem wants her country back?' Ruth said slowly, when she was done. 'I don't think the Weal will mind to sell her Port Naar, it's been a drain on Yarwan's budget for ages. The reclaimer dig sites however... Saul will never give those up.'

'He won't have to,' Shaw said. 'Jem would give him concessions for each dig – as long as he shares the finds with us. But that's for later, I want to discuss this with Eskandar first.' She looked at Nate. 'How's Amsalon?'

'Sleeping a lot, eating a lot, cursing even more,' Nate said. 'He's got a whole heap of anger built up, that guy.'

'Amsalon needs something to do,' Ruth said. 'He dreams of going back and taking an ax to that guild system they have.'

Shaw thought of Ricco and the possibility of getting an airship monopoly. 'Perhaps he'll get his wish,' she said. 'Did anything happen here?'

'I engaged a banker,' Ruth said. 'It's not part of my job, but I knew you'd want him. Besides, when you put up an advertisement, there should be someone to interview the candidates.'

'You're right,' Shaw said. 'I'm glad you did it; I wouldn't have known what questions to ask,'

Ruth grinned. 'I did that, at least. He's one of the Wainschilts of the Weal Bank; a nephew, and bored to tears in that mausoleum of theirs. He's still young, in his mid-twenties; a sporting-mad mountaineer, boatman, swordsman – he nearly begged for the job, so I signed him on and sent him to Smalkand. Healer Tymon gave him an in-depth mind search and he came up safe. Roza was wildly enthusiastic and last I heard they were happily counting the gold and opening accounts for everybody. The National Bank of the Pasandir Peaks for all your money.' She grinned. 'He wrote a business plan. Offices in Seatome and Dvarghish, for starters. Locations, personnel, the lot, everything very modern. Not for him the dusty plush of the Weal Bank; everything sleek, fast and to the point. Here it is.' She shoved a stack of paper across the desk.

Shaw picked up the neatly written sheets. 'Sounds brilliant,' she said. She opened the stapled plan, but she couldn't concentrate.

Something else was tugging at her mind and for a moment she sat staring at her hands, deep in thought.

'What are you thinking of?' Nate asked. 'The bank?'

'Stupid, but no; Kennan's guys. They looked so dispirited when they went back to Dvarghish, as if all their wins, all the compliments and applause counted for nothing.' She slapped the table. 'I must do something about that first. Ruth, could you get me to meet Queen Maud?'

'Of course,' Ruth said. 'She's not that difficult to see. Why?'

Shaw told her of Kennan and his guys, and Ruth's face clouded over.

'She'll want to know that,' she said. 'It's precisely one of those things I'm here for. I'll ask her.' Ruth sat back and closed her eyes.

Shaw watched her, studying the almost artificial symmetry of her face and the paleness of her gray skin, so much like her father Basil.

Ruth stirred. 'She wants to see them.'

Shaw blinked. 'When?'

Ruth smiled. 'Now.'

'What is she planning?' Shaw asked, suddenly suspicious.

'She didn't say, but knowing Aunt Maud she'll want to hear their stories.'

'And then?'

'She'll go and kick some butts, I suppose.'

'As long as she doesn't hurt my guys, for then I'll kick her,' Shaw said savagely.

'She won't. Let's go. Apologies, Nate; only Shaw and me.'

Shaw pushed the bank plan his way. 'You read it; give me your opinion.'

Nate chuckled. 'For what it's worth. I know something of markets and prices, but banks? You go, but don't buy the palace or anything like that.'

'If I can get a good price?' Shaw waved and walked to the stairs.

'Going out?' Haai-Bo cried from the cafeteria. 'Me coming.'

Ruth sighed but didn't say anything.

It was early morning in Port Dvarghish, and Kennan's warriors were about to go to bed after their night watch. They sat in the cafeteria dressed in kilts and their massive muscularity.

'Sorry, guys,' Shaw said as she dropped in a chair at their table. 'No sleep for the brave; I need you to come with me.'

'Where to?' Kennan asked tiredly. 'Not another fight, surely?'

'To Brannoe,' Shaw said, and she saw him stiffen. 'The queen wants a report from you guys.'

'More trouble!' he snarled.

'Not for you,' Shaw said. 'Queen Maud wants to hear how you guys were treated.'

'She'll never believe us,' Kennan said, his face contorted in a wild grimace.

'Get your fine uniforms, brave Kennan,' Haai-Bo said. 'Embrace your duty.'

Kennan wheeled around and shouted an order. His guys looked shocked, and one opened his mouth, but then they filed out to dress. Kennan, his lips a thin line, glanced at Shaw. 'Excuse me for a moment.' He turned and followed his mates.

Within ten minutes they were back, impeccably dressed.

Kennan gave Shaw a challenging look.

'You look fine,' she said. 'Let's go.'

Heads high, they marched to the portal where Ruth was waiting.

'To the Brannoe royal palace, Mr. Mott,' Shaw said.

'Give her my love,' the portal mage said, and off they went.

The public portal in the palace occupied a niche in a large, high corridor built of the traditional Kell redstone. Only here the walls were polished to a smoothness equaling marble. The corridor was an enormous structure, rising high over their heads like the crowns of giant trees, and full of people.

Kennan's boys were as glassily pale as a Kell could get. They followed Ruth and Shaw as if they were marching toward a hopeless battlefield.

*Ruth must be well known here,* Shaw thought. *Everyone is nodding and bowing to her.* None even spared a glance for the six boys or for her, and she glared through her monocle at a formally dressed courtier.

'Are we invisible?' she asked Ruth in a loud voice.

The other girl looked startled, then grinned. 'In court circles, yes. They know me because I am my fathers' daughter, but your fame hasn't reached this far.'

Shaw sniffed. 'Yet.'

The wyrmling came winging down. 'My dear Shaw,' he said. 'I shall sing your praise. Hold up your arm.' He draped his body across her shoulders and looked around regally.

Now people noticed, and she caught the whispered 'wyrmcaller's people', which was slightly better. Suddenly she laughed.

'I'm being silly,' she said.

'You should take a trumpeter,' Haai-Bo said. 'My memories remember the Arrangh riding down this hall on six elephants, with an escort of three hundred armed warriors.'

'I'm not a clan lord,' Shaw said. 'And certainly not the M'Arrangh boss. I'm just a foolish girl who shouldn't let her ventures go to her head. Besides, where would I get an elephant?'

'Hizmyr,' Haai-Bo said.

They had nearly reached the end of the corridor, and a robed servant came to meet them.

'Lady Ruth; welcome. The queen expects you.'

They followed him to a large room furnished more like a gym than an office.

Queen Maud watched them enter, standing before her desk, clad in simple leather armor. Her face was stern and she had her muscled arms crossed over her chest. Shaw had never met her before, but her likeness to Kellani was unmistakable.

'My dear Ruth,' the queen said.

'Aunt Maud.' The two kissed briefly. 'This is Ms. Shaw Harwans.'

'Our up and coming business tycoon,' the queen said. 'Well met, Shaw.' They shook hands, and then Maud looked at Haai-Bo. 'Welcome to you as well, golden one.'

'Haai-Bo, advisor to the rich and powerful,' the wyrmling said. 'Your servant, great Queen.'

She lifted an eyebrow. 'Archaic speech,' she said.

'I must yet adapt to the changed times,' Haai-Bo said. 'This one will learn modern diplomatese.'

Maud smiled. 'Listen well then,' she said. 'Ms. Harwans, are these the boys?'

'Yes, Ma'am,' Shaw said. 'Kennan and his squad serve us with great courage, fighting robbers and jinni regardless of danger to themselves. I feel they have been unjustly treated.'

'We'll see,' the queen said. 'Ruth, you must have many friends to greet. Shaw, you will stay, please.'

Ruth smiled and closed the door behind her as she left.

The queen turned to the boys. 'Kennan.'

'Kennan's Axed reporting, Ma'am Queen,' the boy said, in a clear, emotionless voice and he saluted while staring hard over the queen's shoulder. Shaw marveled at his self-control.

The queen walked around the motionless boys, inspecting each of them critically.

'At ease,' she said at last, and the six boys relaxed a hair's thickness.

'Tell me how you became what you are, Kennan,' the queen said. 'In your own words.'

Still looking over Maud's shoulder, the boy told of his mother and the cowardice he didn't know about. He told of her execution, of his own public dismissal, the humiliation, and the struggle to survive on his own. He spoke of his search to find the others, to build them into a unit and arrange for training. It was simply told, without bragging, and the queen listened impassively. When he was done, she nodded. 'Thank you.' She waved at the boy next to him. 'Your turn.'

For nearly an hour she stood and listened as each boy told the sorrow of his life, and so did Shaw.

When the last one fell silent, the queen brought her hands together. A very senior tigress entered, a grizzled, much-decorated general, scarred by many battles. Her lined face was bitter and her eyes hard as she saluted the queen.

'You heard?' Maud said.

'Yes,' the tigress said. 'It's a mortal disgrace.'

'So it is,' the queen agreed. 'My orders in this have been clear. You will personally arrest those responsible. I will do unto them what they did to these boys.'

'Ma'am,' the tigress general said, and hurried out.

'Kennan,' the queen said. 'Before you came in, I had read your files. Each of you had excellent progress reports, without even the smallest black marks to your names. Yet your Judgment of Dismissal papers spoke of disobedience, laziness and incompetence. Your own words confirmed my suspicion of something else. All officers involved in your dismissals have been vocal in their refusal to accept males in the army.' The queen slapped the files with a big hand. 'This was an attempt to rid the army of six male warriors, in flagrant disobedience of my orders. Rest assured I will not accept this.' She walked quickly around her desk and opened a drawer.

'Warriors,' she said as she came back. 'I am pleased to reinstate you as tiger cubs in the Kell army. Kennan, you have shown true leadership, discipline and integrity. You are hereby promoted to First.

'Now about your future. You may honorably continue on detached duty, serving the Pasandir Trading Co. This will count as active duty, not cub training. You will dye your hair, warriors.' She threw a bottle of some red fluid at Kennan, who caught it instinctively.

Maud chuckled. 'Well done.'

Kennan saluted glassy-eyed.

The queen lifted a big fist and inspected it as if it were a weapon. 'I'm glad you told me, Shaw. Be assured I will make a highly visible example of those traitors. I'll show them public shaming!' She relaxed and smiled. 'Now you must excuse me, paperwork won't wait.'

Shaw grinned. 'I know. Thank you for your time, Ma'am. It is a great relief to have this resolved.'

'For me as well,' the queen said grimly. 'I can do without rebels in the army.'

Outside, Ruth was waiting. 'All is settled?'

Kennan stared at her, his eyes wet, for once at a loss for words.

'They're fully vindicated,' Shaw said.

Ruth nodded. 'Well done, soldiers. We can go back then.'

She pulled out her handportal, and moments later they had returned to the warehouse.

'Well?' Shaw asked, watching her squad leader.

Kennan looked at her. His lips moved, but no words came out. Suddenly the tears won from his self-control and he cried. Shaw reached up to draw her arms around his massive chest and patted his back.

'Thank you,' he said and wiped his face. Then he stepped back and turned to his guys. 'Alright, you lot. Stop sniveling. Let's dye our hair like proper warriors.'

'Yes, First,' they said joyfully, and ran to their room.

'What's wrong with those guys?' the head girl said in amazement as Shaw and Ruth walked to the portal. 'They weren't crying, were they?'

'We've seen Queen Maud,' Shaw said. 'Kennan's warriors have been reinstated with the highest honor. Don't blame them for a bit of emotion.'

'That's beautiful!' the head girl said, brightening. 'We must have a party.'

# CHAPTER 23 – SABOTAGE

*There is someone knocking on my door.* Shaw sat up in bed and listened. Darn, there *was* someone knocking. Hurriedly she got up and looked outside.

'Sorry to wake you,' Squad leader Yens said. 'Young Wyon just brought a message; there's a fire at the WyDir hangars in Dvarghish. That was all he knew. I asked him to wait for you.'

'Curse it!' Shaw cried. 'Call Nate, will you. I must dress.'

A frantic five minutes later, Shaw found Wyon dozing on the stairs to the entresol. He jumped up when she prodded him.

'Sorry,' he said. 'Been working late last night. I'm awake now.'

'Tell me what you know,' Shaw said.

''s not much,' the boy said, yawning. 'A guard runner brought the message, told us to warn the management. "Fire in the hangars at the aerodrome; nobody hurt," she said. That's it.'

Shaw nodded. 'You go back to bed,' she said. 'Nate and I will port to the aerodrome.'

Nate hurried in, buttoning his tunic. 'Fire?'

'Come,' Shaw said. She turned to the young hedgemage on duty. 'You got the Port Dvarghish Aerodrome coordinates?'

'Got all aerodromes,' he said proudly. 'Been porting clerks all over the Weal, lately.'

'Good job,' Shaw said. 'Send us to Dvarghish.'

'Wait, wait, *wait*!' Haai-Bo's high voice cried. 'Me, I come!' He flashed down the stairs and clutched Shaw's tunic. '*Now* we can go.'

They arrived at the aerodrome gates. Across the field, the big WyDir Mines hangars were burning lustily, with three fire carts spouting ineffective beams of water into the flames.

'Whoosh!' Haai-Bo muttered. 'Big blaze that is.'

'It's a goner,' Nate said as they hurried over the field.

'Yeah,' Shaw said. Then she saw a woman in a WyDir uniform standing with a guardswoman, and she hurried over to them.

'Here is Ms. Harwans!' the guardswoman said.

The other woman turned around. 'It's gone,' she said dully. 'It's gone, ma'am.' She was too shocked to wonder at meeting her new boss here in the middle of the night.

'We'll rebuild,' Shaw said. 'How did it happen?'

'Arson,' the aerodrome guard said. She nodded at an elderly Vanhaari in a dark robe. 'He's our elementalist; he says someone used a firebomb.'

The Vanhaari joined them and nodded. 'Hot night,' he said. 'It's arson indeed. An incendiary device exploded inside the building and spread a flammable liquid, probably lamp oil. That was all it needed.'

'Why would someone destroy our hangars?' Shaw said.

'The bid, ma'am. I...' The second woman wrung her hands. 'Pardon, I'm the hangar manager Lines. They called me from home to... to...'

'I know,' Shaw said. 'It's a darned helpless feeling, seeing your place burn.' She shivered and was grateful for Nate's hands on her shoulder.

'What was that about a bid?' Nate asked.

'The bid for the bulk ore contracts, sir. The news came in today; we got the contract.' She cursed softly. 'After we put our competing offer up, two men came to see me. They didn't give their names, or anything, just a warning not to outbid Brynnyr Gunny if we wanted to stay in business. I kicked them out of my hangar.'

'Rightly so,' Shaw said. 'What kind of men were they? Kell?'

'No; though they weren't *small* men, they were pale of face, with high cheekbones and short, straight hair. Rough types.'

'Garthans?' Nate said, surprised.

'This Brynnyr Gunny business stinks,' Shaw said. She turned her back on the flames. 'We need new hangars; who handles that?'

'You'll find the aerodrome manager in the tower, ma'am,' the guard said. 'She's always called when there's an emergency.'

'Thanks.' Shaw gripped Nate's arm and strode away. 'Garthans! Don't say this is a pirate job?'

'Wait!' a voice called.

Shaw looked around and saw Yerene, the *Triumph* reporter, hurrying after them.

'*Disaster at the Aerodrome*,' the young woman said brightly. 'Our readers will love that. Can you tell me who did it?'

'Write that we're absolutely in the dark,' Shaw said. 'No idea who, how or why.'

'But the guard said...'

'We want to catch the villains, so let's soothe them with our ignorance.'

Yerene smiled. 'Sure. *No idea, the great lady said, looking desperately puzzled.* But who *do* you think did it? Who are those Brynnyr Gunny fellows?'

'We really don't know,' Shaw said. 'But we'll find out.'


At the tower, they found the aerodrome manager watching the fire from the high windows, while the controller on duty communicated with an approaching airship.

'...no, the fire is under control. It's only a few hangars; there is no danger. Yes, it is the WyDir Mines place. No, I haven't seen anyone from Salmon Street yet. You know the bigwigs, Captain; they're all asleep while their hangars burn.'

The controller was both mindspeaking, and vocalizing for her superior in the room.

Shaw coughed and the aerodrome manager wheeled around.

'You can't come in here,' she said. 'This tower is off limits.' Then she stiffened as she looked at Shaw. 'Ms. Harwans?'

'Yes, I came to see the damage for myself.'

'Wait, Captain,' the controller said, waving her hands. 'Someone from headquarters just came in. Hang on.'

'What's the matter?' Shaw said.

'The Seatome-to-Dvarghish skipper, ma'am,' the controller said. 'He just had a near-miss collision with another airship. An unauthorized airship. He's a tad upset.'

'Tell him I'll be over when he has moored,' Shaw said. She turned to the aerodrome manager. 'You're in charge here. How could anyone sabotage those hangars?'

'Sabotage?' the manager said, taken aback. 'I haven't had a report yet.'

'I spoke with the guard and the elementalist on the spot. Arson by way of a firebomb. I thought our aerodromes would have better security.' Shaw took a deep breath. 'I'll expect reports, but for now I need a new hangar immediately.'

'I need an authorization from Salmon Street, then I'll have the builders in right away,' the manager said. She was a woman of forty-odd years, with her hair cut in the military fashion, but her bearing lacked that special toughness that characterized the Kell warrioress.

*A bureaucrat,* Shaw thought. *How did she get this job?*
'Call those builders now. I authorize you to replace those hangars. In the meantime, their work must go on. What is the protocol?'

'Protocol?' the manager stared at her helplessly. 'There isn't any. This never has happened. I need orders from Salmon Street.'

'You are the one in charge here,' Shaw snapped. 'Improvise.'

'I... could ask the army for a couple of large tents,' the manager said. 'We must buy new gear, I'm afraid.'

'See to it,' Shaw said impatiently. 'Darnation! I shouldn't be telling you your job. Arrange things! Call the army and send someone to one of the other aerodromes for spare tools – use the portal at our Dvarghish warehouse for speed. We've got mining contracts to meet!' She whirled around to the controller. 'Now, what's that about an unauthorized airship?'

'I haven't seen any,' the controller said quickly, tapping her control desk with nervous fingers. 'Caught a whiff of a foreign mind some time ago; it *could* have been from an airship, but I'm not sure.' She glanced at Shaw. 'It was a muffled thought, very strange.'

'Was that long after the fire started?' Nate asked.

'An hour,' the controller said. 'I'd discovered the flames just before one o'clock and gave the alarm. Fire carts were here inside ten minutes, our manager a few minutes later. The airship captain called six minutes ago. It's now ten past two.'

'An hour,' Nate said. 'If there is a connection between the fire and that ship, why did it take an hour?'

'You mean there could be more mayhem?' the manager said.

'I don't know,' Nate said. 'I'm just wondering.'

'Darn,' the manager said. 'I'd better ask the Castle to have the whole aerodrome searched as well.'

Shaw stared at her in exasperation. 'Yes. Though by now I suppose it's too late.'

Haai-Bo stirred. 'No mice, no organization; 't is not a stout keep, this.' He didn't exactly snigger, but the aerodrome manager wilted in her boots.

'What do you know of Brynnyr Gunny?' Nate asked grimly.

The manager's face twitched. 'It's only a name to me, sir. They got the last bulk contract for the mines, but I never saw anyone representing them. They certainly haven't a station here.'

'Unless they're using unauthorized hangars too,' Shaw muttered.

She turned to the door. 'Should you find out something definite about the fire, this strange ship or the Gunny people, I'd appreciate it if you would inform me.'

The aerodrome manager nodded jerkily. 'I will.'

'I have cleared the incoming ship to moor at Tower Twelve, ma'am,' the controller called.

'Thank you both for your cooperation,' Shaw said and she managed no to slam the door as she left.

'What a scoop!' Yerene said as they crossed the aerodrome field. 'Unauthorized landings? Our readers will want to know how security can be this lax, that strangers can land and walk around our aerodrome setting fire to buildings and nobody does anything. Where is the army? Where are the search parties? The big outcry? Ooh, our readers will love that!'

'I don't,' Shaw said bitterly. 'That's not the publicity I'm aiming for.'

They managed to arrive at Tower Twelve in time to see the airship come alongside. It was a large, gleaming vessel, with the WyDir emblem blazing on her sides. An airman jumped out and fastened the mooring lines to the tower. When he had secured the ship, the captain appeared. He was a dignified older Vanhaari in an expensive uniform.

He saluted and shook hands with each passenger as they stepped onto the mooring platform.

Shaw and Nate waited at the foot of the stairs, watching the passengers pass. One small girl gave a shout and pointed. 'Look, Mom, that girl has a snake!'

'Snake?' Haai-Bo said. 'I am a wyrm, dear girl! A very highborn wyrm.'

'A talking snake!' the girl said. 'Would it like a peanut?'

'He would,' Haai-Bo said, but the child's mother only gave them a preoccupied glance and walked on.

'Alas,' Haai-Bo sighed. 'A peanut is such a delicate treat.'

'Admit it, you're simply greedy,' Shaw said.

He flapped his wings. 'Growing, dear; I am growing. It is vulgar, I admit it, but I require more food than is seemly.'

When the last passenger had gone, Shaw hurried up the ladder to the captain's salute.

'Ms. Harwans!' he said. 'Salmon Street informed us of the change in ownership. What a pleasure meeting you and Mr. Nate, and...'

'Yerene is a journalist of the *Trumpet*. She's much interested in our activities. How was your flight?'

'Uneventful, until we arrived here. The journey from Seatome to Dvarghish is beloved by our passengers for its easy luxury.'

'Peanuts,' Haai-Bo said. 'I am sure there are some left.'

The captain blinked. 'A wyrm? Those are creatures we try to avoid.'

'Wisely so,' Haai-Bo said. 'Our revered elders are no longer responsible for their actions. I, on the other hand, am fully by my senses. And hungry.'

The captain smiled. 'Our steward will attend to your needs.' He bowed. 'Allow me to show you round the ship, ma'am.'

The airship was a floating palace of rosewood paneling and brass fittings, white tablecloths and comfortable seats. Curtained windows gave a clear view of the aerodrome and the soft lighting created a pleasant mood. A few bedrooms with heavy covers, a well-equipped kitchen and even a small library made it look like a first class hotel.'

'How long does a journey take?' Nate asked.

'Six hours,' the captain said. 'This is a luxury flight, so we never go over a hundred miles per hour. We serve a tea buffet, a six-course supper and drinks. People often fly with us just to relax and to be away from everyday's hurry for a few hours.' He smiled. 'For passengers with a tighter schedule we have an alternate fast flight. They cover the same distance in three hours, with just a buffet and discrete workspaces. We offer secretarial services and a certified communications mage as well. Both flights are quite popular.'

'You have newspapers?' Shaw said.

'We offer the *Dvarghish Legends*,' the captain said.

'Ah, but we advise the new *Weal Trumpet* and for those with Vanhaari interests, the *Gazette*.' She grinned. 'Of course, we part-own both.' Then she became serious. 'About that near-miss you had.'

'Yes,' the captain said. 'Let us go to the bridge.'

Up front they met the co-pilot, a younger man with a thin smile, and the handler, busily checking his gas and air bags.

'The near-collision,' the co-pilot said. 'I had the wheel, as the captain was speaking with Control. All was quiet. We had seen the fire and wondered what had happened, but apart from that the night was quiet as always. Until a dark shape rose up right before us. I sent our nose down and prayed, and we felt the turbulence of the stranger's passing drumming against our outer skin. We were so low we could almost touch the goats. Then it was gone and everything was as before. I brought us back to our proper height, and circled round for a second approach. Nothing more happened, and we moored as always.'

'I commend you for your alertness,' Shaw said. 'Did you notice anything about that airship?'

The co-pilot shrugged. 'I wasn't watching too closely,' he said. 'It was big; a lot bigger than us.'

'It was a WTB ship,' the handler said suddenly. 'I shouldn't have looked, but your wriggling kicked me out of my concentration.'

'What's WTB?' Shaw asked.

'The Weal Transport Board,' the captain said. 'Are you sure you saw that? They're government, after all.'

'Positive, sir,' the handler said.

'Thank you,' Shaw said. She remembered the cargo agent telling her that Brynnyr Gunny Co. used a WTB freighter for its ore contracts. 'Really helpful. How did the passengers take the sudden maneuver?'

'I explained it had been a flock of geese,' the captain said. 'Only one passenger lost his balance, but there were no casualties. I described the enormous size of the birds and the damage they would have caused, and everyone was properly understanding.'

Shaw smiled grimly. 'They don't know half. Thank you, gentlemen; you run a fine ship. When will you be sailing back, Captain?'

'One o'clock tomorrow, ma'am. We'll retire to the aerodrome hotel for our eight hours' sleep, while the ground staff cleans up the ship.'

'Then I won't keep you,' Shaw said.


'What was the *point* of that fire?' Shaw said as they walked back to the burning hangar.

'To scare us, maybe,' Nate said. 'No, they should've done that before we got the contract.'

'Guard your holdings,' Haai-Bo said suddenly. 'How safe is this contract?'

'Eh? What do you mean?' Shaw said, her thoughts somewhere else.

'The begrudged bid. What would break the contract? Something fragile we are not looking at?'

'Darn,' Shaw said. 'The bulk ship.' She broke into a run.

At the scene of the fire, the hanger manager sat watching the fire burn lower.

'That ship we need for the contract,' Shaw said abruptly. 'Where is it stationed?'

'The bulk ship? That's no secret; it's at the Brannoe Airship Yard,' the woman said. Suddenly she stiffened. 'You don't say...'

'Nate, get a steamcart,' Shaw said urgently. 'Without that ship our contract is worthless, isn't it?'

The hangar manager nodded. 'We'd never get a replacement in time.'

'We'll go to Brannoe. I've arranged things with the aerodrome manager; she will handle rebuilding the hangars. You had better call on her and discuss what must be done.'

As the woman hurried away, a steamcart came roaring. Shaw jumped in the back. 'To the Peaks Pier warehouse.'

'Me too,' Yerene said. 'The *Trumpet* is on the scent.'


'The WyDir Yard is straight ahead,' the guard at the Brannoe Aerodrome gate said. 'The guard commander is doing her rounds. Why?'

'I need her,' Shaw said. 'We just came from Dvarghish; some foul criminal burned down the Line hangars. I want to make sure our ship here is secure. Kindly get hold of your commander and ask her to go to the yard. Then wake up whoever is in charge there and tell them I want to see them right now.'

'And who might you be?' the guard said. 'That you expect us all jumping?'

'M'dear Shaw,' Haai-Bo said. 'You really need to have your face known. Put it on a coin, or something, that people get to recognize you. Behold the High Merchant Shaw Harwans, Grand Proprietor of the Pasandir Trading Company and of WyDir and countless other important ventures. Your boss.'

The guard stared. 'Ah, *now* I remember. There was an announcement of your taking over WyDir. Apologies, ma'am, I hadn't expected you here in the middle of the night. Darn, you're not this lady I read about in the *Trumpet*, are you? The one who saved those guys at that Yavam place?'

'Guessed in one,' Shaw said. 'Now, shall we get cracking?'

'Sure,' the guard said, and saluted. 'Great story that was, ma'am.'

She shouted and two uniformed girls came running. 'Number one will find the commander. Ask her to go to the WyDir Yard right away. Number two, run into the city and get the yard manager. Tell her to come over on the double; boss alarm.'

Both girls took off at a fast trot.

'Thank you,' Shaw said. 'We'll be at the yard.'

'You think they'll be coming here?' Nate asked as they walked away. 'Tonight?'

'If they're determined to stop us fulfilling that contract, what else would they do? It's the logical step. And why not tonight? It's at most an hour and a half by air from Dvarghish to Brannoe.'

Nate pulled out his bludgeon. 'Are you armed?'

'My knives. And this.' Shaw took a long bronze pistol from her coat pocket. 'Smalkand issue. I had Hella show me how it works. Don't think I'll hit an ox at five paces. Still, it might frighten someone.'

'Oehh,' Haai-Bo said. 'How deliciously dangerous! Me, I'll bite. It is below me, but perhaps my teeth can convince them to drop dead.'

They walked round the yard hangar in silence, listening.

Nothing, only the scratch, scratch of Yerene's pen as she wrote.

*Would they really come right now?* Shaw thought. *It sounds so logical, but mind-drugged jinni slaves aren't good at thinking.*

'*Assassin!*' Haai-Bo launched himself into the air and flew away round the building. '*Creepy-guy in the bushes; bad mischief-maker! Attack!*'

'Darnation! He's already here!' Shaw whispered, and ran into the dark, clutching her pistol. There she saw a big man waving an arm at Haai-Bo.

'Stop right there!' she cried.

Something flashed past her ear and instinctively she took a spurt, pulling the trigger as she ran. The man reared up and dropped backwards to the ground. Behind her was the sound of breaking glass, followed by a wild explosion of light and heat.

'Nate!' she screamed as she turned around. He had been right behind her! A pool of liquid burned fiercely and the wall behind it turned black, but there was no trace of Nate, or Yerene.

Again she shouted and then she heard him answer. She ran back to the corner and found him sitting down, clutching his ankle. To the side, Yerene was busily writing.

'Darn,' Nate said through his teeth. 'I tripped.'

Shaw sat down beside him and burst into tears.

'Now,' Nate said, patting her shoulder. 'It's but an ankle, even if it hurts. Did I hear a shot?'

'I thought you were dead,' she said and hiccupped. 'Come and look.'

She jumped up and helped him limp around the corner. When he saw the dying flames and the dead man with Haai-Bo hovering over him, he stiffened. 'What happened?'

'He threw his bomb thing at me,' she said, gripping his arm hard. 'It was a lot of fire, some burning fluid, and if you had been behind me...' She shuddered.

'So you shot him.'

'Less than five paces; I didn't miss,' she said in a strangled voice.

'Here now, what's all this?' an official voice barked. A squad of big shapes came running, swords drawn.

'Another sabotage attempt!' Shaw snapped. 'In Dvarghish they burned our hangar. We guessed our freight ship was next, so we ported here. While we were waiting for you, that character attacked us, so I shot him.'

'There should be an illegal airship moored around here,' Nate added. 'It probably is a fake Weal Transport Board freighter. I strongly suggest you stop them from escaping.'

'You're Ms. Harwans?' the guard commander asked. She gave a few curt orders, and four of her girls ran off to search the aerodrome.

Nate limped to the dead man. 'Another Garthan,' he said.

'What's wrong with your ankle?' one of the remaining guards said.

'Twisted,' Nate said.

'Sit down; I'll give it a dose of Gathea's mercy.' The guard grabbed the ankle and before Nate had time to cry out, Shaw saw his face relax.

'That's fast,' he said.

The guard grinned. 'I wasn't suited for wisewoman, but the goddess still loves me.'

Then a steamcart came roaring, and dumped two people in WyDir tunics.

'What the heck's going on?' the biggest of the two said in a heavy bass voice. She was a massive woman, built like a professional wrestler, with the battered face to match.

'You're the yard manager?' Shaw said coolly. 'Then I requested your presence.'

'Ms. Harwans!' the woman said, uncomprehending. 'At this hour? What's wrong?'

'Someone tried to sabotage the yard. They're after the freighter. I want you to light up the whole place and get a bunch of soldiers. This place is to be watched day and night.'

A guard came back. 'WTB freighter at tower eight,' she reported.

'Call the others and wait out of their sight,' the commander said. 'I'll be with you in a moment.' She turned to the yard manager. 'You can get guards at the palace barracks. Tell them I want them here, and you'll pay for them. Now we'll have a look at that funny ship.'

'We'll be coming,' Shaw said. 'Nate? Can you walk?'

He grinned at the healer guard. 'Never better.'

Off they went; the guards in that miles-devouring run of the Kell soldier and Yerene in their wake, gripping her notebook like a sword. Shaw wasn't a Kell, nor particularly athletic and her silly eye didn't help, but she'd be darned if she'd drop behind, so she followed them with Nate beside her.

'Whooo!' Haai-Bo cried, flying overhead. 'See us go to war!'

'Curse the villains,' the guard commander muttered as they came near tower eight and found the black shape of the darkened airship overhead. 'They're not cleared to be there.'

'I sense people inside, Commander,' the healer guard said. 'But their minds are very faint; I doubt Control would have caught them when they approached the aerodrome.'

They ran up the wooden stairs and into the airship's corridor without a second's hesitation.

'You're under arrest!' the commander cried. Several big men came running, brandishing long staves.

'To the bridge,' Shaw said to Nate. 'We don't want them to take off.'

On the bridge, a wide compartment lined with windows, a pockmarked Garthan at a control panel was desperately trying to disengage the mooring line from the inside.

'Curse you!' he cried as they ran in. 'I'll blow her first!'

His hand went to a big red handle, but then Nate's bludgeon caught him in the neck. Shaw heard the bones break as the man slumped to the floor.

The commander ran in. 'Ah, you're already here. Fine thinking, ma'am. No idea who those fellows are, but up to no good, I'd say.'

'This is no WTB ship,' Shaw said. 'Those controls are marked in a foreign language. I'd bet you she's been stolen somewhere up north.'

'We captured us some live ones,' the commander said. 'They'll tell us all they know.'

*If they're not under a compulsion,* Shaw thought.

Then a big shadow appeared in the doorway and the commander froze.

'Well, Ms. Harwans, we meet again,' a voice said.

Shaw turned around. 'Queen Maud? It's the middle of the night.'

'Not really; it is close on five o'clock,' the queen said. 'My day has already begun.'

'You're the famous Purser Shaw?' A heavily built Vanhaari came forward, hands outstretched. 'I'm Jurgis, Kellani's father.' He shook hands with Nate and Yerene as well. 'Good to see you aren't afraid of action, Shaw. You even got a wyrmling?'

'Haai-Bo, advisor extraordinaire,' the wyrmling said. 'I do not recognize the uniform, but I'm sure you are worthy of my attention.'

'Mwah,' Lord Jurgis said, tongue-in-cheek. 'I'm only the queen's husband and the Spellstor's brother. Second-rate, as both of them.'

'Spellstor!' Haai-Bo waved his wings, eyes whirling. 'My memory is old, too old for modern times, but Spellstors are never second-rate. I know *them*.'

'That wyrmling is wise,' Jurgis said solemnly. 'Very wise.'

The queen made a fun-derogatory sound Shaw remembered from Kellani. Then she turned to the guard commander. 'At ease; don't mind us. I received a report of Ms. Harwans arriving here, crying "Danger!" and I was curious. Perhaps Shaw would care to enlighten me?'

'Sure,' Shaw said, and she told of the contract, of the mysterious Brynnyr Gunny Co. and the WTB, of the fire at Dvarghish Aerodrome and their rushing to Brannoe.

'I don't think it is the Weal Trading Board's duty to act as subcontractor for a private company,' Lord Jurgis said.

'So I thought,' Shaw said. 'But this is no WTB ship. It seems to me more like our *Pewbara*, which we captured from pirates, who had stolen it up north somewhere.'

'We will find out if WTB has any role in this,' Maud said grimly. 'Again I thank you for bringing matters to my attention.'

'Do we want this vessel?' Lord Jurgis muttered.

'Not me,' the queen said. 'I'm not in the shipping business. Perhaps Ms. Harwans could find a use for her?'

'I'm sure we can,' Shaw said. 'WyDir offers ore transport for half what Brynnyr Gunny asked. So you're making a good investment, Ma'am.'

The queen grinned. 'Done, then. We'll go home; Jurgis and I were walking the cats, and we don't want them to get impatient.'

'To be sure,' Jurgis said. 'We're running. Every morning, ten miles. She walks the cats. I could ride them, but walk? Never.' With a wave and a nod he followed the queen out.

The commander breathed out. 'She gave you the ship,' she said, and there was a hint of respect in her voice. 'The queen must think highly of you, ma'am.'

'It's the wyrmcaller connection,' Shaw said.

'My humans move in the highest circles,' Haai-Bo said. 'That is why I advise them.' He closed his eyes as Shaw stroked his neck.

'You're not purring, are you?' she said, surprised.

'Who? Me?' the wyrmling said. 'Certainly not! That would be beneath my dignity, ma'am. I'm merely, ah, vocalizing my breathing.'

'Sure,' Shaw said, smiling,

The guard commander shook her head. 'A strange creature.' She coughed and looked at Shaw. 'I will inform the people at the yard, ma'am. They'll send someone over to take charge of this vessel.'

# CHAPTER 24 – SURPRISE!

'A chart,' Nate said. 'For once, our enemies used a chart.' He had been prowling around the ship, checking cupboards and drawers. Now he stood bowed over the map table in the navigation room as Shaw joined him, still carrying Haai-Bo.

'What does it say?'

Nate shrugged. 'Good question. It has no points I can recognize, so we'll need a local to translate it.' He peered closely at the chart. 'Someone used it to set out a route, and then erased the details. They shouldn't have used a sharp pencil, for it left a visible trace.

Shaw felt a terrible weariness come over her. 'Silly of them,' she said drowsily.

'Very,' Nate said. 'Why don't you sit down for a moment?'

Shaw dropped into a chair and closed her eyes.

The bass voice of the yard manager woke her.

'Queen Maud *gave* us the ship?' The woman said it with the same sense of wonder the guard commander had shown earlier. 'That's too kind of her; we can certainly use a second bulk carrier!'

'She looks in good shape,' a male voice said. 'Only those controls are strange.'

Shaw forced herself to stand up and join them.

'You're a pilot?' she asked, blinking against the bridge lights.

The man was small for a Kell, and almost slender, but his voice carried the snap of command. 'I'm the skipper of the bulk carrier,' he said. 'Yard manager called me that some idiot had thought to sabotage my boat, so I came. Instead I find we now have two ships. Extremely well done, ma'am, if I may say so.'

'We were lucky,' Shaw said. 'You think you can sail her?'

'We need to trace the controls first, to find out what each of them does. That will take quite a while. But once we know what does what, we can sail her.'

Shaw smiled. 'If we translate the labels for you, would that make it easier?'

'It would!' the pilot said. 'What strange lingo is it?'

'Qoori,' Shaw said. 'I'm almost sure we have a translator on hand. Haai-Bo, can you tell us what those labels mean?'

'That's *not* my job,' the wyrmling said querulously. 'I will translate foreign treaties and other important documents. Not something menial like labels.'

'Lothi-Mo did,' Shaw said. 'She was pleased to help us.'

Haai-Bo sighed dramatically. 'Fine! If the princess did so, I suppose I can't do less. But it is *not* an advisor's task.'

Shaw swallowed a pithy retort. 'Thank you,' she said.

He snorted. 'Got a pencil?'


'That helped a lot,' the pilot said when he'd written down what each control did. 'They seem a lot less different from ours than I first feared. I will move her to the yard, so we can check her over. That WTB emblem...'

'Fake,' Shaw said. 'Please replace it with the WyDir logo.'

'One other question before we leave you to it,' Nate said. 'We found a map and we don't recognize a thing. Perhaps you can tell us?'

The pilot joined him at the map table. 'Oh yes, it's a standard chart of the local mines,' he said. 'I have one like it. Here's the central mine with the offices, and here are the several entrances we're to pick up the ore.'

Shaw tapped the map. 'Do all those penciled lines go to mine entrances?'

The pilot studied them. 'All but this one,' he said. 'If it's a mine, it is not one I know.'

'We'll find out,' Shaw said grimly. 'How do we get there?'

'By airship?' the pilot said.

'By broom,' Shaw said.

The pilot nodded and pointed at a small symbol on the map. 'See this point? It's a mountain peak almost straight east from here. It's called Cleft Tooth, because that's what it looks like; a giant tooth split by some godly ax. It's not far; about twenty-five miles from the aerodrome. Beyond that is empty land; all rock and maybe some wild goats.'

'Arrangh territory,' the yard manager rumbled. 'The black clan had several hide-outs there. It took Lord Jurgis and his broomriders five years to find them all.'

'A perfect place for a clandestine operation,' Nate said.

'So it appears,' Shaw said pensively. Then she smiled at the two Kells. 'We must be going. Send Salmon Street a report on this vessel's state, plus the additional cost of any repairs.' She thought of something and paused. 'Airship yard,' she said. 'You build new ships, don't you?'

'Yes,' the yard manager said. 'Though not of late; there is no demand for new vessels.'

'That will change before long,' Shaw said. 'How many airships can you build in a year?'

The woman grinned. 'Two. And that means going all out and having no major repairs to hold us up.' She hesitated. 'If you would restart the Seatome facility, we could make it four.'

'We are hoping to open up new territory,' Shaw said. 'That would mean we'd need a lot of airships in a hurry. I'd like you to prepare both for building and for erecting new yards. Nothing definite yet, but I want you to start running when you get the go-ahead.'

The yard manager clapped her hands together. 'That would be good news,' she said. 'I'll get on to it immediately.'

'We will return to the warehouse,' Shaw said, as Nate put the map away. The two of them left the ship, while Yerene hurried off to get her story ready for the *Trumpet*.

'And now?' Nate said as they walked away to the aerodrome gate.

Shaw cocked an eye at him. 'We'll get Kennan and our brooms, and take a look at that unidentified point on the chart. If there's anything funny going on, I want to know.'

'Go home, eat, nap; no? No.' Haai-Bo sighed. 'Tiring girl you are.'

By the time they were back at the Dvarghish warehouse, it was close on seven o'clock. Officially, Kennan's watch ended at eight, but the first workers were already in, and the new day was slowly starting.

'Are you guys fit enough for a bit of action?' Shaw asked.

'Of course,' Kennan said. 'Those night watches are dull, but hardly tiring. What did you have in mind?'

As Cook brought some much-needed cawah and sandwiches, Shaw told of their nocturnal doings.

When she was done, Kennan looked at her. 'Darn, your night was a lot more interesting than ours. And now you want to know what's at those places on the map?'

'Exactly,' Shaw said. 'Especially that one point the pilot didn't know. And as we're feeling generous; we won't keep all the fun for ourselves. It would mean a broomride into unknown territory.'

'I'll tell the guys to prepare,' Kennan said. 'Cloaks, arms, the lot.'

'Breakfast first,' Shaw said. 'At eight, we'll port to the aerodrome and take it from there.'

The flight from Brannoe Aerodrome to the east wasn't very enervating and after half an hour Shaw saw a curiously split mountain peak in the distance. She pointed and Nate nodded.

Below them, the landscape was of a desolateness that tore at the soul. Barren rocks without a sign of vegetation and the only animal life a flock of crows that followed them as if hoping the riders would all drop dead to provide them with a meal.

Then Kennan spurted past her and signaled Stop. Below them was a narrow valley with what looked like a trail leading up to an old mine shaft halfway the mountainside.

'Wait,' Kennan signaled, and he went down alone, to land close to the mine entrance.

It was a black hole framed by weathered beams, looking creepy in the pale morning light.

The squad leader waved his arm that all seemed safe, and Shaw hurried down.

'A deserted tunnel?' she said.

Kennan grinned. 'Then who'd light that burning torch I noticed inside?'

'Spooks,' Shaw said. She screwed her monocle in her eye and walked to the dark entrance. It was true; in the distance was the vague glow of a light.

*'No one close.'* Haai-Bo said. *'Thoughts after a while; bad thoughts; cannot tell how many.'*

Shaw walked inside and found herself in a corridor the size of an ox-cart, *a mining-cart*, she corrected herself. The floor was hard packed gravel and the walls were solid rock. That was all.

As they neared the torch, Haai-Bo stopped in mid-air, craning his lock neck left and right.

*'Captured thoughts,'* he said and launched himself into the shadows along the wall. Shaw hurried after him and found there was another corridor, ending in a circular hole at least forty feet across.

'There's a rope ladder,' Nate said, peering over her shoulder.

'What's that?' a voice said below their feet. 'I must be losing my mind. That couldn't have been a real wyrmling? Phantom of my imagination, help!'

'Who's down there?' Shaw called.

'Oh Gods, there is someone? Get me out of here! Please!'

*'Boy in hole,'* Haai-Bo said. *'Do not blow him up; he has no wyrm skin.'*

Without a word, Shaw unsheathed her broom.

'Cover me,' she said to the others, and went down into the dimness of what must have been an abandoned shaft or something. On the bottom were barely visible a heap of bedding, an old chair and a wild-eyed Vanhaari guy a few years her senior, with shiny chains rattling on his ankles. The whole place stank of human refuse and desperation.

'Well,' Shaw said, staring around. 'I heard of people sent to the mines as punishment, but this beats all.'

'I'm not one of those, curse it!' the boy shouted. 'It's bandits! Get me out, before they come back.'

*Darn,* Shaw thought. *'Haai-Bo, is he safe?'*

*'Safe he is. Honest mind, no evil thoughts. Hungry, scared, hopeful.'*

'Get up in front of me,' Shaw said curtly.

Clumsy in his eager weakness, the boy sat down and Shaw wrinkled her nose. He smelled like a corpse recovered from a ripe cesspool.

'Up,' she said, trying not to gag.

Back in the corridor, she landed. 'On your feet,' she said. 'Can someone see to his chains?'

She returned her broom to its sheath. 'Now, let's get civil. Who are you?'

The boy hugged himself, shivering. 'I'm Brynnyr Gunny.'

'What!' Nate said, and the tableau froze in astonishment.

'*You* are Brynnyr Gunny?' Shaw said blankly.

'Yes,' the boy said. 'Brynnyr Gunny, President and General Manager of Brynnyr Gunny Co, Dowsers. Call me B.G., they all do.'

'Dowsers?' Nate said.

'I am a geologer; I can sense deposits of iron, coal, crystals or sources of water in the earth. Or treasures. It was to be such a great venture. We were going to search the old places, and find their treasures. The magic treasures.'

'Like the reclaimers do,' Nate said.

He nodded violently. 'Exactly. But I'd keep them for myself, to study and learn.'

'You're a mage?' Shaw asked.

The boy snorted and waved his arms. 'A mage! I'm a warlock, girl. A warlock! I am the son of Altrynn Ryng-Gunny of Spellstor Center, who heads the powerful Department of Mana Studies.' Then he shrunk, and his face worked.

'A warlock,' he whispered. 'There were six of us when we left Spellstor all those weeks ago. Me, Esthel, who is a designer, Latharom the mover mage, healer witch Suzie, battlemage Oskar and Phynn the engineer. We found stuff, not very impressive, but it proved there were magic objects left in Vanhaar. Then somebody mentioned the old M'Arrangh hideout mines near Brannoe. That was a great suggestion! Either we could find Arrangh treasures, or hidden mineral deposits. We took an airship to Brannoe and rode our spelldrakes into the mountains.'

He beat his fists against the wall. 'We felt so safe, so secure! I mean, with all our magic, no bandit would stand a chance against us! What did we know? We had learned about bandits from our books, we'd never seen one until they'd woke us up in the middle of the night, with swords at our throats and little Suzy a hostage. What could we do?' Then they chained us with silver and took us to the mine we had been looking for.

'They laughed, saying how they would have their sport with us and then butcher us all. I warned them my father would come and destroy them – he wouldn't – and then one of them began about ransom. How much would my father pay to have me back? A thousand? More? Ten thousand, I said, knowing well he wouldn't pay a penny either. My father accepts me as long as I don't inconvenience him. At least the bandits didn't kill me. Instead they put me down that hole. I don't know if they ever contacted my father, but they seemed interested in my company.

'After a few days, they came to me with papers bearing my name, The Brynnyr Gunny Co. I wasn't supposed to read them; they only wanted my signature, but I picked up enough to know it was some kind of shipping contract. I signed everything they gave me, for as long as they thought they needed me, they'd keep me alive. They...'

He looked away. 'They killed my friends; boasted of it, how they screamed and...'

'Done,' Kennan said. 'Your chains are off, mate.'

The boy looked at him. 'Thanks!' He took a deep breath. 'My magic, my poor magic, it's dried up and withered.' Without warning he cried, silently, like a weeping statue.

'No need for tears,' Haai-Bo cackled. 'Mana is like bladder; it will refill and you'll piss again.' He flapped his wings. 'Oops, must be more subtle. Coarse days have gone; modern times I must learn.'

'Yeah, kings won't like such talk,' Shaw said. 'Now B.G., where are those bandits?'

'Further on is a series of rooms,' the boy said. 'They're all furnished.' He sighed. 'But no magic and no deposits; this mine is exhausted.'

Kennan coughed. 'Do you know how many bandits there are?'

The boy shrugged. 'When they caught us, there were twelve; all big men, coarse and white-faced.'

Kennan nodded at two of his guys. 'Go and count them. We'll be right behind you.'

The two slipped away without noise and after a few minutes, Kennan gestured to the others to follow.

Fifty yards on, the corridor made a sharp turn to the right, and sloped gently downward. Halfway, they ran into the two scouts.

'Ten men,' they said. 'And there was a large cage in a cave to the right. Whatever they keep inside, it moves about. It stank like an animal. Although...' He glanced at the smelly warlock, but didn't finish.

As they approached the caves, a voice yelled, and a beam of energy splashed the wall over and behind them.

'Curse it! A mage,' Kennan said.

Shaw dropped on her belly, with her long-barreled pistol in the hand, and crept to the first door.

'Careful,' a heavy male voice said. 'They're Kell soldiers. I'll thin them out somewhat first.'

Shaw glanced inside and spied a stocky Vanhaari wriggling his fingers. Closing her bad eye, she took aim and pulled the trigger. The shot reverberated through the caves and the mage arched backwards. His beam went up and raked the ceiling. A hail of stones and dust came down, blinding her for a moment. Then Kennan yelled, and his guys ran inside, swinging their swords.

'You all right?' Nate said, as he crouched beside her.

Shaw sneezed. 'Powdered.'

'I can see that,' Nate said. 'You got a face mask, girl.'

'No matter.' Shaw grimly drew her knives. 'Let's go and draw some blood.'

Together, they ran into the room. A tall Garthan turned to her, clutching an ax in both hands.

'You'll die!' he yelled, his eyes blood red. He lifted his ax, and then staggered as something hard smashed into his face, drawing blood. Shaw swung her knife and buried it under the bandit's breastbone. He gasped, and dying, managed a last blow. Nate caught it on his sword, and Shaw's second knife entered the bandit's neck. Blood spurted as he fell.

'Idiot!' Shaw said contemptuously. She turned around and there was B.G., balancing a stone in his hand. When he noticed her looking, he smiled wryly.

'Applied Ballistics. That's about all I'm fit for right now.'

'It was a timely throw,' Shaw said. 'Watch out!'

A bandit jumped the warlock, bearing the boy down to the ground. The bandit, his face twisted into a grimace, raised his arm to strike. Shaw grabbed his wrist and rammed her knife in the man's armpit. He bellowed and dropped his sword. B.G. still clutched his stone and the blow he gave the bandit ended any last vestige of fighting spirit.

Kennan came running. 'We got them all,' he said. 'What do we do with the live ones?'

'Put them down that nice hole. On the way back, we'll warn the aerodrome to pick them up.'

The squad leader saluted. Then he glanced at the warlock. 'I'd have a look in that cave to the right,' he said. 'I think those bandits lied to you.'

'What?' The boy's pale gray complexion turned dark, then splotchy as he hurried away.

'We better go with him,' Nate said. 'He doesn't look all that stable on his pins to me.'

They found him on his knees, gripping the bars of a large cage. 'You're not dead!' he said. 'They said you were dead! They said!'

'B.G.?' a girl said in a hoarse voice. 'They... you'd betrayed us. You were livin' in clover on the money you were making them.' She shook her head slowly. 'You're not looking very clovery.'

'I wouldn't betray you,' the boy cried. 'I didn't! They threw me into a hole in the ground, in chains! They lied to all of us.'

One of Kennan's guys came with a large key. 'We didn't have to swim for this one,' he said. 'Let's check if it's the right one.'

It was, and the cage door swung open with a loud clang. A large Vanhaari with a battered face crept outside first and clambered upright.

'Dang, dang, dang!' he muttered. Then he offered a shaking, very dirty paw. 'Blessed day, I am Oskar, who once believed he was a battlemage.'

Shaw's skin crawled as they shook hands. 'I'm Shaw, of the Pasandir Trading Co.'

'Dang,' Oskar said again as he stared at her. 'The wyrmcaller's guys.'

'Move, darn you! We all want out,' the girl said. She was even skinnier than Shaw, with a well-born dove gray skin under the filth. Her white hair had been crew cut, but was growing out unevenly, giving her a ragged scarecrow-look. She gripped the bars of the cage and pulled herself up before looking at Shaw. 'I'm Esthel of Andercast. I'm a warlock and I will *not* greet you on my knees,' she said past clenched teeth. Then she turned to the cage. 'Come on, Suzie, where's your pride, girl?'

'I... can't,' the second girl said. 'I'm so tired.'

'Make an effort,' the boy behind her said. 'I ain't got the energy to push you.'

'Come,' Shaw said, and she wrestled the contents of her stomach down as she leaned into the soiled cage. 'Give me your hands.' She gripped the girl's wrists, and unceremoniously dragged her outside. 'There you are.' Then she looked at the last two boys. 'And you, gentlemen? Will you manage alone?'

'Me? Yeah.' The next boy shook his long, matted hair out of his eyes. 'Guess I can still crawl around. Phynn, come on, man.'

One after another, the last two crept from the cage.

B.G. turned to Shaw. 'Thank you,' he said. 'I... No words to say it properly.'

'No need,' Shaw said. 'Now sit down while we do a quick search of the place.' She looked at Kennan and Nate. 'We want papers, maps, anything that tells us more about those guys.'

The old Arrangh living quarters consisted of four large rooms, one of which furnished as sleeping quarters. Most of the furniture was old and long unused, and the few crates and barrels were empty.

'Here's a bag of money,' Kennan said, returning with a hefty leather sack. 'Guess it would be a waste to leave it behind.'

Shaw grinned. 'Good thinking.' She accepted the bag and nearly sagged to her knees. 'Gods! That's heavy.'

'It's mostly gold,' the squad leader said without a hint of a smile. ''bout sixty pounds, I'd say.'

'You carry it,' Shaw said. 'Anything else?'

'A stack of Brynnyr Gunny notepaper,' Nate said. He looked around. 'And I found this on the mage you shot.' He handed her a scribbled message.

'WyDir letterhead?' she said. '*Hynks is blown. Lord Nimmendal's orders are to carry on as usual, more directions will follow. B.*' She looked at Nate. 'What is this?'

'A link,' Nate said. 'It means Hynks was somehow connected to this Brynnyr Gunny business. That's why he told our Cargo agent to stop bidding for those bulk contracts.'

'Would that B be Benffald?' Shaw said. 'Was he working for Nimmendal of Angsthafn?'

Nate shrugged. 'It would seem so. We haven't found any other boss type jinni yet; if this Nimmendal is a prince, perhaps he is the top dog in the Weal?'

'We run into the beast often enough,' Shaw said. 'I'll ask Ruth what her people know of the big rat. Now let's get out of here.'

She hurried over to B.G. and his friends. 'Time to go. We'll take you guys to our Smalkand headquarters. You need lots and lots of hot water and a good healer, food and beds. We only carry handportals for Kell, so we'll make it in two steps. Kennan, you go to the aerodrome first and report our findings to the guard commander. Ask her to pick up the bandits, for I most surely won't. Tell her we will send our report to the Weal Council. After that you're to go home and sleep. And that's an order, Squad leader.'

He grinned. 'Don't worry; I sleep like a log these days. It must be something in the air.'

Shaw touched his shoulder. 'I'm sure it is.' She waited until the Kells had gone. 'Are you ready?'

The warlock Esthel let go of the cage bars and took a few steps. 'Curse you, legs,' she muttered. 'Behave!' Then she squared her shoulders. 'Ready.'

The others all nodded. Phynn cried soundlessly, hiding his face behind one hand and with the other holding on to Latharom's shoulder.

'We'll be off,' Shaw said and twisted her handportal. Moments later, they were in the Dvarghish warehouse.

'Rescue party,' Shaw said quickly to the curious workers. 'No questions now; we'll tell you later. Kennan's guys have something else to do first.' They hurried the length of the warehouse to the portal. 'Mr. Mott?'

The portal mage hurried from his little office. 'Ma'am?'

'Smalkand, please.'

'Darn!' Esthel cried. 'You have a...'

'Portal?' she finished as they appeared in Smalkand's entry hall.

Shaw grinned. 'Several, in fact,' she said as they walked to the cafeteria. 'We'll show you everything, but first you need to be fit for society.'

The girl's face blanketed out as she looked down at her soiled clothes. 'Yes,' she said, and for the first time her voice shook. 'Please!'

Shaw looked around and waved at Willow, who came hurrying to meet them.

'You bring us guests?' she said.

Shaw saw her nose twitch at the visitors' rank smell, but the former Clammer boss was used to a lot and she didn't comment.

'These folks have been prisoners of bandits for weeks,' Shaw said. 'Tymon must look them over first. Then they need to bathe and have clean clothes. After that, food. I'd like the loan of the office, for I have a lot of questions for them while we eat. Lastly, they need sleep.'

'Bath, yes. Clothes, sure; our regular pirate issue. We'll prepare the rest. Tymon is on his way, he'll meet them at the washroom.' Willow smiled at the six. 'Follow me; I'll show you where you can clean up.'

As they left, Shaw turned to Nate. 'Cawah.' She stumbled a little and relaxed gratefully against Nate's arm around her waist.

'Up you go,' he said, and helped her onto the tall barstool.

'What's with the mask, Shaw?' the boy serving them asked, as he eyed her dust-caked face curiously. 'You guys had a party?'

'A battle,' Nate said. 'Killing bandits in the mountains of Kell.'

In minutes, a crowd had gathered and Shaw listened sleepily as Nate told of the arson attack, their capture of the freighter and the surprising end of their hunt for Brynnyr Gunny.

After a while Tymon clambered onto the stool on her other side. 'Those fellows are a mess,' he said immediately. 'Idiot kids, running from their so safe warlock bubble to play the big adventure-book heroes. Warlocks and a home-schooled battlemage with no idea of the world. Now they know, and it shocked their clean little souls.'

'Are they safe?' Shaw asked. She rubbed her eyes and tried to focus her tired mind.

'They are what they say they are, if you mean that,' Tymon said. 'No compulsions or hidden motives, just six upset fools. Oscar and that B.G. guy are more or less serviceable; I'm not sure of the others. Best keep them here for a week; that gives me time to observe them.'

'I'll talk it over with them,' Shaw said. 'They can assist Imooga, if they can be trusted to keep our secrets.'

'You mean don't blab to the parents?' Tymon snorted. 'I don't think they will. They left Spellstor Center because they wanted a change. We can give them that and pay them too. They have nothing to gain by betraying us.' The healer drained his lemonade. 'Do what you wish with those guys. I'd say hire them. It would be interesting to find out what a warlock can do outside their protective upper-class cocoon. And that little witch, I could use someone for the lighter healing.' He slid off his stool. 'Back to work.'

'Thanks,' Shaw said.

'No thanks necessary.' Tymon paused. 'When I saw them, I wondered if I'd feel animosity towards them. They are the kind of kids who belittled Martha and me at school, with their swollen air of superiority. But I felt nothing; they were just guys who needed my help. That's a victory, isn't it?'

'Yes!' Shaw said. 'A big one.'

Tymon smiled and hurried away.

# CHAPTER 25 – GREAT PLANS

It took them another hour before B.G. and his friends came back, clean and strangely different in their pirate clothes.

'Feeling better?' Shaw asked.

B.G. nodded jerkily. 'I hadn't realized how *foul* I'd become. Gods! Me, Altrynn Ryng-Gunny's son! It's a joke, a sick joke we played on ourselves.'

'I wouldn't say that. You were unprepared, but you guys had the right idea,' Shaw said. 'Let's go sit down somewhere quiet and the kitchen will bring you grub. Nothing fancy, but enough to tide you over till dinner.'

When they entered the wyrmcaller's office even the warlocks stared.

'This *is* a grand place,' B.G. said. 'I didn't think there was anything like this in the Weal, outside Spellstor and Casterglade.'

'I wouldn't call Queen Maud's palace at Brannoe a hovel,' Shaw said. 'But we're not in the Weal, mate. This is Smalkand Keep, headquarters of the Pasandir Trading Company and the de facto capital of the Peaks.'

'Dang!' the battlemage Oskar said. 'We've gone foreign?'

The door opened and three kids brought platters of food and drink. 'There you have it,' a girl said. 'That should fill your bellies, folks.'

Haai-Bo let out a long sigh. 'Food!' he said, landing squarely in the middle of the table. 'Finally!'

'Glutton!' Shaw said. 'You had two meals already, today.'

'I hunger,' he said with dignity.

'This food is for our guests. Here, have a piece of bread and a banana. Now be polite and let the others eat.'

Grumbling, the wyrmling retired with his snack.

There was fresh bread, meats and cheese, honey and homemade jams, a platter of baked fish, milk and fruits; the six had just enough restraint not to start stuffing their mouths, but they ate with a ravenous quickness.

'Dang!' Oskar said finally and sat back kneading a narango before peeling it. 'That was the best meal ever.'

Shaw looked at him as he sat at ease, seemingly unperturbed by their ordeal.

'What are your plans?' she asked. 'We could port you to Spellstor Aerodrome, if you want to go home.'

'No!' B.G. said a little too loud. 'I'm not going back.' He covered his face in his hands. 'I couldn't stand their homilies.'

'Indeed not,' Esthel said slowly. Her face was calm, her shoulders straight, but her hands on the table shook.

'You're a warlock, like B.G.?' Shaw asked.

She clenched her fingers and tried to control them. 'I am. B.G. and I, we're among the few warlocks born after the war. There are about ten of us, of which Argyra of Spellstor is the eldest. She's the Lord Spellstor's daughter. Ever since I was old enough to understand, I knew I would go to Casterglade one day and join my uncle's team of portal builders,' Esthel said. 'When I grew older, I found I didn't want to.'

'Why not?' Nate said when she fell silent.

'It's dull; they haven't made any real progress in fifteen years. Besides, I'm interested in other matters. I'm a designer; I see so many things here I want to discover why they work. Those lamps, your power sources, my fingers itch to screw them open.'

Shaw grinned. 'Don't, there are easier ways. Here at Smalkand are five Thali engineers making things. If you're interested, ask Imooga. If she wants your help, we'll hire you. We don't pay warlock wages; I think those Thali make six unis per week.'

Esthel brightened perceptibly. 'I don't care for money; I want to do things I like, useful things. I'll have a word with your engineers.'

Oskar paused, his fingers leaking sweet narango sap. 'If we're talking opportunities; I'm a battlemage, trained by the instructor at Spellstor.'

'So you didn't go to the Magic Institute?' Shaw asked.

'No. See, our parents are battlemages too; they are part of the Spellstor Defense, an elite corps. They didn't think my going to the Magic Institute had any additional value.'

'It would've broadened your outlook,' Nate said mildly. 'Did you ever fight anything?'

'Targets,' Oskar said. 'Endless rows of targets. And yes, I can ride a broom and shoot.'

'Shoot targets,' Nate said.

'No live practice,' Oskar added. 'They didn't want to risk my safety.' He grimaced. 'So I did that myself. Ain't I foolish?'

Shaw shrugged. 'No; I'd say you are half-trained. You mastered the theory, and now it's time to start the real work.'

'Dang.' Oskar wiped his fingers on his napkin. 'I graduated.'

Shaw stared at him. 'You have read a book; does that make you a scholar?'

'Naturally not,' B.G. said.

'You have thrown magic at a target. That doesn't make you a battlemage,' Shaw said.

Oskar gripped the table and cursed. 'What must I do to become what I thought I was?'

'Go and kill,' Haai-Bo cried from the backrest of the wyrmcaller's chair. He stretched his wings. 'Kill pirates, kill robbers, kill silly jinn. How else would you learn?'

Shaw grinned. 'Exactly. You can join us and I bet you'll get experience soon enough. What about the others? Suzie?'

The second girl was small, even for a Vanhaari, with large eyes and hair that looked like it had never seen a comb.

'I'm a witch,' she said. 'A healer.' She snorted. 'They don't need me in Spellstor Center. I'm not of warlock stock.'

'Suzie!' Esthel said.

'Well, it's true, isn't it?' the girl said. 'They had me brewing potions for their blasted visitors' store. What job is that?'

'Can you heal?' Shaw said. 'Wounds and broken limbs and such?'

'Yes! A mage or wisewoman will do it quicker, neater and more often, but you won't die with me around.' Suzie shook, gripping the edge of the table with her hands.

'How do you diagnose yourself?'

'Shock. Needs confirmation of ability and a redirection of purpose.' She glanced at Phynn, resting his head on his arms. 'That goes for all of us.'

'No wonder.' Shaw looked her over. 'You can mindspeak?'

'Of course,' she said. 'We all can do that. I can use a knife, too.'

Shaw grinned and showed the blades strapped to her arms. 'Excellent choice. Latharom, what about you?'

'I'm a mover mage,' he said. 'Not a glamorous study, but should B.G. find some buried treasure, I could dig it up faster than anyone else.' He looked at his hands. 'If only they'd stop shaking.'

'Does that hamper your moving?' Shaw asked.

'No, it hampers my self-assurance.' He sighed. 'I'm not as bad as old Phynn, though.'

'I can't stop c-crying,' the third boy said. 'It's idiotic, but I c-can't.'

'For the moment you guys better stay here and get your feet back on the ground. Let me tell you about us first.' Once more, Shaw recounted the story of the wyrmcaller, Divine Bodrus and the prophecy, of Clam Street, the pirates and Brisa. Then she went on to the PTC, WyDir and the

Brynnyr Gunny business. As she told of the fire at the hangers and the illegal landings, B.G.'s face became darker and darker.

'They used my name for that?' he burst out. 'Now all the Weal searches for Brynnyr Gunny, the criminal?'

'Hardly on that scale,' Nate said. 'Don't worry; Shaw will explain things in her report to the Lord Spellstor.'

'Gods!' Esthel muttered. 'We'll never dare to show our faces at the Center again.'

'They will forget,' Haai-Bo cackled. 'Stay away a while and they'll forget. Humans aren't wyrms; they have tiny memories.'

'There's truth in that,' Shaw said. 'While I spoke I realized I may have a job for you.'

'Let's hear it,' B.G. said.

'Ever heard of Nanstalgarod?'

'That's the Hellesands Desert,' B.G. said. 'Port Naar and all those reclaimer dig sites.'

'Yes. Five centuries ago, that was a fertile country, until the water ran out and the soil became exhausted. The Weal holds on to Port Naar only reluctantly; it is too far from their territory and it is a drain on their budget.' She smiled. 'For us it would be a handy stop on the way north. But I want to know more of the place. I'd like you to go there and check the place over. It's a hot, dry, miserable hole where nothing grows and there is only one well for all. The navy has its water brought in by ship. What can we do to make it less of a dump?'

'So we first need to see if there's any more water,' B.G. said.

'We'd need to dig wells,' Latharom said. 'That will take time.'

'Pumps,' Phynn said without raising his head.

'I don't think a hand pump...' Oskar began.

Phynn looked up and stared at him with red-rimmed eyes. 'Not that, idiot! I mean a big pump.' He gestured wildly, nearly knocking his plate to the ground. 'Look around ya; these guys here must have a power source other than steam. But what?'

'It's called a mana generator,' Nate said. 'It gathers and stores natural mana to use as a power supply.'

The engineer gripped the table. 'Yeah, I heard a whisper, something the Spellstor said somewhere some time ago; mana directly from the Intermedium.'

'That, too,' Nate said. 'It's what powers the keep. The generators are for the small stuff. I suppose they will power a pump. You should discuss this with Imooga, our lead engineer.'

Phynn nodded, gripping the table. 'I must do something or I go bats.'

'As soon as you're fit, B.G., Latharom and Phynn go to Port Naar,' Shaw said. 'We have handportals, so you can return here for meals and sleep. Esthel?'

'I found I'm not cut out for the life of an adventuress,' she said firmly. 'If I'm given a choice, I'd rather stay here. Sorry, B.G.'

'I understand,' B.G. said. 'I failed you; our companions' agreement broke when I let us all be captured.'

'No!' Esthel said sharply. 'It's not that! The gods know I don't blame you for those bandits; we were all stupidly overconfident. No, I discovered even before our capture I wasn't an outdoors type.'

B.G. reached over the table to catch her trembling hands. 'No matter,' he said. 'Above all, we're friends.'

'Oskar,' Shaw said. 'What are your plans?'

He shrugged. 'I feel a failure,' he said. 'As a battlemage I proved lacking, but I can't do anything else.'

'Do you want action?' Shaw asked. 'I won't blame you if you say no, but if you want to train the battle in battlemage you had better come with us.'

'Where are you going?' Oskar asked.

'As soon as our ship comes out of the dockyard we'll be sailing north, to the lands beyond Nanstalgarod,' Shaw said. 'I can almost guarantee we'll be fighting pirates. We'll carry a squad of Kells on board, but they're all melee fighters, so you might give them ranged back-up.'

She grinned. 'You don't have to make a career of it. If after some time you think you've learned enough, you can rejoin B.G. with a lot more experience in your pockets.'

'The ship needs a healer too.' Shaw looked at Suzie. 'If you're interested. Or you could stay and assist Tymon. I don't need your answers now; sleep on it.

'Nate and I will return to Seatome. I will report your joining us to the Lord Spellstor. Discreetly; his daughter Ruth is my management secretary, so I'll let her handle it. I will tell him of the Brynnyr Gunny thing; legally, your father needs to hear. If there is anything, give me a shout.'

'To bed, to bed,' Haai-Bo said. 'A nap is good for healthy minds.'

'Sleep,' Phynn muttered. 'I wish I could get blind drunk first.'

'You're out of luck,' Shaw said. 'No alcohol in our organization. You'll have to do it on your strength of mind, mate.'

'I know,' he said. 'I asked them already.' His face twitched. 'I'll think of water pumps instead.'

When they had gone, Shaw sat back in her chair and yawned.

'We did enough today; time to go home,' Nate said.

Shaw took his arm. 'Yes. We'll go to Dvarghish, to see if Kennan has returned; then to Seatome and bed.'

Kennan's guys were back, and the center of an admiring group of warehouse workers listening to their adventures.

The squad leader came to his feet, slightly embarrassed. 'We'll go to bed in a minute,' he said.

'Talk it off your chest first,' Shaw said. 'You're not standing any watches tonight, and that's an order.'

He wanted to protest, but Shaw gave him her best monocle stare, and he capitulated with a smile. 'Yes, ma'am. We reported as ordered and the aerodrome commander was pleased the matter had been resolved. She promised to have the army send a squad to pick up the bandits.

'Yerene was here, looking for you. She wasn't happy she missed the last bit, so I told her the army was going to the mine. Mott ported her out to Brannoe and I'm sure she'll manage to visit the scene of the fight. Our action will look glorious in the newspapers.'

'So it will,' Nate said. 'Good show. Take it easy; Shaw and I are going home and get some shut-eye too.'

It was dark and quiet when they returned to Old Wharf. As they stepped from the portal, Ruth came down the stairs and stopped in surprise. 'You're back!'

'Finally,' Nate said. 'What time is it?'

'A little past midnight,' Ruth said. 'Did that fire take so much of your time?'

Shaw giggled. 'Darn, I'd almost forgotten that's all you people have heard. We'll tell you the whole story tomorrow, but we found Brynnyr Gunny Company.'

'You did?' Ruth said. 'And?'

Shaw stared at her. 'You must know him. He's a young warlock.'

'What!' Ruth threw up her hands in consternation. 'Gunny? That wouldn't be old Ryng-Gunny's whelp?'

Shaw grinned. 'That's the one. It's all right, he isn't a criminal.'

Ruth shook her head as Shaw told her. 'Those idiots!' she said finally. 'Those stupid, simplistic fool kids!'

'They had a good idea,' Shaw said. 'I do think their education is lacking. If I were your father Basil, I'd take a long look at the schooling those Spellstor kids get. They had no idea of the world and its dangers; Oskar, their battlemage, had never fired on anything but targets, yet he graduated. I don't think Kellani would approve.'

Ruth grunted. 'Probably not.'

'Anyway, I hired the lot of them,' Shaw said. 'Even after their ordeal, none of them wanted to go back to Spellstor. Now...'

'Now we go and sleep,' Nate said firmly. 'No more talking; bed-time.'

'Nap! Long nap,' Haai-Bo said. 'Was good day, but lo-ong!' The wyrmling cackled softly and made a beeline for his spot in the kitchen.

'I should see if there's any news,' Shaw said.

'Tomorrow.' Nate steered her outside and towards the house.

'Darn you,' she said, without moving away from his arm round her waist.

He grinned. 'I love you too.' Then he kissed her quickly, pushed her inside before him and closed the front door. 'Good night.'


NOT THE END

Shaw's story will continue in

*Book #5 – HIGH MERCHANT*

# LIST OF NAMES

Abia, Captain of the *Drakon*; sister to Sylas
Amaj Mir, a Kalbakar lord, Marshal of Smalkand
Amsalon Illansor, the Grand Guildmistress' grandson
Ancho-Dar, the Wyrm Queen
Barlett, Emmett, journalist
Basil, Lord Spellstor, Naudin's father, ruler of Vanhaar
Benffald, Mr., WyDir's Northern line manager
Benwar, Squad leader, at Smalkand
Beth, portal mage, Smalkand
Brynnyr Gunny (B.G.), a warlock dowser
Callogan, a mover mage
Chagan, Qoori 1Off *Marigold*
Darquine of Piright, High Merchant Proprietor of the MCTC
Dowa, a seamstress girl
Eghol of Unwaar, ruler, High Singer of Aera
Eskandar, Wyrmcaller of Kalbakar
Esthel of Andercast, warlock
Ghol, Mrs., of Ghol's Sewery
Grim, a Yavam Island girl
Haai-Bo, an advisor wyrmling
Hella, Quartermaster, Smalkand
Howwil, ledger keeper
Hynks, WyDir senior director
Imooga of the White Shore Clan, Thali engineer, cousin of Ulaataq;
Inns, Messrs, two auditors
Isambar, captain of *Fayaafa*
Jakop, a Yavam Island boy
Jathira, Guildlady, a Hizmyran guild agent
Jazzaunt Hathwaari, Prince of Hizmyr
Jem, Princess of Nanstalgarod
Jinnbane, the historic hero who banished the jinn; Skandar Jinnbane
Jurgis of Kell-Spellstor, Lord; First Broom, Kellani's father
Justym of Marroth, Unwaari skysinger; Vystyn's great grandson
Kashim, Lieutenant 5th Troop, the babyface
Kavid-Jar, the, Spirit of Mountain; Bodrus' avatar
Keena of the Weevils, mage
Kellani of Kell-Spellstor, broomrider
Kennan, Squad leader PTC at Dvarghish
Kier, portal mage, Old Wharf
Latharom, a mover mage
Leolynn of Kell-Allastar, Captain *Maiden of Allastar*

Llynsing, a pawnbroker in Seatome
Lomillor, Varan, Seatome warehouse manager
Lothi-Mo, a royal wyrmling
Martha, mage instructor, twin to Tymon
Maud of the Kell, Queen, mother of Kellani
Miyra of Brisa, Captain *Marigold*
Morgan, WyDir secretary
Mott, portal mage, Smalkand
Myk of the Weevils, engineer *Marigold*
Na'a of the Arrangh, Kell wisewoman, healer of Gathea
Nate, Director of Operations PTC
Naudin of Maiwar, mindmage
Nimmendal, the First Chair of Brisa (jinni prince Hyloman)
Oskar, a battlemage
Oychak, Thali engineer
Phynn, an engineer
Pomfrith (D), banker of Seatome
Ricco, *Drakon*'s purser, a PTC employee
Roza, ledger keeper
Ruth of Spellstor, Warden of Winsproke, sister to Naudin
Satthyba, the Grand Guildmistress of Hizmyr
Saul of Spellstor, Lord, Warden of Spellstor; Chief Reclaimer
Shaw (Ashawta) Harwans, managing director PTC
Siolde of Seedgraft, Witch, mother of Naudin
Suzie, a witch healer
Sylas, Abia's brother, teacher
Tamyas, Captain *Sashu*
Tangrid IV Tangridi, pilot *Pewbara*
Teodar, the Kavid Jar
Tiu-Ti, a wyrmling boy
Tomar, portal mage.
Tymon, chief healer Smalkand, twin to Martha
Ulaataq of the White Shore Clan, Thali engineer
Uthur, a Yavam Island boy
Varan Lomillor, warehouse manager PTC Old Wharf
Vence, 1Off *Drakon*, brother to Perre
Wainschilt, banker at Smalkand
Wanei, Prince, *Sashu*'s 1Mate
Willow, keepmistress Smalkand
Wrachazd, the lich king of Nanstalgarod
Wylmer, Captain Githeon; captain of *Killarn Ranni*
Wylmer, Mr., Captain Wylmer's father
Wyon, a Kell boy
Xailin, Qoor 3Off *Drakon*, Imperial Princess of Qoor

Yarwan, Commodore; Naudin's father
Yens Rowe-Yens, squad leader PTC Seatome
Yerene M'Dannish, of the *Weal Trumpet*, Port Dvarghish


Aera, Sky Goddess
AZZA, the Universe Maker
Chottapan, Sea God
Demetea, Goddess of the Wild Things
Gathea, Nature, the Mother
Gorm & Otha, the Siblings of Battle
Kallianura, Defender of the Home
Lumentis, God of Knowledge
Ratla, Mother of Thieves
Tenaaz, God of Trade
the Thi-a-Yuuk, the Great Grandmother of the Ice
Zenyunthalata, God of the Lands


liber = Weal gold coin, 20 unis or 400 pennies
uni = Weal silver coin, 1/20 liber or 20 pennies
penny = smallest Weal copper coin